DAY OF
CONFESSION

ATTENTION SCHOOLS AND CORPORATIONS:
WARNER books are available at quantity
discounts with bulk purchase for educational,
business, or sales promotional use. For
information, please write to: SPECIAL SALES
DEPARTMENT, WARNER BOOKS, 1271 AVENUE
OF THE AMERICAS, NEW YORK, N.Y. 10020.

Also by Allan Folsom

The Day After Tomorrow

DAY OF CONFESSION

ALLAN FOLSOM

WARNER
VISION
BOOKS

A Time Warner Company

for Karen and Riley,
and for Ellen

WARNER BOOKS EDITION

Copyright © 1998 by Allan R. Folsom
All rights reserved.

Warner Vision is a registered trademark of Warner Books, Inc.

Cover design by Jackie Merri Meyer and Diane Luger
Photo by Scala/Art Keglourse

Warner Books, Inc.
1271 Avenue of the Americas
New York, NY 10020

Visit our Web site at
www.warnerbooks.com

 A Time Warner Company

Printed in the United States of America

Originally published in hardcover by Little, Brown and Company.
First International Paperback Printing: May 1999
First United States Paperback Printing: July 1999

10 9 8 7 6 5 4 3 2 1

Acknowledgments

FOR TECHNICAL INFORMATION AND ADVICE I am especially grateful to Alessandro Pansa, head of the Central Operative Service of the Italian National Police; Father Gregory Coiro, media relations director for the Catholic Archdiocese of Los Angeles; Lèon I. Bender, M.D.; Gerald Svedlow, M.D.; Niles Bond; Marion Rosenberg; Imara; Gene Mancini, senior biological consultant; Master Gunnery Sergeant Andy Brown and Staff Sergeant Douglas Fraser, United States Marine Corps; and Norton F. Kristy, Ph.D.

I am additionally grateful to Alessandro D'Alfonso, Wilton Wynn, Nicola Merchiori, and, particularly, Luigi Bernabò, for their assistance in Italy.

I am indebted as well to Larry Kirshbaum and Sarah Crichton, and, as always, to the wizardry of Aaron Priest. Finally, a most particular thanks to Frances Jalet-Miller for her excellent suggestions and enduring patience in reworking the manuscript.

The Characters

Harry Addison

Father Daniel Addison—Harry's younger brother, a priest in the Vatican and private secretary to Cardinal Marsciano

Nursing sister Elena Voso

Hercules, a dwarf

The Vatican

Giacomo Pecci, Pope Leo XIV

The pope's *Uomini di fiducia,* "Men of trust"

    Cardinal Umberto Palestrina

    Cardinal Nicola Marsciano

    Cardinal Joseph Matadi

    Monsignor Fabio Capizzi

    Cardinal Rosario Parma

Father Bardoni, an aide to Cardinal Marsciano

The Vatican Police

Jacov Farel, head of the Vatican Police

The Italian Police

Homicide Detective Otello Roscani

Homicide Detective Gianni Pio

Homicide Detective Scala

Homicide Detective Castelletti

Gruppo Cardinale—The special task force set up
by decree of the Italian Ministry of the Interior to
investigate the murder of the cardinal vicar of Rome

Marcello Taglia, Gruppo Cardinale Chief Prosecutor

The Chinese

Li Wen, a state water-quality inspector

Chen Yin, a merchant of cut flowers

Yan Yeh, president of the People's Bank of China

Jiang Youmei, Chinese ambassador to Italy

Zhou Yi, Jiang's foreign minister

Wu Xian, general secretary of the Communist Party

The Freelancers

Thomas Jose Alvarez-Rios Kind, international terrorist

Adrianna Hall, World News Network correspondent

James Eaton, first secretary to the counselor for Political
Affairs, United States Embassy, Rome

Pierre Weggen, Swiss investment banker

Miguel Valera, a Spanish communist

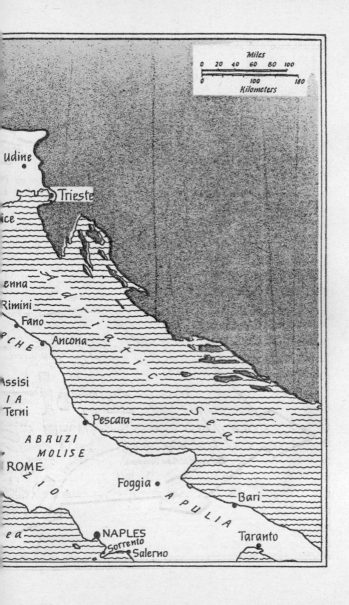

VATICAN CITY

*The wall surrounding Vatican City
is an international boundary*

| 0 | 50 | 100 | 150 | 200 metres |

| 0 | 200 | 400 | 600 feet |

Old
Gardens

Vatican Radio

Fountain of
the Eagle

New Gardens

Monument
to St. Peter

Lourdes
Gardens

St. Martha's
Chapel

Civil
Administr
Building

Ethiopian
College

Church
St Step

Heliport

Railway

Mosaic
Studio

Tower of San Giovanni

Railwa
Station
(St
P

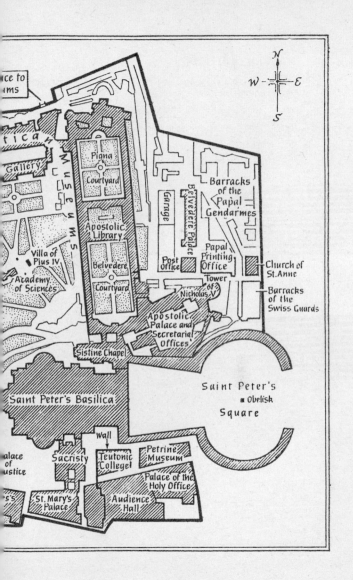

N
W E
S

Entrance to Museums

Gallery

Piona Courtyard

Museums

Garage

Belvedere Palace

Barracks of the Papal Gendarmes

Apostolic Library

Belvedere Courtyard

Post Office

Papal Printing Office

Church of St. Anne

Villa of Pius IV

Academy of Sciences

Tower of Nicholas V

Barracks of the Swiss Guards

Apostolic Palace and Secretarial Offices

Sistine Chapel

Saint Peter's
■ Obelisk
Square

Saint Peter's Basilica

Wall

Palace of Justice

Sacristy

Teutonic College

Petrine Museum

Palace of the Holy Office

's

St. Mary's Palace

Audience Hall

Prologue

Rome. Sunday, June 28.

TODAY HE CALLED HIMSELF S AND LOOKED startlingly like Miguel Valera, the thirty-seven-year-old Spaniard spinning in a light, drug-induced sleep across the room. The apartment they were in was nothing, just two rooms with a tiny kitchen and bath, the fifth floor up from the street. The furnishings were worn and inexpensive, common in a place rented by the week. The most prominent pieces were the faded velvet couch on which the Spaniard reclined and the small drop leaf table under the front window, where S stood looking out.

So the apartment was nothing. What sold it was the view—the green of the Piazza San Giovanni and across it, the imposing medieval Basilica of St. John in the Lateran, the Cathedral of Rome and "mother of all churches," founded by the Emperor Constantine in the year 313. Today the view from the window was even better than its promise. Inside the basilica, Giacomo Pecci, Pope Leo XIV, was celebrating mass on his seventy-fifth birthday, and an enormous crowd overflowed the piazza, making it seem as if all Rome were celebrating with him.

Running a hand through his dyed-black hair, S glanced at Valera. In ten minutes his eyes would open. In twenty he would be alert and functional. Abruptly S turned and let his gaze fall on an ancient black-and-white television in the corner. On its screen was a live broadcast from the mass inside the basilica.

The pope, in white liturgical vestments, watched the faces of the worshipers in front of him as he spoke, his eyes meeting theirs energetically, hopefully, spiritually. He loved and they loved in return, and it seemed to give him a youthful renewal despite his age and slowly declining health.

Now the television cameras cut away, finding familiar faces of politicians, celebrities, and business leaders among those inside the packed basilica. Then the cameras moved on, fixing briefly on five clergymen seated behind the pontiff. These were his longtime advisers. His *uomini di fiducia*. Men of trust. As a group, probably the most influential authority within the Roman Catholic Church.

—Cardinal Umberto Palestrina, 62. A Naples street urchin and orphan become Vatican secretariat of state. Enormously popular within the Church and carried in the same high regard by the secular international diplomatic community. Massive physically, six foot seven and 270 pounds.

—Rosario Parma, 67. Cardinal vicar of Rome, tall, severe, conservative prelate from Florence in whose diocese and church the mass was being celebrated.

—Cardinal Joseph Matadi, 57, prefect of the Congregation of Bishops. Native of Zaire. Broad shouldered, jovial, widely traveled, multilingual, diplomatically astute.

—Monsignor Fabio Capizzi, 62, director general of the Vatican Bank. Native of Milan. Graduate of Oxford and Yale, self-made millionaire before joining the seminary at age thirty.

—Cardinal Nicola Marsciano, 60, eldest son of a Tuscan farmer, educated in Switzerland and Rome, president of the Administration of the Patrimony of the Apostolic See; as such, chief overseer of the Vatican's investments.

CLICK.

The gloved hand of *S* turned off the television, and he stepped again to the table in front of the window. Behind him Miguel Valera coughed and moved involuntarily on the sofa. *S* glanced at him, then looked back out the window. Police barricades had been set up to keep the crowd from the cobblestones directly in front of the basilica, and now mounted police on horseback took up positions on either side of its bronze central entrance gate. Behind them and to the left, out of sight of the crowd, *S* could see a dozen dark blue vans. In front of them stood a phalanx of riot police, also out of sight, but ready if needed. Abruptly four dark Lancias, unmarked cars of the Polizia di Stato, the police force protecting the pope and his cardinals outside the Vatican, pulled up and stopped at the foot of the basilica's steps, waiting to take the pope and his cardinals back to the Vatican.

Suddenly the bronze gates swung open and there was a roar from the crowd. At the same time seemingly every church bell in Rome began to ring. For a moment nothing happened. Then, above the din of the bells, *S* heard a second roar as the pope appeared, the white of his cassock standing out clearly against a sea of red as his men of trust walked close behind him—the group surrounded tightly by security men wearing black suits and sunglasses.

Valera groaned, his eyes flickered, and he tried to roll over. S glanced at him, but only for an instant. Then he turned and lifted something covered with an ordinary bath towel from the shadows beside the window. Setting it on the table, he took away the towel and put his eye to the scope of a Finnish sniper rifle. Instantly his view of the basilica magnified a hundredfold. In the same moment, Cardinal Palestrina stepped forward and fully into its circular frame, its crosshairs meeting directly over his broad grin. S took a breath and held it, letting his gloved forefinger ease against the trigger.

Abruptly Palestrina stepped aside, and the rifle's scope came tight on Cardinal Marsciano's chest. S heard Valera grunt behind him. Ignoring him, he swung the rifle left through a blur of cardinal red until he saw the white of Leo XIV's cassock. A split second later the crosshairs centered between his eyes just above the bridge of his nose.

Behind him Valera yelled something out loud. Again, S ignored him. His finger tightened against the trigger as the pope lurched forward, past a security man, smiling and waving at the crowd. Then, abruptly, S swung the rifle right, bringing the mesh of crosshairs full on the gold pectoral cross of Rosario Parma, the cardinal vicar of Rome. S gave no expression, simply squeezed the trigger three times in rapid succession, rocking the room with thundering discharge and, two hundred yards away, showering Pope Leo XIV, Giacomo Pecci, and those around him with the blood of a man of trust.

1

Los Angeles. Thursday, July 2, 9:00 P.M.

THE VOICE ON THE ANSWERING MACHINE resonated with fear.

"Harry, it's your brother, Danny. . . . I . . . don't mean to call you like this . . . after so much time. . . . But . . . there's . . . no one else I can talk to. . . . I'm scared, Harry. . . . I don't know what to do . . . or . . . what will happen next. God help me. If you're there, please pick up— Harry, are you there?—I guess not. . . . I'll try to call you back."

"Dammit."

Harry Addison hung up the car phone, kept his hand on it, then picked it up again and pushed REDIAL. He heard the digital tones as the numbers redialed automatically. Then there was silence, and then the measured "buzz, buzz," "buzz, buzz" of the Italian phone system as the call rang through.

"Come on, Danny, answer . . ."

After the twelfth ring Harry set the receiver back in its cradle and looked off, the lights of oncoming traffic dancing over his face, making him lose track of where he was—in a limousine with his driver on a race to the airport to make the ten-o'clock red-eye to New York.

It was nine at night in L.A., six in the morning in Rome. Where would a priest be at six in the morning? An early mass? Maybe that's where he was and why he wasn't answering.

"Harry, it's your brother, Danny. . . . I'm scared. . . . I don't know what to do. . . . God help me."

"Jesus Christ." Harry felt helplessness and panic at the same time. Not a word or a note between them in years, and then there was Danny's voice on Harry's answering machine, jumping out suddenly among a string of others. And not just a voice, but someone in grave trouble.

Harry had heard a rustling as though Danny was starting to hang up, but then he had come back on the line and left his phone number, asking Harry to please call if he got in soon. For Harry, soon was moments ago, when he'd picked up the calls from his home machine. But Danny's call had come two hours earlier, at a little after seven California time, just after four in the morning in Rome—what the hell had *soon* meant to him at that time of day?

Picking up the phone again, Harry dialed his law office in Beverly Hills. There had been an important partners' meeting. People might still be there.

"Joyce, it's Harry. Is Byron—?"

"He just left, Mr. Addison. You want me to try his car?"

"Please."

Harry heard the static as Byron Willis's secretary tried to connect with his car phone.

"I'm sorry, he's not picking up. He said something about dinner. Should I leave word at the house?"

There was a blur of lights, and Harry felt the limo lean as the driver took the cloverleaf off the Ventura Freeway and accelerated into traffic on the San Diego, heading south toward LAX. Take it easy, he thought. Danny could be at mass or at work or out for a walk. Don't start driving yourself or other people crazy when you don't even know what's going on.

"No, never mind. I'm on my way to New York. I'll get him in the morning. Thanks."

Clicking off, Harry hesitated, then tried Rome once more. He heard the same digital sounds, the same silence, and then the now-familiar "buzz, buzz," "buzz, buzz" as the phone rang through. There was still no answer.

Italy. Friday, July 3, 10:20 A.M.

FATHER DANIEL ADDISON DOZED LIGHTLY in a window seat near the back of the tour bus, his senses purposefully concentrated on the soft whine of the diesel and hum of the tires as the coach moved north along the Autostrada toward Assisi.

Dressed in civilian clothes, he had his clerical garments and toiletries in a small bag on the overhead rack above, his glasses and identification papers tucked into the inside pocket of the nylon windbreaker he wore over jeans and a short-sleeved shirt. Father Daniel was thirty-three and looked like a graduate student, an everyday tourist traveling alone. Which was what he wanted.

An American priest assigned to the Vatican, he had been living in Rome for nine years and going to Assisi for almost as long. Birthplace of the humble priest who became a saint, the ancient town in the Umbrian hills had given him a sense of cleansing and grace that put him more in touch with his own spiritual journey than any place he'd ever been. But now that journey was in shambles, his faith all but destroyed. Confusion, dread, and fear overrode everything. Keeping any shred of sanity at all was a major psychological struggle. Still, he was on the bus and going. But with no idea what he would do or say when he got there.

In front of him, the twenty or so other passengers chatted or read or rested as he did, enjoying the cool of the coach's air-conditioning. Outside, the summer heat shimmered in waves across the rural landscape, ripening crops, sweetening vineyards, and, little by little, decaying the few ancient walls and fortresses that still existed here and there and were visible in the distance as the bus passed.

Letting himself drift, Father Daniel's thoughts went to Harry and the call he'd left on his answering machine in the hours just before dawn. He wondered if Harry had even picked up the message. Or, if he had, if he'd been resentful of it and had not called back on purpose. It was a chance he had taken. He and Harry had been estranged since they were teenagers. It had been eight years since they'd spoken, ten since they'd seen each other. And that had been only briefly, when they'd gone back to Maine for the funeral of their mother. Harry had been twenty-six then, and Danny twenty-three. It was not unreasonable to assume that by now Harry had written his younger brother off and simply no longer gave a damn.

But, at that moment, what Harry thought or what had kept them apart hadn't mattered. All Danny wanted was to hear Harry's voice, to somehow touch him and to ask for his help. He had made the call as much out of fear as love, and because there had been nowhere else to turn. He had become part of a horror from which there was no return.

One that would only grow darker and become more obscene. And because of it, he knew he might very well die without ever being with his brother again.

A movement down the aisle in front of him shook him from his muse. A man was walking toward him. He was in his early forties, clean shaven, and dressed in a light sport coat and khaki trousers. The man had gotten on the bus at the last moment, just as it was pulling out of the terminal in Rome. For a moment Father Daniel thought he might pass and go into the lavatory behind him. Instead, he stopped at his side.

"You're American, aren't you?" he said with a British accent.

Father Daniel glanced past him. The other passengers were riding as they had been, looking out, talking, relaxing. The nearest, a half dozen seats away.

"—Yes . . ."

"I thought so." The man grinned broadly. He was pleasant, even jovial. "My name is Livermore. I'm English if you can't tell. Do you mind if I sit down?" Without waiting for a reply, he slid into the seat next to Father Daniel.

"I'm a civil engineer. On vacation. Two weeks in Italy. Next year it's the States. Never been there before. Been kind of asking Yanks as I meet them where I should visit." He was talky, even pushy, but pleasant about it, and that seemed to be his manner. "Mind if I ask what part of the country you're from?"

"—Maine . . ." Something was wrong, but Father Daniel wasn't sure what it was.

"That would be up the map a bit from New York, yes?"

"Quite a bit . . ." Again Father Daniel looked toward the front of the bus. Passengers the same as before. Busy with what they were doing. None looking back. His eyes came back to Livermore in time to see him glance at the emergency exit in the seat in front of them.

"You live in Rome?" Livermore smiled amiably.

Why had he looked at the emergency exit? What was that for? "You asked if I was American. Why would you think I lived in Rome?"

"I've been there off and on. You look familiar, that's all." Livermore's right hand was in his lap, but his left was out of sight. "What do you do?"

The conversation was innocent, but it wasn't. "I'm a writer . . ."

"What do you write?"

"For American television . . ."

"No, you don't." Abruptly Livermore's demeanor changed. His eyes hardened, and he leaned in, pressing against Father Daniel. "You're a priest."

"What?"

"I said you're a priest. You work at the Vatican. For Cardinal Marsciano."

Father Daniel stared at him. "Who are you?"

Livermore's left hand came up. A small automatic in it. A silencer squirreled to the barrel. "Your executioner."

At the same instant a digital timer beneath the bus clicked to 00:00. A split second later there was a thundering explosion. Livermore vanished. Windows blew out. Seats and bodies flew. A scything piece of razor-sharp steel decapitated the driver, sending the bus careening right, crushing a white Ford against the guardrail. Bouncing off it, the bus came crashing back through traffic, a screaming, whirling, twenty-ton fireball of burning steel and rubber. A motorcycle rider disappeared under its wheels. Then it clipped the rear of a big-rig truck and spun sideways. Slamming into a silver-gray Lancia, the bus carried it full force through the center divider, throwing it directly into the path of an oncoming gasoline tanker.

Reacting violently, the tanker driver jammed on his brakes, jerking the wheel right. Wheels locked, tires shrieking, the enormous truck slid forward and sideways, at the same time knocking the Lancia off the bus like a billiard ball and sending the burning coach plunging off the highway and down a steep hill. Tilting up on two wheels, it held for a second, then rolled over, ejecting the bodies of its passengers, many of them dismembered and on fire, across the summer landscape. Fifty yards later it came to a rest, igniting the dry grass in a crackling rush around it.

Seconds afterward its fuel tank exploded, sending flame and smoke roaring heavenward in a fire storm that raged until there was nothing left but a molten, burned-out shell and a small, insignificant wisp of smoke.

3

Delta Airlines flight 148, New York to Rome.
Monday, July 6, 7:30 A.M.

DANNY WAS DEAD, AND HARRY WAS ON HIS
way to Rome to bring his body back to the U.S. for burial.
The last hour, like most of the flight, had been a dream.
Harry had seen the morning sun touch the Alps. Seen it glint
off the Tyrrhenian Sea as they'd turned, dropping down over
the Italian farmland on approach to Rome's Leonardo da
Vinci International Airport at Fiumicino.

"Harry, it's your brother, Danny. . . ."

All he could hear was Danny's voice on the answering
machine. It played over and over in his mind, like a tape on a
loop. Fearful, distraught, and now silent.

"Harry, it's your brother, Danny. . . ."

Waving off a pour of coffee from a smiling and pert flight
attendant, Harry leaned back against the plush seat of the

first-class cabin and closed his eyes, replaying what had happened in between.

He'd tried to call Danny twice more from the plane. And then again when he checked into his hotel. Still, there had been no answer. His apprehension growing, he'd called the Vatican directly, hoping to find Danny at work, and what he'd learned, after being passed from one department to another and being spoken to in broken English and then Italian and then a combination of both, was that Father Daniel was "not here until Monday."

To Harry that had meant he was away for the weekend. And no matter his mental state, it was a legitimate reason why Danny was not answering his phone. In response, Harry had left a message on his answering machine at home, giving his hotel number in New York in the event Danny called back as he said he would.

And then Harry had turned, with some sense of relief, to business as usual and to why he had gone to New York—a last-minute huddle with Warner Brothers distribution and marketing chiefs over this Fourth of July weekend's opening of *Dog on the Moon*, Warner's major summer release, the story of a dog taken to the moon in a NASA experiment and accidentally left there, and the Little League team that learns about it and finds a way to bring him back; a film written and directed by Harry's twenty-four-year-old client Jesus Arroyo.

Single and handsome enough to be a movie star, Harry Addison was not only one of the entertainment community's most eligible bachelors, he was also one of its most successful attorneys. His firm represented the cream of multimillion-dollar Hollywood talent. His own list of clients had either starred in or were responsible for some of the highest-grossing movies and successful television shows of the past five years. His friends were household names, the same people who stared weekly from the covers of national magazines.

His success—as the daily Hollywood trade paper *Variety* had recently put it—was due to "a combination of smarts, hard work, and a temperament markedly different from the savagely competitive young warrior agents and attorneys to whom the 'deal' is everything and whose only disposition is 'take no prisoners.' With his Ivy League haircut and trademark white shirt and dark blue Armani suit, the Harry Addison approach is that the most beneficial thing for everyone is to cause as little all-around bleeding as possible. It's why his deals go through, his clients love him, the studios and networks respect him, and why he makes a million dollars a year."

Dammit, what did any of that mean now? His brother's death overshadowed everything. All he could think of was what he might have done to help Danny that he hadn't. Call the U.S. Embassy or the Rome police and send them to his apartment. Apartment? He didn't even know where Danny lived. That was why he had started to call Byron Willis, his boss and mentor and best friend, from the limo when he'd first heard his brother's message. Who did they know in Rome who could help? was what he had intended to ask but hadn't because the call had never gone through. If he had, and if they had found someone in Rome, would Danny still be alive? The answer was probably no because there wouldn't have been time.

Christ.

Over the years how many times had he tried to communicate with Danny? Christmas and birthday cards formally exchanged for a short while after their mother's death. Then one holiday missed, then another. Finally nothing at all. And busy with his life and career, Harry had let it ride, eventually accepting it as the way it was. Brothers at opposites. Angry, at times even hostile, living a world apart, as they always would. With both probably wondering during the odd quiet moment if he should be the one to take the initiative and find a way to bring them back together. But neither had.

And then Saturday evening as he'd been in the Warners New York offices celebrating the huge numbers *Dog on the Moon* was realizing—nineteen million dollars with Saturday night, Sunday, and Monday still to come, making a projected weekend gross of thirty-eight to forty-two million—Byron Willis had called from Los Angeles. The Catholic archdiocese had been trying to reach Harry and was reluctant to leave word at his hotel. They'd traced Willis through Harry's office, and Byron himself had chosen to make the call. Danny was dead, he'd said quietly, killed in what appeared to be a terrorist bombing of a tour bus on the way to Assisi.

In the emotional gyration immediately afterward, Harry canceled his plans to return to L.A. and booked himself on a Sunday-evening flight to Italy. He would go there and bring Danny home personally. It was the last and only thing he could do.

Then, on Sunday morning, he'd contacted the State Department, requesting the U.S. Embassy in Rome arrange a meeting between himself and the people investigating the bombing of the bus. Danny had been frightened and distraught; maybe what he had said might help shed some light on what had happened and who had been responsible. Afterward, and for the first time in as long as Harry could remember, he had gone to church. And prayed and wept.

BENEATH HIM, HARRY HEARD the sound of the landing gear being lowered. Looking out, he saw the runway come up and the Italian countryside fly past. Open fields, drainage ditches, more open fields. Then there was a bump and they were down. Slowing, turning, taxiing back toward the long, low sunlit buildings of Aeroporto Leonardo da Vinci.

THE UNIFORMED WOMAN behind the glass at Passport Control asked him to wait and picked up the telephone. Harry saw himself reflected in the glass as he waited. He was still in his dark blue Armani suit and white shirt, the way he was described in the *Variety* article. There was another suit and shirt in his suitcase, along with a light sweater, workout gear, polo shirt, jeans, and running shoes. The same bag he had packed for New York.

The woman hung up and looked at him. A moment later two policemen with Uzi submachine guns slung over their shoulders walked up to her. One stepped into the booth and looked at his passport, then glanced at Harry and motioned him through.

"Would you come with us, please?"

"Of course."

As they walked off, Harry saw the first policeman ease the Uzi around, his right hand sliding to its grip. Immediately two more uniformed police moved in to walk with them as they crossed the terminal. Passengers moved aside quickly, then turned to look back when they were safely out of the way.

At the far side of the terminal they stopped at a security door. One of the policeman punched a code into a chrome keypad. A buzzer sounded, and the man opened the door. Then they went up a flight of stairs and turned down a corridor. A moment later they stopped at another door. The first policeman knocked, and they entered a windowless room where two men in suits waited. Harry's passport was handed to one of them, and the uniforms left, closing the door behind them.

"You are Harry Addison—"

"Yes."

"The brother of the Vatican priest Father Daniel Addison."

Harry nodded. "Thank you for meeting me . . ."

The man who held his passport was probably forty-five, tall and tanned, and very fit. He wore a blue suit, over a lighter blue shirt with a carefully knotted maroon tie. His English was accented but understandable. The other man was a little older and almost as tall but with a slighter build and salt-and-pepper hair. His shirt was checkered. His suit, a light brown, the same as his tie.

"I am Ispettore Capo Otello Roscani, Polizia di Stato. This is Ispettore Capo Pio."

"How do you do . . ."

"Why have you come to Italy, Mr. Addison?"

Harry was puzzled. They knew why he was there or they wouldn't have met him as they had. "—To bring my brother's body home. . . . And to talk with you people."

"When had you planned to come to Rome?"

"I hadn't *planned* to come at all . . ."

"Answer the question, please."

"Saturday night."

"Not before?"

"Before? No, of course not."

"You made the reservations yourself?" Pio spoke for the first time. His English had almost no accent at all, as if he were either American himself or had spent a lot of time in the U.S.

"Yes."

"On Saturday."

"Saturday night. I told you that." Harry looked from one to the other. "I don't understand your questions. You knew I was coming. I asked the U.S. Embassy to arrange for me to talk to you."

Roscani slid Harry's passport into his pocket. "We are going to ask you to accompany us into Rome, Mr. Addison."

"Why?—We can talk right here. There's not that much to tell." Suddenly Harry could feel sweat on his palms. They were leaving something out. What was it?

"Perhaps you should let us decide, Mr. Addison."

Again, Harry looked from one to the other. "What's going on? What is it you're not telling me?"

"We simply wish to talk further, Mr. Addison."

"About what?"

"The assassination of the cardinal vicar of Rome."

THEY PUT HARRY'S LUGGAGE IN THE TRUNK and then rode in silence for forty-five minutes, not a word or a glance between them, Pio at the wheel of the gray Alfa Romeo, Roscani in the back with Harry, taking the Autostrada in from the airport toward the ancient city, passing through the suburbs of Magliana and Portuense and then along the Tiber and across it, passing the Colosseum, and moving into Rome's heart.

The Questura, police headquarters, was an archaic five-story brownstone-and-granite building on Via di San Vitale, a narrow cobblestone street off Via Genova, which was off Via Nazionale in the central city. Its main entrance was through an arched portal guarded by armed uniformed police and surveillance cameras. And that was the way they came in, with the uniforms saluting as Pio wheeled the Alfa under the portal and into the interior courtyard.

Pio got out first, leading them into the building and past a large glassed-in booth where two more uniformed officers watched not only the door but also a bank of video monitors. Then there was a walk down a brightly lit corridor to take an elevator up.

Harry looked at the men and then at the floor as the elevator rose. The ride in from the airport had been a blur, made worse by the silence of the policemen. But it had given him time to try and get some perspective on what was happening, why they were doing this.

He knew the cardinal vicar of Rome had been murdered eight days earlier by an assassin firing from an apartment window—a crime analogous in the U.S. to killing the President or other hugely celebrated person—but his knowledge was no more than that, limited to what he'd seen on TV or scanned in the newspaper, the same as several million others. That Danny had been killed in the bombing of a bus shortly afterward was an obvious, even logical, line to follow. Especially considering the tenor of his call to Harry. He'd been a Vatican priest, and the murdered cardinal a major figure within the Church. And the police were trying to see if there was some connection between whoever killed the cardinal and those responsible for bombing the bus. And maybe in some way there was. But what did they think he knew?

Obviously it was a bad time and the police were reeling anyway because so public and outrageous a crime had happened in their city, and on their watch and on television. It meant every detail of their investigation would be under the closest scrutiny of the media and therefore even more emotionally charged than it already would have been. The best thing, Harry decided, was to try to put his own feelings aside and simply answer their questions as best he could. He knew nothing more than what he'd wanted to tell them in the first place, which was something they would soon find out.

5

"WHEN DID YOU BECOME A MEMBER OF THE Communist Party, Mr. Addison?" Roscani leaned forward, a notepad at his sleeve.

"Communist Party?"

"Yes."

"I am most certainly not a member of the Communist Party."

"How long had your brother been a member?"

"I wasn't aware that he was."

"You are denying he was a Communist."

"I'm not denying anything. But as a priest he would have been excommunicated . . ."

Harry was incredulous. Where did this come from? He wanted to stand up and ask them where they got their ideas and what the hell they were talking about. But he didn't. He just sat there in a chair in the middle of a large office, trying to keep his composure and go along with them.

Two desks were at right angles in front of him. Roscani was behind one—a framed photograph of his wife and three teenage boys next to a computer whose screen was a mass of brightly colored icons. An attractive woman with long red hair sat at the other, like a court stenographer, entering the text of what they said into another computer. The sound of the keys as she typed made a dull staccato against the noisy grind of an aging air conditioner under the lone window, where Pio stood, leaning against the wall, arms folded over his chest, expressionless.

Roscani lit a cigarette. "Tell me about Miguel Valera."

"I don't know a Miguel Valera."

"He was a close friend of your brother."

"I'm not familiar with my brother's friends."

"He never spoke of Miguel Valera." Roscani made a note on the pad next to him.

"Not to me."

"Are you certain?"

"Detective, my brother and I were not close. . . . We hadn't spoken for a long time . . ."

Roscani stared a moment, then turned to his computer and punched something up on the screen. He waited for the information to come up, then turned back.

"Your telephone number is 310-555-1719."

"Yes . . ." Harry's defensive antenna suddenly went up. His home number was unlisted. They could get it, he knew. But why?

"Your brother called you last Friday at four-sixteen in the morning Rome time."

That was it. They had a record of Danny's calls.

"Yes, he did. But I wasn't home. He left word on my answering machine."

"Word. You mean a message?"

"Yes."

"What did he say?"

Harry folded one leg over the other, then counted to five and looked at Roscani. "—That's what I wanted to talk to you about in the first place."

Roscani said nothing. Just waited for Harry to continue.

"He was frightened. He said he didn't know what to do. Or what would happen next."

"What did he mean by *happen next*?"

"I don't know. He didn't say."

"What else did he say?"

"He apologized for calling the way he did. And said he would try and call back."

"Did he?"

"No."

"What was he frightened of?"

"I don't know. Whatever it was, it was enough to make him call me after eight years."

"You had not spoken in eight years?"

Harry nodded.

Roscani and Pio exchanged glances.

"When was the last time you saw him?"

"Our mother's funeral. Two years before that."

"You had not spoken with your brother in all that time. And then he calls you, and very shortly afterward he is dead."

"—Yes . . ."

"Was there a particular reason you and your brother were at odds?"

"—No. Some things just build up over time."

"Why were you the one he chose to call now?"

"He said . . . there was no one else he could talk to . . ."

Once again Roscani and Pio exchanged glances.

"We would like to hear the message on your machine."

"I erased it."

"Why?"

"Because the tape was full. It wouldn't have recorded anything else."

"Then there is no proof there was a message. Or that you or someone in your home did not actually speak with him."

Abruptly Harry sat forward. "What are you insinuating?"

"That perhaps you are not telling the truth."

Harry had to work to hold down his anger. "First of all, no one was in my house when the call came. Secondly, when it came in, I was at Warner Brothers studios in Burbank, California, talking about a movie contract for a writer-director I represent and about the opening of his new film. For your information, it just came out this past weekend."

"What is the name of this film?"

"Dog on the Moon," Harry said flatly.

Roscani stared for a moment, then scratched his head and made a note on the pad in front of him.

"And the name of this writer-director," he said without looking up.

"Jesus Arroyo."

Now Roscani did look up.

"A Spaniard."

"Hispanic-American. A Mexican to you. Born and grown up in East L.A." Harry was getting angry. They were pressing him without telling him anything. Acting as if they thought not only Danny but also he were guilty of something.

Roscani stubbed his cigarette into an ashtray in front of him. "Why did your brother murder Cardinal Parma?"

"What—?" Harry was stunned, taken completely off guard.

"Why did your brother kill Rosario Parma, the cardinal vicar of Rome?"

"That's absurd!" Harry looked at Pio. Nothing showed. He was the same as he'd been before, arms still folded over his chest, leaning against the wall by the window.

Roscani picked up another cigarette and held it. "Before Father Daniel joined the Church he was a member of the United States Marine Corps."

"Yes." Harry was still reeling, trying to grasp the magnitude of their accusations. Clear thinking was impossible.

"He trained with an elite unit. He was a highly decorated marksman."

"There are thousands of highly decorated marksmen. He was a *priest*, for God's sake!"

"A priest with the skill to put a tight three-shot pattern into a man's chest at two hundred yards." Roscani stared at him. "Your brother was an excellent shot. He won competitions. We have his records, Mr. Addison."

"That doesn't make him a murderer."

"I'll ask you again about Miguel Valera."

"I said I never heard of him."

"I think you have . . ."

"No, never. Not until you brought his name up."

The stenographer's fingers were running steadily over the keyboard, taking it all down; what Roscani said, what he said, everything.

"Then I will tell you—Miguel Valera was a Spanish Communist from Madrid. He rented an apartment across the Piazza San Giovanni two weeks before the shooting. It was from that apartment the shots were fired that killed Cardinal Parma. Valera was still there when we arrived. Hanging from a pipe in the bathroom, a belt around his neck. . . ." Roscani tapped the cigarette's filter end on the desk, compacting the tobacco. "Do you know what a Sako TRG 21 is, Mr. Addison?"

"No."

"It's a Finnish-made sniper rifle. The weapon used to kill Cardinal Parma. It was found wrapped in a towel behind the couch in the same apartment. Valera's fingerprints were on it."

"Just his . . . ?"

"Yes."

Harry sat back, hands crossed in front of his chin, his eyes on Roscani. "Then how can you accuse my brother of the murder?"

"Someone else was in the apartment, Mr. Addison. Someone who wore gloves. Who tried to make us think Valera acted alone." Roscani slowly put the cigarette in his mouth and lit it, the match still alive in his hand. "What is the price of a Sako TRG 21?"

"I have no idea."

"About four thousand U.S. dollars, Mr. Addison." Roscani twisted the burning match between his thumb and forefinger, putting it out, then dropped it in the ashtray.

"The apartment had been rented at nearly five hundred U.S. dollars a week. Valera paid for it himself in cash. . . . Miguel Valera was a lifelong Communist. A stonemason who worked little. He had a wife and five children he could barely afford to feed and clothe."

Harry stared at him, unbelieving. "Are you intimating that my brother was the other person in the room? That he bought the gun and gave Valera money for the rent?"

"How could he, Mr. Addison? Your brother was a priest. He was poor. He was paid only a small stipend by the Church. He had very little money at all. Not even a bank account. . . . He did not have four thousand dollars for a rifle.

Or the equivalent of one thousand dollars in cash to pay for the rental of an apartment."

"You keep contradicting yourself, Detective. You tell me the only fingerprints on the murder weapon belonged to Valera and in the same breath want me to believe it was my brother who pulled the trigger. And then you carefully explain how he could afford neither the gun nor the apartment. Where are you coming from?"

"The money came from someone else, Mr. Addison."

"Who?" Harry glanced angrily at Pio, then back to Roscani.

The policeman stared for a moment and then his right hand came up, smoke rising from the cigarette between his fingers, the fingers pointed directly at Harry.

"You, Mr. Addison."

Harry's mouth went dry. He tried to swallow but couldn't. *This* was why they had so carefully met him at the airport and brought him to the Questura. Whatever had happened, Danny had become a prime suspect and now they were trying to tie him in. He wasn't going to let them. Abruptly he stood, pushing his chair back.

"I want to call the U.S. Embassy. Right now."

"Tell him," Roscani said in Italian.

Pio moved from the window and crossed the room. "We did know you were coming to Rome. And what flight you were on, but it wasn't for the reason you thought." Pio's manner was easier than Roscani's, the way he stood, the rhythm of his speech—or maybe it was just that he sounded American.

"Late Sunday we requested help from the FBI. By the time they found where you were, you were on your way here." He sat down on the edge of Roscani's desk. "If you want to talk to your embassy you have every right. But understand that when you do, you will very quickly be talking to the LEGATS."

"Not without a lawyer." Harry knew what the LEGATS was. It stood for legal attachés, the name for FBI special agents assigned to U.S. embassies overseas who work in liaison with the local police. But the threat made no difference. Overwhelmed and shocked as he was, he wasn't about to let anyone, the Rome police or the FBI, continue this kind of questioning without someone very well versed in Italian criminal law standing beside him.

"Richieda un mandato di cattura." Roscani looked at Pio.

Harry reacted angrily. "Talk in English."

Roscani stood and walked around his desk. "I told him to call for an arrest warrant."

"On what charge?"

"—A moment." Pio looked at Roscani and nodded toward the door. Roscani ignored him and kept staring at Harry, acting as if Harry himself had killed Cardinal Parma.

Taking him aside, Pio said something in Italian. Roscani hesitated. Then Pio said something else. Roscani relented and they went out.

Harry watched the door close behind them and turned away. The long-haired woman at the keyboard was staring at him. Ignoring her, he walked to the window. It was something to do. Through its heavy glass he could see the narrow cobblestone street below and across it a brick building. At the far end was what looked like a fire station. It felt like a prison.

What the hell had he walked into? What if they were right and Danny had been involved with the assassination? But that was crazy. Or was it? As a teenager Danny had had problems with the law. Not much, but some, like a lot of restless kids. Petty theft, vandalism, fighting, just generally getting into trouble. It was one of the reasons he had gone into the marines, as a way to get some discipline in his life. But that had been years ago; he was a grown man when he died and had been a priest for a long time. To envision him as a killer was impossible. Yet—and Harry didn't want to think about it, but it was true—he would have learned how in the Marine Corps. And then there was the phone call. What if that had been why he had called. What if he had done it and there was no one else he could talk to?

There was a sound and the door opened and Pio came in alone. Harry looked past him, waiting for Roscani to follow but he didn't.

"You have hotel reservations, Mr. Addison?"

"Yes."

"Where?"

"At the Hassler."

"I will arrange to have your luggage taken there." Reaching into his jacket, Pio took out Harry's passport and handed it to him. "You'll need it when you check in."

Harry stared at him. "I can go . . . ?"

"You must be tired—from your grief and from your flight." Pio smiled gently. "And from a confrontation with the police you were hardly prepared for. From our view necessary perhaps, but not very hospitable. I would like to explain what has happened and what is happening. . . . Just the two of us, Mr. Addison. . . . A quiet place at the end of the street. Do you like Chinese?"

Harry kept staring. Good cop, bad cop. Just like in the U.S. And right now Pio was the good one, the friend on Harry's side. It was why Roscani had led the questioning. But it was clear they weren't quite done with him and this was their way of continuing it. What it meant was, bottom line, he had no choice.

"Yeah," he said finally, "I like Chinese."

6

"MERRY CHRISTMAS from the Addisons"

HARRY COULD STILL SEE THE CARD, THE
decorated tree in the background, the posed faces smiling
from it, everyone wearing a Santa Claus hat. He had a copy
of it somewhere at home, tucked in a drawer, its once bright
colors slowing fading, now almost pastels. It was the
last time they were all together. His mother and father would
have been in their mid-thirties. He was eleven, Danny eight,
and their sister, Madeline, almost six. Her sixth birthday
came on January first, and two weeks later she died.

It was a Sunday afternoon, bright and clear and very cold.
He and Danny and Madeline were playing on a frozen pond
near their home. Some older kids were nearby playing
hockey. Several of them skated toward them, chasing after
the puck.

Harry could still hear the sharp crack of the ice. It was
like a pistol shot. He saw the hockey players stop short. And

then the ice just broke away where Madeline was. She never made a sound, just went under. Harry screamed to Danny to run for help, and he threw off his coat and went in after her. But there was nothing but icy black.

It was nearly dark when the fire department divers brought her up, the sky beyond the leafless trees behind them a streak of red.

Harry and Danny and their mother and father waited with a priest in the snow as they came across the ice toward them. The fire chief, a tall man with a mustache, had taken her body from the divers and wrapped it in a blanket and held it in his arms as he led the way.

Along the shore, a safe distance away, the hockey players, their parents and brothers and sisters, neighbors, strangers watched in silence.

Harry started forward, but his father took him firmly by the shoulders and held him back. When he reached shore, the fire chief stopped, and the priest said the last rites over the blanket without opening it. And when he had finished, the fire chief, followed by the divers still with their air tanks and wet suits, walked on to where a white ambulance was waiting. Madeline was put inside and the doors were closed and the ambulance drove off into the darkness.

Harry followed the red dots of taillights until they were gone. Finally he turned. Danny was there, eight years old, shivering with the cold, looking at him.

"Madeline is dead," Danny said, as if he were trying to understand.

"Yes . . . ," Harry whispered.

It was Sunday, January the fifteenth, nineteen seventy-three. They were in Bath, Maine.

*   *   *

PIO WAS RIGHT, Ristorante Cinese, Yu Yuan, on Via delle Quattro Fontane *was* a quiet place at the end of the street. At least it was quiet where he and Harry sat, at a highly lacquered back table away from the red-lanterned front door and spill of noontime customers, a pot of tea and large bottle of mineral water between them.

"You know what Semtex is, Mr. Addison?"

"An explosive."

"Cyclotrimethylene, pentaerythritol tetronitrate, and plastic. When it goes off it leaves a distinctive nitrate residue along with particles of plastique. It also tears metal into tiny pieces. It was the substance used to blow up the Assisi bus. That fact was established by technical experts early this morning and will be announced publicly this afternoon."

The information Pio was giving him was privileged, and Harry knew it, part of what Pio had promised. But it told him little or nothing about their case against Danny. Pio was just doing what Roscani had done, giving him only enough information to keep things going.

"You know *what* blew up the bus. Do you know who did it?"

"No."

"Was my brother the target?"

"We don't know. All we know for certain is that we now have two different investigations. The murder of a cardinal and the bombing of a tour bus."

An aging Oriental waiter came up, glancing at Harry and grinning and exchanging pleasantries in Italian with Pio. Pio ordered for both by rote, and the waiter clapped his hands, bowed crisply, and left. Pio looked back to Harry.

"There are, or rather, were, five ranking Vatican prelates who serve as the pope's closest advisers. Cardinal Parma was one. Cardinal Marsciano is another. . . ." Pio filled his glass with mineral water, watching Harry for a reaction that never came. "Did you know your brother was Cardinal Marsciano's private secretary?"

"No . . ."

"The position gave him direct access to the inner workings of the Holy See. Among them, the pope's itinerary. His engagements—where, when, for how long. Who his guests would be. Where he would enter and exit what building. The security arrangements. Swiss Guards or police or both, how many—Father Daniel never mentioned things like that?"

"I told you, we weren't close."

Pio studied him. "Why?"

Harry didn't respond.

"You hadn't spoken to your brother for eight years. What was the reason?"

"There's no point getting into it."

"It's a simple question."

"I told you. Some things just build up over time. It's old business. Family things. It's boring. Hardly about murder."

For a moment Pio did nothing, then picked up his glass and took a drink of mineral water. "Is this your first time in Rome, Mr. Addison?"

"Yes."

"Why now?"

"I came to bring his body home. . . . No other reason. The same as I said before."

Harry felt Pio starting to push, the way Roscani had earlier, looking for something definitive. A contradiction, a diverting of the eyes, a hesitation. Anything to suggest Harry was holding something back or was flat out lying.

"Ispettore Capo!"

The waiter came grinning, as he had before. Making

room on the table for four steaming platters, setting them between the men, chattering in Italian.

Harry waited for him to finish, and when he left, looked at Pio directly. "I'm telling you the truth. And have been all along. . . . Why don't you keep your promise and tell me what you haven't, the particulars of why you think my brother was involved in the cardinal's murder?"

Steam rose from the platters, and Pio gestured for Harry to help himself. Harry shook his head.

"All right." Pio took a folded sheet of paper from his jacket and handed it to Harry. "The Madrid police found it when they went through Valera's apartment. Look at it carefully."

Harry opened the paper. It was an enlarged photocopy of what looked like a page taken from a personal phone book. The names and addresses were handwritten and in Spanish, the corresponding telephone numbers to the right. Most, from the heading, seemed to be from Madrid. At the bottom of the page was a single phone number, to its left was the letter *R*.

It didn't make sense. Spanish names, Madrid phone numbers. What did it have to do with anything? Except that maybe the *R* at the bottom of the page referred to Rome, but the number beside it had no name at all. Then it came to him.

"Christ," he said under his breath and looked at it again. The telephone number beside the *R* was the one Danny had left on his answering machine. Abruptly he looked up. Pio was staring at him.

"Not just his phone number, Mr. Addison. Calls," Pio said. "In the three weeks leading up to the killing, Valera placed a dozen calls to your brother's apartment from his cellular phone. They became more frequent toward the end, and of shorter duration, as if he were confirming instructions. As far as we've been able to tell, they were the only calls he made while he was here."

"Telephone calls do not make killers!" Harry was incredulous. Was this it? All they had?

A newly seated couple looked in their direction. Pio waited for them to turn back, then lowered his voice.

"You were told there is evidence of a second person in the room. And that we believe it was that second person and not Valera who killed Cardinal Parma. Valera was a Communist agitator, but there is no evidence he ever fired a gun. I remind you your brother was a decorated marksman trained by the military."

"That's a fact, not a connection."

"I'm not finished, Mr. Addison. . . . The murder weapon, the Sako TRG 21, normally takes a .308 Winchester cartridge. In this case it was loaded with American-made Hornady 150-grain spire-point bullets. They are bought primarily at specialty gun shops and used for hunting. . . . Three were taken from Cardinal Parma's body. . . . The rifle's magazine holds ten rounds. The remaining seven were still there."

"So?"

"Valera's personal phone directory was what sent us to your brother's apartment. He wasn't there. Obviously he had gone to Assisi, but we didn't know that. Because of Valera's directory we were able to get a warrant to search . . ."

Harry listened, saying nothing.

"A standard cartridge box holds twenty rounds of ammunition. . . . A cartridge box containing ten Hornady 150-grain spire points was found inside a locked drawer in your brother's apartment. With it was a second magazine for the same rifle."

Harry felt the wind go out of him. He wanted to respond, to say something in Danny's defense. He couldn't.

"There was also a cash receipt for one million seven hundred thousand lire—just over one thousand U.S. dollars, Mr. Addison. The amount Valera paid in cash to rent the apartment. The receipt had Valera's signature. The handwriting was the same as that on the telephone list you have there."

"Circumstantial evidence. Yes, it is. And if your brother were alive, we could ask him about it and give him the opportunity to disprove it." Anger and passion crept into Pio's voice. "We could also ask him why he did what he did. And who else was involved. And if he had been trying to kill the pope. . . . Obviously we can't do any of that. . . ." Pio sat back, fingering his glass of mineral water, and Harry could see the emotion slowly fade.

"Maybe we will find out we were wrong. But I don't think so. . . . I've been around a long time, Mr. Addison, and this is about as close to the truth as you get. Especially when your prime suspect is dead."

Harry's gaze shifted off, and the room became a blur. Until now he had been certain they were mistaken, that they had the wrong man, but this changed everything.

"What about the bus . . . ?" He looked back, his voice barely a whisper.

"Whatever Communist faction was behind Parma's murder, killing one of their own to shut him up? . . . The Mafia doing something else entirely? . . . A disgruntled bus company employee with access to, and knowledge of, explosives? . . . We don't know, Mr. Addison. As I said, the bombing of the bus and the cardinal's murder are separate investigations."

"When will all this be made public?"

"Probably not while the investigation continues. After that we will, in all likelihood, defer to the Vatican."

Harry folded his hands in front of him and stared at the table. Emotions flooded. It was like being told you had an incurable disease. Disbelief and denial made no difference, the X rays, MRIs, and CT scans stared back from the wall just the same.

Yet, for all of that—for all the evidence the police had presented, one solid piece stacked upon the another, they still had no absolute proof, as Pio had admitted. Moreover, no matter what he had told them about the substance of Danny's phone message, only he had heard Danny's voice. The fear and the anguish and the desperation. It was not the voice of a murderer crying out for mercy to the last bastion he knew, but of someone trapped in a terrible circumstance he could not escape.

For some reason, and he didn't know why, Harry felt closer to Danny now than he had since they were boys. Maybe it was because his brother had finally reached out to him. And maybe that was more important to Harry than he knew, because the realization of it had come not as a thought but as a rush of deep emotion, moving him to the point where he thought he might have to get up and leave the table. But he hadn't, because in the next moment another realization had come: he wasn't about to have Danny condemned to history as the man who had killed the cardinal vicar of Rome until the last stone had been turned and the proof was absolute and beyond any doubt whatsoever.

"Mr. Addison, it will be another day at least, perhaps more, before the identification procedures are complete and your brother's body can be released to you. . . . Will you be staying at the Hassler the entire time you are in Rome?"

"Yes . . ."

Pio took a card from his wallet and handed it to him. "I would appreciate it if you kept me informed of your movements. If you leave the city. If you go anywhere where it would be difficult for us to reach you."

Harry took the card and slipped it into his jacket pocket, then his eyes came back to Pio.

"You won't have any trouble finding me."

7

Euro Night Train, Geneva to Rome.
Tuesday, July 7, 1:20 A.M.

CARDINAL NICOLA MARSCIANO SAT IN THE
dark, listening to the methodic click of the wheels as the
train picked up speed, pushing southeast out of Milan toward
Florence and then Rome. Outside, a faint moon touched the
Italian countryside, bathing it in just enough light for him to
know it was there. For a moment he thought of the Roman
legions that had passed under the same moon centuries
before. They were ghosts now, as one day he would be, his
life, like theirs, scarcely a blip on the graph of time.

Train 311 had left Geneva at eight-twenty-five the night
before, had crossed the Swiss-Italian border just after midnight, and would not arrive in Rome until eight the next
morning. A long way around, considering it was only a two-
hour flight between the same cities, but Marsciano had
wanted time to think and to be alone without intrusion.

As a servant of God he normally wore the vestments of his office, but today he traveled in a business suit to avoid attracting attention. To that same end his private compartment in the first-class sleeping car had been reserved under the name N. Marsciano. Honest, yet simple anonymity. The compartment itself was small, but it provided what he needed: a place to sleep, if he ever could; and, more important, a moving station to receive a call on his cellular phone without fear it would somehow be intercepted.

Alone in the darkness, he tried not to think of Father Daniel—the accusations of the police, the evidence they had discovered, the bombed bus. Those things were past, and he dared not dwell on them, even though he knew at some point he would have to confront them again personally. They would have everything to do with his future, the future of the Church, and whether either could survive.

He glanced at his watch, its digital numbers a transparent green in the dark.

1:27

The Motorola cell phone on the small table beside him remained silent. Marsciano's fingers drummed on the narrow arm of his chair, then pushed through his gray-white hair. Finally he leaned forward and poured what was left of the bottle of Sassicaia into his glass. Very dry, very full-bodied, the stately red wine was expensive and little known outside Italy. Little known because the Italians themselves kept it a secret. Italy was filled with secrets. And the older one got, the more there seemed to be and the more dangerous they became. Especially if one were in a position of power and influence, as he was at age sixty.

1:33

Still the phone remained silent. And now he began to worry that something had gone wrong. But he couldn't let himself think that way until he knew for sure.

As he took a sip of the wine, Marsciano's gaze shifted from the phone to the briefcase lying flat on the bed beside it. Inside, tucked away in an envelope beneath his papers and personal belongings, was a nightmare. An audiocassette that had been delivered to him in Geneva Sunday afternoon during lunch. It had come in a package marked *URGENTE* and had been delivered by messenger with no return address or indication of who had sent it. Once he had listened to it, however, he knew instantly where it had come from and why.

As president of the Administration of the Patrimony of the Apostolic See, Cardinal Marsciano was a man in whose hands rested the ultimate financial decisions for the investment of the Vatican's hundreds of millions of dollars in assets. And as such, he was one of the very few who knew exactly how much those assets were worth and where they were invested. It was a position of solemn responsibility and by its very nature open to those things men in high station are always heir to—the corruption of mind and spirit. Men who fell to such temptations usually suffered from greed or arrogance or both. Marsciano was afflicted by neither. His suffering came from a cruel intermingling of profound loyalty to the Church, grievously misplaced trust, and human love; made worse, if that were possible, by his own high position within the Vatican.

The tape recording—in light of the murder of Cardinal Parma and the timing of its delivery—only pushed him farther into darkness. More than simply threaten his own personal safety, by its very existence it raised other, more far-reaching questions: *What else was known? Whom could he trust?*

The only sound was that of the wheels passing over the rails as the train drew ever closer to Rome. Where was the call? What had happened? Something had to have gone wrong. He was certain now.

Abruptly the phone rang.

Marsciano was startled and for a moment did nothing. It rang again. Recovering, he picked up.

"*Si.*" His voice was hushed, apprehensive. Nodding almost imperceptibly, he listened. "*Grazie,*" he whispered finally and hung up.

8

Rome. Tuesday, July 7, 7:45 A.M.

JACOV FAREL WAS SWISS.

He was also Capo dell'Ufficio Centrale Vigilanza, the man in charge of the Vatican police, and had been for more than twenty years. He had called Harry at five minutes after seven, waking him from a deep sleep and telling him it was imperative they talk.

Harry had agreed to meet with him, and now, forty minutes later, was being driven across Rome by one of Farel's men. Crossing the Tiber, they drove beside it for a few hundred yards, then turned down the colonnaded Via della Conciliazione, with the unmistakable dome of St. Peter's in the distance. Harry was certain that was where he was being taken, to the Vatican and to Farel's office somewhere deep inside it. Then abruptly the driver veered off to the right and through an arched portal in an ancient wall and into a neighborhood of narrow streets and old apartment buildings. Two blocks later he made a sharp left to stop in front of a small trattoria on Borgo Vittorio. Getting out, he opened the door for Harry and escorted him into the trattoria.

A lone man in a black suit stood at the bar as they came in. His back to them, his right hand rested beside a coffee cup. He was probably five foot eight or nine, heavy-set, and what little hair he might have had left had been shaved to the skull, leaving the top of his head shining in the overhead light.

"Thank you for coming, Mr. Addison." Jacov Farel's English was colored by a French accent. His voice was husky, as if he'd chain-smoked for years. Slowly the hand pulled away from the coffee cup and he turned. Harry hadn't been able to see the power of the man from the back, but he could now. The shaved head, the broad face with the flattened nose, the neck as thick as a man's thigh, the burly chest tight against his white shirt. His hands, big and strong, looked as if they'd spent most of their fifty-odd years wrapped around the handle of a jackhammer. And then there were his eyes, deep-set, gray-green, unforgiving—abruptly they flashed toward the driver. Without a word, the man took a step backward and left, the click of the door sounding behind him as it closed. Then Farel's eyes shifted to Harry.

"My responsibilities are different from those of the Italian police. They protect a city. The Vatican is its own state. A country inside Italy. Therefore I am accountable for the safety of a nation."

Instinctively Harry glanced around. They were alone. No waiter, no barman, no customers. Just he and Farel.

"The blood of Cardinal Parma splattered my shirt and my face when he was shot. It also fell on the pope, soiling his vestments."

"I'm here to do anything I can to help," Harry said, quietly.

Farel studied him. "I know you talked to the police. I know what you told them. I read the transcripts. I read the report Ispettore Capo Pio wrote after he met with you privately. . . . It's what you didn't tell them that interests me."

"What I didn't tell them?"

"Or what they didn't ask. Or what you left out when they did, purposely, or because you didn't remember or perhaps because it didn't seem important."

Farel's presence, considerable before, now seemed to fill the entire room. Harry's hands felt suddenly damp and there was sweat on his forehead. Again he looked around. Still no one. It was after eight. What time did the staff come to work? Or people come in off the street for breakfast or coffee?—Or had the trattoria been opened for Farel alone?

"You seem uncomfortable, Mr. Addison . . ."

"Maybe it's because I'm tired of talking to the police when I've done nothing and you people keep acting like I have. . . . I was happy to meet with you because I believe my brother is innocent. And to show you I'm willing to cooperate any way I can."

"That's not the only reason, Mr. Addison . . ."

"What do you mean?"

"Your clients. You have to protect them. If you had called the United States Embassy as you threatened—or arranged for an Italian lawyer to represent you in your talks with the police—you knew there was a very good chance the media would find out. . . . Not only would our suspicions about your brother be made public, they would learn about you as well. Who you are, and what you do, and who you personally represent. People who would not want to be linked, however distantly or innocently, to the murder of the cardinal vicar of Rome."

"Who do you think I represent that—?"

Abruptly, Farel cut him off, naming half a dozen of his superstar Hollywood clients in rapid succession.

"Should I keep on, Mr. Addison?"

"How did you get that information?" Harry was shocked and outraged. The identity of his firm's clients was carefully guarded. It meant Farel had not only been digging into his background but also had connections in Los Angeles capable of getting him whatever he asked for. A reach and power that was frightening.

"Your brother's guilt or innocence aside, there is a certain practicality to things. . . . That's why you're talking to me, Mr. Addison, alone and of your own free will and will continue to do so until I am done with you. . . . You have to protect your own success." His left hand found its way up to caress his skull just over his left ear. "It's a nice day. Why don't we go for a walk . . . ?"

THE MORNING SUN was beginning to light the top floors of the buildings around them as they came out and Farel turned them left, onto Via Ombrellari—a narrow cobblestone street without sidewalks, the apartment buildings interrupted here and there by a bar or restaurant or pharmacy. A priest walked by across from them. Farther down, two men noisily loaded empty wine and mineral water bottles into a van outside a restaurant.

"It was a Mr. Byron Willis, a partner in your law firm, who informed you of your brother's death."

"Yes . . ."

So Farel knew that, too. He was doing the same thing Roscani and Pio had done, trying to intimidate him and get him off guard, let him know that no matter what anyone said, he was still a suspect. That Harry knew he was innocent made little difference. Law school years had made him more aware than most of the long history of jails, prisons, and even gallows that had been peopled with the guiltless, men and women charged with crimes far less grievous than the one being investigated here. It was unnerving, if not frightening. And Harry knew it showed, and he didn't like it. Moreover, Farel's digging into his professional world gave everything a calculated spin. One that gave the Vatican policeman added power, because it let him inside Harry's life, and told him there was nowhere he could go that Farel couldn't find out about.

Harry's concern about publicity had been one of the first things he'd addressed yesterday, as soon as he'd left Pio and checked into his hotel, calling Byron Willis at his home in Bel Air. By discussion's end they'd enumerated, almost word for word, the reasons Farel had just given for Harry's keeping a low profile. They'd agreed that, tragic as it was, Danny was dead, and since whatever involvement he'd had or not had in the murder of Cardinal Parma was being kept quiet, it was best for all of them to let it stay that way. The risk that Harry's clients might be revealed and his situation exploited was something neither they, nor he, nor the company needed, especially now, when the media seemed to rule everything.

"Did this Mr. Willis know Father Daniel had contacted you?"

"Yes. . . . I told him when he called to notify me of what had happened . . ."

"You told him what your brother said."

"Some of it. . . . Most of it. . . . Whatever I said, it's in the transcripts of what I told the police yesterday." Harry felt the anger begin to rise. "What difference does it make?"

"How long have you known Mr. Willis?"

"Ten, eleven years. He helped me get into the business. Why?"

"You are close to him."

"Yes, I guess . . ."

"As close to him as to anyone?"

"I guess so."

"Meaning you might tell him things you would tell no one else."

"What are you getting at?"

Farel's gray-green eyes found Harry's and held there. Finally his gaze moved off and they continued to walk. Slowly, deliberately. Harry had no idea where they were going or why. He wondered if Farel did, if it was simply his manner of interrogation.

Behind them, a blue Ford turned the corner, drove slowly for a half block, then pulled over and stopped. No one got out. Harry glanced at Farel. If he was aware of the car, he didn't acknowledge.

"You never spoke with your brother directly."

"No."

Farther down, the men loading bottles finished, and their van pulled from the curb. Parked beyond it was a dark gray Fiat. Two men sat in the front seat. Harry glanced back. The other car was still there. The block was short. If the men in the cars belonged to Farel, it meant they had essentially sealed off the street.

"And the message he left on your answering machine . . . you erased."

"I wouldn't have done it if I had known how things were going to turn out."

Abruptly Farel stopped. They were nearly to the gray Fiat, and Harry could see the men in the front seat watching them. The one at the wheel was young and leaned forward in his seat almost eagerly, as if he hoped something would happen.

"You act like you don't know where we are, Mr. Addison." Farel smiled slowly, then swept his hand at the yellow stained and paint-peeled four-story building in front of them.

"Should I?"

"Number one-twenty-seven Via Ombrellari—you don't know?"

Harry looked down the street. The blue Ford was still there. Then his eyes came back to Farel.

"No, I don't."

"It's your brother's apartment building."

9

DANNY'S APARTMENT WAS ON THE GROUND
floor, small and exceedingly Spartan. Its cubicle of a living
room faced a tiny back courtyard and was furnished with a
reading chair, small desk, floor lamp, and bookcase, all of
which looked as though they had come from a flea market.
Even the books were secondhand, most of them old and
dealing with historical Catholicism, with titles such as *The
Last Days of Papal Rome, 1850–1870, Plenarii Concilii Bal-
timorensis Tertii, The Church in the Christian Roman
Empire.*

The bedroom was sparer yet—a single, blanket-covered
bed and a small chest of drawers, with lamp and telephone
on top, which served as a bedside table. His closet was as
meager. A suit of the classic priest's vestments—black
shirt, black slacks, and black jacket all on one hanger. A
pair of jeans, a plaid shirt, worn gray sweat suit, and pair
of old running shoes. The chest of drawers revealed a
white clerical collar, several pairs of well-worn underwear,

three pairs of socks, a folded sweater, and two T-shirts, one with the logo of Providence College.

"Everything just as he left it when he went to Assisi," Farel said quietly.

"Where were the cartridges?"

Farel led him into the bathroom and opened the door of an ancient commode. Inside were several drawers, all of which had locks that had been pried open, presumably by the police.

"The bottom drawer. In the back behind some toilet tissue."

Harry stared for a moment, then turned and walked slowly back through the bedroom and into the living room. On the top shelf of the bookcase there was a hot plate he hadn't noticed before. Beside it was a lone cup with a spoon in it, and next to that a jar of instant coffee. That was it. No kitchen, no stove, no refrigerator. It was the kind of place he might have rented as a freshman at Harvard, when he had no money at all and was there only because he'd earned an academic scholarship.

"His voice—"

Harry turned. Farel stood in the bedroom doorway watching him, his shaved head looking suddenly too large and disproportionate to his body.

"Your brother's voice on the answering machine. You said he sounded frightened."

"Yes."

"As if he might be afraid for his life?"

"Yes."

"Did he mention names? People you would both know. Family? Friends?"

"No, no names."

"Think carefully, Mr. Addison. You hadn't heard from

your brother in a long time. He was distraught." Farel stepped closer, his words running on. "People tend to forget things when they're thinking about something else."

"If there had been names I would have told the Italian police."

"Did he say why he was going to Assisi?"

"He didn't say anything about Assisi."

"What about another city or town?" Farel kept pushing. "Somewhere he had been or might be going?"

"No."

"Dates? A day. A time that might be important—"

"No," Harry said. "No dates, no time. Nothing like that."

Farel's eyes probed him again. "You are absolutely certain, Mr. Addison . . ."

"Yes, I'm absolutely certain."

A sharp knock at the front door drew their attention. It opened, and the eager driver of the gray Fiat—Pilger, Farel called him—entered. He was even younger than Harry had first thought, baby-faced, looking as if he were barely old enough to shave. A priest was with him. Like Pilger, he was young, probably not thirty, and tall, with dark curly hair and black eyes behind black-rimmed glasses.

Farel spoke to him in Italian. There was an exchange, and Farel turned to Harry.

"This is Father Bardoni, Mr. Addison. He works for Cardinal Marsciano. He knew your brother."

"I speak English, a little, anyway," Father Bardoni said gently and with a smile. "May I offer my deepest condolences . . ."

"Thank you . . ." Harry nodded gratefully. It was the first time anyone had acknowledged Danny in any context outside of murder.

"Father Bardoni has come from the funeral home where your brother's remains were taken," Farel said. "The necessary paperwork is being processed. The documents will be ready for your signature tomorrow. Father Bardoni will accompany you to the funeral home. And the following morning, to the airport. A first-class seat has been reserved for you. Father Daniel's remains will be on the same plane."

"Thank you," Harry said again, right now wanting only to get out from under the authoritarian shadow of the police and take Danny home for burial.

"Mr. Addison," Farel warned, "the investigation is not over. The FBI will follow up for us in the States. They will want to question you further. They will want to talk to Mr. Willis. They will want the names and addresses of relatives, friends, military associates, other people your brother may have known or been involved with."

"There are no living relatives, Mr. Farel. Danny and I were the last of the family. As for who his friends or associates were, I couldn't say. I just don't know that much about his life. . . . But I'll tell you something. I want to know what happened as much as you do. Maybe even more. And I intend to find out."

Harry looked at Farel a beat longer. Then, with a nod to Father Bardoni, he took a final look around the room, a last, private moment to see where and how Danny had lived, and started toward the door.

"Mr. Addison."

Farel's voice rasped sharply after him, and Harry turned back.

"I told you when we met that it's what you haven't said that interests me. . . . It still does. . . . As a lawyer you should know the most insignificant pieces sometimes make the whole. . . . Things so seemingly unimportant, a person might pass them on without realizing it."

"I've told you everything my brother said to me."

"So you say, Mr. Addison." Farel's gaze narrowed and his eyes grasped Harry's and held there. "I was washed with the blood of a cardinal. I will not bathe in the blood of a pope."

The Hotel Hassler. Still Tuesday, July 7, 10:00 P.M.

"GREAT! GREAT! I LOVE IT! . . . HAS HE called in? . . . No, I didn't think he would. He's where? . . . Hiding?"

Harry stood in his room and laughed out loud. Telephone in hand, his shirt open at the neck, sleeves rolled up, shoes off, he turned to lean against the edge of the antique desk near the window.

"Hey, he's twenty-four, he's a star, let him do what he wants."

Signing off, Harry hung up and set the phone on the desk among the pile of legal pads, faxes, pencil stubs, half-eaten sandwich, and crumpled notes. When was the last time he'd laughed, or even felt like laughing? But just now he'd laughed, and it felt good.

Dog on the Moon was a monster hit. Fifty-eight million

dollars for the three-day holiday weekend, sixteen million more than Warner Brothers' highest estimates. Studio number crunchers were projecting a total domestic gross of upward of two hundred and fifty million. And as for its writer-director, Jesus Arroyo, the twenty-four-year-old barrio kid from East L.A. Harry had found six years ago in a special writing program for troubled inner-city teenagers and had mentored ever since, his career was blasting off the planet. In little more than three days he had become the new *enfant terrible,* his golden future assured. Multi-picture contracts worth millions were being overtured to him. So were demands for guest appearances on every major television talk show. And where was baby Jesus in all this? Partying in Vail or Aspen or up the coast looking at Montecito real estate? No? He was—*hiding!*

Harry laughed again at the purity of it. Intelligent, mature, and forceful as Jesus was as a filmmaker, at heart he was really a shy little boy who, following the biggest weekend of his career, could not be found. Not by the media, not by his friends, his latest girlfriend, or even his agent—whom Harry had been on the phone with. No one.

Except Harry.

Harry knew where he was. Jesus Arroyo Manuel Rodriguez was his full name, and he was at his parents' house on Escuela Street in East L.A. He was with his mom and his hospital custodian dad, and his brothers and sisters, and cousins and aunts and uncles.

Yes, Harry knew where he was, and he could call him, but he didn't want to. Let Jesus have his time with his family. He'd know what was going on. If he wanted to be in touch he would be. Much better to let him celebrate in his own way and let all the other stuff, including the congratulatory call from his lawyer, come later. Business did not yet rule his life as it did Harry's and the lives of most everyone else who was a success in the entertainment world.

There had been eighteen calls waiting for Harry to return when he'd checked in yesterday. But he'd answered none of them, just gone to bed and slept for fifteen hours, emotionally and physically exhausted, the idea of business as usual impossible. But tonight, after his encounter with Farel, work had been a welcome relief. And everyone he'd talked to had congratulated him on the big success of *Dog* and the bright future of Jesus Arroyo, and had been kind and sympathetic about his own personal tragedy, apologizing for talking business under the circumstances and then—all those things said—talking business.

For a time it had been exhilarating, even comforting, because it took his mind off the present. And then, as he'd ended the last call, he realized no one he had talked to had any idea that he was dealing with the police or that his brother was the prime suspect in the assassination of the cardinal vicar of Rome. And he couldn't tell them. As much as they were friends, they were business friends, and that was all.

For the first time, it came to him how singular his life really was. With the exception of Byron Willis—who was married and had two young children and still worked as many hours as Harry did and maybe more—he had no genuine friends, no soul mates of any kind. His life moved too quickly for those kinds of relationships to develop. Women were no different. He was part of Hollywood's inner circle, and beautiful women were everywhere. He used them and they used him; it was all part of the game. A private screening, dinner afterward, sex, and then back to business; meetings, negotiations, telephones, maybe seeing no one at all socially for weeks at a time. His longest affair had been with an actress and lasted little more than six months. He'd been too busy, too preoccupied. And until now it had seemed all right.

Turning from the desk, Harry went to the window and looked out. The last time he'd looked, the city had been a dazzle of early-evening sun. Now it was night, and Rome sparkled. Below him, the Spanish Steps and the Piazza di Spagna beyond teemed with people—a mass congregation of coming and going and just being, with little collections of uniformed police here and there making sure none of it got out of hand.

Farther away he could see a convergence of narrow streets and alleyways, above which the orange-and-cream-colored tile rooftops of apartments, shops, and small hotels fingered out in ancient orderly blocks until they reached the black band of the Tiber. Across it was the lighted dome of St. Peter's, that part of Rome where he'd been earlier in the day. Beneath it sprawled Jacov Farel's domain, the Vatican itself. Residence of the pope. Seat of authority for the world's nine hundred and fifty million Roman Catholics. And the place where Danny had spent the final years of his life.

How could Harry know what those years had been like? Had they been enriching or merely academic? Why Danny had gone from the marines to the priesthood he didn't know. It was something he had never understood. Not surprising, because at the time they were barely talking, so how could he have asked at all without sounding judgmental? But looking out now at the lighted dome of St. Peter's, he had to wonder if it was something there, inside the Vatican, that had driven Danny to call him, and afterward sent him to his death.

Who or what had he been so frightened of? And where had it originated? At the moment, the key seemed to be the bombing of the bus. If the police could determine who had done it and why, they would know if Danny himself had been the target. If he had been the target, and the police knew who the suspects were, then they would all be a major step closer to confirming what Harry still believed in his heart— that Danny was not guilty and had been set up. For some unknown reason altogether.

Once more, he heard the voice and the fear.

"I'm scared, Harry. . . . I don't know what to do . . . or . . . what will happen next. God help me."

11

11:30 P.M.

HARRY WOUND HIS WAY DOWN THE VIA
Condotti to the Via del Corso and on, unable to sleep, looking in shop windows, just wandering with the late crowd. Before he'd gone out he'd called Byron Willis in L.A., telling him about his meeting with Jacov Farel and alerting him to the probability of a visit from the FBI, then discussing with him something deeply personal—where Danny should be buried.

That twist—one that, in the crush of everything, Harry hadn't considered—had come in a call from Father Bardoni, the young priest he'd met at Danny's apartment, informing him that, as far as anyone knew, Father Daniel had no will, and the director of the funeral home needed to advise the funeral director in the town where Danny was to be interred about the arrival of his remains.

"Where would he want to be buried?" Byron Willis had asked gently. And Harry's only answer was "I don't know . . ."

"You have a family plot?" Willis had asked.

"Yes," Harry had said. In their hometown of Bath, Maine. In a small cemetery overlooking the Kennebec River.

"Would that be something he would like?"

"Byron, I . . . don't know . . ."

"Harry, I love you and I know you're pained, but this is going to have to be your call."

Harry had agreed and thanked him and then gone out. Walking, thinking, troubled, even embarrassed. Byron Willis was the closest friend he had, yet Harry had never once spoken to him of his family in more than a passing way. All Byron knew was that Harry and Danny had grown up in a small seacoast town in Maine, that their father had been a dockworker, and that Harry had received an academic scholarship to Harvard when he was seventeen.

The fact was, Harry never talked about the details of his family at all. Not to Byron, not to his roommates in college, not to women, not to anyone. No one knew about the tragic death of their sister, Madeline. Or that their father had been killed in a shipyard accident barely a year later. Or that their mother, lost and confused, had remarried in less than ten months, moving them all into a dark Victorian house with a widowed frozen-food salesman who had five other children, who was never home, and whose only reason to marry had been to get a housekeeper and baby-sitter. Or that later, as a young teenager, Danny had been in one scrape after another with the police.

Or, that both brothers had made a pact to get out of there as soon as they were able, to make the long grimness of those years a thing of their past, to leave and never come back—and promised to help each other do it. And, how, by different routes, both had done so.

With that in mind, how in hell could Harry take Byron Willis's suggestion and bury Danny in the family plot? If he wasn't dead it would kill him! Either that or he'd come up out of the grave, grab Harry by the throat, and throw him in instead! So what was Harry supposed to tell the funeral director tomorrow when he asked him where the remains should be sent after they and Harry arrived in New York? Under different circumstances it might have been amusing, even funny. But it wasn't. He had until tomorrow to find an answer. And at the moment, he hadn't a clue.

HALF AN HOUR LATER Harry was back at the Hassler, hot and sweaty from his walk, stopping at the concierge desk to get his room key, and still with no solution. All he wanted was to go up, get into bed, and drop into the total escape of deep, mindless sleep.

"A woman is here to see you, Mr. Addison."

Woman? The only people Harry knew in Rome were police. "Are you sure?"

The concierge smiled. "Yes, sir. Very attractive, in a green evening dress. She's waiting in the garden bar."

"Thank you." Harry walked off. Someone in the office must have had an actress client visiting Rome and told her to look Harry up, maybe to help take his mind off things. It was the last thing he wanted at the end of a day like this. He didn't care who she was or what she looked like.

SHE WAS SITTING alone at the bar when he came in. For a moment the long auburn hair and emerald green evening dress threw him off. But he knew the face; he'd seen

her a hundred times on television, wearing her trademark
baseball cap and L. L. Bean–type field jacket, reporting
under artillery fire from Bosnia, the aftermath of a terrorist
bomb blast in Paris, refugee camps in Africa. She was no
actress. She was Adrianna Hall, top European correspondent
for WNN, World News Network.

Under almost any other circumstance Harry would have
gone out of his way to meet her. She was Harry's age or a little older, bold, adventuresome, and, as the concierge said,
very attractive. But Adrianna Hall was also media, and that
was the last thing he wanted to confront now. How she found
him he didn't know, but she had, and he had to figure out
what to do about it. Or maybe he didn't. All he had to do was
turn and leave, which was what he did, glancing around, acting as if he were looking for someone who wasn't there.

He was almost to the lobby when she caught up with him.

"Harry Addison?"

He stopped and turned. "Yes . . ."

"I'm Adrianna Hall, WNN."

"I know . . ."

She smiled. "You don't want to talk to me . . ."

"That's right."

She smiled again. The dress looked too formal for her.
"I'd had dinner with a friend and I was on my way out of the
hotel when I saw you leave your key with the concierge. . . .
He said you told him you were going for a walk. I took a
chance you wouldn't go too far—"

"Ms. Hall, I'm sorry, but I really don't want to talk to the
media."

"You don't trust us?" This time she smiled with her eyes.
It was a kind of natural twinkle that teased.

"I just don't want to talk. . . . If you don't mind, it's late."

Harry started to turn, but she took his arm.

"What would make you trust me—at least more than you do now?" She was standing close, animated, breathing easily. "If I told you I knew about your brother? That the police picked you up at the airport? That today you met with Jacov Farel . . . ?"

Harry stared at her.

"You don't have to gape. It's my business to know what's going on. . . . But I haven't said anything to anyone but you, and I won't until an official okay is given."

"But you want to see what I'm about anyway."

"Maybe . . ."

Harry hesitated, then smiled. "Thanks—as I said, it's late . . ."

"What if I told you I found you very attractive and that was the real reason I waited for you to come back?"

Harry tried not to grin. This was the kind of thing he was used to at home. A direct and very confident sexual come-on that could be done by either male or female—and taken by the other party either in fun or seriously, depending on one's mood. Essentially it was a playful crumb tossed out to see what, if anything, would happen next.

"On the one hand I'd say it was flattering. On the other I'd say it was a particularly underhanded and politically incorrect approach to probing a story." Harry put the ball back in her court and held his ground.

"You would?"

"Yes, I would."

An elderly threesome came out of the bar and stopped beside them to talk. Adrianna Hall glanced at them, then looked back to Harry, dipped her forehead slightly and lowered her voice.

"Let me see if I can give you a slightly different approach, Mr. Harry Addison. . . . There are times when I just like to fuck strangers." She never took her eyes from him when she said it.

HER APARTMENT WAS SMALL and neat and sensual. It was one of those things, sex that comes right up from nowhere. Heat that just happens. Somebody strikes a match and the whole place goes up.

Harry made it clear from the beginning—when he'd answered her and said, "So do I"—that the subject of either Danny or the murder of the cardinal vicar of Rome was off limits, and she'd agreed.

They'd taken a cab, then walked a half block, talking about America. Mostly politics and sports—Adrianna Hall had grown up in Chicago, moving to Switzerland when she was thirteen. Her father had been a player for the Chicago Blackhawks and later a coach for the Swiss national hockey team—and they were there.

There was a click as she closed the door. Then she turned and came to him in the darkness. Mouth open, kissing him roughly, her tongue exploring his. The back of his hands so gently and expertly running over the top of her evening gown, teasing her breasts. Feeling her nipples harden as he did. Her hands opening his slacks, taking down his shorts. Taking his hardness in her hand, stroking him, then lifting her skirt and rubbing him against the thin silk of her underwear. All the while kissing and deep breathing as if it were for all time. And Harry slipping off her underwear, sliding her dress over her head. Unhooking her bra and throwing it into the darkness as she eased him down onto the couch, slipping his shorts from his ankles and moving up, taking him into her mouth. His head rolling back, letting her, then raising up on his elbows to watch as she did. Thinking he had never felt so enormous in his life. Finally, after minutes, easing her head away, lifting her up, carrying her through the orderliness of the living room—a giggle in the dark as she gave him directions—down a short hallway to her bedroom. Waiting, vamping really, as she pulled a condom from a nearby drawer—swearing under her breath, struggling to tear open the foil—then, succeeding, taking it out, and easing it down around him.

"Turn over," he whispered.

Her smile enraptured him as she did, so that she faced the head of the bed. And he mounted her from behind, feeling the insertion into her warmth, beginning the stroking, the slow in and out, that he sustained almost forever.

Her moaning stayed in his mind for a long time. By Harry's count he'd come five times in two hours, not bad for a thirty-six-year-old. How, and if, she kept score of her own orgasms he had no idea. What he remembered was her not wanting him to fall asleep there. Just kissing him once more and telling him to go back to his hotel, because in two hours she had to get up and go to work.

12

AGAIN HARRY GLANCED AT THE CLOCK.
Time crept. If he slept at all, he didn't know. He could still smell Adrianna's perfume. It was almost masculine, like citrus and smoke. Getting up, going to work in two hours, she'd said. Not just to work like most people, but to the airport and a plane to Zagreb and then into the Croatian backcountry for a story on human rights abuses committed by Croats against Croatian Serbs who had been driven from their homes and slaughtered. It was who she was and what she did.

He remembered, somewhere during their circus, breaking his own rule of not talking about Danny and asking what she knew about the investigation into the bombing of the Assisi bus.

And she'd answered directly, not once, even in tone, accusing him of trying to use her. "They don't know who did it . . ."

He'd looked at her in the darkness—her bright eyes watching his, the gentle rise and fall of her breasts as she breathed—trying to judge if she was telling him the truth. And the truth was, he couldn't tell. So he let it go. In two days he would be gone, and the only time he would see her again would be on television, in her baseball cap and L. L. Bean field jacket, reporting some kind of struggle from somewhere. What mattered now, as he watched her, moved down to caress her breasts, encircle her nipples with his tongue, one and then the other, was that he wanted her once more. And once more after that. And then again, until there was nothing left, everything gone from his mind but this thing that was Adrianna. Selfish, yes. But it wasn't entirely one-sided. The idea, after all, had been hers.

Running his fingers slowly up the inside of her thigh, he'd heard her whimper as he reached the sticky wetness where her legs came together. Fully aroused, he was easing up, about to mount her, when abruptly she shifted, rolling him over and getting on top, pulling his erection sharply inside her.

Moving back, she dug her feet into the tuft of the bed and then leaned forward, hands on either side of his head, eyes wide open, watching him. Slowly she began her work, sliding up and down the length of him. Masterfully. Her full weight behind each calculated thrust. And then, like a rower listening to the cadence of her coxswain, she picked up the beat. Moving faster, and faster, then still. The jockey testing the heart of the creature beneath her. Riding loud and hard and with no mercy. Until she became the thoroughbred herself. Pounding the inside rail. Tasting the Crown and thundering savagely toward the finish. In the blink of an eye she'd made it a new game. What before had been desire had suddenly become a leviathan competition.

Nor had she made a mistake in choosing Harry. Long ago having vowed to master the fine art of "swordsmanship," he watched her every move, then met her stride for stride. Thrust for thrust. Beast against beast. A heart-stopping, all-out match race. A thousand to one as to who would explode first.

They crossed the line together. A howling, sweating, photo finish of orgasmic pyrotechnics that left them sprawled side by side and gasping for air, wholly spent, their inner workings worn raw. Quivering in the dark.

Harry had no idea why, but in that moment a far-off part of him stood back and wondered if Adrianna had picked him—not because he might be a lead player in a major story and it was secretly her style to establish an early personal relationship—not either because she simply liked to have sex with strangers—but for another reason altogether . . . because she was afraid of tomorrow—of going to Zagreb. Because maybe this was one time too many and something would happen and she would die somewhere in the Croatian countryside. Maybe what she wanted was to breathe as much more life as she could before she went. And Harry just happened to be the one she chose to help her do it.

4:36

Death.

In the dark of room 403 at the Hotel Hassler, there were shutters closed and drapes drawn against the approaching dawn, and yet sleep still did not come to Harry. The world spun, faces danced past.

Adrianna.

The detectives Pio and Roscani.

Jacov Farel.

Father Bardoni, the young priest who was to escort him and Danny's remains to the airport.

Danny.

Death.

Enough! Turning on the light, Harry threw back the covers and got up, going to the small desk by the telephone. Picking up his notes, he reviewed business deals he'd worked in the hours before he'd gone out. A television contract to pick up a series star for a fourth year at an increase of fifty thousand per episode. An agreement for a top screenwriter to do a month's polish on a script that had been rewritten four times already. Writer's fee, five hundred thousand dollars. A deal in the works for two months for a major A-list director to shoot an action film on location in Malta and Bangkok for a flat fee of six million against ten percent of the first dollar box office gross, finally done. Then undone a half hour later because the male star, for reasons unknown, abruptly pulled out. Two hours and half a dozen phone calls later, the star was back in, but by now the director was considering other offers. A call to the star at lunch at a trendy West L.A. restaurant, another to the studio head in his car somewhere in the San Fernando valley, and still another to the director's agent ended in a four-way conference call to the director at home in Malibu. Forty minutes later the director was back on the picture and getting ready to leave for Malta the following morning.

By the time it was over, Harry had negotiated deals worth, give or take, seven and a half million dollars. Five percent of which, roughly three hundred and seventy-five thousand dollars, went to his firm, Willis, Rosenfeld and Barry. Not too shabby for somebody working on anxiety, autopilot, and very little sleep in a hotel room halfway around the world. It was why he was who he was and doing what he did . . . and why he was paid what he was paid, plus bonus, plus profit sharing, plus. . . . Suddenly it all felt very hollow and unimportant.

Abruptly Harry shut out the light and closed his eyes against the dark. When he did, shadows came. He tried to push them away, tried to think of something else. But they came anyway. Shadows moving slowly along a distant iridescent wall, then turning and coming toward him. Ghosts. One, two, three, and then four.

Madeline.

His father.

His mother.

and then

Danny . . .

13

THEIR FOOTSTEPS WERE SILENT AS THEY came down the stairs. Harry Addison, Father Bardoni, and the director of the funeral home, Signore Gasparri. At the bottom Gasparri turned them left and down a long, mustard-colored corridor with pastoral paintings of the Italian countryside decorating the walls.

Deliberately, Harry touched his jacket pocket, feeling the envelope Gasparri had given him when he'd come in. In it were Danny's few personal belongings recovered at the scene of the bus explosion—a charred Vatican identification, a nearly intact passport, a pair of eyeglasses, the right lens missing, the left cracked, and his wristwatch. Of the four, it was the watch that told most the true horror of what had happened. Its band burned through, its stainless steel scorched, and its crystal shattered, it had stopped on July 3 at 10:51

A.M., scant seconds after the Semtex detonated and the bus exploded.

Harry had made the burial decision earlier that morning. Danny would be interred in a small cemetery on the west side of Los Angeles. For better or worse, Los Angeles was where Harry lived and where his life was, and despite the emotional ride he was on now he saw little reason to think he would change and move elsewhere. Moreover, the thought of having Danny nearby was comforting. He could go there from time to time, make certain the grave site was cared for, maybe even talk to him. It was a way that neither would be alone or forgotten. And, in some ironic way, the physical closeness might help assuage some of the distance that had been between them for so long.

"Mr. Addison, I beg you"—Father Bardoni's voice was gentle and filled with compassion—"for your own sake. Let past memories be the lasting ones."

"I wish I could, Father, but I can't . . ."

The thing about opening the casket and seeing him had come only in the last minutes, on the short drive from the hotel to the funeral home. It was the last thing on earth Harry wanted to do, but he knew that if he didn't do it, he'd regret it for the rest of his life. Especially later on, when he got older and could look back.

Ahead of them, Gasparri stopped and opened a door, ushering them into a small, softly lit room where several rows of straight-backed chairs faced a simple wooden altar. Gasparri said something in Italian, and then left.

"He's asked us to wait here . . ." Father Bardoni's eyes behind his black-rimmed glasses reached out with the same feeling as before, and Harry knew he was going to ask him again to change his mind.

"I know you mean well, Father. But please don't . . ."

Harry stared at him for a moment to make sure he understood, then turned away to look at the room.

Like the rest of the building, it was old and worn with time. Its plaster walls, cracked and uneven, had been patched and patched again and were the same earthen yellow as the hallway outside. In contrast to the dark wood of the altar and the chairs facing it, the terra-cotta floor seemed almost white, its color faded by years, if not centuries, of people coming to sit and stare and then leave, only to be replaced by others who had come for the same reason. The private viewing of the dead.

Harry moved to one of the chairs and sat down. The grisly process of identifying and then examining the bodies of those killed on the Assisi bus for explosive residue had been managed quickly and pragmatically by a larger-than-usual staff at the request of an Italian government still shaken by the murder of Cardinal Parma. The task completed, the remains had been sent from the morgue—the Istituto di Medicina Legale at the City University of Rome—to various funeral homes nearby, there to be placed in sealed caskets for return to their families for burial. And despite the investigation surrounding him, Danny had been treated no differently. He was here now, somewhere in Gasparri's building, his mutilated body, like those of the others, sealed away for transport home and final disposition.

Harry could have left it that way, maybe *should* have left it that way—his casket unopened; just taken him back to California for interment. But he couldn't. Not after all that had happened. What Danny looked like didn't matter. He needed to see him one last time, to make one final gesture that said, *I'm sorry I wasn't there when you needed me. I'm sorry we somehow got locked into the years of bitterness and misunderstanding we did. That we never got to talk about it,*

or work through it, or even try to understand. . . . To say sim-
ply, Goodbye and I love you, and always did, no matter
what.

"Mr. Addison"—Father Bardoni had moved up and was
standing beside him—"for your own good. . . . I have seen
people as strong and determined as you crumble as they witness the unspeakable. . . . Accept God's way. Know your
brother would want you to remember him as he was."

There was a sound as the door behind them opened and a
man with close-cropped gray-white hair entered. He was
nearly six feet tall and handsome and carried with him an
aura that was both aristocratic and at the same time kind and
humane. He wore the black cassock and red sash of a cardinal of the Church. A red zucchetto was on his head, and a
gold pectoral cross hung from a chain around his neck.

"Eminence . . ." Father Bardoni bowed slightly.

The man nodded, his eyes going to Harry. "I am Cardinal
Marsciano, Mr. Addison. I came to offer my deepest sympathies."

Marsciano's English was excellent, and he seemed to be
comfortable speaking it. The same was true of his manner;
his eyes, his body language, everything about him comfortable and comforting.

"Thank you, Eminence . . ." Friend of power brokers and
world celebrities, Harry had never once been in the presence
of a cardinal, let alone a man of Marsciano's stature within
the Church. Having been brought up Catholic, no matter
how nonreligious, how totally non-churchgoing he was now,
Harry was humbled. It was as if he were being visited by a
head of state.

"Father Daniel was my personal secretary, and had been
for many years . . ."

"Yes, I know . . ."

"You are waiting here now, in this room, because it is your wish to see him . . ."

"Yes."

"You had no way of knowing, but Father Bardoni called me while you were with Signore Gasparri. He thought perhaps I would have better luck in dissuading you than he." The slightest hint of a smile rose then left. "I have seen him, Mr. Addison. I was the one the police asked to identify the body. I have seen the horror of his death. What the proud inventions of mankind can do."

"It doesn't matter. . . ." Marsciano's presence aside, Harry was resolute; what he had chosen to do was deep and very personal, between Danny and himself. "I hope you can understand."

Marsciano was silent for a long moment. Finally he spoke. "Yes, I can understand."

Father Bardoni hesitated, then left the room.

"You are very much like him," Marsciano said quietly. "That is a compliment."

"Thank you, Eminence."

Immediately a door near the altar opened and Father Bardoni came back in. He was followed immediately by Gasparri and a heavy-set man wearing a crisp white jacket who pushed a hospital gurney. On it was a small wooden coffin no bigger than a child's. Harry felt his heart catch in his throat. Inside it was Danny, or what was left of him. Harry took a deep breath and waited. *How do you prepare for something like this? How does anyone?* Finally he looked to Father Bardoni.

"Ask him to open it."

"Are you certain?"

"Yes."

Harry saw Marsciano nod. Gasparri hesitated, and then in one motion leaned forward and removed the lid from the casket.

For a moment Harry did nothing. Then, steeling himself, he stepped forward and looked down. As he did, he heard himself gasp. The thing was on its back. Most of the right torso was gone. Where there should have been a face there was a crushed mass of skull and matted hair, with a jagged hole where the right eye would have been. Both legs had been sheared off at the knee. He looked for the arms, but there were none. What made the whole thing even more obscene was that someone had pulled on a pair of underpants, as if to protect the viewer from the indecency of the genitals, whether they were there or not.

"Oh, God," he breathed. "Oh, fucking God!" Horror and disgust and loss swept over him. The color drained from his face, and he had to put out his hand to keep his balance. Somewhere he heard the rattle of Italian, and it took a moment before he realized Gasparri was talking.

"Signore Gasparri apologizes for what your brother looks like," Father Bardoni said. "He wants to cover him again, to take him away."

Harry's eyes lifted to Gasparri. "Tell him no, not yet . . ."

Fighting everything in him, Harry turned to look at the mutilated torso once more. He had to pull himself together. To think. To say silently to Danny what needed to be said. Then he saw Cardinal Marsciano gesture and Gasparri move forward with the lid. At the same time something else registered.

"No!" he said sharply, and Gasparri froze where he was. Reaching out, Harry touched the cold chest, then ran his fingers down under the left nipple. Suddenly he felt his legs turn to rubber.

"Are you all right, Mr. Addison?" Father Bardoni moved toward him.

Abruptly Harry pulled away and looked up. "It's not him. It's not my brother."

DAY OF CONFESSION
fingers down under the left nipple. Suddenly he felt his legs
turn to rubber . . . .
"Are you all right . . ." . . . . Father Bardoni moved
toward him.
Abruptly Harry pulled away and pushed up. "It's not him,
it's not my brother."

HARRY DIDN'T KNOW WHAT TO THINK OR
how to feel. That it might be someone other than Danny in
the casket had never occurred to him. That after everything—the police work, the investigations by how many
agencies, the recovery of the personal articles, the identification of the body by Cardinal Marsciano, the death cer-
tificate—they could have made this kind of error was
unconscionable.

Cardinal Marsciano put a hand on his sleeve. "You are
weary and filled with grief, Mr. Addison. In circumstances
like this our hearts and emotions do not always let us think
clearly."

"Eminence," Harry said sharply. They were all staring at
him—Marsciano, Father Bardoni, Gasparri, and the man in
the starched white jacket. Yes, he was tired. Yes, he was filled
with grief. But his thinking had never been clearer in his life.

"My brother had a large mole under his left nipple. It's
called a third breast. I've seen it a thousand times. Medically

it's known as a supernumerary nipple. Whoever's in that casket has no mole under his left nipple. That person is not my brother. It's as simple as that."

CARDINAL MARSCIANO closed the door to Gasparri's office, then gestured toward a pair of gilded chairs in front of the funeral director's desk.

"I'll stand," Harry said.

Marsciano nodded and sat down.

"How old are you, Mr. Addison?"

"Thirty-six."

"And how long has it been since you last saw your brother without his shirt or with it, for that matter? Father Daniel was not merely an employee, he was a friend. Friends talk, Mr. Addison. . . . You had not seen him for many years, had you?"

"Eminence, that person is not my brother."

"Moles can be removed. Even from priests. People do it all the time. I should imagine you, in your business, would know that better than I."

"Not Danny, Eminence—especially not Danny. Like most everyone else, he was insecure growing up. What made him feel better about himself was when he had things other people didn't. Or did things differently from those around him. He used to drive our mother crazy opening his shirt and showing his mole to people. He liked to think it was some kind of secret baronial mark, and that he was really descended from royalty. And unless he changed deeply and immeasurably since then, he would never have had it removed. It was a badge of honor, it kept him apart."

"People do change, Mr. Addison," Cardinal Marsciano spoke gently and quietly. "And Father Daniel did change a great deal in the years I knew him."

For a long moment Harry stared, saying nothing. When he did speak, he was quieter but no less adamant. "Isn't it possible there was a mix-up at the morgue? That maybe another family has Danny's body in a sealed casket without knowing it? . . . It's not unreasonable to imagine."

"Mr. Addison, the remains you saw are those I identified." The cardinal's response was sharp, even indignant. "Presented to me by the Italian authorities." No longer the comforter, Marsciano had suddenly become acerbic and authoritative.

"Twenty-four people were on that bus, Mr. Addison. Eight survived. Fifteen of the dead were positively identified by members of their own families. That left only one. . . ." For the briefest moment Marsciano's manner reverted and his humanity returned. "I, too, had hopes that a mistake had been made. That it was someone else. That perhaps Father Daniel was still away, unaware of what had happened.

"But I was confronted by fact and evidence." Marsciano's edge returned. "Your brother was a frequent visitor to Assisi and more than one person who knew him saw him get on the bus. The transport company was in radio contact with the driver along the way. His only stop was at a toll station. Nowhere else. Nowhere where a passenger could have gotten off prior to the explosion. And then there were his personal belongings found among the wreckage. His reading glasses, which I knew only too well from the many times he left them on my desk, and his Vatican identification were in the pocket of a shredded jacket still on the remains. . . . We cannot change the truth, Mr. Addison, and mole or not, and whether you want to believe it or not, the truth is he is dead." Marsciano paused, and

Harry could see his mood shift once more and something darker come into his eyes.

"You have encountered the police and Jacov Farel. So have we all. . . . Did your brother conspire to kill Cardinal Parma? Or perhaps even the Holy Father? Did he actually fire the shots? Was he, at heart, a Communist who despised us all? I cannot answer. . . . What I can tell you is that for the years I knew him he was kind and decent and very good at what he did, which was controlling me." The hint of a smile flickered, then left.

"Eminence," Harry said, intensely. "Did you know he'd left a message on my answering machine only hours before he was killed?"

"Yes, I was told . . ."

"He was scared, afraid of what would happen next. . . . Do you have any idea why?"

For a long moment Marsciano said nothing. Finally he spoke, directly and quietly. "Mr. Addison, take your brother from Italy. Bury him in his own land and love him for the rest of your life. Think, as I do, that he was falsely accused and that one day it will be proven so."

FATHER BARDONI SLOWED the small white Fiat behind a tour bus, then turned onto Ponte Palatino, taking Harry from Gasparri's and back across the Tiber to his hotel. Midday Rome was loud, with bright sun and filled with traffic. But Harry saw and heard only what was in his mind.

"Take your brother from Italy and bury him in his own land," Marsciano had said again as he'd left, driven away in a dark gray Mercedes by another of Farel's black-suited men.

Marsciano had not talked of the police and Jacov Farel without purpose; his not answering Harry's query, too, had been deliberate. His charity had been in his indirectness, leaving it to Harry to fill in the rest—a cardinal had been murdered, and the priest thought to have done it was dead. So was his colleague in the murder. So, too, were fifteen others who had been on the Assisi bus. And whether Harry wanted to believe it or not, the remains of that priest, the suspected assassin, were officially and without question those of his brother.

To make certain he understood, Cardinal Marsciano had done one more thing: turned and looked at Harry severely as he'd walked down the steps to his car, his glance more telling than anything he'd said or implied. There was danger here, and doors that should not be opened. And the best thing Harry could do would be to take what had been offered and leave as quickly and quietly as possible. While he still could.

15

Ispettore Capo, Gianni Pio
Questura di Roma
sezione omicidi

HARRY SAT IN HIS HOTEL ROOM, TURNING
Pio's card over in his hand. Father Bardoni had dropped him
off just before noon, saying he would pick him up at six-
thirty the following morning to take him to the airport.
Danny's casket would already be there, checked in. All
Harry would have to do would be board the plane.

The trouble was, even in the shadow of Marsciano's
warning, Harry couldn't. He could not take a body home and
bury it for all time as Danny's when he knew in his heart it
was not. Nor could he take it home and, by burying it, make
it easy for the investigators to officially close the book on the
murder of the cardinal vicar of Rome; an act that, for all
intents, would brand Danny forever as his killer. And this,

after his meeting with Marsciano, was something Harry was more certain than ever was not true.

The problem was what to do about it, and how to do it quickly.

It was twelve-thirty in the afternoon in Rome, three-thirty in the morning in Los Angeles. Whom could he call for help there right now who would be able to do anything other than be sympathetic? Even if Byron Willis or someone in the office could arrange for a prominent Italian attorney to represent him in Rome, it wouldn't happen in the next few hours.

And even if it did, then what? They would meet. Harry would explain what had happened. And he would be back to square one. This wasn't simply about a misidentified corpse, it was about an investigation of murder on the highest levels. In no time, they would all be under an intense media spotlight, and he, his firm, and his clients would make world news. No, he had to find another way. Come from the inside, ask the help of someone who already knew what was going on.

Again Harry looked at Pio's card. Why not the Italian homicide investigator? They had developed a relationship of sorts, and Pio had encouraged further communication. He had to trust someone, and he wanted to believe he could trust Pio.

12:35

Someone in Pio's office who spoke English said the *ispettore capo* was out but took Harry's name and number, saying he would call back. That was all. That he would call back. No idea when.

12:55

What to do if Pio didn't call? Harry didn't know. The best he could do was put his faith in the policeman and his professionalism and hope he would call back sometime before six-thirty tomorrow morning.

1:20

Harry had taken a shower and was shaving when the phone rang. Immediately he picked the receiver from the mount over the sink, smearing it with Ralph Lauren gel.

"Mr. Addison—"

It was Jacov Farel.

"Something new has come up concerning your brother. I thought it might interest you."

"What is it?"

"I'd rather you saw for yourself, Mr. Addison. My driver will pick you up and take you to a site near the scene of the bus explosion. I will meet you there. Will ten minutes give you enough time?"

"Yes."

"Good."

THE DRIVER'S NAME was Lestingi or Lestini. Harry didn't quite get the pronunciation, nor did he ask again, because the man apparently spoke no English. Dressed in aviator sunglasses, off-white polo shirt, jeans, and running shoes, Harry simply got into the rear seat of a maroon Opel and sat back as they drove off, staring at the blur of Rome as they wound through it.

The idea of another encounter with Farel was disturbing enough, but projecting what he might have found at the site of the explosion troubled Harry even more. Obviously, whatever it was would not be something in Danny's favor.

Up front, Lestingi or Lestini, in the trademark black suit of Farel's soldiers, slowed for a toll plaza, took a ticket, and accelerated out onto the Autostrada. Immediately the city fell away. Ahead were only vineyards and farms and open land.

As the Opel pushed north, with only the hum of its tires and the whine of its engine for sound, as they passed signs for the towns of Feronia, Fiano, and Civitella San Paolo, Harry thought about Pio and wished it had been he who had called him and not Farel. Pio and Roscani were tough policemen, but at least there was something human about them. Farel—with his presence and bulk and raspy voice and the way his glassy stare cut through you—seemed more like some kind of beast, ruthless and without conscience.

Maybe it was because he had to be. Maybe it was because, as he said, he was accountable for the safety of a nation—and of a pope. And maybe, over time, that kind of strain and responsibility unknowingly turned you into something that, at heart, you were not.

16

TWENTY MINUTES LATER FAREL'S DRIVER
swung off the Autostrada, paid the toll, and they moved off
once more, turning onto a country highway, passing a gas
station and a large building housing farm equipment. Then
there was nothing but the road and cornfields on either side
of it. They drove on, a mile, then two, then three. The bus
had blown up on the Autostrada, and they were rapidly moving away from it.

"Where are we going?" Harry asked suddenly.

The driver looked at him in the rearview mirror and shook
his head. *"Non capisco inglese."*

In the last minutes they had passed no other traffic. Harry
looked over his shoulder, then out through the windshield.
The corn was lush, higher than the car. Dirt farm roads cut
off left and right, but they kept on. Five miles now. Harry's
uneasiness grew. Then he felt the car begin to slow. He
watched the speedometer drop, 80 kilometers, 60, 40, 20.
Abruptly the driver swung right, turning off the highway
and starting down a long, rutted lane. Instinctively, Harry
glanced at the door locks to see if they were down, if the driver controlled them electronically from up front.

There were none.

Only holes in the leatherette trim where they'd been. Then he realized this was a police car, and the rear seats of police cars never had door locks. They were always locked and could be opened only from the outside.

"Where are we going?" Harry said it louder this time. He could feel the thump of his heart against his chest. His palms were sticky with sweat.

"Non capisco inglese."

Again the driver glanced at him in the mirror. Then Harry saw his foot press down on the accelerator. The car picked up speed, bucking and jolting over the uneven road. Corn rows flew past. Behind them was a curtain of dust. Harry put out a hand to keep his balance. Sweat trickled down from under his arms. For the first time in his life he felt real fear.

Without warning the road turned, and they rounded a bend. Ahead was a clearing and a modern two-story house. A gray Alfa Romeo was parked on dry grass alongside a tiny three-wheel farm vehicle. The Opel slowed and then stopped. The driver got out and walked around the car, his footsteps crunching on the gravel. Then he pulled the door open and motioned for Harry to get out.

"Fuck," Harry swore under his breath. He got out slowly, watching the man's hands, trying to decide what to do if he moved them. Then he saw the door to the house open. Two men came out. Farel was one and—Harry felt a huge surge of relief cut through him—Pio was the other. A man and two young boys followed. Harry looked off and at the same time let out a deep sigh. Behind the house, on the far side of a row of trees, traffic flowed on the Autostrada. They had done nothing but make a large circle off the highway and come up on the house from behind.

17

"THE *ISPETTORE CAPO* WILL TELL YOU."
Farel's eyes held on Harry, but only for a moment. Then he turned, and he and Pio walked to the rear of the Alfa Romeo. It was only as Pio opened the trunk that Harry realized both men wore surgical gloves and that Pio carried something in a clear plastic bag.

Putting whatever it was in the trunk, Pio pulled off the gloves and found a notebook. Filling out some kind of form, he signed it and handed it to Farel, who scrawled his own signature on it, pulled off the top copy, and, folding it, slid it into his jacket pocket.

With a nod to the man who had followed them from the farmhouse, Farel glanced once more at Harry, then got into the Opel. There was the roar of engine and spinning of wheels in the gravel and then Farel and the man who had driven Harry out from Rome were gone, with only swirling dust to suggest they'd been there at all.

"Grazie," Pio said to the man standing with the two boys. *"Prego,"* the man said, then gathered the youngsters and took them back into the house.

Pio looked to Harry. "The boys are his sons. They found it."

"Found what?"

"The gun."

Pio took Harry to the back of the car and showed him what he'd put in the trunk. It was what remained of a pistol, sealed inside a clear evidence bag. Through the plastic, Harry could see a small automatic with a silencer attached to the barrel. Its blue metal was scorched, its polymer grips all but melted.

"It's still loaded, Mr. Addison." Pio looked at him. "It was probably thrown clear when the bus overturned; otherwise the ammunition would have gone off and the weapon would have been destroyed."

"Are you concluding that it belonged to my brother?"

"I'm not concluding anything, Mr. Addison. Except, most pilgrims to Assisi do not carry automatic pistols mounted with silencers. . . . For your information, the make is a Llama XV. Small-frame auto-pistol." Pio slammed the trunk shut. "It was made in Spain."

THEY RODE WITHOUT SPEAKING. Past the high cornstalks. Down the dirt road. The Alfa banging over its ruts. The dust kicking up behind them. At the country highway, Pio turned left, toward the entrance to the Autostrada.

"Where's your partner?" Harry tried to break the quiet.

"At his son's confirmation. He took the day off."

"I called you . . ."

"I know—why?"

"About what happened at the funeral home . . ."

Pio made no reply, just kept driving, as if he were waiting for Harry to finish.

"You don't know?" Harry was genuinely surprised. He was certain Farel had learned of it and would, at the very least, have informed Pio.

"Know what?"

"I was at the funeral home. I viewed my brother's remains. The body is not his."

Pio's head came around. "Are you certain?"

"Yes."

"The funeral home made a mistake. . . ." Pio half shrugged. "Unfortunately it happens. It is especially understandable under the circum—"

Harry cut him off. "The remains are the same as those Cardinal Marsciano identified at the morgue."

"How do you know?"

"He was there, he told me."

"Marsciano came to the funeral home?"

"Yes."

Pio seemed genuinely surprised, his reaction honest and instantaneous. It was enough for Harry to tell him the rest. In thirty seconds he explained about Danny's mole and the reasons why he would never have had it removed. About his private meeting with Marsciano in Gasparri's office, and the cardinal's insistence that the body was his brother's and that he accept the fact and get out of the country with it while he could.

Pio stopped at the tollbooth, picked up a ticket, and swung them onto the Autostrada toward Rome.

"You're certain the mistake is not yours . . ."

"No, it's not." Harry was adamant.

"You know his personal belongings were found where the remains were recovered . . ."

"I have them here." Harry touched his jacket. The envelope Gasparri had given him was still in his pocket. "His passport, watch, his glasses, the Vatican ID—they may have been his. The body isn't."

"And you think Cardinal Marsciano knows that . . ."

"Yes."

"You are aware he is one of the most powerful and prominent men in the Vatican."

"So was Cardinal Parma."

Pio studied Harry, then glanced in the rearview mirror. A dark green Renault was a half mile back, holding speed with them, and had been for some time.

Pio looked back to the road ahead, accelerating past a truck hauling lumber, then pulled into the lane in front of it.

"You know what I would be thinking if I were you." Pio kept his eyes on the road.

"Is my brother still alive? And if he is, where is he?"

Harry looked at Pio, then turned away. That Danny might still be alive was a thought that came the moment he realized the corpse was not his. But he hadn't let himself think about it. Couldn't let himself think about it. Danny had been on the bus. Those who survived were accounted for. So, for Danny to still be alive wasn't possible. Any more than it was possible for Madeline to have remained alive all that time under the ice. Yet Harry had stayed there watching, an eleven-year-old shivering in his wet and freezing clothes, refusing to go home and change, while the fire department divers worked. Yes, Madeline was down there in the icy, black water, freezing cold and wet as he, but she was still alive, he knew it. But she wasn't. And neither was Danny. To think so was not only unrealistic but far too painful to even consider.

"Anyone would have thought about it, Mr. Addison. When there is a change of facts, hope is natural. What if he were still alive? I would like to know that too. . . . So, one way or another, why don't we attempt to find out?" Pio smiled, not unselfishly, and glanced in the mirror once more.

They had reached the bottom of a long hill with the lumber truck now almost a mile behind. Then Pio saw a car come into the passing lane beside it, accelerate, and then cut back into the travel lane in front of it.

The green Renault.

18

IT WAS AFTER FOUR WHEN THEY CAME OFF the Autostrada, moving with traffic down Via Salaria toward the center of the city. Pio had been alert the whole time, watching the green Renault in the mirror. He'd been expecting it to follow them off at the toll exit and was prepared to radio for assistance if it had. But it hadn't and instead stayed on the Autostrada.

Still, its presence, the way it had remained with them for so long made him nervous, and he kept an eye on the road behind them as he unveiled his thoughts to Harry.

The idea, he told him, would be to use the gun found at the bus site as a reason to keep Harry in Rome for further questioning and to once again visit the victims of the Assisi bus. Querying the survivors to determine if any had seen a man with a gun onboard; a question that would not have come up earlier because there had been no reason to suspect a gunman and because most still suffered from some degree of shock. There was a chance, of course, the gun had been used against a passenger, but because of the silencer, the others would not have heard it. It would have been a bold move, one made by a professional. But done right, in all probability it would have worked. The victim, appearing to be doing nothing more than sleeping, would not have been found until the bus had reached the terminal and everyone else had gotten off and dispersed.

Using that possibility as justification would give them a chance to carefully reexamine everyone. The living and the dead. They would start with the eight survivors and go from there. Some were still hospitalized, others had been sent home. If Father Daniel was not among them—and Pio was certain he would not be—then they would move on to the dead, professing to be looking for gunshot wounds, something that could have easily been overlooked earlier, considering the condition of the corpses and the gun's small caliber. In that way each set of remains could be carefully examined once more, this time from a different perspective, because they would be looking for one person in particular, Father Daniel. And, if after everything, his body was still not there, then it would be safe to begin to suspect that the accused killer of the cardinal vicar of Rome was still somewhere among the living.

Roscani would know their real purpose, but only he. No one else would be told, not even Farel.

"I must tell you truthfully, Mr. Addison." Pio stopped for a red light. "We can go just so far before Farel finds out. When he does, he may terminate everything."

"Why?"

"Because of what Cardinal Marsciano said to you. Because if what has happened has to do with Vatican politics, Farel will end it right there. The case will be closed, and we will have no authority to pursue it. The Vatican is a sovereign state and not part of Italy. Our job is to cooperate with the Holy See and help them any way we can. And if they do not invite us in, we cannot go."

"Then what?"

The light changed, and Pio moved the Alfa Romeo off, shifting through the H of the manual transmission. "Then nothing. Unless you go to Farel. And Farel, I can assure you, will not help you."

Harry saw Pio glance in the mirror again. He had done it several times while they were on the Autostrada, and he'd thought nothing of it. A driver being cautious. But now they were on city streets, and this was the third time in the last few minutes.

"Something wrong?"

"I don't know . . ."

A small white Peugeot was two cars behind them. Pio had been watching it ever since they'd turned onto Via Salaria. Now he turned left onto Via Chiana and then right onto Corso Trieste. The Peugeot moved out in traffic, staying with them.

Ahead was a cross street bordering a small park, and Pio took it fast, downshifting suddenly and making a sharp right without a signal. The Alfa leaned heavily, its tires screeching. Immediately Pio slowed, his eyes on the mirror. The Peugeot came into view but did not turn, just continued on.

"Sorry." Pio accelerated again. They were in a quiet neighborhood separated by the park. Old buildings interspersed with new. Big trees, lush bushes, and everywhere oleander in bloom. Pio turned a corner and again glanced at the mirror.

The Peugeot.

It had just cut in from a side street and was accelerating toward them. Instinctively Pio slid a 9mm Beretta from a clip under the dash and put it on the seat beside him. At the same time he reached for the car's radio.

"What's going on?" Fear stabbed at Harry.

"Don't know." Pio glanced in the mirror. The Peugeot was right behind them. The windshield was heavily tinted. It was impossible to see the driver. Downshifting quickly, he stepped hard on the accelerator.

"Ispettore Capo Pio—," he said into the radio.

"Look out!" Harry yelled too late.

A truck abruptly pulled out of a side street blocking the road. A tremendous squeal of tires was followed by a deadening crash as the Alfa hit the truck full on. The force pitched Pio forward, his head slamming off the steering wheel. Harry flew forward, then was jolted back by his safety belt.

Instantly the door beside him was pulled open. He saw a face for the briefest moment, then something hit him hard and everything went black.

Pio looked up to see his own gun in the gloved hand of a stranger. He tried to move, but his seat belt held him in. Then he saw his gun buck in the stranger's hand and thought he heard a thundering explosion. But he was wrong. There was nothing but silence.

19

Hospital St. Cecilia. Pescara, Italy.
Still Wednesday, July 8, 6:20 P.M.

NURSING SISTER ELENA VOSO PASSED THE
man at the door and went into the room. Her patient was as
she'd left him, on his side, sleeping. Sleeping was what she
called it, even though from time to time he opened his eyes
and was able to blink in response when she squeezed a finger
or toe and asked if he could feel it. Then his eyes would close
and he would be as he was now.

It was approaching six-thirty, and he needed to be turned
again. The man at the door would help with that, as whoever
was on duty did every two hours to prevent the destruction of
muscle tissue, which could lead not only to bedsores but kid-
ney failure. Coming in at her call, he would take the shoulders while she took the feet, easing her charge carefully from
his back and onto his side, being especially careful of the IV
and of his broken legs, set in blue fiberglass casts, and the
bandages covering his burns.

Michael Roark, age 34. Irish citizen. Home, Dublin. Unmarried. No children. No family. Religion, Roman Catholic. Injured in an automobile accident near this Adriatic seacoast town, Monday, July 6. Three days after the terrible explosion of the Assisi bus.

Elena Voso was a member of the Congregation of Franciscan Sisters of the Sacred Heart. At twenty-seven, she had been a nursing sister for five years, working in the long-term-care ward at the Hospital of St. Bernardine in the Tuscan city of Siena. She had come to this small Catholic hospital on a hill overlooking the Adriatic only yesterday, assigned to this patient as part of a new kind of program for the Order. It was a way to expose younger nursing sisters to situations away from their home convents, preparing them for future emergencies where they might be called upon to go almost anywhere on short notice. And, though no one had said so, she also believed she had been sent because she spoke English and could communicate with the patient as he progressed, if he progressed.

"My name is Elena Voso. I am a nursing nun. Your name is Michael Roark. You are in a hospital in Italy. You were in an automobile accident."

It was a string of words she had said over and over, trying to comfort him, hoping he could hear and understand. It wasn't much, but it was something she knew she would like someone to say to her if she were ever in a similar situation. Especially since he had no relatives and therefore no familiar face he might recognize.

The man outside the door was named Marco. He worked from three in the afternoon to eleven at night. A year or two older than Elena, he was dark and strong and handsome. He said he was a fisherman and worked at the hospital when the fishing was slow. She knew he had been a *carabiniere*, a member of the national police, because he had told her so. She had seen him talking with other *carabinieri* earlier in the day, when she'd walked along the *lungomare,* the road along the seashore, during a short respite from her duties. She had seen the bulge under his hospital jacket and knew he had a pistol there.

The turning of Michael Roark done, Elena checked the fluid in the IV, then smiled at Marco and thanked him. Afterward she went into the next room, which was where she could sleep or read or write letters, and where she would be immediately available at any moment.

Her room, like Roark's, was a hospital room with its own toilet and shower, small closet, and bed. She was grateful especially for the toilet and shower, where, unlike in the communal bathrooms of the convent, she could be totally alone. Her being, her body, her thoughts private, except to God.

Now, as she closed the door and sat down on the bed, intending to write a letter home, she glanced at the red glow of the audio monitor on the bedside table next to her. The sound of her patient's steady breathing was clearly audible, the monitor's electronics so advanced that it seemed almost as if he were there beside her.

Lying back against the pillow, she closed her eyes and listened to his breathing. It was strong and healthy, even vital, and she began to imagine that he was there, alongside her, alert and well, as muscular and handsome as she knew he must have been before his injuries. The longer she listened, the more sensual his breathing seemed to become. In time she began to feel the press of his body against hers. Felt herself breathing with him, as if the rise and fall of their chests were the same. Her breathing became deeper, overriding his. She felt her own hand touch her breast, and she reached out, wanting to touch him and to keep touching him, exploring him in a way far more provocative and passionate than any way she had when she cared for his wounds.

"Stop it!" she whispered to herself.

Abruptly she got up from the bed and deliberately went into the bathroom to wash her face and hands. God was testing her again, as He had been more and more frequently over the past two years.

When exactly the feelings had begun she wasn't sure, nor had there been anything in particular to precipitate them. They had just started, rising seemingly from nowhere. And they'd astonished her. They were deep and sensual and erotic. Profound physical and emotional hungers she'd never experienced in her life. Feelings she could talk to no one about—certainly not to her family, who were strict and tradition bound in the way of old Italian Catholic familes; certainly not to the other nuns, and most assuredly not to her mother general—yet the feelings were there just the same and made her pulse with an almost unmanageable desire to be unclothed and in a man's arms, and to be a woman with him in the fullest sense. And, increasingly, not just a *woman*, but one wild and lusty, like the Italian women she'd seen in the cinema.

There had been times early on when she'd passed the emotions off as nothing more than the extension of an adventurous spirit; one that had always been physical and brave and, on occasion, overly impulsive. One time, visiting Florence as a teenager, and to the horror of her parents, who were with her, she'd run to a car that had just been in a terrible collision with a taxi, pulling the unconscious driver from it seconds before it burst into flame. Another time, when she was older, she'd been on a picnic with nursing nuns from St. Bernardine and had climbed to the top of a hundred foot radio tower to bring down a young boy who had scaled it on a dare, but who, once at the top, had become frozen with fear, unable to do more than cling there and cry.

But finally she'd realized physical courage and sexual desire were not the same. And with that she'd suddenly understood.

This was God's doing!

He was testing her inner strength, and her vows of chastity and obedience. And each day He seemed to test her a little more. And the more He did, the more difficult it became to overcome. But somehow she always did, her subconscious suddenly making her aware of what was happening, enabling her to abruptly bring herself back from the edge. The same as she had now. And, in doing so, giving her the courage and conviction to know she had the fortitude to withstand His purposeful temptations.

As if to prove it, she let her mind go to Marco standing guard outside the door. His strapping body. His bright eyes. His smile. If he was married he hadn't said, but he wore no wedding ring, and she wondered if he spent his off hours bedding women at will. He was certainly handsome enough to do so if he wanted. But, if he did, he would do so with other women, not her. To her he was simply a man doing his job.

Seeing him in that light, she knew it was safe to think about him any way she wished. He said he had been trained as a nursing aide, as supposedly the others had been. But if he was only that, why did he carry a pistol? That question alone made her think of the others—the stocky Luca, who came on at eleven at night on the shift following Marco's, and Pietro, who began at seven in the morning when Luca left. She wondered if they were armed as well. If they were, why? In this peaceful seacoast town, what threat could there possibly be?

20

ROSCANI WALKED AROUND THE CAR. OUTSIDE, beyond the police barricades, faces stared at him, wondering who he was, if he was anyone of importance.

A second body had been found in the bushes just off the sidewalk twenty feet behind the Alfa. Shot twice. Once in the heart, once above the left eye. An elderly man with no identification.

Roscani had left it to Castelletti and Scala, the other *ispettori capi* from homicide. His principal interest was the Alfa Romeo. Its windshield cracked, its front end was smashed into the truck it had hit full on, just missing the gas tank behind the driver's door.

Pio's body had still been there when he arrived. He'd studied it without touching, had it photographed and videotaped, and then it was taken away, the same as had been done with the body in the bushes.

There should have been a third body, but there wasn't. The American, Harry Addison, had been riding with Pio, coming back into the city from the farmhouse location where they had recovered the Spanish-made Llama pistol. But Harry Addison was gone. So was the pistol, the ignition keys still in the trunk lock, as if someone had known exactly where the gun was and where to find it.

Inside the Alfa, what appeared to be the murder weapon, Pio's own 9mm Beretta, lay on the backseat on the driver's side, as if it had been casually tossed there. Bloodstains were on the passenger side, on top of the seat by the door, just below the headrest. Shoe prints were in the carpet beneath it—not terribly distinct, but there just the same. Fingerprints were everywhere.

Tech crews were dusting, taking samples, marking them, putting them in evidence bags. Police photographers were on the scene as well. Two of them. One taking photographs with a Leica, the other making a video record with a modified Sony Hi-8.

And then there was the truck—a large Mercedes delivery vehicle reported stolen earlier that afternoon, its driver long gone.

Ispettore Capo Otello Roscani got behind the wheel of his dark blue Fiat and drove slowly around the barricades and past the faces watching him. The glare of police work lights illuminated the scene like a movie set, filling in the darkness for the faces and providing additional light for media cameras, which were there in frenzy.

"Ispettore Capo!"

"Ispettore Capo!"

Voices shouted. Men and women. Who did this? Does it have to do with the murder of Cardinal Parma? Who was killed? Who was suspected? And why?

Roscani saw it all, heard it all. But it didn't matter. His mind was focused on Pio and what had happened in the moments immediately preceding his death. Gianni Pio was not a man to make mistakes, but late this afternoon he had, somehow letting himself be compromised.

At this point—without an autopsy, without lab reports—questions were all Roscani had. Questions and sadness. Gianni Pio was godfather to his children and had been his friend and partner for more than twenty years. And now, as he headed back across Rome toward the Garbatella section, where Pio had lived—going to see Pio's wife and his children, where Roscani knew his own wife already was, giving what little comfort she could—Otello Roscani tried to keep his personal feelings at a distance. As a policeman he had to, and out of respect for Pio he had to, because they would only get in the way of what had become his primary objective.

The finding of Harry Addison.

21

Still Wednesday, July 8. Same time.

THOMAS KIND STOOD IN THE DARKNESS, WATCH-ing the man in the chair. Two others were in the room with him, dressed in coveralls, standing somewhere behind him. They were there to help if he needed it, which he would not. And to do the work afterward, which should be simple enough.

Thomas Kind was thirty-nine, five foot ten and very slim, a hundred and forty pounds at most, and in superb condition. His hair was cut short and jet-black, as were his slacks, shoes, and sweater, which made him difficult—if not impossible—to see in the darkness. Besides the paleness of his skin, the only color about him was the deep blue of his eyes.

The man in the chair stirred, but that was all. His hands and feet were bound and his mouth closed, pinched tight by thick tape.

Thomas Kind stepped closer, watched for a moment, then walked completely around the chair.

"Relax, comrade," he said quietly. Patience and calmness were everything. It was how he lived each day. Even tempered, waiting for the right moment. It was the sort of thing Thomas Jose Alvarez-Rios Kind, native Ecuadorean born of an English mother, might put on his résumé. Patient. Painstaking. Well educated. Multilingual. Add to that, one-time actor—and also one of the world's most-hunted terrorists.

"Relax, comrade." Harry heard the phrase again. A male voice, the same as before. Calm. In accented English. Harry thought he felt someone moving past him, but he couldn't be sure. The throbbing of his head overrode everything. All he knew was that he was sitting up and that his hands and feet were bound and there was tape across his mouth. And then there was the darkness that was all-pervasive. No shadows, no light spill from behind a door seam. Only dark.

He blinked. Then blinked again, twisting his head from side to side, trying to find some bit of light. But there was none. Suddenly it came to him that whatever had happened, wherever he was, whatever day this was, he was blind!

"NO! NO! NO!" he screamed, his voice garbled by the tape covering his mouth.

Thomas Kind stepped closer.

"Comrade," he said with the same unhurried quietness. "How is your brother? I understand he is alive and well."

Immediately the tape was torn from Harry's mouth. And he cried out as much in surprise as from the sting of it.

"Where is he?" The voice was closer than it had been.

"I don't . . . know . . . if . . . he's alive . . ." Harry's mouth and throat felt like sandpaper. He tried to make enough moisture to swallow but couldn't.

"I asked about your brother . . . where he is . . ."

"Could—I—please—have some—wa—ter?"

Kind lifted a small remote control. His thumb found a button and touched it.

Instantly, Harry saw a pinpoint of light in the distance and he started. Did he really see it, or was it an illusion?

"Where is your brother, comrade?" This time the voice came from behind his left ear.

Slowly the light began to move toward him.

"I . . ."—Harry tried again to swallow—"don't . . . know . . ."

"Do you see the light?"

"Yes."

The pinpoint came closer.

"Good."

Kind's thumb slid to another button.

Harry saw the light alter its track and shift ever so slightly. Moving toward his left eye.

"I want you to tell me where your brother is." The voice had changed sides and whispered in his right ear. "It's very important that we find him."

"I don't know."

The light was now moving toward his left eye alone and growing steadily brighter. The throbbing inside his head had been forgotten with the terror of his blindness. But with the light it began again. A slow, steady drumming that grew stronger with the approaching luminescence.

Harry jerked sideways, trying to turn his head, but something hard prevented it. He twisted the opposite way. Same thing. Then he pressed back. But nothing he did could turn him away from the light.

"So far you have not felt pain. But you will."

"Please—" Harry turned his head as far as he could, squeezing his eyes closed.

"That won't help." The timbre of the voice was suddenly different. The first voice had been a man's, this time it sounded like a woman's.

"I—have—no—idea if—my broth—er is—even—alive. How could I—know—where he—is?"

The light's pinpoint narrowed, its beam rising up, moving over Harry's left eye, searching, until it found the center.

"Don't, please . . ."

"Where is your brother?"

"Dead!"

"No, comrade. He's alive, and you know where he is . . ."

The light was only inches away now. Becoming brighter. And brighter. Its pinpoint sharpened even more. The pounding inside his head grew. The light came closer, a needle pushing from the outside in, toward the back of his brain.

"STOP!" Harry screamed. "MY GOD! STOP! PLEASE!"

"Where is he?" Male.

"Where is he?" Female.

Thomas Kind shifted from one voice to the other, playing both man and woman.

"Tell us and the light will stop." Male.

"The light will stop." Female.

The voices calm, even quiet.

The pounding became thunderous. Louder than anything Harry had ever heard. An enormous booming drum inside his head. The light crept on, toward the center of his brain, a white-hot needle searing toward the sound. Trying to mate with it. Brighter than anything he'd ever seen, or could ever imagine. Brighter than a welding arc. The core of the sun. Pain became everything; it was so terrible he was certain even death would not end it. He would take its horror with him into eternity.

"I DON'T KNOW! I DON'T KNOW! I DON'T KNOW! GOD! GOD! STOP IT! STOP IT! PLEASE!—*PLEASE . . . PLEASE . . .*"

CLICK.

The light went out.

22

*Rome. Harry Addison's room, the Hotel Hassler.
Thursday July 9, 6:00 A.M.*

NOTHING HAD BEEN TOUCHED. HARRY'S BRIEF-
case and working notes were on the table next to the telephone as he'd left them. The same for his clothes in the
closet and his toiletries in the bathroom. The only difference
was that a bug had been placed in each of the two telephones,
the one by the bed, the other in the bathroom, and a tiny surveillance camera had been mounted behind the light sconce
facing the door. Just in case he came back. This was part of
the plan put in motion by Gruppo Cardinale, the special task
force set up by decree of the Italian Ministry of the Interior
in response to passionate appeals by legislators, the Vatican,
the Carabinieri, and the police in the wake of the murder of
the cardinal vicar of Rome.

The murder of Cardinal Parma and the bombing of the
Assisi bus were no longer separate investigations but were

now considered components of the same crime. Under the umbrella of Gruppo Cardinale, special investigators from the carabinieri, Squadra Mobile of the Italian police, and DIGOS, the special unit that investigates criminal acts with suspected political motive, all reported to the head of Gruppo Cardinale, ranking prosecutor Marcello Taglia; and while the highly respected Taglia did indeed coordinate the activities of the various police agencies, there was no doubt in anyone's mind who Gruppo Cardinale's true *"Il responsabile,"* the man in charge, was—Ispettore Capo Otello Roscani.

8:30 A.M.

Roscani stared, then turned away. He knew all too well what the circular saw did in an autopsy. Cutting into the skull, taking the cap off so that the brain could be removed. And then the rest of it, taking Pio apart almost piece by piece, looking for anything that would tell them more than they already knew. What that might be Roscani didn't know, because he already had enough information to establish Pio's killer beyond what he believed was reasonable doubt.

Pio's 9mm Beretta had been confirmed as the murder weapon, and several clear prints had been found on it. Most were Pio's, but two were not—one, just above the left grip, the other on the right side of the trigger guard.

A query to the Los Angeles bureau of the FBI had, in turn, accessed the files of the California Department of Motor Vehicles in Sacramento, requesting a copy of the driver's license thumbprint of one Harry Addison, 2175 Benedict Canyon Drive, Los Angeles, California. Less than thirty minutes later, a computer-enhanced copy of Addison's thumbprint had been faxed to Gruppo Cardinale headquarters in Rome. The whorl pattern and measured ridge tracings matched perfectly with those on the print lifted from the left grip of the gun that had killed Gianni Pio.

For the first time in his life Roscani grimaced at the sound of the saw as the morgue doors closed behind him, and he walked down the hallway and up the steps of the Obitorio Comunale. Something he had done a thousand times in his career. He had seen policemen dead. Judges dead. The bodies of murdered women and children. Tragic as they were, he'd been able to distance himself professionally. But not now.

Roscani was a cop, and cops got killed all the time. It was a truth drummed into you day after day at the institute. One you were supposed to accept going in. It was tragic and sad, but it was reality. And when it came, you were supposed to be prepared to deal with it professionally. Pay homage and move on; without anger, outrage, or hatred for the killer. It was part of what you were trained for in the career you chose.

And you thought you were trained—until the day you walked around your partner's body and saw the blood and shredded flesh and shattered bone. The grotesque work the bullets had done. Then saw it all over again when the medical people began their work in the morgue. That was when you knew you weren't prepared for it at all. No one could be, no matter what he was trained for, or taught, or what anyone else said. Loss and rage stormed through you like wildfire, overtaking everything. It was why—whenever cops were killed—every policeman who could, sometimes from across continents, came to the funeral. Why five hundred uniformed men and women on motorcycles were not uncommon, riding in solemn procession in honor of a fallen comrade—one who might have been only a year on the force, a rookie on foot patrol, but who was still a member of the brotherhood.

ANGRILY ROSCANI SHOVED OPEN a side door and stepped into the morning sun. Its warmth should have been a welcome relief from the coldness of the rooms below, but it wasn't. Taking the long way around the building, he tried to let his emotions fade, but they didn't. Finally, he turned a corner and walked down a ramp to the street where he'd parked his car. Sadness and loss and anger were crushing him.

Leaving his car, he stepped off the curb, waited for traffic to pass, then crossed the street and started to walk. He needed what he called *"assoluta tranquillità,"* a kind of splendid silence, that quiet time when he was alone and could think things through properly. Especially now, time alone to try and walk off the emotion, to begin to think things through as an investigator for Gruppo Cardinale, not as the shattered, enraged partner of Gianni Pio.

Time for silence and to think.

To walk and walk and walk.

23

THOMAS KIND PULLED BACK A WINDOW curtain and watched as the men in coveralls emerged from the building and took Harry Addison across the courtyard. He had what he needed from him, or at least as much as he knew he was going to get; now the men in coveralls simply needed to get rid of him.

HARRY COULD SEE only from his right eye. And that was more shadow than image. His left eye had no feeling or sight whatsoever. His other senses told him that he was outside and being walked across a hard surface by, he thought, two men. Somewhere he had the vaguest memory of sitting on a stool or something like it, of taking directions and saying words out loud that were spoken to him through an earphone by the same voice that had spoken to him before. He remembered that only because of the fuss someone else had made about fitting the device in his ear. Most of the argument was in Italian. But part had been fought in English. It was the wrong size. It wouldn't work. It would show.

Abruptly a male voice beside him spoke sharply in Italian—the same man, he thought, who had argued about the earphone while trying to fit it. A moment later, a hand shoved him from behind and he nearly stumbled. His recovery cleared his thoughts enough to tell him that while his hands were still bound behind him, his feet had been freed. He was walking on his own, and he thought he could hear traffic. His mind cleared to another level, telling him that if he could walk, he could run. The hand shoved him again. Hard. And he fell, crying out as he hit the ground and felt his face scrape the pavement. He tried to roll over, but a foot stamped on his chest, holding him there. Somewhere nearby came the sound of a man straining, then there was a clank, and he heard something heavy, like iron scraping stone, sliding past his ear. Then he was lifted up by his shoulders and put over an edge. His feet touched steel and he was forced down the rungs of a ladder. Instantly what little light there was faded, and stench dominated everything.

A second male voice farther off cursed and then echoed. There was the sound of rushing water. The smell was overpowering. And then Harry knew. He'd been brought into the sewer. An exchange came in Italian.

"Prepararsi?"

"Si."

Harry felt a jarring between his wrists. There was a snap, and his hands came free.

CLICK. The unmistakable metallic sound of a gun being cocked.

"Sparagli." Shoot him.

In reflex reaction Harry stepped backward, throwing his hands in front of his face.

"Sparagli!"

Immediately there was a thundering explosion. Something slammed into his hand. Then his head. The force threw him backward into the water.

Harry did not see the face of the gunman who stepped over him. Or of the other man who held the flashlight. Harry did not see what they saw; the enormous volume of blood covering the left side of his face, matting his hair, a trickle of it washing away in the flow of water.

"Morto," a voice whispered.

"Si."

The gunman knelt down and rolled Harry's body over the edge into a deeper, faster rush of water, then watched as it floated away.

"I topi faranno il resto."

The mice will finish it.

24

The Questura, police headquarters.

HARRY ADDISON SAT THERE, A BANDAGE OVER his left temple, dressed in the off-white polo shirt, jeans, and aviator sunglasses he wore when he left the Hotel Hassler at little after one-thirty yesterday afternoon. Nearly thirty hours earlier.

The fifteen-second video of the fugitive Harry Addison had come anonymously to Sala Stampa della Santa Sede, the press office of the Holy See, at 3:45 that afternoon, with a request it be sent immediately to the pope. Instead it had been put on a shelf and not opened until approximately 4:50. Immediately it had been sent to Farel's office and, after being viewed by a junior staff member, sent to Farel himself. By six o'clock Farel, Gruppo Cardinale prosecutor Marcello Taglia, Roscani, along with Castelletti and Scala, the homicide detectives assigned to Pio's murder, and a half dozen others were sitting in the dark of a video room viewing it together.

"Danny, I'm asking you to come in. . . . To give yourself up." Harry spoke in English, and an interpreter from Roscani's office translated into Italian.

As far as they could tell, Harry was sitting on a wooden stool in a darkened room, alone. The wall behind him appeared to be covered with a textured and patterned wallpaper. That and Harry, his dark glasses, and the bandage on his forehead were all that was visible.

"They know everything. . . . Please, for me. . . . Come in . . . please. . . . Please . . ." There was a pause and Harry's head started to come up as if to say something more, then the tape abruptly ended.

"Why wasn't I told the priest might still be alive?" Roscani looked at Taglia and then Farel as the lights came up.

"I learned of it only moments before this video was brought to my attention," Farel said. "The incident happened yesterday, when the American asked that the casket be opened, and when it was, swore the remains were not those of his brother. . . . It could be the truth, it could be a lie. . . . Cardinal Marsciano was there. He felt the American was emotionally overwrought. It was only this afternoon, when he learned of the circumstances of Pio's death, he sent Father Bardoni to tell me."

Roscani got up and crossed the room. He was irritated. This was something he should have been told of immediately. Besides, there was no love lost between him and Farel.

"And you and your people have no idea where the video came from."

Farel's eyes locked on Roscani's and stayed there. "If we knew, Ispettore Capo, we would have done something about it, don't you think?"

Taglia, slim and dressed in a dark pinstripe suit, and with

a bearing that suggested an aristocratic upbringing, intervened and spoke for the first time.

"Why would he do it?"

"Ask for the casket to be opened?" Farel looked to Taglia. "Yes."

"From what I was told he was overcome with feeling; he wanted to see his brother to tell him good-bye. . . . Blood runs deep, even with murderers. . . . Then when he saw the body was not Father Daniel, he reacted in surprise, without thinking."

Roscani came back across the room, working to ignore Farel's abrasiveness. "Suppose that's true and he made a mistake—why, a day later, does he assume the man is still alive and beg him to come forward? Especially when he's wanted for murder himself?"

"It's a gamble," Taglia said. "They're worried that if he is alive, what he might reveal if he is caught. They have his brother call him in so they can kill him."

"This same brother who so emotionally asked to look at a hideous corpse now wants to kill him?"

"Maybe that was the reason." Farel sat back in his chair. "Maybe it was more calculated than it appears. Maybe he had a sense that everything was not as it seemed."

"Then why did he say so out loud? Father Daniel was officially dead. Why didn't he leave it that way? It's not likely the police would search for a dead man. If he were alive, he could have gone after him quietly."

"But where to look?" Taglia said. "Why not let the police help find him?"

Roscani shook a cigarette from a pack and lit it. "But they send the video to the pope instead of here. Why? There's been enough publicity, they know who we are."

"Because," Farel said, "they want it released to the media. Gruppo Cardinale might do it, they might not. By sending the video to the Holy Father, they hoped he would intervene personally. Ask me to pressure you to release it. All of Italy knows how shocked and horrified he was by the cardinal vicar's murder and how much it would mean to him to have his assassin caught and brought to justice."

"And did he ask you?" Roscani said.

"Yes."

Roscani stared at Farel for a moment, then walked off.

"We have to assume they've calculated the odds," Farel continued, ignoring Roscani. "They know if we choose not to give it to the media, we would be losing a major chance to have the public help us fish for him. If we do, and he is alive and sees the story on television or reads about it in the newspapers and decides to do what his brother asks, we might very well get to him before they do. Thereby giving him the chance to tell us the very thing they are so concerned about."

"Evidently it is a chance they are willing to take," Taglia said.

"Evidently . . ." Putting out his cigarette, Roscani let his eyes wander from Taglia to Farel and then to Castelletti, Scala, and the others.

"There is one other concern." Farel stood up, buttoning his suit coat. "If the media are given the video, we must provide a photograph of the priest and, more significantly, details of what, until now, has been highly confidential . . . the Vatican cleric who murders a Roman cardinal. . . . I have consulted with secretariat of state Cardinal Palestrina, and he agrees that no matter the pope's personal feelings, if this becomes public, the Holy See will be exposed to a scandal unknown for decades. And at a time when the Church's influence is quite the opposite of hugely popular."

"We're talking about *murder*." Roscani was looking directly at the Vatican policeman.

"Be respectful of your personal passions, Ispettore Capo. You will remember that they, among other things, were why you were not selected to head the investigation." Farel stared at Roscani for a long moment, then turned to Taglia.

"I am confident you will make the right decision . . ."

With that, he walked out.

25

ONCE AGAIN ROSCANI HAD TO WORK TO IGNORE Farel. The Vatican policeman was gruff, direct, abrasive when it suited him, putting the Holy See before anything else, as if it and only it had any stake here. It was what you got when you dealt with him, especially if you were from a police force outside his control, and if you were, like Roscani, a person far more introspective, and a great deal less political. Roscani's daily life was devoted to grinding it out and doing the best job he possibly could, whatever it was and whatever it took. It was an attribute he'd learned from his father—a taskmaster and maker and seller of leather goods who had died of a heart attack in his own shop at eighty while trying to move a hundred-pound anvil; the same attribute that he tried to instill in his sons.

So, if you were like that and you realized it, you did your best to disregard people like Farel altogether, and devote your energies to things more positive and useful to what you were doing. Like Scala's comment after Farel had gone, about what they had seen on the video, pointing out the bandage on Harry Addison's forehead and suggesting that most probably he had been injured when Pio's car collided with the truck. If so, and if a medical professional had treated him and they could find that person, it would give them a direction the man had gone.

And Castelletti, not to be outdone, had picked up the videocassette itself and written down the manufacturer and manufacturer's batch code number printed on the back. Who knew where a trace like that could go, what it might turn up? Manufacturer, to wholesaler, to a store chain, to a certain store, to a clerk who might remember selling it to someone in particular.

And then the meeting was over, with the room emptying of everyone but Roscani and Taglia, Taglia with a decision to make, Roscani to hear it.

"You want to give the video to the media. And, like the TV show *America's Most Wanted*, let the public help us find them," Taglia said softly.

"Sometimes it works."

"And sometimes it drives fugitives farther from sight. . . . But there are other considerations. What Farel was talking about. The delicate nature of the whole thing. And the diplomatic implications that could rise between Italy and the Vatican. . . . The pope may wish one thing personally, but Farel did not mention Cardinal Palestrina without reason. . . . He is the real keeper of the Vatican flame and how the world views the Holy See."

"In other words, diplomatically, scandal is worse than murder. And you are not going to release the video."

"No, we are not—Gruppo Cardinale will continue to treat the hunt for fugitives as classified and confidential. All pertinent files will continue to be protected." Taglia stood. "I'm sorry, Otello. . . . *Buona sera.*"

"*Buona sera . . .*"

The door closed behind Taglia, and Roscani was left alone. Frustrated, emasculated. Maybe, he thought, his wife was right. For all his dedication, the world was neither just nor perfect. And there was little he could do to change it. What he could do, however, was to stop railing so hard against it; something that would make his life and his family's a little easier. But the reality was that he could do as little to change himself as he could the world. He had become a policeman because he did not want to go into his father's business and because he had just been married and wanted stability before starting a family, and because the profession itself had seemed both exciting and noble.

But then something else had happened: victims' lives began to touch his on an everyday basis, lives torn apart, ripped often irreparably by senseless violence and intrusion. His promotion to homicide made it worse: for some reason, he began to see the murdered, whatever their age, not so much as themselves but as someone's children—his own, at three or four or eight or twelve—each deserving to live life to its end without such terrible and vicious interruption. In that, Cardinal Parma was as much a mother's son as Pio had been. It made finding the guilty all the more imperative. Get them before they did it again. But how often had he gotten them, only to have the courts, for one reason or another, let them go? It had driven him to rail against injustice, within the law or without. He was fighting an unwinnable war, but the thing was, he kept fighting anyway. And maybe the reason he did was simply that he was his father's son and, like him, had grown up to be a bulldog.

Abruptly, Roscani reached out and picked up the TV's remote, then pointed it at the large-screen television. There was a click as it came on. He hit REWIND and then PLAY and watched the video again. Saw Harry on the stool, watched him talk behind dark glasses.

"Danny, I'm asking you to come in. . . . To give yourself up. . . . They know everything. . . . Please, for me. . . . Come in . . . please. . . . Please . . ."

Roscani saw Harry pause at the end, then start to say something more just as the tape itself ended. He hit REWIND once more and played it again. And then again. And again. The more he watched, the more he felt the anger build inside him. He wanted to look up and see Pio come through the door, smiling and easy as always, talking about his family, asking Roscani about his. Instead he saw Harry, Mr. Hollywood in sunglasses, sitting on a stool, begging his own brother to give himself up so that he could be killed.

CLICK.

Roscani shut off the television. In the semidarkness the thoughts came back. He didn't want them to, but they did. How he would kill Harry Addison when he got him. And there was no doubt at all that he would get him.

CLICK.

He turned the TV back on and lit a cigarette, forcefully blowing out the match afterward. He couldn't allow himself to think like that. He wondered how his father would have reacted if he had been in his place.

Distance was what he needed. And he got it by playing the tape again. And once more. And once more after that. Forcing himself to watch it coldly, analytically, the experienced policeman looking for the smallest piece of something that would help.

The more he watched, the more two things began to intrigue him—the textured, patterned wallpaper barely visible behind Harry; and what happened just before the end, when Harry's head started to come up with his mouth open as if to say something more, but he never did because the tape finished. Sliding a small notebook from his jacket, he made a note.

—Have video image computer enhanced/wallpaper.

—Have English-speaking lip reader analyze unspoken word(s).

REWIND.

PLAY.

Roscani hit the MUTE button and watched in silence. When it was finished, he did the same thing and watched it again.

26

Rome. The Vatican Embassy to Italy,
Via Po. Same time.

IN THEIR FIRST PUBLIC APPEARANCE SINCE
the murder of the cardinal vicar of Rome, the pope's remaining men of trust—Cardinal Umberto Palestrina, Cardinal Joseph Matadi, Monsignor Fabio Capizzi, and Cardinal Nicola Marsciano—mixed freely with the members of the Council of Ministers of the European Union, who were in Rome for a meeting on economic relations with emerging nations, and who had been invited to an informal cocktail party given by Archbishop Giovanni Bellini, the apostolic nuncio to Italy.

Of the four it was the Vatican secretariat of state, the sixty-two-year-old Palestrina, who seemed most at ease. Dressed not in the clerical garments the others wore but in a simple black suit with white Roman collar, and unmindful of the plainclothes Swiss Guards watching the room, the cardinal moved affably from one guest to the next, chatting energetically with each.

Palestrina's size alone—two hundred and seventy pounds over a six-foot seven-inch frame—turned heads. But it was the unexpected intensity of the rest of him—the grace with which he moved, his broad smile and riveting gray eyes under an unruly shock of stone-white hair, the iron grip of his hand as he took yours, addressing you directly and most often in your own language—that so took you off guard.

To watch him work the room, and revel in it—renewing old friendships, making new ones, then moving on to the next, made him seem more a politician on the stump than the second-most powerful man in the Roman Catholic Church. Yet it was as a representative of that Church, of the pope himself, that he and the others were here, their presence, even in the shadow of grave tragedy, speaking for itself, reminding all that the Holy See was tirelessly and unremittingly committed to the future of the European Community.

Across the room, Cardinal Marsciano turned from the representative of Denmark and glanced at his watch.

7:50

Looking up, he saw Swiss investment banker Pierre Weggen enter the room. With him—and immediately causing a turn of heads and a very noticeable drop in the conversation level across the room—were Jiang Youmei, the Chinese ambassador to Italy, his foreign minister, Zhou Yi, and Yan Yeh, the president of the People's Bank of China. The People's Republic of China and the Vatican did not have official diplomatic relations, and had not since the

Communist takeover of China in 1949, yet here were its two ranking diplomats to Italy and one of the new China's most influential business leaders striding into the Vatican Embassy in public view with Weggen.

Almost immediately Palestrina crossed to greet them, bowing formally then smiling broadly and taking the hand of each, and afterward motioning for drinks and chatting happily as if they were his old and dear friends. Chatting, Marsciano knew, in Chinese.

China's expanding relationship with the West, coupled with its rapid emergence as a towering economic power, had had little or no effect on the all but nonexistent relations between Rome and Beijing. And while there remained no formal diplomatic communication between them, the Holy See, under Palestrina's careful posturing, was attempting to pry open the door. His immediate goal was to arrange a papal visit to the People's Republic.

It was an objective that had far-reaching implications because, if his overture was accepted, it would be a sign that Beijing was not simply opening its doors to the Church but was ready to embrace it. Which was something, Palestrina was certain, China had no intention of doing—today, tomorrow, or, in all likelihood, ever; making his objective exceedingly ambitious at best. Yet, the secretariat of state was no wallflower. And moreover, the Chinese were here, and publicly.

That they were here was due chiefly to Pierre Weggen, with whom they had worked for years and whom they trusted implicitly. Or, as implicitly as any Oriental trusted any Westerner. Seventy, tall, and genteel, Weggen was a preeminent international investment banker. World renowned and immensely respected, he functioned primarily as liaison between major multinational companies looking to create global working partnerships. At the same time, he continued to work as a private counselor to longstanding clients and friends; the people, companies, and organizations who, over the years, had helped build his reputation.

It was a client base that had always been and still remained confidential. The Vatican was among them. And Nicola Marsciano, the man responsible for Vatican investments, had spent the entire afternoon sequestered in a private apartment on Via Pinciana with Weggen and a battery of lawyers and accountants he'd brought with him from Geneva.

For more than a year Marsciano and Weggen had been belt-tightening the Holy See's portfolio, narrowing the range of investments to focus on energy, transportation, steel, shipping, heavy equipment; corporations, companies, and spin-off companies that specialized in major international infrastructure development—the building and rebuilding of roads, waterways, power plants, and the like in emerging nations.

The Vatican's investment strategy was the kingpin in Palestrina's mandate for the future of the Holy See, and was why the Chinese had been invited here to mingle and why they had come, to show that China was a modern country that shared the same economic concerns for emerging nations as did her European friends. The invitation had been out of goodwill, giving the Chinese a way to quietly intermingle and to discreetly establish a presence—and at the same time to be stroked by Palestrina.

Yet *emerging nations* in the plural was not on Palestrina's agenda. One nation, in the singular, was: China herself. And outside of a very few—Pierre Weggen and the pope's remaining men of trust—no one, not even the Holy Father, had any idea of the secretariat's real objective, which was to see the Vatican become a wholly anonymous yet major partner and influencer in the future of the People's Republic, economic and otherwise.

The initial step was tonight, with the hand holding of the Chinese. The second would take place tomorrow, when Marsciano would present the newly revised "Emerging Nation Investment Strategies" to a commission of four cardinals charged with him in overseeing the Church's investments for ratification.

The session would be tumultuous because the cardinals were conservative and not open to change. It would be Marsciano's job to convince them, to show in exhaustive detail the regions his extensive research had targeted—Latin America, Eastern Europe, and Russia. China would be there, of course, but hidden within the sweeping term *Asia*—Japan, Singapore, Thailand, Philippines, China, South Korea, Taiwan, India, etc.

The trouble was it was a deliberate fabrication. Unethical and immoral. A calculated lie designed to give Palestrina exactly what he wanted without ever divulging it.

Moreover, it was only the beginning of Palestrina's plan. China, the secretariat understood all too well, was, for all its openness, still at heart a closed society, tightly controlled by an authoritarian Communist guard. Yet authoritarian or not, China was modernizing quickly; and a modern China with one-quarter of the world's population and its accompanying economic leverage would, with little doubt and in little time, become the most formidable power on earth. With that truth came the obvious—control China and you control the world. And that was the heart and soul of Palestrina's plan—the domination of China in the next century, reestablishing the Catholic Church and its influence in every city, town, and village. And, within a hundred years, to create a new Holy

Roman Empire. With the people of China answering no longer to Beijing but to Rome, the Holy See would become the greatest superpower on earth.

It was madness, of course—and to Marsciano an all too clear illustration of Palestrina's progressively deranged thinking—but there was nothing any of them could do about it. The Holy Father was enamored with Palestrina and had no knowledge of his plan whatsoever. Furthermore, slowed by precarious health and an exhausting daily schedule, and trusting Palestrina as he would trust himself, the pope had all but handed the global directives of the Holy See over to his secretariat of state. So to go to the Holy Father would be doing nothing more than going to Palestrina himself because, if called, the secretariat would deny everything, and his accuser would be summarily shipped off to a parish unknown and never heard from again.

And therein was the true horror of it. Because, with the exception of Pierre Weggen, who believed in Palestrina fully, the others—Marsciano, Cardinal Matadi, Monsignor Capizzi, the remaining three most influential men in the Catholic Church—were all in one way or another terrified of Palestrina. Of his physical size, of his ambition, of his exceptional ability to find a man's weakness and then exploit it to further his own ends, and—perhaps most frightening of all—the tremendous force of his character once you became the focus of his attention.

They were terrified, too, of the madmen who worked for him: Jacov Farel, who was, on the one hand, the very public and outspoken chief of the Vatican police, and on the other, the secretive and ruthless henchman to Palestrina's ambition; and the terrorist Thomas Kind, who had assassinated Palestrina's archfoe, Cardinal Parma, in their presence and in the presence of the Holy Father, and in the presence of Palestrina, who had ordered it done, and then calmly stood beside him as he was shot down.

Marsciano had no idea how the others felt, but he was certain none despised his own weakness and fear more than he.

Once again he looked at his watch.

8:10

"Eminence." Pierre Weggen approached with Yan Yeh. The president of the People's Bank of China was quite short, and trim, his dark hair flecked with gray.

"You remember Yan Yeh," Weggen said.

"Of course." Marsciano smiled and took the Chinese banker's hand firmly. "Welcome to Rome."

They had met once before, in Bangkok, and except for a few terse moments when Palestrina had purposefully challenged the banker about the future of the Catholic Church in the new China and been told coldly, directly, and authoritatively that the time was not right for a rapprochement between Beijing and Rome, Marsciano had found Yan Yeh to be personable, outgoing, even witty, and with seeming genuine concern for the well-being of people, whoever they were.

"I think," Yan Yeh said, a twinkle in his eye as he lifted a glass of red wine and touched it to Marsciano's, "the Italians should give us Chinese a good lesson in wine making."

Just then Marsciano saw the papal nuncio enter and approach Palestrina, taking him aside, away from the Chinese ambassador and foreign minister. The two spoke briefly, and he saw Palestrina glance his way before leaving the room. It was a small gesture, insignificant to anyone else. But for him it was everything, because it meant he had been singled out.

"Perhaps," Marsciano said, turning back to Yan Yeh, "an arrangement could be made." He smiled.

"Eminence." The nuncio touched the cardinal's sleeve.

Marsciano turned. "Yes, I know. . . . Where do you want me to go?"

27

MARSCIANO STOPPED BRIEFLY AT THE BOT-
tom of the stairway, then walked up. At the top, he turned
down a narrow hallway, stopping at an elaborately paneled
door. Turning the knob, he entered.

The late sun cut sharply through the lone window divid-
ing the ornate meeting room in half. Palestrina stood on one
side of it, partly in shadow. The person with him was little
more than a silhouette, but Marsciano didn't need to see him
to know who it was. Jacov Farel.

"Eminence . . . Jacov." Marsciano closed the door behind
him.

"Sit down, Nicola." Palestrina gestured toward a group-
ing of high-backed chairs that faced an ancient marble fire-
place. Marsciano crossed the shaft of sunlight to do as he had
been asked.

As he did, Farel sat down opposite him, crossing his feet
at the ankles, buttoning his suit coat, then his gaze coming
up to Marsciano's and holding there.

"I want to ask you a question, Nicola, and I want you to
answer with the truth." Palestrina let his hand trail lightly

across the top of a chair, then took hold of it and pulled it around to sit down directly in front of Marsciano. "Is the priest alive?"

Marsciano had known, from the moment Harry Addison declared the remains were not his brother's, that it was only a matter of time before Palestrina came with his questions. He was surprised it had taken this long. But the interval had given him the chance to prepare himself as best he could.

"No," he said, directly.

"The police believe he is."

"They are wrong."

"His brother disagreed," Farel said.

"He merely said the body was not that of his brother. But he was mistaken." Marsciano worked to seem dispassionate and matter-of-fact.

"There is a videotape in the possession of Gruppo Cardinale made by Harry Addison himself, asking his brother to give himself up. Does that sound like someone who was mistaken?"

For a moment Marsciano said nothing. When he did speak, it was to Palestrina and in the same tone as before. "Jacov was there beside me at the morgue when the evidence was presented and the identification made." Marsciano turned toward Farel. "Is that not true, Jacov?"

Farel said nothing.

Palestrina studied Marsciano and then rose from his chair and walked toward the window, his enormous body blocking the sunlight. Then he turned, so that he stood wholly in shadow, with nothing visible except the dark hugeness of his form.

"The top is taken from a box. A moth flies out to disappear in the breeze. . . . How did it survive where it was? Where did it go when it flew away?" Palestrina came back toward them.

"I grew up a *scugnizzo,* a common Neapolitan street urchin. My only teacher was experience. Sitting in the gutter with your head bleeding because you had been lied to but had believed you had been told the truth. . . . From it you learned. And you took care so that it wouldn't happen again. . . ." Palestrina stopped at Marsciano's chair and looked down at him.

"I will ask you once more, Nicola—for the good of the church. Is the priest alive?"

"No, Eminence. He is dead."

"Then we are finished here." Palestrina glanced at Farel, then abruptly left the room.

His sensibilities all but frozen, Marsciano watched him go. Then, knowing Palestrina would question his policeman about his manner after he left, Marsciano gathered himself and looked to Farel. "He is dead, Jacov," he said. "Dead."

ONE OF FAREL'S plainclothes guards stood at the bottom of the stairs as Marsciano came down, and the cardinal passed him without a glance.

Marsciano's entire life had been given to God and the Church. He was as strong yet simple as his Tuscan background. Men like Palestrina and Farel lived in a world beyond his, one that he had no place in and feared greatly, yet circumstance and his own competence had placed him there.

"For the good of the Church," Palestrina had said because he knew the Church and its sanctity were Marsciano's weakness, that he revered them nearly as much as he revered God, because to him they were close to one and the same. Give me Father Daniel, Palestrina was telling him, and the Church will be saved from the spectacle of a trial and the public scandal and degradation certain to come with it if it is true he is alive and the police get him. And he would be right, because if he did, Father Daniel, already presumed dead, would simply vanish. Farel or Thomas Kind would see to that. He would be judged guilty within the Church and the matter of Cardinal Parma's murder put to rest.

But giving up Father Daniel only to have him murdered was not something Marsciano was prepared to do. Under the noses of Palestrina and Farel and Capizzi and Matadi, he had called upon all the resources at his command in an attempt to get away with the impossible; to have Father Daniel declared dead when he knew he was not. And were it not for Father Daniel's brother, it might have worked. But it hadn't. In result, he had no choice but to continue the charade and, with it, hope to buy time. But he had done poorly, of that there was little doubt.

His attempt to reassure Farel he had been telling the truth after Palestrina left had been feeble and had fallen on deaf ears. His fate, he knew, had been sealed with the secretariat's glance at his policeman as he'd walked from the room. With it, he'd taken Marsciano's liberty. From that moment on, he would be watched. Wherever he went, whoever he saw or spoke with, whether on the telephone or in the corridor, even at home, would be monitored and reported. First to Farel and then from Farel to Palestrina. What it amounted to was house arrest. And there was nothing at all he could do about it.

Once again he looked at his watch.

8:50

All he could do was pray there had been no glitches. That by now they were gone, safely out of there as planned.

28

Pescara. Still Thursday, July 9, 10:35 P.M.

NURSING SISTER ELENA VOSO RODE ON A FOLD-down jump seat in the back of an unmarked beige van. In the dimness she could see Michael Roark next to her. He lay on his back on a gurney, staring at the IV hanging overhead as it swung with the motion of the truck. Across from her was the handsome Marco, while up front, the heavy-set Luca drove, guiding the van deliberately through the narrow streets as if he knew exactly where he was taking them, though none had spoken of it.

Elena had not been prepared when, little more than an hour earlier, her mother general had called from her home convent of the Congregation of Franciscan Sisters of the Sacred Heart in Siena to tell her the patient in her charge was to be moved by private ambulance that night and she was to accompany him, continuing to give him the care she had been. When she asked where he was being moved, where

they were going, she was simply told "to another hospital."
Very shortly afterward Luca had arrived with the ambulance
and they were on their way. Leaving Hospital St. Cecilia
quickly and quietly, with hardly a word spoken between
them, as if they were fugitives.

Crossing the Pescara River, Luca took a number of side
streets before ending up in a slow parade of traffic along
Viale della Riviera, a main thoroughfare that paralleled the
beach. The night was steamy hot, and scores of people
ambled along the sidewalk in shorts and tank tops, or
crowded the pizzerias that sat along the edge of the sand.
Because of their route Elena wondered if perhaps they were
going to another hospital in the city. But then Luca turned
away from the ocean and drove a zigzag course through the
city, which took them past the massive railroad terminal
before swinging northeast on a main highway out of town.

Through it all Michael Roark's gaze shifted, from the IV
to her, to the men in the van, and then back to her. It made
her think that his mind was working, that somewhere he was
trying to put it all together and understand what was happening. Physically he seemed as well as could be expected, his
blood pressure and pulse remained strong, his breathing as
normal as it had been all along. She had seen the EKG and
EEG results of tests done prior to her arrival that reflected a
strong heart and a functioning brain. The diagnosis was that
he had suffered acute trauma; and that aside from the burns
and broken legs, the main damage and the one bearing the
closest watching had been a severe concussion. He could
recover from it fully, partially, or not at all. Her job was to
keep his body operative while the brain attempted to heal
itself.

Smiling gently at Michael Roark's gaze, she looked up to
see Marco watching her as well. Two men examining her at

the same time—the thought tickled her, and she grinned. Then quickly she looked away, embarrassed she had reacted so openly. In doing so, she saw for the first time that dark curtains covered the van's rear windows. Turning back, she looked at Marco.

"Why are the windows covered?"

"The truck was rented. It came that way."

Elena hesitated. "Where are we going?"

"Nobody told me."

"Luca knows."

"Then ask him."

Elena glanced forward at Luca at the wheel, then back to Marco. "Are we in danger?"

Marco grinned. "So many questions."

"We are directed to leave, suddenly, almost in the middle of the night. We drive as if to make it impossible to follow us. The truck windows are covered over, and you . . . carry a gun."

"Do I . . ?"

"Yes."

"I told you I was a *carabiniere* . . ."

"Not anymore."

"But still on reserve. . . ." Abruptly Marco turned toward the front. "Luca, Sister Elena wants to know where we're going."

"North."

Crossing his arms over his chest, Marco leaned back and closed his eyes. "I'm going to sleep," he said to Elena. "You sleep, too. We have a long way to go."

Elena watched him, then looked to Luca at the wheel and saw his features briefly as he lit a cigarette. She had seen the bulge under his jacket as he helped load her patient into the truck, verifying what she had suspected earlier, that he carried a gun as well. And though no one had mentioned it, she knew Pietro, the morning man, was following in his car behind them.

Beside her Michael Roark had closed his eyes. She wondered if he was dreaming, and if so, what his dreams might be like. And where they were taking him. Or if he was simply going without knowing, as she was, down a darkened road toward a destination unknown, in the company of armed strangers.

And she wondered, as she had before, who he was that he would need such men. She wondered who he was at all.

29

Rome. Same time.

SUDDENLY THERE WAS THE SENSATION OF
being walked on by hundreds of tiny feet. Light, nimble feet.
Small. Like those of rodents. With what seemed like super-
human effort Harry opened one eye and saw them. Not mice.

Rats.

They were on his chest, his midsection, on both legs.
Fully aware, he shouted. Screamed. Trying to shake them
off. Some disappeared, but others clung there. Ears up.
Watching him with tiny red eyes.

Then he smelled the stench.

And remembered the sewer.

Everywhere was the sound of rushing water, and he felt
the wet and realized he was in the water and it was washing
past him. Raising himself up, he turned his head and with his
one good eye saw more of them. Hundreds. Higher up on dry

ground. Watching, waiting. It was why more hadn't come. They were aware of the water, too. Only the bravest had ventured across the shallow flow where he was.

Above him was the semicircle of ancient stone that made up the ceiling. And the same stone supplemented by worn concrete lined the walls of either side and the sluice where he lay. Here and there dim lightbulbs encased in wire provided the illumination for what little vision he had.

Vision.

He could see!

At least a little.

Lying back, he let his right eye close, and abruptly everything faded. For a moment he remained still, then, gathering himself, opened his left eye.

Black. Nothing at all.

Immediately he opened his right eye and the world came back. Dim lights. Stone. Concrete. Water.

Rats.

He saw the two closest to his right eye inch forward. Noses moving. Teeth bared. The bravest of the brave. As if they knew. Take out that eye and he would see nothing at all. He was theirs.

"GET AWAY!" he screamed and tried to struggle up. He felt their claws dig and hold, staying where they were.

"GET AWAY! GET AWAY! GET THE FUCK AWAY!"

He thrashed from side to side, his voice echoing off the stone. Trying with everything to throw them off. Then he fell sideways into deeper water. He felt it rush over him, the force taking him with it. He was sure he felt them let go. Sure he heard their shrill squeaks as they tried to make higher ground without drowning. Sure he heard the hundreds of others shrieking in a terrible uproar of shared fear. He opened his mouth, bellowing against the sound, trying to get air. But it filled with water and he choked as he was swept away. The only thing clear in his mind was the taste of it; foul and filled with his own blood.

30

Friday, July 10, 1:00 A.M.

A HAND TOUCHED HARRY'S FACE, AND HE groaned, shivering. The hand retreated, a moment later to return with a damp cloth to wipe his face and again clean the wound on his forehead. Then moving a little to scrub gently the dried blood that matted his hair.

Somewhere far off came a vague rumbling and the ground shook, and then both sound and movement stopped. Then he felt a tugging at his shoulders and he opened his eyes, or rather the one eye that could see. When he did, he started. An oversized head stared down at him, the eyes glistening in the dim light.

"Parla Italiano?" A man was sitting on the ground beside Harry, his voice high-pitched and accented in a strange, singsong way.

Harry turned his head slowly to look at him.

"Inglese?"

"Yes . . . ," Harry whispered.

"American?"

"Yes . . . ," Harry whispered again.

"Me, too, once. Pittsburgh. I came to Rome to be in a Fellini movie. I never was. And I never left."

Harry could hear the sound of his own breathing. "Where am I . . . ?"

The face smiled. "With Hercules."

Suddenly another face appeared, looking down at him, too. It was that of a woman. Dark skinned, maybe forty, her hair turned up in a bright bandana. Kneeling down, she touched his head, then reached across and lifted his left hand. It was bandaged heavily. Her eyes went to the man with the enlarged head, and she said something in a language Harry had never heard. The man nodded. The woman glanced back at Harry, then stood abruptly and left. After a moment there was a sound like a heavy door opening and then closing.

"You have the use of only one eye. . . . But soon the other will come back. She has said so." Hercules smiled again. "I am to wash your wounds twice every day and to change the bandage on your hand tomorrow. The one on your head can remain for a time. . . . She has told me that, too."

Again came the rumbling and again the ground shook.

"This my house. Where I live," Hercules said. "A boarded-up part of the Metro, an old work tunnel. I have existed here for five years—and no one knows. Well, except for a few such as her. . . . Pretty good, eh?" He laughed and then reached out and pulled himself up with an aluminum crutch. "I have no use of my legs. But my shoulders are huge and I am very strong."

Hercules was a dwarf. Three and half feet, four feet tall at most. His head was large, almost egg shaped. And his shoulders *were* huge, as were his arms. But that was most all of him. His waist was tiny, his legs little more than spindles.

Limping to a darkened wall behind him, Hercules plucked something from it. When he turned back, he had a second crutch.

"You were shot . . ."

Harry stared blankly. He remembered none of it.

"Very lucky. The gun was small caliber. The bullet hit your hand and bounced off your head. . . . You were in the sewer. I fished you out."

Harry stared at him with his one good eye, uncomprehending, his mind straining to adjust, as if fighting to come out of a deep sleep, to move from an endless dream to reality. For some reason his thoughts went to Madeline, and he saw her, arms and legs askew, her hair floating out from her head in the black water under the ice, and he wondered if this was what it had been like for her—moving from some kind of terrifying reality to a dreamlike state, shifting back and forth between one and the other until she went finally into her last deep sleep.

"You do not feel pain?"

"No . . ."

Hercules grinned. "Because of her medicine. She is a Gypsy who knows healing. I am not Gypsy, but I get along with them. They give me things, I give them things. We do favors. That way we respect and do not steal from each other. . . ." A giggle erupted, and he let it run, then became serious again. "Nor I from you, Father."

"Father . . . ?" Harry looked at him blankly.

"Your papers were in your jacket, Father Addison . . ." Hercules leaned on his crutches and swept his hand to the side.

Nearby, Harry's clothes hung on a makeshift rack to dry.

On the ground next to them, carefully laid out to dry as well, was the envelope Gasparri had given him. Next to it were Danny's personal effects—his scorched watch, his broken glasses, his charred Vatican identification, and his passport.

Like an acrobat Hercules suddenly dropped the length of his crutches to sit on the ground next to Harry, face-to-face as before. As if he had abruptly pulled up a chair.

"We have a problem, Father. Decidedly you would want me to tell someone of your condition. Most probably the police. But you are not ready to walk, and I can tell no one you are here because then my home would be found out. Understand?"

"Yes . . ."

"Best you rest anyway. With good fortune, as early as tomorrow you will be able to stand and then go where you wish."

Suddenly Hercules reversed his earlier motion and abruptly pulled himself up on his crutches.

"I am leaving for a time. Sleep without fear. You will be safe."

With that he swung off and disappeared in the darkness, the sound of him echoing until there was the creak of wood, the same as when the woman left—a heavy door opening and closing.

Harry lay back and for the first time was aware of a pillow under his head and a blanket covering him. "Thank you," he whispered. Again he heard the vague rumbling and felt the ground shake as a Metro train passed in the distance. Then exhaustion overtook him and he closed his eyes and thoughts of Hercules and everything else faded away.

31

Beverly Hills, California. Thursday, July 9, dusk.

BYRON WILLIS LET OUT A DEEP BREATH AND hung up the phone. Turning off Sunset and onto Stone Canyon Road, he switched on the Lexus's headlights and saw them illuminate the ivy-covered walls guarding the massive, elegant estates he wound past. What had happened was impossible. Harry Addison, *his* Harry Addison, the guy whom he brought into the firm and loved like a brother and who had an office down the hall, was suddenly on the run in Italy, wanted for the murder of a Rome detective. And Harry's brother was accused of the assassination of the cardinal vicar of Rome. And it had happened bang, bang. Like an auto accident. Already the media were tying up the office switchboard, trying to get a statement from him and the other partners.

"Son of a bitch!" he said out loud.

Whatever the hell had happened, Harry was going to need all the help he could get, and so was the firm. The night was going to be spent fending off the media and making certain their clients knew what had happened and telling them to say nothing when the reporters pounced. At the same time he would be trying to find Harry and get him the best legal representation in Italy.

Slowing, Byron Willis saw the satellite trucks and the gaggle of media gathered in front of the security gates of his home at 1500 Stone Canyon Road. Pressing the remote that opened the gates, he waited for people to clear, then drove through, waving politely, doing his best to ignore them. On the far side he stopped, making certain no one slipped past as the gates closed. Then he drove on, his headlights cutting an easy path through the darkness, illuminating the long, familiar drive up to his house.

"Dammit," he breathed.

In an instant a friend's world was turned upside down. It made him realize his own situation only more. Another late meeting, another coming home after dark. His wife and two young sons were away at the family vacation house in Sun Valley. A wife and two young sons whom, even when they were home, he barely saw, even on weekends. God only knew what lay around any corner. Life was rich and to be lived thoroughly, and the demands of work should not be allowed to take up so much of it. And in that moment he made a resolve that once the business with Harry had been worked through—and it *would* be worked through—he would cut his time at the office and begin to enjoy the rewards life had presented him.

Another push of the remote, and the door to his garage swung open. Usually the garage lights came on when the door opened, but for some reason this time they didn't, and he didn't know why. Opening the car door, he stepped out.

"Byron—," a male voice said in the dark.

Byron Willis started and swung around to see the vaguest outline of a figure coming toward him.

"Who are you?"

"A friend of Harry Addison."

Harry? What the hell did that mean? Suddenly, fear stabbed through him. "How did you get in here? What do you want?"

"Not much."

There was a dance of flame and the smallest sound, as if someone had spit. Willis felt something hit him hard in the chest. Instinctively he looked down, wondering what it was. Then he felt his knees begin to buckle. The sound came again. Twice. The man stood right in front of him.

Byron Willis looked up. "I don't understand . . ."

They were the last words he ever said.

32

Rome. Friday July 10, 7:00 A.M.

THOMAS KIND WALKED ALONG THE PATHWAY
above the Tiber, waiting impatiently for the cell phone in his
pocket to ring. He was dressed in a beige seersucker suit and
blue-striped shirt open at the throat. A white panama hat was
tilted down over his face to protect him both from the early
sun and the possible inquiring face, the one that might recognize him and alert the authorities.

Moving under an umbrella of shade trees, he walked
another dozen paces to a place he had seen as he approached,
a point where the flowing Tiber washed against the granite
walls directly below him. Glancing around and seeing nothing but the rush of early traffic passing on the roadway
beyond the trees, he opened his jacket and reached into his
waistband, taking out an object wrapped in a white silk
handkerchief. Leaning forward casually, he rested his elbows on the protective balustrade over the water, a tourist

stopped to gaze out over the river, and let the object fall from the handkerchief. A moment later he heard the splash and slowly straightened up, absently wiping the handkerchief across the back of his neck. Then he walked on, the Spanish-made Llama pistol washing somewhere along with the current at the bottom of the river.

Ten minutes later he entered a small trattoria just off Piazza Farnese, ordered a cold espresso from the bar, and sat down at a table near the back, still waiting for the call and the information that yet had not come. Taking the phone from his jacket, he dialed a number, let it ring twice, then punched in a three-digit code and hung up. Sitting back, he picked up his glass and waited for the return call.

Thomas Jose Alvarez-Rios Kind had become famous in 1984 for killing four undercover French antiterrorist police in a botched raid in a Paris suburb and had been the darling of the media and the terrorist underground ever since. Becoming, as journalists liked to call him, a latter-day Carlos the Jackal, a terrorist of fortune, willing to serve the highest bidder. And through the late 1980s and into the 1990s, he had served them all. From remnants of Italian Red Brigades to the French Action Directe. From Muammar al Qaddafi to Abu Nidal, and work for Iraqi intelligence in Belgium, France, Britain, and Italy. Then to Miami and New York as a debt payer for the master *traficantes*, the leaders of the Medellín drug cartel. And later, as if they needed help, coming back to Italy as a contractor for the Cosa Nostra, assassinating Mafia prosecutors in Calabria and Palermo.

All of which allowed him to echo publicly the words of Bonnot, the leader of a murderous gang operating in Paris in 1912, and later used by Carlos himself—"I am a celebrated man." And he was. Over the years his face had graced not only the front pages of the world's major newspapers, but also the covers of *TIME, Newsweek,* even *Vanity Fair. 60 Minutes* had profiled him twice. All of which put him in a different class entirely from the long succession of other freelancers who had eagerly worked for him.

The trouble was he was increasingly certain he was mentally ill. At first he thought he had simply lost track. He had started out to become a revolutionary in the truest sense, traveling from Ecuador to Chile as an idealistic teenager in 1976 and taking up a rifle in the streets of Santiago to avenge the slaughter of Marxist students by the soldiers of fascist General Augusto Pinochet. Then came an ideological life in London with his mother's family, attending exclusive British schools before studying politics and history at Oxford. Immediately afterward there had been a clandestine meeting with a KGB operative in London, followed by an offer to train him as a Soviet agent in Moscow. On the way there, he had stopped in France. And with it had come the business with the Paris police. And then, and all at once, fame.

But in the last months, he had begun to sense that he was not driven by ideology or revolution at all, but rather by the exploit of terror itself or, more explicitly, by the act of killing. It was more than something that gave him pleasure, it was sexually arousing. To the extent that it had replaced the sex act altogether. And each time—though he wanted to deny it—the feeling magnified in intensity and became ever more gratifying. A lover to be found, stalked, and then butchered in the most ingenious way that came to him at the time.

It was awful. He hated it. The idea terrified him. Yet, at the same time, he craved it. That he might be ill was a thought he desperately tried to refute. He wanted to think he was only tired, or, more realistically, having the thoughts of a person approaching middle age. But he knew it wasn't true and something was wrong, because progressively he felt off balance, as if some part of him was weighted more heavily than the rest. It was a situation made all the worse because there was absolutely no one he could talk to about it without fear of being caught or turned in or compromised in some other way.

The abrupt chirp of the phone at his elbow jolted him back to the present. Instantly he picked up.

"*Oui*." Yes, he said, speaking in French, nodding several times in response. It was news he had been waiting for, and it came in two parts: the first was confirmation that a potential problem in the U.S. had been tidied up—If Harry Addison had purposely or inadvertently passed on troublesome information to Byron Willis, it no longer made a difference. The subject had been eliminated.

The second was more difficult because it had involved extensive telephone research and the results had taken far longer to get than he anticipated. But, late or not, they were here and they were welcome.

"Yes," he said finally. "Pescara. I'm leaving now."

33

"WARM TEA," HERCULES SAID. "CAN YOU swallow?"

"Yes . . . ," Harry nodded.

"Put your hands around it."

Hercules guided the cup to him and helped Harry grasp it, the bandage on his left hand, like an oversized mitten, making what should have been a simple process awkward.

Harry drank and gagged.

"Terrible, isn't it? Gypsy tea. Strong and bitter. Drink it anyway. It will help you heal and bring back your sight."

Harry hesitated, then took the tea down in a series of long gulps, trying not to taste it. Hercules watched him carefully as he drank, moving from side to side and then back again as an artist might while studying a subject. When he was finished, Hercules snatched the cup away.

"You are not you."

"What?"

"You are not Father Daniel but his brother."

Harry put an elbow under himself and raised up. "How do you know that?"

"First, from the picture on the passport. Second, because the police are looking for you."

Harry started. "The police?"

"It was on the radio. You are wanted for murder—not the one your brother is wanted for. The cardinal vicar, that's a big one. But yours is big enough."

"What are you talking about?"

"The policeman, Mr. Harry Addison. The police detective named Pio."

"Pio is dead?"

"You did a good job."

"*I* did a—?"

In an instant it came back. Pio glancing in the mirror of the Alfa Romeo. Then sliding his gun onto the seat. At the same time Harry saw the truck directly in front of them. Heard his own voice scream for Pio to *look out!*

And now another part of it returned too. Something he hadn't remembered until this moment. It was a *sound.* Terribly loud. A thunderous boom that repeated quickly. A gun being fired.

And then he remembered the face. There and then gone, like a flashbulb illuminating something for a millisecond. It had been pale and cruel. With a half smile. And then, for some reason, although he didn't know why, he remembered the deepest blue eyes he had ever seen.

"No . . . ," Harry said, his voice barely audible. Stunned, his eyes found Hercules.

"I didn't do it."

"It makes no difference, Mr. Harry, if you did or you

didn't. . . . All that matters is the authorities think you did. Italy has no capital punishment, but the police will find a way to kill you anyhow."

Suddenly Hercules pulled himself up. Leaning on his crutch, he looked down at Harry. "They say you are a lawyer. From California. You make money from movie stars and are very rich."

Harry lay back. So that was it. Hercules wanted money and was going to extort it from him, threatening him with the police. And why not? Hercules was a common criminal living in filth under the Metro, and Harry had fallen into his lap. And whatever reason he had had for saving his life, with the new turn of events, he suddenly found he had saved a golden goose.

"I have some money, yes. But I can't get it without the police knowing where I am. So, even if I wanted to give it to you, I couldn't."

"It does not matter." Hercules leaned closer and grinned. "You have a price on you."

"Price?"

"The police have offered a reward. One hundred million lire. About sixty thousand dollars, U.S. A lot of money, Mr. Harry—especially to those who have none."

Finding his other crutch, Hercules abruptly turned his back and pushed off as he had earlier, swinging away into the darkness.

"I didn't kill him!" Harry shouted.

"The police will kill you anyway!" Hercules' voice echoed until it was lost in the distant rumbling of a Metro train passing at the end of his private tunnel. Afterward came the sound of the great door as it opened and thudded closed.

And then there was silence.

34

Cortona, Italy.

THE PLACE WHERE THEY BROUGHT MICHAEL
Roark was not a hospital but a private home—Casa Alberti, a
restored, three-story stone farmhouse, named for an ancient
Florentine family. Sister Elena saw it through the early mist
as they drove through the iron gate and started up the long
gravel drive.

Leaving Pescara they had circumvented the A14 Autostrada, taken the A24, and then rejoined the A14 to the north.
Driving along the Adriatic coast to San Benedetto and then
Civitanova Marche, they turned west sometime after midnight, later passing Foligno, Assisi, and Perugia before
climbing into the hills to find Casa Alberti just east of the
ancient Tuscan city of Cortona at daybreak.

Marco had unlocked the gate and opened it, walking up
the drive in front of the van as Luca drove toward the house.

Pietro, following in his car, had locked the gate behind them, then gone into the house first, checking it carefully before turning on the lights and letting them in.

Elena had watched without a word as, a few moments later, Marco and Luca carried the gurney up the steps and into the house and then up to the large second-floor suite that was to become Michael Roark's hospital room. Opening the shuttered window, she had seen see the red globe of the sun just beginning to rise over the farmland in the distance.

Now, below her, Pietro came out of the house and moved his car to the front of the van so that it blocked the driveway, as if to make it all but impossible for another vehicle to get past and up to the house. Then she heard the engine stop and saw Pietro walk to the trunk and take out a shotgun. A moment later, he yawned and got back in the car with the door open, then folded his arms over his chest and went to sleep.

"Do you need anything?"

Marco stood in the doorway behind her.

"No." She smiled.

"Luca will sleep in the room upstairs. I will be down in the kitchen if you need me."

"Thank you . . ."

Marco looked at her and then left, closing the door behind him. Almost at once, Elena felt her own weariness. She had dozed off and on during most the trip, but her senses and thoughts had kept her on edge. Now they were here at the Casa, and the thought of sleep was suddenly and overwhelmingly seductive.

To her right was a large bathroom with a tub and separate shower. To the left was a small nook with a bed and closet and a room divider for privacy.

In front of her Michael Roark was in a deep sleep. The trip, she knew, had exhausted him. He'd remained awake for a good deal of it. His eyes going from her to the men in the van and then back to her, as if he were trying to understand where he was and what was happening. If he'd been afraid, she hadn't seen it, but perhaps it was because of her constant reassurance, telling him her name and his, over and over, and the names of the men who were with them, friends taking him to a place where he could rest and recover. And then an hour or two before they'd arrived at the farmhouse, he'd fallen into the sound sleep he was in now.

Opening the medicine kit Marco had brought up and set on the chair, she took out the arm wrap with its pump and gauge and took his blood pressure, studying him as she did. His face beneath the bandages covering his head was gaunt, and she knew he had lost weight. She wondered what he had looked like before. What he might look like again when he began to recover and take solid food and rebuild his strength.

Finishing, she stood, and put the blood pressure gauge away. His blood pressure was the same as it had been that afternoon, the same as it had been when she'd first arrived in Pescara. Not better. Not worse. Simply unchanged. She marked it on his chart, then took off her habit, pulled on the light cotton sleeping gown, and got into bed, hoping to close her eyes for forty-five minutes or at most an hour. As she did, she looked at her watch.

It was eight-twenty in the morning, Friday, July 10.

35

Rome. Same time.

CARDINAL MARSCIANO WATCHED THE PRESS
conference on a small television in his library. It was live,
impromptu, and filled with anger. Marcello Taglia, the man
in charge of Gruppo Cardinale, had been cornered as his car
entered police headquarters, and he had stepped out to confront the mass of reporters and respond to their questions
head on.

Where the videotape of the American attorney Harry
Addison had come from he did not know, Taglia said. Nor
did he have any idea who had leaked it to the press. Nor did
he know who had leaked the photograph and speculation
surrounding Addison's brother, Father Daniel Addison, a
prime suspect in the murder of the cardinal vicar of Rome
and thought killed in the bombing of the Assisi bus, but now
possibly alive and in hiding somewhere in Italy. And, yes, it
was true, a reward of one hundred million lire had been

offered for information leading to the arrest and conviction of either of the American brothers.

Abruptly the cameras cut away from Taglia and went to the television studio, where an attractive anchorwoman behind a glass desk introduced the video of Harry. When it was over, photographs of both brothers were put on the screen and a telephone number given that anyone seeing either man could call.

CLICK.

Marsciano turned off the television and stared at the empty screen, his world darker yet. It was a world that in the following hours could become even more impossible, if not unbearable.

Shortly he would sit before the four other cardinals who made up the commission overseeing the investments of the Holy See and present the new, and intentionally misleading, investment portfolio for ratification.

At one-thirty the meeting would break, and Marsciano would take the ten-minute walk from Vatican City to Armari, a small family-run trattoria on Viale Angelico. There, in a private upstairs room, he would meet with Palestrina to report on the outcome. It was an outcome upon which rested not only Palestrina's "Chinese Protocol" but also Marsciano's own life, and with it, the life of Father Daniel.

Purposefully he had fought to keep the thought from his mind for fear it would weaken him and show him as desperate when he went before the cardinals. But, as the clock ticked forward, and as much as he battled to keep it locked away, the memory crept forward, chillingly, almost as if Palestrina had willed it.

And then, with a rush, it was there, and he saw himself in Pierre Weggen's office in Geneva the evening of the day that the Assisi bus had exploded. The phone had rung, and the call was for him. It was Palestrina informing him, in one breath, that Father Daniel had been on the bus and was presumed dead; and, in the next—Father in heaven! Marsciano could still feel the awful stab of Palestrina's words delivered in a voice so calm they were like the brush of silk—"the police have found sufficient evidence to prove Father Daniel guilty of the assassination of Cardinal Parma."

Marsciano remembered his own shout of outrage and then seeing Weggen's quiet grin in response, as if the investment banker knew full well the content of Palestrina's call, and then the continuing voice of Palestrina as he went on unmoved.

"Moreover, Eminence, if your presentation to the council of cardinals should fail, resulting in the investment proposal voted down, the police will soon discover that the road from Parma's murder does not end with Father Daniel but leads directly to you. And I can safely surmise that the first question the investigators will ask is if you and the cardinal vicar were lovers. A denial, of course, would be futile, because there would be sufficient evidence—notes, letters of a lurid and very personal sort, found in the private computer files of you both. . . . Think then, Eminence, of seeing your face and his on the cover of every newspaper and magazine, on every television screen around the globe. . . . Think of the repercussions throughout the Holy See, and the utter disgrace it would bring to the Holy Church."

Trembling and horrified, and certain without doubt who had been responsible for the bombing of the bus, Marciano had simply hung up. Palestrina was everywhere. Twisting the screw, tightening his hold. Efficient, controlled, ruthless. Larger, more terrifying and detestable than Marsciano could ever have imagined.

*   *   *

TURNING IN HIS CHAIR, Marsciano looked out the window. Across the street he could see the gray Mercedes waiting to take him from his apartment to the Vatican. His driver was new and a favorite of Farel's, the baby-faced plainclothes member of the Vatican police, Anton Pilger. His housekeeper, Sister Maria-Louisa, was new as well. As were his secretaries and office manager. Of his original staff only Father Bardoni remained, and only because he knew how to access computer files and understood the shared database with Weggen's Geneva office. Once the new portfolio was accepted, Marsciano was certain Father Bardoni would be gone, too. He was the last of the truly loyal, and his going would leave Marsciano wholly alone in the nest of Palestrina's vipers.

36

HARRY MOVED UNSTEADILY IN THE DARK-
ness, his head still aching from the smack of the ricocheting
bullet, his back against the rough of the tunnel wall, with his
good hand stretched out along it trying to find Hercules'
great door. He had to get out before the dwarf came back.
Who knew what he would bring with him when he did?
Friends? The police? What must sixty thousand dollars mean
to a creature like him?

Where was the door? It couldn't be this far. What if he
had gone past it in the dark?

He stopped. Listening. Hoping for the distant rumble of a
Metro train that might give him some clue to where he was.

Silence.

It had taken most of his strength just to dress, collect
Danny's things, and get out of Hercules' den. What he would
do once he was out and away he didn't know, but anything
was better than staying there and waiting for whatever Hercules had planned.

Behind and in front was blackness. Then he saw it. A pin-point of light in the distance. The end of the tunnel. He felt relief shudder through him. Back against the wall he started toward it. The light became brighter. He walked faster. Now his foot touched something hard. He stopped. Put his foot up to feel it. Steel. It was a rail. He looked back. The light was closer. He flashed on the machine of torture his captors had used. It couldn't be the same. Where was he? Had he never left there at all?

Then he felt the ground rumble under him. The light was racing toward him. Then he knew! He was in a live tunnel. The light rocketing toward him was a Metro train. Turning, he ran back the way he had come. The light became brighter and brighter. His left foot slipped on the rail and he nearly fell. He heard the shriek of the train whistle. Then the scream of steel as the driver slammed on the brakes.

Suddenly rough hands grabbed him and threw him against the tunnel wall. He saw the lights inside the train as it slid past inches from him. The faces of startled passengers. Then it was past. Screeching to a stop fifty yards down the track.

"Are you crazy?"

Hercules was in his face, his hands on Harry's jacket, holding him in an iron grip.

Yells of trainmen came from down the track. They were climbing out, coming toward them with flashlights.

"This way."

Hercules spun him around and into a narrow side tunnel. A moment later he shoved him up a work ladder, then fol-lowed himself, crutches hanging on one arm, swinging up behind him like a circus performer.

Behind them they heard the shouts and calls of the

trainmen. Hercules stared angrily at him, then moved him forward down another narrow tunnel full of wiring and ventilation equipment.

They went on that way, Harry in front, Hercules directly behind, for what seemed like a half mile or more. Finally they stopped under the light of a ventilation shaft.

For a long moment Hercules said nothing, just listened then, satisfied they hadn't been followed, looked to Harry.

"They will report that to the police. They will come and search the tunnels. If they find my place, they will know you were there. And I will have nowhere to live."

"I'm sorry . . ."

"At least we know two things. You are well enough to walk, even run. And you are no longer blind."

Harry *could* see. He hadn't had time to even think about it. He'd been in darkness. Then had come the light of the train and seeing the passengers inside. Not with one eye but two.

"So," Hercules said. "You are free." With that he slung a small bound package from his shoulder and pushed it at Harry.

"Open it."

Harry stared, then did as the dwarf said. Undoing the package, he unrolled its contents. Black trousers, black shirt, black jacket, and the white clerical collar of a priest, all worn but serviceable.

"You will become your brother, eh?"

Harry stared, incredulous.

"All right, maybe not your brother, but a priest. Why not? Already you are growing a beard, changing your appearance. . . . In a city filled with priests, how better to hide than in the open . . . ? In the pants' pocket are a few hundred thousand lire. Not much, but enough for you to gather your wits and see what you would do next."

"Why?" Harry said. "You could have turned me over to the police and collected the reward."

"Is your brother alive?"

"I don't know."

"Did he kill the cardinal vicar?"

"I don't know."

"There, you see. If I had given you to the authorities, you could never have answered the questions: If your brother lives. If he is a murderer. How do you know unless you find out?—Not forgetting that you yourself are wanted for the murder of a policeman. It makes it twice as interesting, eh?"

"You could have had enough money to last you a long time."

"But the police would have to give it to me. And I cannot go to the police, Mr. Harry. Because I myself am a murderer. . . . And if I had someone else do it and offered some sort of arrangement, they might take the money and never come back. . . . You would be in prison, and I would be no better off than I am now. . . . What good is that?"

"Then why?"

"Do I help you?"

"Yes."

"To let you out, Mr. Harry, and see what you can do. How far your wits and courage will take you. If you are good enough to survive. To find answers to your questions. To prove your innocence."

Harry studied him carefully. "That's not the only reason, is it?"

Hercules moved back on his crutches and for the first time Harry saw sadness in him. "The man I killed was wealthy and drunk. He tried to smash my head with a brick because of what I look like. I had to do something and did.

"You are a handsome, intelligent man. If you use what you have, you have a chance. . . . I have none. I am an ugly dwarf and murderer, condemned to a life beneath the streets. . . . If you win your game, Mr. Harry, maybe you will remember me and come back. Use your money and what you know to help me. . . . If I am still alive, any Gypsy will know how to find me."

A feeling of warmth and true affection crept over Harry, making him feel as if he stood in the presence of an extraordinary human being. And he cocked his head, smiling at the sheer curiosity of it. A week ago he'd been in New York on business, one of the youngest, most successful entertainment lawyers in Hollywood. His life had seemed charmed. He was on top of the world, with only higher to go. Seven days later, in a turn of circumstance beyond imagination, he stood bandaged and dirty in a cramped air shaft above the Rome Metro—wanted for the murder of an Italian policeman.

It was a nightmare that defied belief but all too real just the same. And in the middle of it, a man brutalized by life, who had little or no hope of ever being free again—a crippled dwarf who had rescued him and helped nurse him back to health—hung on his crutches inches away in a deep chiaroscuro of light, asking for his help. One day in the future, if he could remember.

By his simple request, Hercules had effected a grace Harry barely knew existed. Saying gently that he truly believed one person, if he wished, could use what he had learned in life to do something of value for another. It was pure and honest and had been asked with no expectation that it would ever be carried out.

"I will do the best I can," Harry said. "I promise you."

37

A cafeteria in Stazione Termini,
Rome's main railroad terminal. 9:30 A.M.

ROSCANI WATCHED HIM WALK OUT TOWARD
the trains and disappear into the crowd. He would finish his
coffee and take his time leaving, making certain no one had
the impression they knew each other or had left together.

Enrico Cirelli had been just another face ordering coffee.
He'd taken it from the counter and come to the table where
Roscani was having his own coffee and reading the morning
paper. No more than a dozen words had been exchanged
between them, but they were all Roscani needed.

An electrician, Cirelli had been north on a job and had
come back only yesterday. But for Roscani it was worth the
wait. As a ranking member of the Democratic Party of the
Left, the new name for the Italian Communist Party, Cirelli
knew as well as he knew his children whatever was happening inside Rome's far left. And the far left, he told Roscani

straight out, had had nothing to do with the murder of Cardinal Parma, the bombing of the Assisi bus, or the killing of Ispettore Capo Gianni Pio. If there were outside factions at work, a splinter group, he didn't know. But if they existed, he would find out.

"*Grazie,*" Roscani had said, and Cirelli had simply stood and walked out. There was no need for the party leader to acknowledge the appreciation. Roscani would reciprocate later. When it was needed.

Finally Roscani stood and walked out himself. By now the Harry Addison video would have played on every channel of Italian television. His picture and that of his brother would have been seen in ninety percent of the country.

Roscani had purposely stayed away from the Questura and out of the limelight. It was a decision that had been made when he'd called Taglia at home at three in the morning to inform him Italian television had gotten hold of the video, and also a photo of Father Daniel, complete with pertinent details of the Gruppo Cardinale investigation of him. In response, Taglia had assigned Roscani to discover who had leaked the material. It was an inquiry to be rigorously pursued. One necessary to preserving the integrity of Gruppo Cardinale, not to mention Italian jurisprudence. Yet it was a pursuit both agreed would be difficult at best and might lead nowhere. Since both knew the material had been leaked by Roscani.

Now, as he crossed the terminal and out toward the street, pushing quickly through the tremendous flow of humanity that moved through it, Roscani saw uniformed police watching all of it. And knew there were more watching in other public places—airports, train stations, bus and ship terminals—from Rome to Sicily, and north to the borders at France, Switzerland, and Austria. Knew, too, that because of the media, the general populace would be on the lookout for them as well.

As he pushed through the glass doors and out into the bright sunshine, walking across toward his car, the immense scope of the Gruppo Cardinale manhunt began to sink in. He felt his eyes begin to narrow and realized he was watching faces, too. That was when he knew the feelings and emotions he thought he had put aside and buried under the guise of distance and professionalism hadn't been left behind at all. He could feel their heat coming up through him.

Whether Father Daniel was alive or dead was a guess—conjecture one way or the other. But Harry Addison was somewhere out there. It was only a matter of time before he would be recognized. When that happened he would be pinpointed and watched. People in harm's way would be quietly evacuated. And then, when the time was right, probably after dark, one man would go in after him alone. He would wear a flak jacket and be armed, both with a gun and memories of a fallen comrade.

That man would be Roscani himself.

Friday, July 10, 9:50 A.M.

HARRY ADDISON STEPPED OUT OF THE METRO
and into bright July sunshine at Manzoni Station. He wore
Hercules' costume and looked, he assumed, like a priest
who'd had a bad night. A stubble beard, one bandage on the
hairline at his left temple, another on his left hand, which
kept together his thumb, index, and middle fingers.

The thing that jolted him to hard reality was his picture,
side by side with Danny's, on the covers of *Il Messagero* and
La Repubblica, Italian-language newspapers that lined either
side of a news and magazine kiosk near the station. Turning,
he walked off in the other direction.

The first thing was to clean up to keep from drawing
attention to himself. Ahead of him two streets came together
with a small café on the corner. He went in, hoping to find a
rest room where he could wash his face and hands and wet
back his hair so that he was at least presentable.

A dozen people were inside, and not one looked up as he entered. The lone barman was at the coffee machine and had his back to the room. Harry walked past, assuming the rest room, if there was one, was at the rear. He was right, but someone was inside and he had to wait. Stepping back, he leaned against the wall near a window, trying to determine what to do next. As he did, he saw two priests pass by outside. One was bare headed, but the other wore a black beret that was pulled jauntily forward and to the side like some twenties Parisian artist. Maybe it was the style, maybe not, but if one priest could do it, why not two?

Abruptly the lavatory door opened and a man came out. He stared briefly at Harry as if in recognition, then passed by and went back into the café.

"Buon giorno, padre," he said as he did.

"Buon giorno," Harry said after him, then stepped into the lavatory and closed the door. Locking it with a flimsy slide-bolt, he turned to the mirror.

What he saw startled him. His face was gaunt, his skin pallid, his beard filled in more than he'd realized. When he'd left L.A., he'd been in good shape. A hundred and ninety pounds, over six feet two inches. He was certain he'd lost considerable weight. How much, he didn't know, but under the black of the priest's clothing he looked exceptionally slim. The weight loss, with the beard, had changed his appearance considerably.

Washing his face and hands as best he could, considering the bandages, he wet his hair and slicked it back with his palms. Behind him he heard a sound and saw the doorknob rattle.

"Momento," he said instinctively, suddenly wondering if that was the correct word or not.

From outside, an impatient knock on the door was

followed by an angry rattle of the doorknob. Unlocking the door, he opened it. An irate woman stared at him. That he was a priest had no effect at all. Obviously, her business was urgent. Nodding politely, he pushed past her, walked the length of the café and out into the street.

Two people had seen him face-to-face; neither had said a word. Yet he had been seen at a place with a name, and later—hours or moments—they might see his photo and remember. And remembering, call the police. What he needed to do was distance himself from the café as quickly as possible.

39

ROSCANI RAN ALONG THE TRACK, SCALA AND
Castelletti right behind him. Work lights flooded the tunnel.
Uniformed police in flak jackets and carrying submachine
guns were everywhere. So were Metro officials and the driver of the train that had nearly hit the fugitive.

"There were two of them. The American and a small man
with crutches. Maybe a midget."

Roscani had taken the call as he was leaving the railroad terminal on his way back to the Questura. It had come
late, nearly an hour after the men had been sighted. Rush
hour, the driver complained. Fearing he'd hit the men, he'd
stopped the train and come back but had seen nothing. He'd
reported it and gone on. It wasn't until he was taking a break
and saw Harry's picture on the cover of *Il Messagero* that he
made the connection with the man in the tunnel.

"You're certain it was him," Roscani pressed.

"He was only for the smallest moment in the train's head-
light. But yes, as sure as I can be. He had a bandage of some
kind on his head."

"Where could they have gone?" Roscani turned to a tall, mustached Metro official.

"Anywhere. In this section there are many original tunnels, for one reason or another no longer in use."

Roscani hesitated. The stations at either end of this part of the tunnel had been shut down, passengers taken out and shifted to buses under the close eye of a phalanx of police. But it was only a matter of time before the entire Metro would begin to suffer from the closing.

"There are maps of these tunnels?"

"Yes."

"Get them." He looked to Scala. "Go to Mr. Addison's hotel room. Find something he has worn recently, something not laundered. Bring it back here as quickly as you can."

Scala looked back. He understood. "You want dogs."

"Yes."

HARRY MOVED QUICKLY along the sidewalk, already sweating with the July heat. Leaving the area of the café was one thing. His picture stared out from newspapers on every kiosk he passed. It was not only frightening, it was bizarre, as if he had been transported to another planet where everyone on it was looking for him. Suddenly he stopped, thunderstruck at the sound of his own voice. He was passing an electronics store. In the window was a bank of televisions. Large screen to small. And he was on every one of them, wearing dark glasses and sitting on a stool, dressed in the sport coat he had left behind with Hercules. His voice was coming from a small speaker just above the front door.

"Danny, I'm asking you to come in. . . . To give yourself up. . . . They know everything. . . . Please, for me. . . . Come in . . . please. . . . Please . . ."

Now the picture cut to an interior of a television station. A male broadcaster sat at a news desk speaking in Italian. He heard his name and Danny's. Then there was a video clip of the murder of the cardinal vicar of Rome. Police were everywhere, ambulances, a glimpse of Farel, a brief shot of the Holy Father's car as it sped him from the scene.

Suddenly Harry was aware of other people standing on the sidewalk watching the televisions. Turning his head, he moved away. Dazed. Where had the video come from? Vaguely he remembered the business with the earphone, someone talking into it. Vaguely remembered repeating what was said, then thinking something was wrong and trying to do something about it. Then being hit and everything going black again. Now he realized what it was. He had been tortured to reveal Danny's whereabouts, and when they realized he didn't know, they'd forced him into making the video, then taken him away to kill him.

Stepping off a curb, he waited for a car to pass, then crossed the street. The photos in the newspapers had been bad enough, but now his face was on every television screen in the country. Maybe even worldwide. Thank God for the dark glasses. They had to have helped some in disguising him. At least a little.

Directly ahead was an arched portal in an ancient wall. It reminded him of a similar wall near the Vatican that Farel's driver had taken him through on the way to meet the Vatican policeman. He wondered if this was the same wall, if he was close to the Vatican itself. He didn't know Rome, he'd simply popped out of a subway station somewhere in the middle of it and started walking. It was no good; he could be going in circles for all he knew.

Abruptly he walked into the deep shade of the portal. For an instant the shade and cool were a relief from the bright sun and July heat. Then he reached the far side and stepped back into the sunlight again. As he did, and for the second time in minutes, he stopped dead.

Little more than a half block in front of him was a swarm of police vehicles near the entrance to a metro station. Mounted police on horseback kept a gathering crowd at bay. To one side were several ambulances and parked media cars, including two satellite trucks.

People were suddenly rushing past him toward what was happening, and he stepped back, trying to get some idea of where he was. It didn't help. All he saw was a massive intersection of converging streets. Via La Spezia. Via Sannio. Via Magna Grecia. And Via Appia Nuova, where he stood.

"What's goin' on, Father?" The accent was young and New York.

Harry started. A teenager wearing a T-shirt with the words END OF THE DEAD over a likeness of Jerry Garcia had come up next to him, his round-faced girlfriend beside him. Both were staring at the mass of activity down the block.

"I don't know, I'm sorry," he replied. Then he turned and started back the way he had come. He knew very well what was going on. The police were looking for him.

Heart pounding, he picked up his pace as more people hurried past him. Across the street to his left was a large expanse of green and beyond it a large and apparently very old church.

Quickly he crossed the street and started across the piazza toward it. As he did, two police cars flew past, bumper to bumper, in a wail of sirens. He kept on.

Ahead was the church. Huge, ancient, beckoning. A refuge from the turmoil behind him. Numbers of people—tourists, it looked like—were on the steps. Some were turned, looking in the direction he was coming from, drawn by what was going on. Still others were more intent on the church itself. This was a city, what did he expect? People were everywhere. He had to take the chance, for a short while at least, that he could lose himself among them and not be recognized.

Crossing the cobblestones he went up the steps and into the crowd. People barely noticed as he pushed between them to enter through an enormous set of open bronze doors.

Inside, despite the people, it was all but silent. And Harry stopped with others coming in to look, a tourist priest taken in by the spectacle. The central nave in front of him was a good fifty feet wide and probably five or six times that in length. Above him, the ornately carved and gilded ceiling rose ninety feet or more over the equally ornate polished marble floor. High windows just below ceiling level allowed an inpouring of dramatic, downward rays of light. Along the walls, ornate statuettes and frescoes surrounded twelve enormous statues of the Apostles. Harry's refuge, it seemed, was not only a church but also a grand cathedral.

To his left a group of Australian tourists worked their way along the wall toward the massive altar at the far end. Quietly, he joined them, walking slowly, observing the artwork, continuing to play the out-of-towner, like any other. So far he had seen only one person look at him, and that was an elderly woman who seemed to be looking more at the bandage on his forehead than at him.

For the moment he was all right. Fearful, confused, exhausted, he let himself drift, feeling the breath of the cathedral's centuries, wondering who had passed through, and under what circumstances.

Pulling himself back he saw they had reached the altar, and several of the Australians broke from the group to cross themselves and kneel on benches in front of it, bowing their heads in prayer.

Harry did the same. As he did, emotion swept him. Tears came to his eyes, and he had to fight to hold back a sob. Never had he felt as lost or frightened or alone as he did now. He had no idea where to go or what to do next.

Still kneeling, he turned and looked over his shoulder. The Australian group was filing out, but other people were coming in. With them came two security guards. Watching the crowds. Making their presence known. They wore white shirts with epaulets, and dark pants. It was hard to tell from the distance, but it looked as if they carried two-way radios on their belts.

Harry turned back. Stay where you are, he told himself. They won't approach unless you give them reason. Take your time. Think it through. Where to go next. What to do. Think.

Noon.

THE DOGS SNIFFED AND STRAINED AGAINST their harnesses, leading their handlers forward—with Roscani, Scala, and Castelletti scrambling after them—through a series of dirty, dimly lit tunnels to finally stop at the end of an air shaft above Manzoni Station.

Castelletti, the smallest of the three detectives, pulled off his jacket and crawled into the air shaft. At the far end he found the cover loosened. Sliding it off, he stuck his head out and looked down onto a public walkway that led out of the station itself.

"He went out here." Castelletti's voice echoed as he inched his way backward on elbows and knees.

"Could he have come in that way?" Roscani yelled back.

"Not without a ladder."

Roscani looked to the lead dog handler. "Let's find where he came in."

Ten minutes later they were back in the main tunnel, following the path Harry had taken when he left Hercules' encampment, the dogs following by the scent from a pullover sweater taken from Harry's room at the Hotel Hassler.

"He's in Rome for only four days—how the hell does he know his way around here?" Scala's voice bounced off the walls, the harsh beam of his flashlight cutting a path behind the dogs and their keepers, whose own flashlights lit the way ahead for their animals.

Suddenly the lead dog stopped, its nose upward, sniffing. The others stopped behind it. Quickly, Roscani moved ahead.

"What is it?"

"They've lost the scent."

"How? They got this far. We're in the middle of a tunnel. How could they—?"

The lead handler moved past his animal, sniffing the air himself.

"What is it?" Roscani came up beside him.

"Smell."

Roscani sniffed. Then sniffed again.

"Tea. Bitter tea."

Stepping forward, he flashed his light on the tunnel floor. There it was, scattered over the ground for fifty or sixty feet. Tea leaves. Hundreds, thousands of them. As if they had been broadcast by the handful for the very purpose of throwing the dogs off.

Roscani picked a few from the floor and brought them to his nose. Then let them fall in disgust.

"Gypsies."

41

The Vatican. Same time.

MARSCIANO LISTENED PATIENTLY AS JEAN Tremblay, cardinal of Montreal, read from the thick dossier on the table before him.

"Energy, steel, shipping, engineering and construction, energy, earth-moving equipment, construction and mining, engineering equipment, transportation, heavy-duty cranes, excavators." Tremblay turned the dossier's pages slowly, skipping over the names of corporations listed, emphasizing instead the businesses in which they were engaged. "Heavy equipment, construction, construction, construction." Finally he closed the document and looked up. "The Holy See is now in the construction business."

"In a manner of speaking, yes," Marsciano answered Cardinal Tremblay directly, fighting the dryness in his mouth, trying not to hear the echo of his own voice inside his head as he spoke. Knowing that to show weakness would be to lose. And if he lost, Father Daniel would be lost too.

Cardinal Mazetti of Italy, Cardinal Rosales of Argentina, Cardinal Boothe of Australia—like members of a high court, each man sat with his hands folded on top of the now-closed dossiers, staring at Marsciano across from them.

MAZETTI: Why have we gone from a balanced portfolio to this?

BOOTHE: It's too heavily weighted and ungainly. A world recession would leave us and every one of these companies literally stuck in the mud. Factories frozen, equipment parked like so many multi-ton sculptures, useless, except to look at and marvel at the expense.

MARSCIANO: True.

Cardinal Rosales smiled and raised his elbows to lean on his chin. "Emerging economies and politics."

Marsciano lifted a glass of water and drank, then set the glass down. "Correct," he said.

ROSALES: And the guiding hand of Palestrina.

MARSCIANO: His Holiness believes the Church should extend, in both spirit and manner, encouragement to less fortunate countries. Help them take their place in the expanding world marketplace.

ROSALES: His Holiness or Palestrina?

MARSCIANO: Both.

TREMBLAY: We are to encourage world leaders to bring the emerging nations up to speed in the new century, while at the same time profiting from it?

MARSCIANO: Another way to look at it, Eminence, is that we are following our own beliefs, and in doing so, attempting to enrich them.

The meeting was running long. It was nearly one-thirty and time to break. And Marsciano did not want to report to Palestrina that a vote had not yet been taken. Moreover, he knew that if he let them go now without a positive consensus, they would talk about it among themselves at lunch. The more they talked, the more, he knew, they would begin to dislike the entire plan. Maybe even sense there was something intangibly wrong with it, maybe suspect they were being asked to approve something that had other purposes than what was apparent.

Palestrina had purposely kept himself out of it, wanting none to sense his influence over something he ostensibly had no part in. And as much as Marsciano despised him, he knew the power of his name and the respect and fear that came with it.

Pushing back from the table, Marsciano stood. "It is time to break. In all fairness I should tell you I am meeting with Cardinal Palestrina over lunch. He will ask me about your reaction to what has been discussed here this morning. I would like to tell him that in general your response has been positive. That you like what we have done and—with a few minor changes—will approve it by the end of the day."

The cardinals stared back in silence. Marsciano had taken them by surprise and knew it. In essence he had said, "Give me what I want now or risk dealing with Palestrina yourselves."

"Well—?"

Cardinal Boothe raised his hands as if in prayer and stared at the table.

"Yes," he murmured.

CARDINAL TREMBLAY: —Yes.
CARDINAL MAZETTI: —Yes.

Rosales was the last. Finally he looked up at Marsciano. "Yes," he said sharply, then stood and walked angrily from the room.

Marsciano looked to the others and nodded. "Thank you," he said. "Thank you."

42

Still Friday, July 10, 4:15 P.M.

ADRIANNA HALL SAT IN HER TINY OFFICE AT the Rome bureau of World News Network watching the Harry Addison video for something like the tenth time, trying to make some sense of it.

She'd spent less than three hours with him—granted, a very passionate and provocative three hours—but in that short time, after all the men she'd known, the one thing she knew about Harry Addison, if she knew nothing else, was that he was not someone who could kill a policeman. Yet the police believed he had, and had his fingerprints on the murder weapon to prove it. She also knew that a Spanish-made Llama pistol recovered from the scene of the Assisi bus explosion was missing from Pio's car, and the police believed Harry took it as he fled after killing Pio.

Abruptly she put both hands flat on her desk and pushed back in her chair. She didn't know what the hell to think.

Then her phone rang, and for a moment she let it before picking up.

"Mr. Vasko," her secretary said. He was calling for the third time in the last two hours. He hadn't left a call-back number before because he was traveling but said he would call back again. And now he was on the phone.

Elmer Vasko was a former professional hockey player and Chicago Blackhawks teammate of her father's who had later worked with him when he'd coached the Swiss team. In his halcyon days on the ice they'd called him "Moose." Now he was a gentle giant, a kind of distant uncle she hadn't seen for years. And here he was in Rome calling her at the worst of all possible times, when an enormous story was on fire and burning all around her.

Adrianna had come back from Croatia early that morning at her own request when news of the Harry Addison story first broke. Going straight to the Questura, she'd arrived at the tail end of Marcello Taglia's impromptu interview. She'd tried to corner him afterward without success and then looked for Roscani, ending with the same result.

Going home for a shower and quick change of clothes, she'd been drying her hair when the Metro tunnel business happened. She'd gone there on the back of her cameraman's motor scooter with her hair still wet. But the media, all media, were being kept out of the tunnels and away from the action. After an hour, she'd retreated to the studio to start putting the story together and to watch the Harry Addison video for the first time. And then she'd gone out, and when she came back, there were the Elmer Vasko messages. And now he was calling again. She had no choice but to take it.

"Elmer. Mr. Vasko. How are you?" She tried to sound up and gracious even if she wasn't. "Mr. Vasko . . . ?"

The phone was silent and she started to hang up when the voice came on.

"I need your help."

"Oh fuck!" Adrianna felt the breath go out of her.

It was Harry Addison.

HARRY STOOD IN A PHONE BOOTH near a small café across the Piazza della Rotonda from the ancient circular structure that was the Pantheon. By now he had his hat, a black beret bought easily at a corner shop selling hats of all kinds and pulled down to cover the bandage at the top of his forehead. His still-bandaged left hand he kept in his jacket pocket.

"Where are you?" The surprise was gone from Adrianna's voice.

"I . . ."

There'd been no way to know if she was back from Croatia, but he'd taken the chance she was. He'd called her because he'd added up his options and realized she was the only one he could call. The only one who would know what was going on and whom he dared trust. But now that he actually had her on the phone, he wasn't sure if he could trust anyone. She knew the police, relied on her relationship with them for access to stories she might not otherwise have; would she agree to meet him somewhere and then bring the police with her?

"Harry, where *are* you?" Her voice came again, stronger than before.

Again he hesitated. Unsure. The dull ache still in the back of his head, reminding him he wasn't as alert as he might have been.

"I can't help you if you don't talk to me."

A group of schoolgirls suddenly walked past, giggling and joking among themselves. They were loud, and he turned away trying to hear. As he did, he saw two mounted *carabinieri* on horseback slowly crossing the piazza toward him. They were in no hurry, simply on patrol. But still every policeman in the country was on the lookout for him, and he had to take every precaution he possibly could to avoid them. In this case it probably meant staying right where he was until they passed. Turning ever so slightly away from them, he spoke into the phone.

"I didn't kill Pio."

"Tell me where you are."

"I'm scared to death the Italian police are going to kill me."

"Harry, *where* are you?"

Silence.

"Harry, *you* called me. I assume because you trust me. You don't know Rome, you don't know Italian, and if I told you to meet me somewhere, you'd have to ask someone, and that could get you into trouble. If I know where you are, I can come to you. Reasonable?"

The *carabinieri* were closer now. Both young. Both on big white horses. Both with side arms. And they weren't just on patrol, they were watching the people they passed carefully.

"Police on horseback coming toward me."

"Harry, for Crissake, where are you?"

"I . . . don't . . ." Turning, he glanced around, trying not to look at the police but to see a street sign, the name of a building, a café, anything that would tell him where he was. Then he saw it. A plaque on the side of a building twenty feet away.

"Something rotunda."

"Piazza della Rotonda. At the Pantheon?"

"I guess."

"Big circular building with columns."

"Yes."

The *carabinieri* were almost on top of him, their horses moving slowly, their eyes searching the crowd in the piazza, the people at the outdoor cafés surrounding it. Now one officer pulled up and both stopped, only feet away.

"Holy fuck," Harry breathed.

"What is it?"

"They're right here. I could touch the horse."

"Harry, are they looking at you?"

"No."

"Ignore them. They'll move on in a minute. When they're gone, cross the square to the right of the Pantheon. Take any side street and walk two blocks to the Piazza Navona. Near the fountain in the middle are benches. The piazza will be crowded. Pick a bench and I'll find you there."

"When?"

"Twenty minutes."

Harry looked at his watch.

4:32

"Harry?"

"What?"

"Trust me."

Adrianna clicked off. Harry stayed as he was, the phone in his hand. The police were still there. If he hung up and they saw him, he'd have to leave. If he didn't hang up, with one end of the line dead, he took the chance the phone company might report it as a phone suddenly out of service, something the police, in their heightened state of awareness, might be looking for. He looked back. And his heart sank.

Two more *carabinieri* on horseback had ridden up and were talking with the others. Four policemen. Only feet away. Slowly he hung up. He couldn't stay there without making another call, and there was no call to make. He had to do something before one of them looked over and saw him just standing there. And he did. Simply stepped out and walked past them. Moving across the square toward the Pantheon.

One of the *carabinieri* saw him go, even watched him for a moment, then his horse tugged at its bit, and he had to pull him back. When he looked back Harry was gone.

ROSCANI ABSENTLY CRUSHED A CIGARETTE
into the ashtray in front of him as he read the Italian translation of a fax sent down from Taglia's office. It was a notifica-
tion from Special Agent David Harris in the FBI's Los
Angeles office that Byron Willis, a senior partner in Harry
Addison's Beverly Hills law firm, had been shot and killed
outside his home the night before by an assailant or
assailants unknown. The motive appeared to have been rob-
bery. His wallet, wedding ring, and Rolex watch were missing. Los Angeles homicide detectives were working on the
case. An autopsy was pending. Further information would be
forthcoming.

Roscani ran a hand over his eyes. What the hell did this
mean? Without more information he had no choice but to
take the murder as a coincidence. But he couldn't. It was too
close to what was going on. Still, what would be the purpose
of killing Harry Addison's partner? Something he knew
about Harry? Or Father Daniel?

Roscani typed a response memo on his computer and sent it to his secretary for translation and transmission to Harris/FBI/Los Angeles. In it he thanked the FBI for their cooperation and asked to be personally kept advised of new developments, suggesting—what he was certain the FBI was already doing—that they question close friends and business associates of Harry Addison to see if there was some universal thread, a common knowledge some or all might share; and then to put them on alert for their own personal safety.

His phone rang as he finished. It was Valentina Gori, the speech therapist and lip reader he had brought in to analyze the Harry Addison video. She had viewed it a number of times and was downstairs. Did he have time to join her?

HARRY'S FACE WAS FROZEN on the large video screen as Roscani entered, took Valentina's hand, and kissed her on the cheek. Valentina Gori was fifty-two, red-haired, recently a grandmother, and still very attractive. She had a degree in speech therapy from the University of Leuven in Belgium, had studied mime in the French theater in the 1970s, and, afterward, worked as an actress dubbing foreign sound tracks for the Italian film industry while at the same time consulting on speech and speech patterns for both the *carabinieri* and the Italian police. She had also grown up in the same Roman neighborhood as Roscani and knew his entire family. Moreover, when she was twenty-two and he was fifteen, she had stolen his virginity just to show him he wasn't as much in control as he thought he was. It was a relationship they carried to the present. Besides his wife, she was the one person in the world who could look him knowingly in the eye and make him laugh at himself.

"I think you're right. It looks like he is about to say something, or is *trying* to say something just before the tape ends. But I'm not sure he wasn't just looking up."

Turning the remote toward the screen, she touched the PAUSE/STILL button. Harry's mouth began to open as the tape inched forward, and Roscani heard his voice growl with the slow-motion sound. And then they reached his last words. He finished, started to relax, then his head made an awkward and abrupt upward move with his mouth open. That was when the taped ended.

"It almost looks like an *i* . . ."

There was a slow hissing sound, like wind being expelled by an inebriated giant.

"*I* what?" Roscani was locked on the screen and Harry's frozen image.

"I'm not so sure he wasn't just finished and tired and was simply going to let out a breath."

"No, he was trying to say something. Again," Roscani said, and Valentina played it over. In stop motion. Slow motion. At half speed and then normal. Each time Harry reached the same point, there was the brief hissing sound and then the tape was over.

Roscani looked at her. "What else?—How many thousand films have you seen? You must have other ideas about what's going on up there on the screen."

Valentina smiled. "A thousand ideas, Otello. A hundred scenarios. But I can only go from what I see. And hear. And from that, we have a tired man with a lump on his head who has done what has been required of him and would like to rest. Maybe even sleep."

Roscani turned abruptly to look at her. "What do you mean *required* of him?"

"I don't know. It's just a feeling." Valentina winked.

"Occasionally we all do things required of us when our heart isn't entirely in it."

"We're not talking about sex, Valentina," Roscani said flatly.

"No—" This was no time for Valentina to break through his veneer, and she realized it. "Otello, I'm not a psychologist, just an old broad who's been around a little. I look at the screen and see a tired man apparently speaking his mind but who sounds more like he's doing what he thinks somebody wants. Like a child reluctantly clearing the dishes off the table so he can go out to play."

"You think he made the tape against his will?"

"Don't ask me to draw conclusions from the air, Otello. It's far too difficult." Valentina smiled and put a hand on his. "It's not my job, anyway. It's yours."

44

HARRY WATCHED HER COME. WATCHED HER cross the Piazza Navona toward the fountain, sipping something from a plastic Coca-Cola cup, light blue skirt and white blouse, hair turned up in a bun, dark glasses, her walk unhurried. She could have been a secretary or tourist, perhaps wondering whether or not to meet a lover as promised; anything but a journalist about to rendezvous with the most wanted man in Italy. If she had brought the police, he didn't see them.

Now he saw her circle the fountain, half looking, half not. Then, glancing at her watch, she settled on a stone bench twenty feet from a man painting a watercolor of the piazza. Harry waited, still uncertain. Finally he stood up, glancing at the painter as he did. Walking toward her in a wide arc, he came up from behind to sit casually a few feet to her left, facing in the opposite direction. To his surprise she did nothing more than glance his way, then looked off again. Either she was being very careful or his beard and costume worked better than he thought. As bad as things were, the idea she might not know who he was tickled him, and he tilted his head ever so slightly in her direction.

"Would the lady consider screwing a priest?"

She started and looked, and for the briefest instant he thought she was going to slap him. But instead she stared right at him and admonished him out loud.

"If a priest wants to talk dirty to a lady, he ought to do it where people can't see or hear him."

PIANO, OR FLAT, NUMBER 12, as it read on the worn key tag, was on the top floor of a five-story apartment building at 47 Via di Montoro, a ten-minute walk toward the Tiber from the Piazza Navona. It belonged to a friend who was out of town and would understand, Adrianna said. Then she stood abruptly and walked off, leaving the Coca-Cola cup behind. The key was inside it.

Harry had entered the lobby and taken the small elevator to the top, finding number 12 at the end of the hall.

Once inside, he locked the door behind him and looked around. The flat was small but comfortable, with a bedroom, living room, small kitchen, and bath. Men's clothing hung in the closet—several sport coats, slacks, and two suits. A half dozen shirts, several sweaters, socks, and underwear were in a chest of drawers opposite the bed. In the living room was a telephone and small TV. A computer with separate printer sat on a desk in a cubbyhole near the window.

Moving to the window, Harry stood at the edge and looked down at the street. Nothing any different than when he came in. Passing cars, motor scooters, the occasional pedestrian.

Taking off his jacket, he set it on a chair and went into the kitchen. In a cupboard next to the sink he found a glass and started to fill it. Then he had to set it down. The room spun, and it was all he could do to get his breath. Emotion and exhaustion had caught up with him. That he was even alive was a miracle. That somehow he was off the street was a gift from the gods.

Finally he calmed enough to splash some water on his face and begin to breathe normally. How long had it been since he'd left Hercules and come here? Three hours, four? He didn't know. All sense of time was gone. He looked at his watch. It was Friday, July 10. Ten after five in the afternoon. Ten after eight in the morning Los Angeles time. Another breath and his eyes went to the telephone.

No. Can't. Don't even consider it. By now the FBI would have every line to his home and office tapped. If he tried to call, they'd know where he was in a millisecond. The fact was that even if he reached someone without being caught, what could they do? In truth, what could anyone do, even Adrianna? He was caught in a horrendous dream that was no dream at all. Just stark, brutal reality.

And except for that few square feet of apartment where he was, there was absolutely nowhere he could go where he didn't risk being caught and turned over to the police. Even here, how long was he safe? He couldn't stay where he was forever.

Suddenly there was a sound in the other room. A key had been put into the lock. Heart pounding, he pressed back against the kitchen wall. Then came the sound of the door opening.

"Mr. Addison?" a male voice said sharply.

Harry could see the jacket he'd left on the chair in the front room. Whoever had come in would see it, too. Quickly he glanced around. The kitchen was little more than a closet. The only way out, the way he had come in.

"Mr. Addison?" the voice rang out again.

Dammit! Adrianna had set him up for the police. And he'd walked right into it. At his elbow was a butcher block with carving knives. No good. They'd kill him in a second if he came out with a knife in his hand.

"Mr. Addison—are you here?" Whoever it was spoke English and without an accent.

What to do? He had no answer because there was none. Better to just walk out facing them and hope that Adrianna or someone from the media was with them so they wouldn't kill him on the spot.

"I'm here!" he said, loudly. "I'm coming out. I'm not armed. Don't shoot!" Taking a deep breath, Harry raised his hands and stepped into the room.

WHAT HE SAW WAS NOT the police but a sandy-haired man alone, the door closed behind him.

"My name is James Eaton, Mr. Addison. I'm a friend of Adrianna Hall. She knew you needed a place to stay and—"

"Jesus God . . ."

Eaton was probably in his late forties or early fifties. Medium height and build. Dressed in a gray suit with striped shirt and gray tie. The most striking thing about him, other than that he was alone, was his plainness. He looked like the kind of guy who'd made it as far as he could in a bank, who still takes his family to Disneyland, and cuts his lawn on Saturdays.

"I didn't mean to frighten you."

"This is your apartment . . ." Incredulous, Harry lowered his hands.

"Sort of . . ."

"What do you mean *sort of* ?"

"It's not in my name, and my wife doesn't know about it."

That was a surprise. "You and Adrianna."

"Not anymore . . ."

Eaton hesitated, looking at Harry, then he crossed the room and opened a cabinet above the television. "Would you like a drink?"

Harry glanced at the front door. Who was this guy? FBI? Checking him out, making sure he was unarmed and alone?

"If I'd told the police where you were, I wouldn't be standing here offering you a drink. . . . Vodka or scotch?"

"Where's Adrianna?"

Eaton took out a bottle of vodka and poured them each two fingers.

"I work in the U.S. Embassy. First secretary to the counselor for Political Affairs. . . . No ice, sorry." He handed Harry a glass and then walked over and sat down on the couch. "You're in a lot of trouble, Mr. Addison. Adrianna thought it might be helpful if we talked."

Harry fingered his glass. He was overwrought. Beat up. His nerves all over the place. But he had to pull himself back. Be aware enough of what was happening to protect himself. Eaton might be who he said he was and there trying to help him. Or he might not. He could be doing a diplomatic thing. Making sure no feathers got ruffled between the U.S. and Italy when they handed him over to the police.

"I didn't kill the policeman."

"You didn't . . ."

"No."

"What about the videotape?"

"I was tortured, then coerced into making it by the people who I assume did kill him. . . . They took me away afterward. . . . Then they shot me and left me for dead . . ." Harry lifted his bandaged hand. "Except I didn't die."

Eaton sat back. "Who were these people?"

"I don't know. I never saw them."

"Did they speak English?"

"Some. . . . Mostly Italian."

"They killed a policeman and, in essence, kidnapped and tortured you."

"Yes."

Eaton took a pull at his drink. "Why? What did they want?"

"They wanted to know about my brother."

"The priest."

Harry nodded.

"What did they want to know about him?"

"Where he was . . ."

"And what did you tell them?"

"I said I didn't know. Or if he was even alive."

"Is that true?"

"Yes."

Harry lifted his glass and took half the vodka in one swallow. Then he finished it and set the glass on the table in front of Eaton.

"Mr. Eaton, I am innocent. I believe my brother is innocent. . . . And I am scared to death of the Italian police. What can the embassy do to help? There *has* to be *something*."

Eaton looked at Harry for a long moment, as if he were thinking. Finally he stood and picked up Harry's glass. Crossing to the cabinet, he poured them each a second drink.

"By rights, Mr. Addison, I should have informed the consul general the moment Adrianna called. But then he would have been obliged to notify the Italian authorities. I would have betrayed a trust, and you would have been in the jail, or worse. . . . And that wouldn't have done either of us much good."

Harry looked at him, puzzled. "What does that mean?"

"We are in the information business, Mr. Addison, not law enforcement. . . . The job of the counselor for Political Affairs is to know the political climate of the country to which he or she is assigned. In our case that applies not only to Italy but the Vatican. . . . The killing of the cardinal vicar of Rome and the sabotage of the Assisi bus, which I know the police believe are somehow interconnected, involve both.

"As private secretary to Cardinal Marsciano, your brother was in a privileged position within the Church. If he did assassinate the cardinal vicar, it's more than probable he wasn't acting alone. If so, there's every reason to believe that the murder was not an isolated incident but part of a larger intrigue taking place at the highest levels of the Holy See. . . ." Eaton came back and handed Harry his glass. "That's where our interest is, Mr. Addison, inside the Vatican."

"What if my brother didn't do it? What if he wasn't involved at all?"

"I have to believe what the police do, that the Assisi bus was bombed for one reason, to kill your brother. Whoever did it thought he was dead, but now they doubt it and are very fearful of what he knows and what he can tell. And they will do anything to find him and shut him up."

"What he knows. What he can tell . . ." Suddenly Harry understood. "You want to find him, too."

"That's right," Eaton said quietly.

"No, I mean *you*. Not the embassy. Not even your boss. You, yourself. That's why you're here."

"I'm fifty-one years old and still a secretary, Mr. Addison. I have been passed over for promotion more times than you would want to know. . . . I don't want to retire as a secretary. Therefore I need to do something that will make it impossible for them not to raise my standing. Uncovering something going on deep inside the Vatican would do that very well."

"And you want me to help you—" Harry was incredulous.

"Not just me, Mr. Addison. Yourself. What your brother knows—he's the only one who can get you off the hook. You know that as well as I do."

Harry said nothing, just stared.

"If he is alive and in fear of his life. How would he know the video is fake? All he knows is that you want him to come in—and when he gets desperate enough, he's going to have to trust someone. Who better than you?"

"Maybe. . . . But it doesn't matter. Because he doesn't know where I am. And I don't know where he is. Neither does anybody else."

"Don't you think the police are meticulously backtracking through the people who were onboard the bus—both the living and the dead—to see what happened? Find out where he made the switch or where someone made it for him?"

"What good does that do me?"

"Adrianna . . ."

"Adrianna?"

"She is the ultimate professional. She knew about you the first day you came to Rome."

Harry's gaze drifted off. It was why she'd picked him up at the hotel. He'd even accused her of it and tried to walk away. But she'd turned him inside out and back again. The whole time she was setting him up for the story. Not so much then, but for where it might lead. Yes, she was the ultimate professional, the same as he was. And he should have been aware of it all along, because it was the place where they both lived their lives. There, and almost nowhere else.

"Why do you think she called me as soon as she got off the phone with you? She knew what she wanted and what I needed and what I could do for you. She knew that if she played it right, it would work to all our advantages."

"Jesus fucking Christ." Harry ran a hand through his hair and walked away. Then he turned back.

"You've thought it all out. Except for one thing. Even if we did find out where he is, he can't come to me, and I can't go to him."

Eaton took a sip of his drink. "You could as someone else. . . . New name. Passport. Driver's license. If you were careful, you could go anywhere you wanted . . ."

"You can do that . . ."

"Yes."

Harry stared at him. Angry, manipulated, amazed.

"If I were you, Mr. Addison, I would be jubilant. After everything, you actually have two people who want to help you. And can."

Harry continued to stare. "Eaton, you are one goddamned son of a bitch."

"No, Mr. Addison. I'm a goddamned civil servant."

11:00 P.M.

HARRY LAY IN BED IN EATON'S APARTMENT
trying to sleep, the door locked, a chair propped under the
knob, just in case. Trying to tell himself that it was all right.
And that Eaton had been right. Up until now he had been
alone in an impossible situation. Suddenly he had a place to
stay and two people willing to help him.

Eaton had gone out, saying he would get Harry something to eat, suggesting that in the meantime Harry shower
and wash his healing wounds as best he could. But not shave.
For the moment the new beard was protecting him, making
him someone else.

But he wanted Harry to think who he wanted to become.
Something he might know if questioned, a law school pro-
fessor or perhaps a journalist who wrote about the entertainment industry on holiday in Italy, or an aspiring screenwriter
or novelist doing research on ancient Rome.

"I'll remain what I was, a priest," Harry had said when Eaton came back with pizza and a bottle of red wine and some bread and coffee for the morning.

"An American priest is who they are looking for."

"There are priests everywhere. And I would assume more than one is American."

Eaton had hesitated, then simply nodded and gone into the bedroom and brought out two of his shirts and a sweater. Then, pulling a 35mm camera from a drawer, he'd loaded it with film and positioned Harry against a blank wall. He took eighteen photographs. Six with Harry wearing one shirt, six with the other, six with the sweater.

After that he'd left, telling Harry to go nowhere. That either he or Adrianna would be back by noon the next day.

Why?

Why had he chosen to remain a priest? Had he thought it out? *Yes.* As a priest, he could become a civilian at will by a simple change of clothes. And, as he had suggested, how unusual would it be to find any number who were American? Hercules had said, Hide in plain sight. Right next to them. He had, and it had worked. Any number of times. Once right under the nose of the *carabinieri*.

On the other hand Eaton had been right, the police were looking for Danny. And Danny was an American priest. A priest who spoke English with an American dialect would be a natural suspect. People would look at him and wonder if, despite the beard, the face wasn't familiar. And don't forget the reward. A hundred million lire. Some sixty thousand U.S. dollars. Who wouldn't risk a little embarrassment by taking a chance and calling the police, even if it turned out to be the wrong person?

Moreover, what did he know about the priesthood? What if another clergyman engaged him in talk? What if someone asked him for help? Still, the decision had been made, the photos taken, with Eaton certain to give him a background along with his papers.

A priest.

Outside, Harry heard the sounds of Rome at night. Via di Montoro was a side street and a great deal quieter than the din outside his hotel at the top of the Spanish Steps. But still the noise was there. Traffic. The incessant putt of motor scooters. People walking by outside.

Little by little it all became background, drifting into a distant symphony of nothingness. The shower, the clean bed, the whole of the ordeal carried Harry toward sleep, gently forcing him to accept his true exhaustion. Perhaps that was why he had chosen to stay a priest. Simply because it was easy. And because it had worked. And not at all for another reason . . . that he wished in some curious way to understand who Danny really was. To do as Hercules had offhandedly suggested. To, for a while at least, become his brother.

Closing his eyes, he began to drift off. As he did, he saw the Christmas card once more: the decorated tree behind the posed faces smiling from under Santa Claus hats—his mother and father, himself, Madeline, and Danny.

"MERRY CHRISTMAS from the Addisons"

Then the vision faded, and in the dark he heard Pio's voice. It whispered again the thing he had said in the car on the way back to Rome—*"You know what I would be thinking if I were you. . . . Is my brother still alive? And if he is, where is he?"*

MARSCIANO WAS ALONE in his library, his desktop computer dark. The books, which filled every open space floor to ceiling, seemed, in his mood, little more than decorations. The only illumination was from a halogen lamp sitting near the back of his wooden desk. On top of it, and in the lamp's glow, was the envelope that had been delivered to him in Geneva in the package marked *URGENTE*. The same envelope he had brought back with him on the train. Inside it was the audiocassette he had heard once but never played again. Why he wanted to hear it now, he didn't know. But he was drawn to it nonetheless.

Opening a drawer, he set a palm-sized tape player on the desk, then opened the envelope and slid the cassette into it. For a moment he hesitated, then deliberately he pressed the PLAY button. There was a dull whirring as the tape came to speed. Then he heard the voice, hushed but perfectly clear.

"In the name of the Father, and of the Son, and of the Holy Spirit. May God, who has enlightened every heart, help you to know your sins and trust in His mercy."

Then came the other voice: *"Amen.*

"Bless me, Father, for I have sinned," the other voice continued. *"It has been many days since my last confession. These are my sins—"*

Abruptly Marsciano's thumb pushed the STOP button and he sat there, unable to go on, to hear any more.

A confession had been recorded without the knowledge of either the penitent or the priest. The penitent, the confessor, was himself. The priest, Father Daniel.

Filled with horror and revulsion, pushed to the darkest edges of his soul by Palestrina, he had turned to the only place he could. Father Daniel was not only an honorable co-worker and as devoted a friend as he had had in his life, he was a priest given to God, and whatever was said would be protected by the Seal of Confession and would go no farther than the confessional.

Except that it had.

Because Palestrina had recorded it. And he no doubt had had Farel implant electronic devices in other places, private or otherwise—any place Marsciano or the others might go.

Increasingly paranoid, the secretariat was protecting himself on all fronts, playing the stirring military leader he had years earlier told Marsciano he was certain he was. He had been drunk, but in all seriousness and with great pride, he had boasted that from the day he was old enough to know such things, he believed he was the reincarnation of Alexander of Macedon, ancient conqueror of the Persian empire. It was how he had lived his life from then on, and why he had risen to become who he was and in the place he was. Whether anyone else believed it made no difference, because he did. And little by little Marsciano could see him taking on the mantle of a general at war.

How quickly and brutally he had acted after hearing the recording! Marsciano had given his confession late Thursday night, and early Friday morning Father Daniel had left for Assisi, no doubt as horrified as Marsciano and seeking his own solace. There had never been a question in Marsciano's mind who had reached out to stop Danny, blowing up the bus and killing how many innocents in the process. It was the same ruthless disregard for humanity as his stratagem for China, the same cold-blooded paranoia that made him distrust not only those around him but the Seal of Confession, and in that, the canon law of the Church.

It was something Marsciano should have expected. Because, by then, he had seen the true horror of Palestrina unveiled. The specter of it frozen in his memory as if it had been stamped from steel.

*   *   *

ON THE MORNING FOLLOWING the immense public funeral for the cardinal vicar of Rome, the secretariat had called the still deeply shaken remaining members of the cabal—himself; prefect of the Congregation of Bishops, Joseph Matadi; and director general of the Vatican Bank, Fabio Capizzi—to a conference at a private villa in Grottaferata, outside Rome, a retreat Palestrina often used for "introspective" gatherings and the place where he had first presented his "Chinese Protocol."

On arrival, they had been taken to a small, formal courtyard nestled among manicured foliage away from the main house where Palestrina waited at a wrought-iron table, sipping coffee and making entries into a laptop computer. Farel was with him, standing behind his chair like some iron-fisted majordomo. A third person was there as well—a quietly handsome man, not yet forty. Slim and of medium height, he had jet-black hair and piercing blue eyes and was dressed— Marsciano remembered—in a double-breasted navy blazer, white shirt, dark tie, and gray slacks.

"You have not met Thomas Kind," Palestrina said as they sat down, sweeping his hand as if he were introducing a new member of a private club.

"He is helping coordinate our 'situation' in China."

Marsciano could still feel the rush of horror and disbelief and saw the same in the others as well—the sudden, involuntary inward twist of Capizzi's tight, thin lips; the immediate and grave apprehension in the once humor-filled eyes of Joseph Matadi—as Thomas Kind stood up and politely greeted them by name, his eyes fixing on each as he did.

"*Buon giorno,* Monsignor Capizzi.

"—Cardinal Matadi.

"—Cardinal Marsciano."

* * *

MARSCIANO HAD REMEMBERED seeing Kind there a year earlier in the company of a short middle-aged Chinese, but only at a distance, when he and Father Daniel had come for a business meeting with Pierre Weggen. At the time he'd had no idea who he was and hadn't given it much thought, except for the China connection. But now, seeing him this close and being told who he was, and realizing who he was as he looked at you and said your name, was a horrifying experience.

And Palestrina's quiet delight in their not-well-concealed reactions told them, as clearly as if he had announced it, who murdered the cardinal vicar and at whose order. Their summons to the villa had been simply a warning that if any of them secretly harbored the late cardinal's views, disagreed with Palestrina's plan for China and had thoughts of going to the Holy Father or the College of Cardinals about it, they would have Thomas Kind to deal with. It was pure and terrifying Palestrina gall, a theatrical sideshow to his ever-increasing circus of horror. Moreover, it was a clear signal that his war to control China was about to begin.

And afterward, as if it were possible to be more audacious, Palestrina had simply pushed a huge hand through his great white mane and dismissed them.

MARSCIANO'S EYES CAME BACK to the dim light of his study and the tiny recorder on his desk. With his confession he had told Father Daniel of the assassination of Cardinal Parma and of his own complicity in Palestrina's master plan for the expansion of the Church into China—one that would involve not only the surreptitious maneuvering of

Vatican investments but, more horrifically, the deaths of untold numbers of innocent Chinese citizens.

With his confession, and wholly unknowingly, he had condemned Father Daniel to death. The first time, God or perhaps fate had intervened. But once they knew for certain he was still alive, Thomas Kind would take up the hunt. And to escape someone like Kind would be all but undoable. Palestrina would not fail twice.

46

Pescara. Via Arapietra.
Saturday, July 11, 7:10 A.M.

THOMAS KIND SAT BEHIND THE WHEEL OF A
rented white Lancia and waited for someone to open the
door to number 1217, the private ambulance company across
the street.

Glancing in the mirror, he smoothed his hair, then looked
back to the storefront. The shop opened at seven-thirty. Just
because he was early, why should he expect anyone else to
be, especially on a Saturday morning? So he would wait.
Patience was everything.

7:15

A male jogger passed on the sidewalk in front of number 1217. Seventeen seconds later, a boy on a bicycle went by in the opposite direction. Then nothing.

Patience.

7:20

Abruptly two policemen on motorcycles appeared in his rearview mirror. Thomas Kind did not flinch. They approached slowly and then passed. The door across the street remained closed.

Leaning back against the leather seat, Thomas Kind thought about what he knew so far—that a late-model beige Iveco van with the Italian license plate number PE 343552 had left Hospital St. Cecilia at exactly ten-eighteen Thursday night. It had carried a male patient, a nun who was apparently a nurse as well, and two men thought to be male nurses.

The information he had requested and received, finally, from Farel had shown that Hospital St. Cecilia was one of only eight hospitals in all of Italy that, in the last week, had admitted an anonymous patient. More specifically, it was the only hospital whose patient had been male and in his early to mid-thirties. And that patient had been discharged shortly after ten the evening before.

Arriving just after noon yesterday, he had gone directly to St. Cecilia's. A brief look around confirmed what he had suspected and prepared for; that the private hospital had in place a system of security cameras covering not only the hallways and public rooms but also the exits and entrances. It was, he hoped, as extensive as it appeared.

Directed to the administrative offices, he produced a business card identifying him as a sales representative for a security systems company based in Milan and asked to see the hospital's chief of security.

The security chief was out, he was told, and not due back until eight that evening. And Thomas Kind had simply nodded and said he would return then.

By eight-fifteen the two were chatting amiably in the security chief's office. Turning the conversation to business, he asked whether, in light of the bombing of the Assisi bus and the assassination of the cardinal vicar of Rome in what the government feared might be a new wave of terrorist attacks, the hospital had done anything to increase its security situation.

Not to worry, he was told by the assured and surprisingly young security chief. Moments later the two men entered St. Cecilia's security operations center and sat down at a bank of sixteen television monitors taking live feed from surveillance cameras throughout the building. One, in particular, caught Thomas Kind's attention. The one he was looking for. The camera covering the ambulance dock.

"Your cameras operate twenty-four hours a day, every day," he said.

"Yes."

"Do you keep videotape of everything?"

"There." The chief of security pointed to a narrow closet-like hallway where red recording lights of video recorders glowed in the dim light.

"The tapes are kept for six months before they are erased and reused. I designed the system myself."

Thomas Kind could see the pride the man took in his accomplishment. It was something to be applauded and then exploited. And Thomas Kind did, saying how impressed he was with the setup, enthusiastically pulling his chair closer, asking for a demonstration of how the system's video retrieval worked. Asking, for example, if the security chief could pull up a videotaped record of someone arriving or leaving by ambulance at a specific time on a particular day— say, oh, last night about ten.

Only too happy to oblige, the security chief grinned and punched in a number on the master board. A video screen in front of them snapped on. A time/date code showed in the upper right-hand corner of the screen, and then a video of the ambulance dock at the hospital's rear entrance came to life. The security chief fast-forwarded, then brought the tape back to speed as an ambulance arrived. The vehicle stopped, attendants got out, and a patient was taken from the ambulance and disappeared into the hospital. Clearly seen were the faces of the attendants as well as that of the patient. A moment later the attendants returned and the ambulance pulled away.

"You have stop motion," Kind said. "If there were a problem and investigators needed a license plate number—"

"Watch," the security chief said, punching REVERSE and bringing the ambulance back. Then letting it go forward again in stop motion to freeze and hold a frame on a clearly identifiable license plate number.

"Perfect." Kind smiled. "Could we see a little more?"

The tape ran forward, and Kind, with his eye carefully on the running time code, engaged the security chief in conversation through the comings and goings of several more ambulances, until, at nine-fifty-nine, a unmarked beige Iveco van pulled in.

"What is that, a delivery truck?" Kind asked, as he watched a heavy-set man step from behind the wheel and walk out of the camera's view into the hospital.

"Private ambulance."

"Where is the patient?"

"He's picking one up. Watch." The tape fast-forwarded, then came back to speed as the man returned, this time accompanied by a woman who looked like a nursing nun, another man, who appeared to be a male nurse, and a patient on a gurney, heavily bandaged with two IVs hanging from a rack overhead. The heavy-set man opened the door. The patient was put inside. The nursing nun and male nurse got in with him. Then the door was closed and the heavy-set man got behind the wheel and drove off.

"You can retrieve that license number, too, no doubt," Kind said, stroking the security chief again.

"Sure." The security chief stopped the tape, then backed it up. Then forwarded in stop motion and froze. The license number was clearly visible—*PE 343552*. The time/date code in the upper corner—*22:18/9 July.*

Kind smiled. "*PE* is a Pescara prefix. The ambulance company is local."

"Servizio Ambulanza Pescara." The security chief's pride showed again. "You see, we have everything under control."

Smiling in admiration, Thomas Kind pushed the chief's pride button one more time and retrieved the name the anonymous patient had used—Michael Roark.

THE SQUARE BOXED ad in the telephone book gave Thomas Kind the rest. Servizio Ambulanza Pescara was headquartered at 1217 Via Arapietra, directly across the street from where he waited now. The ad also listed the name of the company's *direttore responsabile,* its owner, Ettore Caputo, and alongside showed his photograph. Beneath it were its business hours. Monday through Saturday. 7:30 A.M. to 7:30 P.M.

Kind glanced at his watch.

7:25

Suddenly he looked up. A man had turned the corner across the street and was walking down the block. Thomas Kind watched him carefully, then smiled. Ettore Caputo was four and a half minutes early.

THE PHOTOGRAPH ON THE PASSPORT IN FRONT of him was Harry's, showing him bearded, as he still was. The passport itself was worn, its stiff cardboard covers bent, softened as if it had been carried around for years. It had been issued by the U.S. Passport Agency, New York. The inside pages showed the entry stamps of British, French, and U.S. immigration authorities, but beyond that there was nothing to indicate the course of the traveler's movements because few western European countries stamped passports anymore.

The name beside his photograph was *JONATHAN ARTHUR ROE*—born 18/SEP/65—New York, U.S.A.

On the table next to the passport was a District of Columbia driver's license and a faculty membership card for Georgetown University. The driver's license listed his residence as the Mulledy Building, Georgetown University, Washington, D.C. Both pieces carried his photograph.

In fact, all three photos were different. With Harry wearing either one or the other of Eaton's shirts or his sweater. None looked as if it could have been taken at the same place as another—the room in which he now stood—or at the same time, yesterday evening.

"That's the rest of it." Adrianna Hall slid a letter-sized envelope across the coffee table in front of her. "There's cash there, too. Two million lire, about twelve hundred dollars. We can get more if you need it. But Eaton said to warn you—priests do not have money, so don't spend it like you do."

Harry looked at her, then opened the envelope and took out its contents—the two million in Italian lire, in fifty-thousand lire notes, and the lone sheet of paper with its three neatly typed, single-spaced paragraphs.

"It tells you who you are, where you work, what you do, all of it," Adrianna said. "Or enough for you to fake your way through if someone asks. The instructions are to memorize what's there, then destroy it."

Harry Addison was now Father Jonathan Arthur Roe, a Jesuit priest and associate professor of Law at Georgetown University. He lived in a Jesuit residence on the campus and had taught there since 1994. He had grown up an only child in Ithaca, New York. Both his parents were deceased. The rest gave his background: the schools he had attended, when and where he had joined the seminary, a physical description of Georgetown University and its environs, the Georgetown section of Washington, down to the detail that he could see the Potomac River from his bedroom, but only in fall and winter when the leaves were off the trees.

And then there was the last, and he looked up at Adrianna. "It seems as a Jesuit, I've taken a vow of poverty."

"Probably why he didn't give you a credit card . . ."

"Probably."

Harry turned and walked across the room. Eaton had promised and delivered, giving him everything he needed. All Harry had to do was the rest.

"It's kind of like Charades, isn't it?" He turned back. "You totally become someone else . . ."

"You don't have much choice."

Harry studied her. Here was a woman, like many, one he'd slept with but hardly knew. And except for that one moment in the dark when he'd sensed that some part of her feared her own mortality and was genuinely afraid—not so much to die as to no longer live—he realized he almost knew her better from seeing her on television than he did standing in a room with her.

"You're how old, Adrianna? Thirty-four?"

"I'm thirty-seven."

"All right, thirty-seven. If you could be someone else," he asked seriously, "who would you choose?"

"I never thought about it . . ."

"Take a stab at it, go on. Who?"

Suddenly she crossed her arms in front of her. "I wouldn't be anyone else. I like who I am and what I do. And I've worked like hell to get there."

"You sure?"

"Yes."

"A mother? A wife?"

"Are you kidding?" Her half laugh was both droll and defensive, as if he'd touched some nerve she didn't like touched.

He pushed her. Maybe more than he should have and unfairly, but for some reason he wanted to see more of who she was.

"A lot of women do both, have a career and a home life . . ."

"Not this woman." Adrianna held her ground, if anything becoming more serious. "I told you before, I like to fuck strangers.—You know why? It's not only exciting, it's total independence. And to me that's the most important thing there is, because it lets me do my job the best way I can, lets me go as far as I have to to get to the truth of the stories. . . . Do you think as a mother I'm going to stand out in the middle of a fucking field under artillery fire covering somebody's civil war?—Or, bringing it a little closer home, risk spending the rest of my life in an Italian prison because I provided one of the most wanted men in the country false identity papers?—No, Harry Addison, I would not, because I wouldn't do that to children. . . . I'm a loner who likes it. . . . I make good money, I sleep with who I want, I travel to places even you could only dream of and have access to people most of the world's leaders don't. . . . I get a rush from it, and that rush gives me the balls to cover history like they used to but like nobody but me does anymore. . . . Is it selfish? I don't know what the hell that means. . . . But it's no charade, it's who I am. . . . And if something happens and I lose, the only person who gets hurt is me . . ."

"How does that play when you're seventy?"

"Ask me then."

Harry watched her a moment longer. It was why he felt as he had, that he knew her better on television than here. Her life and her intimacy were right there on the screen. It was who she was and all she wanted to be. And she was very good at it. A week ago he would have said something of the same about himself. Freedom was everything. It gave you incredible opportunities because you could take chances. You trusted your skills and ability and played everything on the surface as hard and fast as it came. And if you lost, you lost. . . . But now he wasn't sure. Maybe it was because he no longer had freedom at all. Maybe there was a price for it he'd never realized. Maybe it was as simple as that. . . . But maybe it wasn't. . . . And there was something else, something he knew he had yet to learn and understand. . . . And all this was a journey to help him find it. . . .

"Where I do go from here . . . and when . . . ," Harry suddenly found himself saying, "who do I communicate with— you or Eaton?"

"Me." Opening her purse, Adrianna took out a small cellular phone and handed it to him. "I know what the police are doing, and I make a hundred telephone calls a day. One more won't raise an eyebrow."

"What about Eaton?"

Adrianna hesitated, then turned her head slightly, the way she did on camera when she was about to explain something.

"You've never heard of James Eaton . . . and he's never heard of Harry Addison, except for what he's read in the papers or seen on TV, or maybe had passed through the embassy about you. . . . You don't know me either, except for that one time we were seen in the hotel together and I was trying to get a statement from you."

"What about all *this*?" Harry leaned forward and spread the Jonathan Arthur Roe passport, the Georgetown ID, the driver's license across the table.

"What happens if I turn left instead of right and walk into the arms of Gruppo Cardinale. What am I supposed to tell Roscani, that I always carry a second set of identification? He's going to want to know how I got it and where."

"Harry." Adrianna smiled warmly. "You are a very big boy. By now you should know your left from your right. . . . If you don't, practice, huh?" Leaning forward she kissed him lightly on the lips. "Don't turn the wrong way," she whispered, and then she left. Turning only at the door to tell him to stay where he was, and when she had news she'd call him.

He stood there and watched the door close behind her. Heard the click of the latch as it did. Slowly his eyes went to the table where the IDs were spread out. For the first time in his life he wished he had taken acting lessons.

48

Cortona, Italy. Still Saturday, July 11, 9:30 A.M.

NURSING SISTER ELENA VOSO FINISHED HER
shopping and came out of the small grocery on Piazza Signorelli with a large bag of fresh vegetables. She had picked
the vegetables carefully, wanting to make a soup that would
be as palatable and nutritious as possible. Not just for the
three men who were with her but for Michael Roark. It was
time at least to try to feed him solid food. Earlier she had
moistened his lips and he had swallowed automatically in
reaction. But when she had tried to get him to sip some water
he'd only looked at her, as if the effort were too much. Still,
if she offered a warm puree of fresh vegetables, perhaps the
aroma itself might be enticing enough to make him at least
attempt to get it down. Even a spoonful was better than nothing, because it would be a beginning, and the sooner he
began taking solid food, the sooner she could get him off the
IV and help him start regaining his physical strength.

Marco watched her come out and turn down the narrow cobblestone street toward the far end, where they had parked the car. Ordinarily he would have walked beside her and carried the bag. But not now, not here today in the bright sunshine. And even though they would drive off in the same car, it was not good that they be seen shopping or walking together. It was something someone might later remember. They were Italians, yes, yet strangers to Cortona—a nun and a man, obviously together, gathering supplies, taking them away. Why? What were they doing? It could be enough for someone to say, "Yes, they were here. I saw them."

Ahead of him Marco saw Elena stop, glance back, then turn and go into a small shop. Marco stopped, too, wondering what she was doing. To his left, a narrow street dropped steeply downward. Below he could see the distant plain and the roads leading up from it to the ancient walled city of the Umbrians and Etruscans, where he now stood. Cortona had been a fortress then; he hoped he would not have to make it one again.

Looking back toward the shop, he saw Elena come out, turn her head toward him, and then walk away in the direction of the car. Five minutes later, she reached a small, silver Fiat, the car Pietro had driven when he followed them north from Pescara. A moment later Marco came up, waited for several pedestrians to pass, then took the bundle from Elena and unlocked the door.

"Why did you go into the store?" he asked as they drove off.

"I'm not allowed?"

"Of course. I just wasn't prepared."

"Neither was I, which was why I went in." She lifted a package from the bag in her lap.

Sanitary napkins.

* * *

BY ELEVEN O'CLOCK both soup and puree were simmering on the kitchen stove and Elena was in the second-floor bedroom with Michael Roark. He was in an armchair, a pillow tucked under each arm, sitting upright for the first time. Marco had helped get him out of bed and into the chair and then had left, anxious to go outside for a cigarette. Above them, Luca slept in a third-floor bedroom. He was the night man, the same as he had been in the hospital in Pescara, sitting in the van outside from eleven at night until seven in the morning. Coming every two hours to help Elena turn her patient. Then going back out to wait and watch.

For what? Or whom? she wondered again, as she had wondered about the men all along.

From the bedroom she could see Marco, smoking and walking the southern periphery of the yard atop a stone wall. Below the wall was the road, and up from it, the gate and the driveway leading up to the house. Across the road was a large farm that went as far as the eye could see into the summer haze. A tractor worked it now, dust rising behind it as it plowed a stretch of open field behind the main house.

Abruptly Pietro appeared, crossing between the cypress trees in front of the window and walking toward Marco, his sleeves rolled up, his shirt open against the growing heat of the day, the gun in his waistband no longer hidden. Reaching him, he stopped, and the men talked. After a moment Marco glanced back at the house, as if he knew the two were being watched.

Elena turned to look at Michael Roark. "Are you comfortable sitting up?" she asked.

He nodded ever so slightly, just a small tip of his head. But it was a definitive response, much more dynamic than his previous blinking in reaction to her squeezing of his thumb or toes.

"I've made something for you to eat. Would you like to try and see if you can get it down?"

This time there was no response. He merely sat looking at her, then moved his eyes away and to the window. Elena watched him. His head, turned as it was against the light, gave him, despite the bandages, a profile she hadn't before seen. She hesitated, studying him a moment longer, then went past him and into the nook that was her part of the room.

Yes, she had turned into the store for sanitary napkins. But the move had been an excuse. Something else had caught her eye: a storefront rack with newspapers and a copy of *La Repubblica* with the bold headline FUGITIVES IN CARDINAL PARMA MURDER STILL AT LARGE, and beneath it, less bold, "Police Screen Victims of Assisi Bus Explosion."

They were both stories she knew of, but in little detail. The assassination of the cardinal had, of course, been the talk of the convent, and then had come the explosion of the Assisi bus. But very shortly afterward she had gone to Pescara and had seen no papers or television since. Yet the moment she'd glimpsed the headlines, she'd reacted, making an instinctive correlation between the headline and Marco and the others—men who were armed and guarded her and her patient twenty-four hours a day. Men who seemed to know a great deal more about what was going on than she did.

Inside the store, she'd picked up the paper and seen photographs of the men the police were looking for. Her mind raced. The bus explosion had taken place Friday. Michael Roark's automobile accident had occurred in the mountains outside Pescara on Monday. Tuesday morning she'd been given the order to go to Pescara. Could not a survivor of the bus explosion be badly burned and in a coma? Perhaps even have broken legs? Could he have perhaps been secretly moved from one hospital to another, or even to a private residence for a day or more before arrangements had been made to bring him to Pescara?

Quickly she'd bought the paper. And then as an afterthought—as a way to hide it from Marco and an unquestionable excuse for why she'd gone into the store—she'd bought the sanitary napkins and had both put into the same brown paper bag.

Back at the house, she'd gone immediately to her nook and put the napkins on a shelf where they could be seen. And afterward she'd carefully folded the newspaper, putting it away under clothing still in her suitcase.

"Dear God," she'd thought over and over. "What if Michael Roark and Father Daniel Addison are the same person?"

Washing her hands and changing into a fresh habit, she'd started to take the newspaper from her suitcase, wanting to hold it up next to her patient. To look at the photograph and see if there was any resemblance at all. But Marco had called her from the staircase, and she had not been able to do so. Putting the paper back, she'd closed the suitcase and gone to see what he wanted.

Now Marco and Pietro were outside and Luca was sleeping. Now there was time.

Michael Roark was still looking out the window, his back to her, as she came in. Moving closer, she folded the paper back and held it up so that the photograph of Father Daniel Addison was level with her patient. The bandages made it difficult to tell; moreover, Michael Roark's beard was growing, while the photo of Father Daniel showed a man clean shaven, but . . . the forehead, the cheekbones, the nose, the way the—

Abruptly, Michael Roark turned his head and looked directly at her. Elena started and jumped back, jerking the paper out of sight behind her as she did. For a long moment he seemed to glare at her and she was certain he knew what she had been doing. Then slowly his mouth opened.

"Wa—a—ah—t—errr," he garbled the word hoarsely. "Wa—a—ah—trrrrrr . . ."

49

Rome. Same time.

WHY, OF ALL TIMES, HAD ROSCANI DECIDED to quit smoking *now?* But as of seven this morning he had just stopped, stubbed the half-smoked cigarette into his ashtray and announced to himself that he no longer smoked. Since then, almost anything had done in place of tobacco. Coffee, gum, sweet rolls. Coffee, gum again. At the moment it was a chocolate *gelato* cone, and he was eating it against the July heat, licking the melting ice cream from his hand as he walked through the noonday crowds and back to the Questura. But neither melting *gelato* nor the lack of nicotine could pull him from the thing on his mind—the missing Llama pistol with the silencer squirreled to its barrel.

It was a thought that had come in the middle of the night and kept him awake for the rest of it. The first thing this morning he'd looked at the "Transfer of Evidence" form Pio and Jacov Farel had both signed at the farmhouse when Farel had transferred possession of the gun found at the Assisi bus site to Pio. Correct and legal. It meant Pio definitely had the gun, and after he was killed, it was gone, along with Harry Addison. But that was only routine detective work, not the thought that had waked him and had eaten at him all morning and still did. All along he'd believed the Spanish-made Llama had been carried by Father Daniel and was a definitive link between him and the dead Spanish Communist Miguel Valera, the man set up to take the blame for the assassination of the cardinal vicar of Rome.

But—and this was the thing—what if the gun had not belonged to Father Daniel at all but to someone else on the bus? Someone who was there to kill him. If that was the case, then they might be looking not at one crime but two: an attempt to murder the priest and the blowing up of the bus itself.

11:30 P.M.

Hot and sticky. The heat that had begun to build the previous week had not let go, and even at this late hour it was still eighty-three degrees.

Trying to get some relief against it, Cardinal Marsciano had changed from his wool vestments into khaki trousers and a short-sleeved shirt and gone outside to the small interior courtyard of his apartment, hoping for a breeze that might lighten the oppressiveness.

The light spill from his library window illuminated the tomatoes and peppers he had planted in late April. They had ripened early and now had fruit that was almost ready to pick. Ripened early because of the heat. Not that it was totally unexpected. It was July, and July was usually hot. For a moment Marsciano smiled, remembering the small two-story Tuscan farmhouse where he had grown up along with his parents and four brothers and three sisters. The heat of summer meant two things—exhaustively long days with the entire family getting up before sunrise and working in the fields almost until dusk and scorpions, by the thousands. Coming in and sweeping them out of the house was a two- or three-times-a-day chore, and one never got into bed or put on a pair of pants or shirt or shoe, for that matter, without shaking it out first. The sting of a scorpion would leave you with a welt and pain you would remember for a long time. The insect was the first of God's creatures he truly despised. But then that was long before he'd known Palestrina.

Filling a watering can, Marsciano soaked the ground beneath his vegetable plants, then set the can back where it had been and wiped the sweat from his forehead. Still there was no breeze, and the night air seemed more stifling than ever.

The heat.

He tried to push it from his mind but he couldn't, because he knew it was what had started Palestrina's China clock ticking. Every day Marsciano watched the papers and the global weather reports on television and scanned the Internet, monitoring as best he could the weather conditions across Asia, the same as he knew Palestrina was doing. Only the secretariat would have a far more comprehensive manner of information gathering than he did, mainly because, in light of his "Chinese Protocol," Palestrina himself had taken up the study of meteorology, becoming a passionate student of the science of weather forecasting. In less than a year he had become a near-expert in the projection of computerized weather forecast models. Additionally, he established personal relationships with a half dozen professional weathercasters around the world with whom he could communicate for advice almost instantly via E-mail. If the secretariat hadn't had a more direct agenda before him, he could have easily settled into a second career as Italy's chief weather expert.

A prolonged spell of hot, humid weather across eastern China was what he was waiting for. With it, the sun-fed algae and its accompanying biological toxins would quickly begin to clot the surface of lakes, polluting the main water supplies of towns and cities along their shores. And when the conditions were right and the algae mass large enough, Palestrina would give the order and his "protocol" would begin. Poisoning the lakes in a way that would be undetectable, making the cause appear to be the algae and the inability of the aging municipal water-filtration systems to correct it.

People would die in huge numbers, and an enormous public outcry would follow. And government leaders would be secretly worried that the provinces might panic and sense Beijing was not capable of running the water system and threaten to pull away from the central government, thereby putting China on the brink of its greatest fear, collapse, in the same way the Soviet Union had collapsed. And these government leaders would respond to a strong, very private recommendation by a longtime trusted ally that a consortium of international construction companies, many already working on projects within China, be quickly brought together to immediately rebuild the country's entire crumbling and near-archaic water-delivery/treatment infrastructure. From canals to reservoirs to filtration plants to dams and hydroelectric plants.

That longtime trusted ally would, of course, be Pierre Weggen. And the companies and corporations to do the work would, of course, be those silently controlled by the Vatican. It was the heart of Palestrina's plan: control China's water and you control China.

And to begin to control the water he needed hot weather, and today it was hot in Italy, and it was hot in eastern China. And Marsciano knew that, save an unlikely and abrupt change of weather over Asia, it was only a matter of days before Palestrina would send word and the horror would begin.

TURNING TO GO INSIDE, Marsciano caught a glimpse of a face at an upper window. Just a glimpse, then it was gone, pulled back quickly—Sister Maria-Louisa, his new housekeeper, or, rather, Palestrina's new housekeeper, put there to let him know he was constantly watched, that no matter what he did, Palestrina sat on his shoulder.

Back inside, Marsciano sat down wearily at his desk and began to go over the final draft of the minutes of the meeting of the day before, the new investment portfolio approved by the council of cardinals. Monday morning he would put it before Palestrina for his signature. And then it would become part of the permanent record.

As Marsciano worked, an immeasurable darkness in the form of questions rose from the depths of his mind, one that lurked in the shadows of his soul as if it were a living thing, rising whenever there was a quiet moment to torment him— what they had allowed Palestrina to become and, more pointedly, his own deeply despised inability to do anything about it himself. Why had he not requested a private meeting with the Holy Father or sent a secretive memo to the College of Cardinals admitting what had happened and what was about to happen and begging for their help to stop it?

The tragedy was that the answers were all too familiar

because he had wrestled with them a hundred times before. The Holy Father was old and altogether devoted to his secretariat of state and therefore would be unswayable to anything said against him. And who presided over the College of Cardinals more than Palestrina himself? His esteem was enormous, his allies everywhere. A charge of this magnitude would either be laughed off or treated with outrage, as if it were heresy, or as if his accuser were deranged.

Making it even more impossible was Palestrina's threat to reveal him as the man who had ordered the murder of Cardinal Parma, the result of a sordid love affair. How could Marsciano defend against a lie like that to the pope or the cardinals? The answer was, he couldn't, because Palestrina held all the cards and could manipulate them at will.

Complicating things further was the fact that what had happened had originated entirely from the secrecy and sanctity of the pope's inner circle, the follow-up to a papal request to find a way to expand the reach of the Church in the next century. Any number of studies had been done and proposals made before Palestrina presented his—deliberately and fully fleshed out. And when he had, Marsciano, like the others, had laughed, taking it as a joke. But it was not a joke. The secretariat was utterly serious.

To Marsciano's horror, only Cardinal Parma voiced opposition. The others—Monsignor Capizzi and Cardinal Matadi—had remained silent. In retrospect Marsciano should not have been surprised. Palestrina had obviously evaluated them all carefully beforehand. Parma, old school, staunchly conservative and unyielding, would never have gone along. But Capizzi, graduate of Oxford and Yale and chief of the Vatican Bank, and Matadi, prefect of the Congregation of Bishops, whose family was among the most prominent in Zaire, were altogether different. Both were highly ambitious political animals who had not reached the pinnacles they had by accident. Profoundly driven and exceedingly canny, each man had a huge following inside the Church. And, knowing full well that Palestrina had no desire for the office himself, each had his eye directly on the papacy, knowing that it was wholly within Palestrina's whim and power to seat either one of them there.

Marsciano was another creature altogether, a man who had achieved what he had because he was not only intelligent and decidedly unpolitical but at heart a simple priest who believed in his Church and in God. It made him truly a "man of trust," an innocent who would find it impossible to conceive that a man like Palestrina could exist inside the modern Church, thereby making it easy to use his faith as an instrument to manipulate him.

Suddenly Marsciano slammed his first down on the table in front of him, in the same instant damning himself for the thousandth time for his weakness and naivete, even his own *godliness,* in pursuit of the calling he had been drawn to his entire life. If his fury and self-realization had come earlier, he might have been able to do something, but by now it was far too late. Control of the Holy See had been all but relinquished to Palestrina by the Holy Father, and the only voice against him, Cardinal Parma's, had been silenced. And Capizzi and Matadi had bowed to their leader and followed him. As had Marsciano himself, hopelessly trapped by the substance of his own character. In result, Palestrina had taken the reins, setting in motion a horror that could not, and would not, be called back. Leaving them all to wait only for the broiling heat of Chinese summer.

$$\boxed{50}$$

Beijing, China. The Gloria Plaza Hotel.
Sunday, July 12, 10:30 A.M.

FORTY-SIX-YEAR-OLD LI WEN CAME OUT OF
the elevator on the eighth floor and turned down the hallway,
looking for room 886, where he was to meet James Hawley,
a hydrobiological engineer from Walnut Creek, California.
Outside, he could see the rain had stopped and the sun was
breaking through the overcast. The rest of day would be hot
and oppressively humid as predicted, with the pattern to continue for several more days.

Room 886 was halfway down the corridor, and the door
to it partway open when Li Wen reached it.

"Mr. Hawley?" he said. There was no reply.

Li Wen raised his voice. "Mr. Hawley." Still there was
nothing. Pushing the door open, he entered.

Inside, the color TV was on to a news broadcast, and a
light gray business suit for a very tall man was laid out on the

bed. Alongside it was a white short-sleeved shirt, a striped tie, and a pair of boxer shorts. To his left, the bathroom door was open and he could hear the sound of a shower running.

"Mr. Hawley?"

"Mr. Li." James Hawley's voice rose over the sound of the water. "Another apology. I've been called to an urgent meeting at the Ministry of Agriculture and Fisheries. About what, I don't know. But it makes no difference—everything you need is in an envelope in the top dresser drawer. I know you have a train to catch. We'll have tea or a drink the next time around."

Li Wen hesitated, then went to the dresser and opened the top drawer. Inside was a hotel envelope with the initials *L. W.* handwritten on the front. Taking it out, he opened it, glanced quickly at its contents, then slid it into his jacket pocket and closed the drawer.

"Thank you, Mr. Hawley," he said at the steam coming from the bathroom door, then quickly left, closing the door behind him. The contents of the envelope were precisely as promised, and there was no need to stay longer. He had little more than seven minutes to leave the hotel, dodge the traffic on Jianguomennan Avenue, and get to his train.

HAD LI WEN FORGOTTEN something and come back to retrieve it, he would have seen a short, stocky Chinese in a business suit exit the bathroom in James Hawley's place. Stepping to the window, he looked out and saw Li Wen cross the street in front of the hotel and walk quickly toward the railroad station.

Turning from the window, he took a suitcase from under the bed, put James Hawley's carefully laid-out clothes into it, and then left, leaving the room key on the bed.

Five minutes later he was at the wheel of his silver Opel, picking up his cell phone and turning onto Chongwenmendong Street. Chen Yin grinned. Publicly he was a successful merchant of cut flowers, but on quite another level he was a master of spoken language and dialect. One that he particularly delighted in using was American English—speaking the way a man like James Hawley, a polite, if harried, hydrobiological engineer from Walnut Creek, California, might, if he existed.

51

Cortona, Italy. Sunday, July 12, 5:10 A.M.
11:10 A.M. in Beijing

"THANK YOU, MY FRIEND," THOMAS KIND SAID in English. Then, clicking off the cellular, he put it on the seat beside him. Chen Yin's call had been within the allocated time window, and the news was as he had expected. Li Wen had the documents and was on his way home. There had been no face-to-face contact. Chen Yin was good. Dependable. And he had found Li Wen, not an easy thing to do—uncover the perfect all-too-accommodating pawn who had all the skills and reasons to do as asked, yet who, if circumstance required, could be disavowed or simply liquidated at any time.

Chen Yin had been paid beforehand, as a deposit in good faith, and once Li Wen had done his job, he would be paid the remainder of what he was owed. Then both would vanish: Li Wen because his usefulness would be over and they dared leave no trace back to them; Chen Yin, because it would be wise for him to leave the country for a time and because his money was out of China anyway, deposited in the Union Square branch of a Wells Fargo bank in downtown San Francisco.

SOMEWHERE A ROOSTER CROWED, the sound bringing Thomas Kind immediately back to the task at hand. Ahead, in the predawn light, he could just see the house. It sat back from the road and behind a stone wall, a layer of mist hanging over the ploughed fields across from it.

He could have gone in just after he'd arrived, at a little past midnight. He would have cut the power, and the night-vision goggles would have given him the advantage. But still the killing would have had to be done in the dark. And against three men in a house he did not know.

So he'd waited, parking the rented Mercedes on an out-of-the-way cul-de-sac a mile away. There he'd field-stripped and checked his weapons in the darkness—twin 9mm Walther MPKs, *mascinen pistole kurz,* machine pistols with thirty-round magazines—then rested, his mind flashing back to the unfortunate happening in Pescara when Ettore Caputo, owner of Servizio Ambulanza Pescara, and his wife had refused to talk to him about the Iveco ambulance that left Hospital St. Cecilia Thursday night for a destination unknown.

Stubbornness was an unfortunate trait in all of them. The husband and wife would not talk, and Thomas Kind was determined to have answers and would not leave without them. His questions were simple: who were the people in the ambulance? and where had they gone?

It had only been when Kind pressed a two-shot .44 magnum derringer against Signora Caputo's forehead that Ettore suddenly had had the urge to talk. Who the patient or passengers were he had no idea. The driver was a man named Luca Fanari, a former *carabiniere* and licensed ambulance driver who worked for him from time to time. Luca had rented the ambulance from him earlier that week and for an unspecified period of time. Where he had gone with it, he did not know.

Thomas Kind pressed the derringer a little more firmly against Signora Caputo's head and asked again.

"Call Fanari's wife, for God's sake!" the signora shouted.

Ninety seconds later Caputo hung up the phone. Luca Fanari's wife had given him a telephone number and an address where to reach her husband, warning him that neither was to be given out under any circumstance whatsoever.

Luca Fanari, Caputo said, had driven his patient north. To a private home. Just outside the town of Cortona.

STREAKS OF DAYLIGHT crossed the sky as Thomas Kind slipped over the wall and approached the house from behind. He wore tight gloves, steel-colored jeans, a dark sweater, and black running shoes. One of the Walther MPKs was in his hand, the other hung from a strap over his shoulder. Both were mounted with silencers. He looked like a commando; which, at this moment, he was.

In front of him he could see the beige Iveco ambulance parked near the side door. Five minutes later he had searched the entire house. It was empty.

52

Rome. 7:00 A.M.

HARRY HAD SEEN THE VIDEO CLIP ON AN English-language channel an hour earlier—a Hollywood trade paper photograph of Byron Willis, exterior shots of their Beverly Hills office building and of Byron's home in Bel Air. His friend, boss, and mentor had been shot to death as he arrived at his home Thursday night. Because of his association with Harry and the events concurrent in Italy, the police had withheld the news pending further inquiry. The FBI was now involved, and investigators from Gruppo Cardinale were expected to arrive in Los Angeles later in the day.

Stunned, horrified, Harry had taken the chance and called Adrianna's office, leaving word to have her call Elmer Vasko immediately. And she had, from Athens an hour later. She'd just returned from the island of Cyprus, where she'd covered a major confrontation between Greek and Turkish politicians and had only just learned of the Willis piece herself and tried to find out more before she called him.

"Did it have to do with me, with what the fuck is going on here in Italy?" Harry was angry and bitter and fighting to hold back tears.

"Nobody knows yet. But—"

"But *what*, for Chrissake?"

"From what I understand, it looked like a professional hit."

". . . God, why?" he whispered. "He didn't know anything."

Pulling himself back, fighting off the dark swirl of emotion, Harry asked her what the status was in the hunt for his brother. Her response was that the police had no leads, that nothing had changed. It was why she hadn't called.

Harry's world was collapsing around him in violence. He'd wanted to call Barbara Willis, Byron's widow. To talk to her, to somehow touch her, try to comfort her and share her terrible pain. He'd wanted to call Willis's senior partners Bill Rosenfeld and Penn Barry to find out what the hell happened. But he couldn't. Not by phone or fax or even E-mail without fear it would be traced to where he was. But he couldn't sit still either; if Danny was alive, it was only a matter of time before they got to him just as they got to Byron Willis. Instantly his thoughts shifted to Cardinal Marsciano and the stance he had taken at the funeral home, telling him to bury the charred remains as if they were his brother's, then warning him forcefully afterward not to press further. Clearly the cardinal knew a great deal more than he was telling. If anyone knew where Danny was now, it would be he.

"Adrianna," he said forcefully, "I want Cardinal Marsciano's home phone number. Not the main number, the private one that hopefully only he answers."

"I don't know if I can get it."

"Try."

53

Still Sunday, July 12.

VIA CARISSIMI WAS A STREET OF STYLISH apartments and town houses bordered on one end by the sprawling gardens of the Villa Borghese, and the elegant, tree-lined Via Pinciana, on the other.

Harry had been watching the ivy-covered, four-story building at number 46 off and on since nine-thirty. Twice he'd dialed Cardinal Marsciano's private number. Twice an answering machine had started to pick up. Twice he'd clicked off the cellular. Either Marsciano wasn't there or he was screening his calls. Harry wanted neither. He couldn't leave a message or give Marsciano the opportunity to leave him hanging while someone put a trace on his call. The best thing was to be patient, at least for a time. Try later and hope the cardinal himself answered.

At noon he dialed again with the same result. Frustrated, he went for a walk in the Villa Borghese. At one o'clock he took a seat on a park bench on the edge of the Villa grounds where he could see the cardinal's residence clearly.

Finally, at two-fifteen, a dark gray Mercedes pulled up in front and stopped. The driver stepped out and opened the rear door. A moment later Marsciano appeared, followed by Father Bardoni. Together the clergymen walked up the steps and went into Marsciano's building. Immediately the driver got behind the wheel and drove off.

Glancing at his watch, Harry took the cellular from his pocket, waited for a young couple to pass by, then hit REDIAL and waited.

"*Pronto,*"—Hello—the cardinal's voice came back strongly.

"My name is Father Roe, Cardinal Marsciano. I'm from Georgetown University in—"

"How did you get this number?"

"I'd like to speak to you about a medical problem . . ."

"What?"

"A third breast. It's called a supernumerary nipple."

There was a sudden pause—and then another voice came on.

"This is Father Bardoni. I work for the cardinal. What can I do for you?"

"Monsignor Grayson at Georgetown School of Law was kind enough to give me the cardinal's number before I left. He said that if I should need help, His Eminence would be more than willing to give it."

HARRY WAITED ON THE BENCH until he saw Father Bardoni come down the steps and start down the block toward him. Getting up, he walked slowly toward a large fountain and the crowd clustered around it, people vainly attempting to escape the oppressive heat and humidity of this July Sunday afternoon. Harry was simply one among them, a priest, young and bearded, doing the same.

Looking back, he watched the young, tall priest with the dark, curly hair cross into the park. He walked casually, as if he were out for a stroll. Yet Harry could see him looking in his direction, trying to find him in the crowd around the fountain. It was the manner of a man not wanting to draw attention to himself or what he was doing, of someone on the spot and uncomfortable. Still, he was coming, and that was enough to tell Harry he'd been right. Danny was alive. And Marsciano knew where he was.

HARRY STOOD WATCHING, HALF HIDDEN
by the children splashing in the fountain in front of him, letting Father Bardoni find him in the crowd. Finally he did.

"You look different . . ." Father Bardoni came up to
stand next to him, his eyes not on Harry but on the children
shrieking and splashing in the fountain. Harry was indeed
thinner, the beard helped, and so did the priest's clothing
and the black beret angled over his forehead.

"I want to meet with His Eminence."

Both men talked quietly, watching the children, smiling
when appropriate, enjoying their antics.

"I'm afraid that's not possible."

"Why?"

"It just is. . . . His schedule is full . . ."

Harry turned to look at him. "Bullshit."

Father Bardoni let his eyes wander past Harry. "On the
hill behind you, Mr. Addison, are several *carabinieri* on
horse patrol. A little closer and to your right are two more on

motorcycles." His eyes came back to Harry. "You are one of the two most wanted men in Italy.... By simply moving toward the police and waving my arms.... Do you understand?"

"My brother is alive, Father. And His Eminence knows where he is. Now, either he can take me to him himself, or we can call the police over here and let them convince him to do the same thing . . ."

Father Bardoni studied Harry carefully, then his gaze caught a man in a blue shirt on the far side of the fountain watching them.

"Perhaps we should go for a walk . . ."

HARRY SAW THE MAN as they left, moving out of the crowd, following them at a distance as they crossed an open grassy area and started down a paved walkway through the park.

"Who is he?" Harry pressed. "The man in the blue shirt."

Father Bardoni took his glasses off, rubbed them on his sleeve, then put them back on. Without them, he seemed stronger and more physical, and the thought crossed Harry's mind that he didn't need them at all, that they were there for effect in an attempt to soften his appearance. That maybe he was more like a bodyguard than a personal secretary. Or, if not that, a man much more involved with what was going on than he seemed to be.

"Mr. Addison—" Father Bardoni glanced over his shoulder. The man in the blue shirt was still following them. Abruptly he stopped. Deliberately letting the man catch up. "He works for Farel," he said quietly.

The man was up to them, nodding as he passed. *"Buon giorno."*

"Buon giorno," Father Bardoni said in return.

Father Bardoni watched him go, then looked to Harry. "You have no idea what's going on, or what you are getting into."

"Why don't you tell me?"

Father Bardoni glanced after the man in the blue shirt. He was still walking up the path, moving away. Once again he took off his glasses and turned back to Harry.

"I will speak with the cardinal, Mr. Addison," Father Bardoni acquiesced for the moment. "I will tell him you wish to meet with him."

"It's more than a wish, Father."

Father Bardoni hesitated, as if he were judging Harry's determination, then slid the glasses back on. "Where are you staying?" he asked. "How can we get in touch with you?"

"I'm not sure, Father. It's best I get in touch with you."

At the end of the pathway, the man in the blue shirt stopped and glanced back. When he did, he saw the two priests shake hands and then Father Bardoni turn and walk off, going back the way he had come. The other priest, the one in the black beret, watched him go, then, taking another path, walked away.

CASTELLETTI TOOK A CIGARETTE FROM A pack on the table in front of him and started to light it. Then he saw Roscani staring at him.

"You want me to go outside?"

"No."

Abruptly Roscani took a bite out of a carrot stick. "Finish what you were saying," he said, then, glancing at Scala, turned to stare at the bulletin board on the wall next to the window.

They were in Roscani's office, their jackets off, sleeves rolled up, talking over the din of the air conditioner. The detectives bringing Roscani current on their separate investigations.

Castelletti had traced the numbers on the Harry Addison videocassette and found it had been bought at a store on Via Frattina, which was little more than a five-minute walk from the Hotel Hassler and the American's room.

Scala, looking for the source of the bandage seen on Addison's forehead in the video, had canvassed every street within a half-mile circumference of the site where Pio had been slain. In that area were twenty-seven physicians and three clinics. None had treated anyone matching Harry Addison's description the afternoon or evening of the murder. Furthermore, Roscani's request to have the video's image computer enhanced to get a more detailed look at the wallpaper behind Addison had proved a failure. There was simply not enough detail to find a clear pattern for a manufacturing source.

Crunching on his carrot, trying to ignore the sweet nicotine smell of Castelletti's cigarette, Roscani listened to it all. They had done their work and found nothing they could use; it was part of the game. Of far more interest was the bulletin board and the 3×5 cards listing the names of twenty-three of the twenty-four victims of the bombing of the Assisi bus. Beside them were photographs, some recent, some old, collected from family archives, mostly of the mutilated dead.

Roscani, like Scala and Castelletti, had looked at the photos a hundred times. Saw them while falling asleep, while shaving, while driving. If Father Daniel was alive, whom had he replaced? Which one of the twenty-three others?

Of the eight who had survived and the sixteen dead, all but one—the remains originally thought to be Father Daniel Addison—had been positively identified; even those five burned beyond recognition had had their identities confirmed through dental and medical records.

The one missing, victim number 24—with no card or name or photograph—was the charred body in the box, the one originally thought to be that of Father Daniel Addison. So far he was without identity. Tests had shown no scars or other visible means of identification. A dental chart had been made from what little was left of the mouth, but as yet there was nothing with which to compare it. And files of missing persons had turned up nothing. And yet someone obviously *was* missing. A Caucasian male, probably in his late thirties or early forties. Five foot nine to six feet and weighing somewhere between——

Suddenly Roscani turned to look at his detectives.

"What if there were twenty-*five* people on the bus, not twenty-four? In the mass of confusion afterward, who could know exactly how many there were? The living and dead are taken to two different hospitals. Extra doctors and nurses are called in. Ambulances are banging around like rush-hour traffic. There are people terribly burned, some without arms or legs. We've got gurneys piling up in hallways. People are running. Yelling. Trying to keep some kind of order and the victims alive at the same time. Add that to whatever else was going on in those emergency rooms at the time. Who the hell sits there keeping track? There isn't enough help to begin with.

"And what did it take afterward? Almost a full day of talking to rescuers, looking at hospital records, talking to bus company people trying to tally up tickets sold. Another day after that working through the identities of the people we had. And in the end, everyone——us included——simply accepted the total count as twenty-four.

"It's not impossible at all to think one person could have been overlooked in that chaos. Someone who was never even formally admitted. Somebody who, if he was ambulatory enough, might have simply wandered off, walked away in the middle of everything. Or, maybe even had help getting the hell out of there.

"Damn it!" Roscani slammed his hand down on his desk. All the while they had been looking at what they had, not at what they didn't have. What they had to do now was go back to the hospitals. Check every record of every admittance that day. Talk to anyone who had been on duty. Find out what had happened to that one victim. Where he might have gone by himself or been taken.

FORTY MINUTES LATER Roscani was on the Autostrada, driving north toward Fiano Romano and the hospital there, a juggler with too many balls in the air, a jigsaw man confounded by the sheer number of pieces. His mind swam and tried to push them away. For a while to think of nothing at all, let his subconscious work. Use the soft hum of the tires over the road as background to his splendid silence, his *assoluta tranquillità*.

Reaching up, he lowered the visor against the glare of the setting sun. God, he wanted a cigarette, and there was a pack still in the glove box. He started to reach for it, then caught himself and instead opened a brown bag on the seat next to him and took out not one of the carrot sticks his wife had cut for him but a large *biscotto,* one of a half dozen he had bought himself. He was about to bite into it when everything came full circle.

He had said nothing to the others about his idea that the Spanish Llama pistol found at the site of the bus explosion might not have belonged to Father Daniel but to someone on the bus who was there to kill him—Why? because there were no facts to back it up, and without some kind of evidence, thinking in that direction was a waste of time and energy. But, fuse that concept with the idea of a twenty-fifth man, and you had your uncounted passenger, perhaps one who bought a ticket at the last minute as he got on, a ticket the driver had not had time to tally before the bus blew up. If that were so, and it was he who was in the box, it would certainly explain why no one had come forward to identify him.

Still, he argued, it was conjecture. On the other hand, it was a feeling that kept coming back, more now than ever. It was a hunch, something all his years of experience told him—there *had* been a twenty-fifth passenger, and he had been onboard to kill Father Daniel. And if he was the assassin—Roscani stared at the horizon—then who blew up the bus? And why?

56

Xi'an, China. Monday, July 13, 2:30 A.M.

LI WEN LIT A CIGARETTE AND SAT BACK, moving his body as far away as he could from the sleeping, overweight man crowding the seat beside him. In fifteen minutes the train would reach Xi'an. When it did he'd get off, and the fat man could have both seats for all he cared. Li Wen had made this same trip in May and then again in June, only that time he'd splurged and traveled in luxury on the Marco Polo Express, the green-and-cream train that follows the route of the old Silk Road, 2,000 miles from Beijing to Ürümqi, the capital of Xinjiang Uygur province, the first great east–west link. The train the Chinese hoped would lure the same monied traveler who frequented the fabled Orient Express from Paris to Istanbul.

But tonight Li rode in the hard-seat class of a packed train that was already almost fours hours behind schedule. He hated the packed trains. Hated the loud music, the weather forecasts, and the "no-news" news that was broadcast cease-lessly over the train's loudspeakers. Beside him the fat man shifted his weight, and his elbow dug into Li's rib cage. At the same time, the middle-aged woman in the seat in front of him hucked up and spit on the floor, angling it to hit between the shoe of the man standing in the aisle beside her and the young man jammed in next to him.

Pushing at the fat man's elbow, Li took a heavy drag on his cigarette. In Xi'an he would change trains, he hoped to one less crowded, and then be on his way to Hefei and his room at the Overseas Chinese Hotel and maybe a few hours' sleep. The same as he had done in May and then again in June. And would again in August. These were the months when the heat grew the algae in the lakes and rivers that provided drinking water for the municipal water supplies throughout his area of Central China. A former assistant pro-fessor of research at the Hydrobiological Institute in Wuhan, Li Wen was a midlevel civil worker, a water-quality-control engineer for the central government. His job was to monitor the bacterial content of the water released for public use by water-filtration plants throughout the region. Today his chores would be the same as always. Arrive by five in the morning. Spend the day and perhaps the next inspecting the plant and testing the water, then record his findings and rec-ommendations for forwarding to the central committee; and move on to the next. It was a gray life and tedious, boring, and, for the most part, uneventful. At least it had been until now.

57

Lake Como, Italy.
Sunday, July 12, 8:40 P.M.

THE SOUND OF THE MOTORS CHANGED
from a whine to a low drone, and nursing sister Elena Voso
could feel the hydrofoil slow as the boat's hull settled into
the water. Ahead, a great stone villa sat on the lake's edge,
and they were moving toward it. In the twilight, she could
see a man on the dock looking toward them, a large rope in
his hand.

Marco stepped down from the pilot house and went out
onto the deck as they neared. Behind her, Luca and Pietro
stood up to unhook the safety straps that had held the gurney
secure on the trip from shore. The hydrofoil was large, able
to seat, she guessed, maybe as many as sixty passengers and
was used for public transportation between the towns sitting
on the edge of the thirty-mile-long lake. But this trip, they
were the only travelers—she, Marco, Luca, and Pietro. And
Michael Roark.

They had left the house in Cortona just after noon the day before. Going quickly, leaving almost everything but Michael Roark's medical supplies behind. A telephone call had come for Luca, and Elena answered. Luca was sleeping, she'd said, but the voice told her to wake him, to tell him that it was urgent, and Luca had taken the call on the upstairs extension.

"Get out, *now*," she'd heard the voice say as she'd returned to the kitchen to hang up. She'd started to listen, but Luca knew she was there and told her to hang up. And she had.

Immediately Pietro had driven off in his car, only to return three-quarters of an hour later at the wheel of another van. Less than fifty minutes after that they were in it, all of them, leaving behind the vehicle they'd come in.

Driving north, they'd taken the A1 Autostrada to Florence and then gone on to Milan to a private apartment in the suburbs where they'd spent the night and most of that day. There Michael Roark had his first real food, rice pudding Marco had bought at a local store. He'd taken it slowly, between sips of water, but he managed, and it had stayed down. But it hadn't been enough, and so she kept him on the IV.

The newspaper she'd bought, with the photograph of Father Daniel Addison, had been left behind in the rush to depart. Whether Roark had seen her hide it away behind her as he'd so abruptly turned toward her she didn't know. All she did know was that the comparison had been inconclusive. He might be the American priest, he might not. Her entire effort had been in vain.

THERE WAS AN ABRUPT ROAR as the propellers reversed, then a gentle bump as the hydrofoil touched the dock. Elena saw Marco toss the mooring line to the man onshore and turned from her musing to see Luca and Pietro lift the gurney and carry it forward to the steps. As they did, Michael Roark raised his head and looked at her, more for comfort and the assurance she was coming with them, she thought, than for anything else. As far as he had come, he could talk only in hoarse, guttural sounds and was still extremely weak. She realized she had become his emotional anchor as well as his caregiver. It was a tender dependency, and for all her nursing experience, it touched her in a way she'd never felt before. She wondered what it meant, whether somehow she was changing. It made her think, too, and ask herself, if he were the fugitive priest, would it make any difference?

Moments later they had him up and out, with Marco leading them up the gangway to bring him ashore. And then Elena was ashore as well, listening as the engines of the hydrofoil revved up, then turning to see the boat pull away in the enveloping darkness, its running lights glowing on the stern, the Italian flag above the pilot house flapping in the wind. Then the vessel picked up speed, and its hull rose out of the water so that the boat stood up on stilts like a huge, ungainly bird. And like that it was gone, the black water closing behind it, washing over its wake. As if it had never been.

"Sister Elena," Marco called, and she turned to follow them up the stone steps toward the lights of the immense villa above.

58

Rome. Same time.

HARRY STOOD IN EATON'S TINY KITCHEN,
staring at the cell phone on the counter. Next to it was a partially eaten loaf of bread and, with it, some cheese he'd
picked up at one of the few stores open on Sunday. By now
Marsciano would know what had transpired between him
and Father Bardoni in the park. And the cardinal would have
made a decision what to do when Harry called.

If he called.

"You have no idea what's going on, or what you're getting into." Father Bardoni's warning hung chillingly in his
mind.

The man in the blue shirt had been one of Farel's policemen, and he had been watching Father Bardoni, not Harry.
Eaton had been certain some dark intrigue was going on at
the highest levels of the Holy See. And maybe that was what
Father Bardoni had been talking about, cautioning Harry that

his intrusion was more than unwelcome—it was very dangerous. Suggesting he was close to drowning them all in his own waves.

Harry looked away from the phone. He didn't know what to do. By pushing Marsciano further he could make things far worse than they already were. But for whom? Marsciano. Farel's people. Anyone else involved. Who?

For no reason he picked up the knife he had used to slice the bread and cheese. It was an everyday kitchen knife, its cutting edge a little bit dull like most. As a knife it wasn't very impressive, but it did the job. Holding it up, he rotated it in his hand, saw the blade glint in the overhead light. Then, with the easiest of motions, he turned and slid it deep into what remained of the bread. The safety and well-being of his brother was all that mattered. All the rest—the Vatican, its power struggles and intrigues—could go to hell.

59

The Hospital of St. John.
Via dell' Amba Aradam, 9:50 P.M.

HARRY WAS ALONE IN THE SMALL CHAPEL,
sitting in a pew three rows back from the altar, his black
beret tucked inside his jacket pocket, his head bowed, seemingly in prayer. He'd been there fifteen minutes when the
door opened and a man in a short-sleeved shirt and what
looked like tan Levi Dockers came in and sat down nearby.

Harry glanced at his watch and then back toward the door.
Marsciano was to have met him there twenty minutes ago. It
was only when he decided he would give the cardinal
another five minutes and then leave that he looked again at
the man who had come in and realized in amazement that it
was Marsciano.

For a long while the cardinal remained still. Head bowed,
silent. Finally he looked up, made eye contact, and nodded
toward a door to the left. Then he stood, crossed himself

before the altar, and pushed through the door. At the same moment, a young couple entered, knelt before the altar and crossed themselves, taking seats together in the front row.

Harry counted slowly to twenty, then got up, made the sign of the cross and went out through the same door Marsciano had taken.

On the far side was a narrow hallway, and the cardinal stood alone in it.

"Come with me," Marsciano said.

Their footsteps echoing on the worn black-and-white tile floor, the cardinal led Harry down the empty corridor and into an older part of the building. Turning down another hall-way, Marsciano opened a door, and they entered a small private room which was another sanctuary for prayer. Dimly lit, more intimate than the first, it had a stone floor and several polished wooden benches facing a simple bronze cross on the wall opposite. Above, on the left and right, high windows, now dark against the night sky, touched the ceiling.

"You wished to see me. Here I am, Mr. Addison." Marsciano closed the door and turned in such a way that the lights of the room cut him at an angle that left his eyes and the top of his head in shadow. Purposeful or not, it under-scored his authority, reminding Harry that whatever else he was, or might be, Marsciano was still a major figure within the hierarchy of the Church. Hugely forceful, and larger than life.

Still, Harry could not let himself be intimidated. "My brother is alive, Eminence, and you know where he is."

Marsciano was silent.

"Who are you protecting him from? The police? . . . Farel?"

Harry knew Marsciano was watching him, the eyes he couldn't see searching his own.

"Do you love your brother, Mr. Addison?"

"Yes . . ."

"Do—you—love—your—brother?" Marsciano asked again. This time more deliberate, demanding, unforgiving. "You were estranged. You did not speak for years."

"He is my *brother*."

"Many men have brothers."

"I don't understand."

"You have been apart all this time. Why is he so important to you now?"

"Because he just is."

"Then why do you risk his life?"

Fire and anger danced in Harry's eyes. "Just tell me where he is."

"Have you thought what you would do if you knew?" Marsciano ignored him, just kept on. "Go to him. Then what? Stay with him where he is? Hide with him forever?— Sooner or later you would realize that you had to face the matter immediately at hand. The police. And when you do that, Mr. Addison, when you come out, you will both be killed. Your brother, because of what he knows. You, because they will think he has told you."

"Just *what* does he know?"

For a long moment Marsciano said nothing, then he stepped forward out of the shadow, the light touching his face, illuminating his eyes for the first time. What was there was no longer a papal aristocrat but a lone man who was twisted and torn and filled with fear. More fear than Harry thought anyone capable of. And it caught him wholly by surprise.

"They tried to murder him once. They are trying again. A hunter has been sent to track and kill him." Marsciano's eyes were riveted on Harry's.

"Number forty-seven Via di Montoro. Do not think you retreated to your apartment this afternoon unnoticed. Do not think your priest's costume will continue to hide you. I warn you with everything I have, to stay away! Because, if you do not—"

"Where *is* he? What the hell does he *know*?"

"—because if you do not, *I* will tell them where he is myself. And if I do, neither of us will hear from him again." Marsciano's voice dropped to a whisper. "That much is at stake . . ."

"The Church." Harry felt the chill, the immensity of it, even as he said it.

The cardinal stared for the briefest moment, then abruptly turned, pulled open the door, and disappeared into the hallway, his footsteps fading to silence.

60

Three hours later. Monday, July 13, 1:20 A.M.

ROSCANI TOOK THE CALL IN THE NUDE,
the way he always slept in the heat of summer. Glancing at
his wife, he put the caller on hold and pulled on a light robe.
A moment later he picked up the phone in his study, clicking
on the desk light as he did.

A middle-aged man and his wife had been found shot to
death in a storage container behind the ambulance company
they owned in Pescara. They had been dead almost thirty-six
hours when anxious family members had discovered them.
Local investigators on the scene at first believed it was a
murder-suicide, but after questioning friends and family,
decided in all probability it was not. And, on the off chance it
might have a connection to the nationwide manhunt, alerted
Gruppo Cardinale headquarters in Rome. Hence, the call
to him.

Pescara. 4:30 A.M.

Roscani walked the murder scene, the storage shed behind Servizio Ambulanza Pescara. Ettore Caputo and his wife had six children and had been married thirty-two years. They fought, Pescara police said, all the time, and about anything. Their battles were loud and violent and passionate. But never had anyone seen one touch the other in anger. And—never—had Ettore Caputo owned a gun.

Signora Caputo had been shot first. Point blank. And then her husband had apparently turned the weapon on himself, because his fingerprints were on it. The weapon was a two-shot .44 magnum derringer. Powerful, but tiny. The kind of weapon few people even knew about unless they were firearm aficionados.

Roscani shook his head. Why a derringer? Two shots didn't give you much room for miss or error. The only positive thing about it was its size, because it was easy to conceal. Stepping back, Roscani nodded to a member of the tech crew, and she moved in with an evidence bag to take the gun away. Then he turned and walked out of the shed and across a parking area to the ambulance company's front office. In the street beyond he could see people gathered in the gray early-morning light watching from behind police barricades.

Roscani thought back to last evening, and what he and his detectives had learned from their singular tours of the hospitals outside Rome. And that was nothing more definitive than the chance they could be right. That there could have been a twenty-fifth passenger on the bus who was never recorded. Someone who could have walked away in the confusion if he was able or taken off by car or—Roscani glanced at a promotional calendar tacked on the office wall as he stepped into the company's office—by private ambulance.

Castelletti and Scala were waiting as he came in. They were smoking and immediately put their cigarettes out when they saw Roscani.

"Fingerprints again," Roscani said, deliberately waving away the smoke that still hung in the air.

"The Spaniard's prints on the assassination rifle. Harry Addison's prints on the pistol that killed Pio. Now the clear prints of a man who allegedly never owned a gun, yet committed a murder-suicide. Each time making it seem obvious who the shooter was. Well we know that wasn't the case with the cardinal vicar. So what about the others? What if we have a *third* person doing the killing, then making sure the prints they wanted on the weapon got there? The *same* third person each time. The same 'he/she,' maybe even 'they,' killed the cardinal vicar. Killed Pio. Did the job here at the ambulance office."

"The priest?" Castelletti said.

"Or our *third* person, someone else entirely." Absently Roscani took out a piece of gum, unwrapped it and put it in his mouth. "What if the priest was in bad shape and was brought by ambulance from one of the hospitals outside Rome to Pescara . . ."

"And this third person found out and came here looking for him," Scala said quietly.

Roscani stared at Scala, then folded the chewing gum wrapper carefully and put it in his pocket. "Why not?"

"You follow that thinking and maybe Harry Addison didn't kill Pio . . ."

Roscani walked off, slowly chewing his gum. He looked at the floor, then at the ceiling. Through the window he could see the red ball of the sun beginning to come up over the Adriatic. Then he turned back.

"Maybe he didn't."

"Ispettore Capo—"

The detectives looked up as an investigator from the Pescara police came in, his face already streaked with sweat from the early heat.

"We may have something else. The chief medical officer has just examined the body of a woman who died in an apartment house fire last night—"

Roscani knew before he was told. "The fire didn't kill her."

"No, sir. She was murdered."

61

Rome. 6:30 A.M.

HARRY WALKED TOWARD THE COLOSSEUM, head down, unmindful of the rush of morning traffic passing on the Via dei Fori Imperiali beside him. At this point, motion was everything. The only way to keep from losing what small splinter of sanity he had left. Cars. Buses. Motor scooters. Roared and putted past. An entire society going about their own personal business, their thoughts and emotions focused wholly and innocently on the day before them, the same way he had every morning of his professional life until he had come to Rome. It had been as routine and comfortable as old shoes.

Up at six, exercise for an hour in the gym off his bedroom, shower, breakfast meeting with clients or potential clients, and into the office, cell phone never more than inches away, even in the shower. The same as now. Cell phone right there, in his pocket. Only it wasn't the same. None of it. The cellular phone was there, but he dared not use it. They could trace it back in an instant to whatever close-by cell site he was using, and the whole area would be filled with police before he knew it.

Suddenly he walked from bright sun to deep shade. Looking up, he saw that he stood in the shadow of the Colosseum. As quickly, his eye caught a movement in the dimness, and he stopped. A woman in a tattered dress stood watching from the base of the ancient arches. Then another stepped in beside her. And then a third, this one holding a baby. Gypsies.

Turning, he saw there were more. Eight or ten at least, and they were beginning to encircle him. Closing in slowly. Singly, and in twos and threes. All were women, and most had children in tow. Quickly Harry glanced back toward the street. There was no one. No groundskeepers. No tourists. No one.

Suddenly he felt a tug on his pants, and he glanced down. An old woman was lifting his pant leg, looking at his shoes. Jerking back, he stepped away from her. It did no good. Another woman was right there. Younger, grinning. Her front teeth gone. One hand held up for money, the other reaching out to caress the material of his trousers. That he seemed to be a priest made no difference. Then something brushed his back and a hand went for his wallet.

In one motion he whirled, his own hand flashing out, coming up hard with a piece of material, dragging a wildly shrieking young woman up with it. The others shrank back, frightened, uncertain what to do. All the while the woman in his grasp thrashed and wailed, screaming as if she were being murdered. Abruptly Harry pulled her close. His face inches from hers.

"Hercules," he said, quietly, "I want to find Hercules."

* * *

THE DWARF SAT with one hand on his hip, the other holding his chin, staring intently at Harry. It was just past noon, and they were on a bench in a small, dusty square across the Tiber in the Gianicolo section of Rome. Midday traffic rumbled past on a boulevard at the square's farthest boundary. But that was the extent of it; other than two elderly men on a bench farther down, they were alone. Except that Harry knew the Gypsies were there, somewhere, out of sight, watching.

"Because of you, the police found my tunnel. Because of you, I now live outdoors instead of in. Thank you very much." Hercules was angry, and put out, literally.

"I'm sorry . . ."

"Yet here you are again. Back, I think, looking for help instead of the other way around."

"Yes."

Hercules deliberately looked off. "What do you want?"

"You, to follow someone. Two people, actually. You and the Gypsies."

Hercules looked back. "Who?"

"A cardinal and a priest. People who know where my brother is . . . who will lead me to him."

"A cardinal?"

"Yes."

Hercules suddenly pulled a crutch under him and stood up. "No."

"I'll pay you."

"With what?"

"Money."

"How are you going to get it?"

"I have it. . . ." Harry hesitated, then took Eaton's money from his pocket. "How much do you want? How much for you and the Gypsies?"

Hercules looked at the money, then at Harry. "That's more than I gave you. Where did you get it?"

"I got it—that's all. . . . How much do you want?"

"More than that."

"How much more?"

"You can get it?" Hercules was surprised.

"I think so . . ."

"If you can get so much money, why don't you ask the people giving it to you to follow the cardinal?"

"It's not that simple."

"Why?—Can't trust them?"

"Hercules, I'm asking for your help. I'm willing to pay for it. And I know you need it . . ."

Hercules said nothing.

"Before, you said you could not collect the reward on me because you would have to go to the police for it. . . . Money can help get you off the street."

"Frankly, Mr. Harry, I would just as soon not be seen with you. The police want you. The police want me. We're bad company. Twice as bad when we're together. . . . I need you as a lawyer, not a banker. When you can do that, come back. Otherwise, *arrivederci.*"

Indignantly, Hercules grabbed for his other crutch. But Harry beat him to it and snatched it away.

Hercules' eyes flashed angrily. "That's not a very good idea."

Harry ignored his protest. "Before, you said you wanted to see what I could do. How far my wits and courage would take me. This is how far, Hercules. In a big circle, right back to you. . . . I tried, it just didn't work . . ." Harry's voice softened, and he looked at Hercules for a long moment, then ever so slowly gave him back his crutch.

"I can't do it alone, Hercules. . . . I need your help."

Harry's last words were barely out when the cellular phone rang in his jacket pocket, its shrill intrusion startling them both.

"—Yes . . . ," Harry answered warily, his eyes darting around the park, as if this were a trick, the police on to him.

"Adrianna!" Quickly Harry turned away, covering his free ear against the sound of the traffic on the boulevard.

Hercules swung up on his crutches, watching intently.

"*Where?*" Harry nodded once, then twice. "—Okay. Yes! I understand. What color?—Okay, I'll find it."

Snapping off the phone, Harry slid it into his pocket, at the same time looking to Hercules.

"How do I get to the main railroad station?"

"Your brother—"

"He's been seen."

"Where?" Hercules could feel the excitement.

"In the north. A town on Lake Como."

"That's five hours by train through Milan. Too long. You would risk being—"

"I'm not going by train. Someone has a car waiting for me at the railroad station."

"A car . . ."

"Yes."

Hercules glared at him. "So, suddenly you have other friends and don't need me."

"I need you to tell me how to get to the station."

"Find it yourself."

Harry stared at the dwarf, incredulous. "First you want nothing to do with me, now you're mad because I don't need you."

Hercules said nothing.

"I *will* find it myself." Abruptly Harry turned and walked off.

"Wrong way, Mr. Harry!"

Harry stopped and looked back.

"You see, you *do* need me."

The wind picked up Harry's hair, and dust danced past his feet. "All right. I need you!"

"All the way to Lake Como!"

Harry glared. "All right!"

In an instant Hercules was up and swinging toward him. Then he was past him, calling over his shoulder.

"This way, Mr. Harry. *This* way!"

62

ROSCANI TURNED TO LOOK AT SCALA AND
Castelletti in the seats behind him, then with a glance at the
jet-helicopter's pilot, turned back to stare out the window.
They had been flying for nearly three hours, north along the
Adriatic coast, over the cities of Ancona, Rimini, and
Ravenna, then inland toward Milan, and finally north again
to drop down over the high hills and sweep across Lake
Como toward the town of Bellagio.

Below, he could see the tiny white wakes of pleasure
boats cutting the deep blue of the lake's surface like decorations on a cake. To his left, a dozen opulent villas surrounded
by manicured gardens dotted the shoreline, and to his right,
the steep hillsides dropped sharply to the lake itself.

They'd been still in Pescara at the scene of the apartment
house fire when he'd taken an urgent call from Taglia. A man
thought to be Father Daniel Addison had been brought to a

private villa on Lake Como by chartered hydrofoil the night before, Gruppo Cardinale's chief had said. The hydrofoil captain had seen the broadcast of the continuing public appeal messages on television and was all but certain who his passenger was. Yet he'd been reluctant to say anything because the villa was very exclusive and he was afraid he might lose his job if he was wrong and accidentally exposed a celebrity of some kind. But then sometime this morning his wife had convinced him he should notify the authorities and let them make the decision.

Celebrity, Roscani thought as the pilot banked sharply left and dropped lower over the water; who the hell cared who got exposed if they were on the right track? Time was more critical than ever.

The body found in the rubble had been that of Giulia Fanari, the wife of Luca Fanari, the man who, records had shown, had rented an ambulance from the slain proprietors of the ambulance company in Pescara. Signora Fanari had been dead before the fire began. Killed by a sharp instrument, probably an ice pick, inserted into the skull at the base of the brain. For all intents she was "pithed," the way a biologist might dispatch a frog he was about to dissect. *Cold blooded* wasn't a description. From the way it had been done, it appeared to Roscani to have been an act performed almost passionately, as if, with each involuntary squirm and muscular jolt the victim gave as her brain was slowly and deliberately crushed inside her skull, the killer was enjoying it. Maybe even sexually. If nothing else, the sheer inventiveness of the act told him the perpetrator was a person with absolutely no concept of conscience. A true sociopath who had complete indifference to the feelings, pain, or well-being of other people. A human being truly evil from birth. And if this sociopath was their illusory *third person*, Roscani could eliminate the "they" of it, because everything told him the murder had been done by one person alone, and he could eliminate the "she" as well, because it would have taken enormous strength to kill Giulia Fanari the way it had been done, meaning, almost without doubt, the creature who did it was a man. And if he had been in Pescara on the trail of Father Daniel and, through his doings there, had learned where he had been taken, it would mean he was a great deal closer to finding Father Daniel than they were.

Which was why, as Roscani watched the ground come up quickly, abruptly becoming obscured in a cloud of dust as the helicopter set down at the edge of a thick woods near the lake, he prayed to God that the injured man delivered to the villa was indeed the priest, and that they would get there first—before the man with the ice pick.

63

THE SCOPE WAS A 1.5–4.5 × ZEISS DIAVARI C, and through it Thomas Kind watched the dark blue Alfa Romeo come down the hill toward Bellagio. The crosshairs cut Castelletti in the middle of his forehead, and a slight shift to the left took Roscani the same way. Then, after a glimpse of a *carabiniere* at the wheel, the vehicle passed, and he stood back. He was uncertain if today he should once again call himself *S*, because he was not sure whether logistics or circumstance would present him with his target.

S for *sniper.* It was a designation he gave himself when he prepared, mentally and physically, to kill from a distance. It had begun as a self-promotion to an elite corps after his first kill, shooting a fascist soldier from an office window in Santiago, Chile, in 1976, as the troops opened fire on a gathering of Marxist students.

Moving the Zeiss down and to the right, he saw the *carabinieri* command post set up just outside the long formal drive leading to the palatial lakeside estate known as Villa

Lorenzi. A move to the right again, and the scope picked up the three police patrol boats idle in the water, a quarter of a mile apart and a hundred yards offshore.

Through Farel, Kind had learned that Villa Lorenzi was owned by the renowned Italian novelist Eros Barbu and that Barbu was traveling in western Canada and had not been at Villa Lorenzi since the previous New Year's Eve, when he had given his annual ball, one of the most famous events in all of Europe. In Barbu's absence, Villa Lorenzi was managed by a black South African poet named Edward Mooi, who lived free of charge, saw after the buildings, and directed the staff of twenty full-time house help and gardeners. And Mooi, at Eros Barbu's order, had given the police permission to search the grounds.

A formal statement from Barbu's attorneys maintained that neither Barbu nor Edward Mooi ever knew or had heard of a Father Daniel Addison, and that neither they nor any of the staff were aware of anyone coming to Villa Lorenzi by boat. Most certainly not someone with a medical staff of four tending him.

Easing back from his craggy perch on a wooded hill overlooking the villa, Thomas Kind lifted the scope again and saw Roscani's Alfa Romeo pull up to the command post just as Edward Mooi came down from the main house at the wheel of a battered three-wheel maintenance vehicle that looked like an old Harley-Davidson motorcycle towing the bed of a small dump truck.

Kind smiled. The poet was wearing a khaki shirt, western jeans, and leather sandals. His long hair, tied in a ponytail that dropped to his shoulders, had touches of gray at the temples and gave him the appearance of a distinguished hippie or an aging biker.

For a moment Mooi and Roscani chatted, then the poet climbed back on his vehicle and led Roscani's car and two large trucks filled with armed *carabinieri* back up the driveway and onto the grounds of the villa proper. Thomas Kind was certain the police would find nothing. But he was equally certain that his target was somewhere there, or at a place close by. So he would wait and watch, and then make his move. Patience was everything.

Hefei, China. The Overseas Chinese Hotel. Tuesday, July 14.

Li Wen rolled over, restless. It was hot and still, and he was unable to sleep. Thirty seconds later he rolled over again and looked at the clock. It was twelve-thirty in the morning. In three hours he would have to get up. In four he would be at work. He lay back. This night, more than any, he needed to sleep, but it didn't come. He tried to erase thought from his mind, not think of what he was about to do, or what Hefei would be like twenty-four hours from now after he had introduced the deadly product of American hydrobiologist James Hawley's formula to the water supply at the treatment plant's clear-water outflow wells. Polycyclic unsaturated alcohol was not a monitored constituent in the water systems, nor could it be detected visually or by taste or odor in the drinking water. Introduced in frozen snowball-like form to melt in the already-treated water, the effect would be to cause severe digestive-system cramping, followed by intense diarrhea, and, ultimately, intestinal bleeding and death within six to twenty-four hours. The amount introduced, calculated at ten-parts-per-million concentration in a glass of drinking water, would have sufficient fatal contamination for one hundred thousand individuals.

Ten parts per million.

One hundred thousand deaths.

Li Wen tried to stop his mind from working, but he could not. Then, in the distance, he heard the crackle of thunder. At almost the same time he felt a breeze and saw the curtains billow slightly at the open window. A front was approaching, and with it would come wind and warm rain. By the time he got up it should have passed, and tomorrow would be muggy and even hotter. Not-so-distant lightning flashed, for an instant lighting up his hotel room. Eight seconds later there was a clap of thunder.

Li Wen moved up on an elbow, alert, his gaze crossing the room. In the corner next to his suitcase was a small refrigerator. Few hotels in China had room refrigerators, especially hotels in the smaller cities like Hefei, away from the major centers, but this one did. It was the reason he had chosen this hotel and asked for this room. Not only was there a refrigerator, but the appliance itself had a freezer, which was even more important because it was where he had frozen the polycyclic "snowballs" after he had blended the formula. And where they would remain until he left for the treatment plant in something over three hours.

Again lightning flashed. For an instant the lights illuminating the hotel sign outside his window went out, then they came back on. Li Wen was wide awake now. Staring in the dark. The last thing he needed was to have the electricity go out.

64

Como, Italy. Still Monday, July 13, 7:00 P.M.

A TROUBLED AND ANXIOUS ROSCANI WORKED
his way across a jammed, hastily set-up communications
room deep inside Como's central carabinieri headquarters. A
dozen uniformed officers manned phone banks set on desks
in the middle of the room, while as many others hacked at
computer terminals plopped down haphazard, wherever they
could fit into the too-small quarters. Others still—anxious,
smoking, drinking coffee—moved in between. It was a war
room set up in hours to coordinate an all-out manhunt after a
search of Villa Lorenzi turned up no sign of the fugitive
priest.

Roscani's destination was an enormous map of the Lake
Como area that covered one entire wall. On it, pinpointed
with small Italian flags, were the locations of roadway
checkpoints where heavily armed Gruppo Cardinale personnel were stopping and searching every vehicle passing

through—a major undertaking, considering the variety of terrain and the number of roads that could be used as escape routes.

Bellagio was at the northern tip of a landmass triangle that jutted northward into the lake. The lake itself extended farther north, while at the same time spilling, in long fingers, down either side of the triangle to Lecco on the southeast and Como on the southwest, with Chiasso and the Swiss border just inland and northwest of it.

Because of its location, Chiasso was the most obvious exit point and was heavily manned, but there were other places still within Italy where the fugitives might hole up and hide to wait out a search. The towns of Menaggio, Tremezzo, and Lenno across the lake to the west. Bellano, Gittana, and Varenna to the east. And then those, like Vassena and Maisano, within the triangle and still others to the west.

It was a massive and intense operation that disrupted almost every household and business in the region; a condition exacerbated by an all-out invasion of the media. They were betting that the alleged assassin of the cardinal vicar of Rome was on the brink of capture and were broadcasting it live to the world.

Roscani was hardly new to large operations, and the disruptive circus atmosphere was part of it. But no matter how well things were organized, their very size made them cumbersome. Things rushed at you, decisions had to be made quickly and by any number of people. Mistakes were inevitable. Under fire you didn't have the *assoluta tranquillità* to be quiet and think things through properly, try to find the logic and approach that could make the difference between success and failure.

A sudden noise at the back of the room made Roscani look up. For an instant he saw a gaggle of media people in the hallway outside shouting questions as Scala and Castelletti came in with the captain and two members of the hydrofoil crew who had allegedly ferried Father Daniel and his medical entourage to Bellagio and Villa Lorenzi.

Roscani followed them across the room and into an alcove where a *carabiniere* pulled a sliding curtain to give them privacy.

"I am Ispettore Capo Otello Roscani. I apologize for the disorder."

The hydrofoil captain smiled and nodded. He was probably forty-five and looked fit. He wore a dark blue double-breasted naval jacket over the same color trousers. His crewmen wore light blue short-sleeved shirts with epaulettes on the shoulders and the same dark blue pants.

"Would you like coffee?" Roscani asked, at their obvious nervousness. "A cig—" Roscani caught himself, then grinned. "I was going to offer you a cigarette, but I have just quit smoking. In all this bedlam, I'm afraid that if I let you smoke, I might give in and join you."

Roscani smiled again and he could see the men relax. It was a calculated gesture on his part, designed for the effect it had, yet he wasn't so sure it wasn't the truth. Still, his admission had put the men at ease, and over the next twenty minutes he learned the particulars of the voyage from Como to Bellagio and was given detailed descriptions of the three men and the woman who had accompanied the man on the gurney. He also learned one other singular piece of information. The hydrofoil had been hired the day before the trip. It had been done through a travel agency in Milan at the behest of a Giovanni Scarso, a man claiming to represent the family of a man badly injured in an automobile accident who wanted him transported to Bellagio. Scarso had paid cash and left. It was only when they had approached Bellagio that one of the men accompanying the sick man had directed them away from the main landing and farther south, to the dock at Villa Lorenzi.

When the session had finished, there was no doubt in Roscani's mind that he had been told the truth and that the patient the crew of the hydrofoil had brought to Villa Lorenzi had indeed been Father Daniel Addison.

Turning to Castelletti and asking him to go over the details once more, Roscani thanked the captain and his crewmen and then left, pushing out from behind the curtain and walking back into the clamor of the war room. Then, as quickly, he left it.

Walking down a narrow corridor, he entered a lavatory, used the urinal, washed his hands, and splashed water on his face. And then, certain it was impossible in this situation to think without a cigarette, he pressed two fingers against his lips and inhaled deeply between them. Sucking in the phantom smoke, feeling the imagined rush of nicotine, finally he leaned back against the wall and used the *assoluta tranquillità* of the rest room to think.

This afternoon he and Scala and Castelletti and two dozen *carabinieri* had scoured every inch of Villa Lorenzi. Yet they had found nothing. Not a trace of Father Daniel or the people with him. That an ambulance might have been waiting somewhere on the villa's grounds and the party simply loaded their patient onboard and escaped was not possible, because Villa Lorenzi had only two access ways, the main driveway and a service road, and both were gated, with the gates operated from inside the villa. A vehicle could not enter or leave without the knowledge and assistance of someone inside. And, according to Mooi, this had not happened.

Of course, as cooperative as Mooi had seemed, he could have been lying. Moreover, there was always the possibility someone else had helped Father Daniel escape without Mooi's knowledge. And then there was the last, the possibility the priest was still there and hidden away and they had missed him.

Once again Roscani inhaled phantom smoke through his fingers, dragging deep into his lungs. At dawn, he and Scala and Castelletti along with a select force of *carabinieri* would go back to Villa Lorenzi unannounced and search again. This time they would take dogs, and this time they would leave nothing unturned, even if they had to dismantle the villa stone by stone to do it.

65

"CHIASSO . . . ," HERCULES SAID AS THEY MOVED away from Milan and up the A9 Autostrada in heavy summer traffic, his eyes intent on Harry at the wheel of the dark gray Fiat Adrianna had left parked across from the railroad terminal in Rome, the keys tossed under the left rear wheel as she'd promised.

Harry didn't respond. He was watching the road in front of him, his mind focused on getting to the city of Como, where he was to meet Adrianna; and then, somehow, across the lake to the town of Bellagio, where Danny presumably was.

"Chiasso," he heard Hercules say again, and he looked over abruptly to see the dwarf staring at him.

"What the hell are you talking about?"

"Did I help you get this far, Mr. Harry? Find your way out of Rome. Onto the Autostrada. Making you go north when you wanted to go south. . . . Without Hercules you would be coming up on Sicily, not Como."

"You were magnificent. I owe you everything I am today. But I still don't know what the hell you're talking about."

Harry suddenly cut right and in behind a fast-moving Mercedes. The drive was taking much too long.

"Chiasso is on the Swiss border. . . . I would like you to take me there. It's why I came."

"So that I would drive you to Switzerland?" Harry was incredulous.

"I am wanted for murder, Mr. Harry . . ."

"So am I."

"But I cannot put on the clothes of a priest and pass for someone else. Nor does a dwarf travel by bus or train unnoticed."

"But he could by private car."

Hercules smiled conspiratorially. "None had been available until now . . ."

Harry glared at him. "Hercules, this is not exactly a pleasure tour. I'm not on vacation."

"No, you are trying to get to your brother. And so are the police. On the other hand, Chiasso is hardly much farther than Como. I get out, you turn around and go back. Nothing to it."

"What if I said no?"

Hercules rose up indignantly. "Then you would be a man whose word cannot be trusted. When I gave you those clothes, I asked you to help me. You said, 'I will do the best I can. I promise you.'"

"I meant with the law and in Rome."

"Under the circumstances I think it would be more sensible for me to take the help now, Mr. Harry. An extra twenty minutes out of your life."

"Twenty minutes . . ."

"Then we are even."

"All right, then we're even."

Very shortly afterward they passed the Como exit, and very soon after that their agreement suddenly became moot. Ahead of them the traffic to Chiasso slowed, narrowing into one lane. Then it stopped. And Harry and Hercules stared into an endless succession of brake lights. Then, in the distance, they saw them. Flak-jacketed, Uzi-carrying policemen walking slowly toward them in the traffic, looking into each vehicle they passed.

"Turn around, Mr. Harry, Quick!"

Harry backed up a few feet, then slammed the Fiat into drive and, with a sharp squeal of tires, swung it in a sharp U-turn, accelerating back the way they had come.

"What the hell was that?" Harry glanced in the mirror.

Hercules said nothing, instead punching on the car's radio. A scan of stations found a newscaster rattling in Italian. The border at Chiasso was a massive police checkpoint, Hercules translated. Every vehicle was being turned inside out in the hunt for the fugitive priest, Father Daniel Addison, who had somehow eluded the police at Bellagio and was thought to be attempting a border crossing into Switzerland.

"Eluded them?" Harry turned to look at Hercules. "Does that mean somebody actually saw him?"

"They didn't say, Mr. Harry . . ."

66

Como. 7:40 P.M.

THE FIAT WAS STOPPED JUST OFF THE AUTO-
strada on the main road leading into Como. Hercules had
asked Harry to pull over, and Harry had. And now they sat
together for one last time, the soft yellow of the evening sky
filling the car with a delicate light and standing in sharp contrast to the harshness of the ongoing stream of bright headlights passing by outside.

"Police or no police, Chiasso is too close not to try. . . .
You understand, Mr. Harry . . ."

"I understand, Hercules. . . . I'm sorry I wasn't able to do
more . . ."

"Then good luck, Mr. Harry." Hercules smiled and suddenly put out his hand, and Harry took it.

"You, too . . ."

And like that, Hercules was out of the car and gone. Harry
watched for a moment as he crossed the street in the path of

oncoming traffic. At the far curb, he looked back and grinned, then swung away on his crutches into the growing twilight. Walking, if that was the word, to Switzerland.

Ten minutes later Harry parked the Fiat on a side street down from the railroad station and wiped the steering wheel and gearshift clean of his fingerprints with a handkerchief. Getting out carefully, locking the car, he made his way to Via Borsieri and then onto Viale Varese, following the street signs for the lake and for Piazza Cavour. He walked at the same pace as the people around him, trying to blend in, to seem nothing more than a priest out to enjoy the warm summer evening.

Now and again someone would nod or smile as he passed. And he would return the pleasantry, and then turn casually and glance back, make sure one of them hadn't recognized him or told others, or wasn't coming back for a closer look.

Crossing a square, watching the signs, he was suddenly aware of people walking more slowly, the crowd thickening. Ahead he could see people gathered at a news kiosk. As he neared, he saw Danny's face staring from the late editions. Each paper carried nearly the same headline:

SACERDOTE FUGGITIVO A BELLAGIO?
Was the fugitive priest in Bellagio?
Quickly he turned away and walked on.

Turning down one street and then another, Harry tried to follow the confusion of signs toward the lakefront and the Piazza Cavour. Dodging a chattering couple walking hand in hand, he turned a corner and stopped. The street directly ahead was blocked off by police barricades. Beyond them were police vehicles, media vans, and satellite trucks. Farther down he could see police headquarters.

"Christ." Harry waited a half second, then moved on, trying to regain his composure. Ahead was a cross street and he went left on a whim, certain he'd find himself back at the police barricades or the kiosk or even the railroad station. Instead he saw the lake, traffic flowing along the boulevard at its edge. Immediately in front of him was a street sign for the Piazza Cavour.

Another half block and he was on the boulevard. To his right was the Palace Hotel, a huge brownstone with a busy outdoor café in front. Festive music played. People ate and drank, white-aproned waiters moving among them. They were normal, everyday people, doing everyday things, yet never knowing how close they sat to a potential climax of the first order had but one of them recognized the bearded priest in the black beret walking past them and sounded the alarm. In seconds the street would be filled with police. It would be like an American action movie. A Gruppo Cardinale showdown with a cop killer, the outlaw brother of the assassin of the cardinal vicar of Rome. Flashing lights. Helicopters. Chiseled extras running everywhere with machine guns and flak jackets. A Lee Harvey Oswald ride at an amusement park. Watch the bad guy get it from all sides. Buy your tickets, be there when it happens.

But none of them did. And then Harry was gone, just someone else walking by. A moment later he turned a corner and entered Piazza Cavour. Directly ahead was the Hotel Barchetta Excelsior.

67

HARRY PRESSED THE BUZZER FOR ROOM 525 and waited, beret in hand, soaked with sweat. From his own rattled nerves as much as from the July heat. Still eighty-some degrees at almost sunset.

He started to push the buzzer again when the door abruptly opened and Adrianna stood there, hair wet from the shower, a white hotel bathrobe around her, a cell phone to her ear. Harry went in quickly, closing the door behind him and locking it.

"He's here now." Adrianna was at the window pulling the curtains, talking into the phone as she did. The television next to the window was on, tuned to the news channel, the sound off. Somebody was doing a standup in front of the White House. As quickly the scene shifted to the British Parliament.

Crossing to a dressing table, Adrianna bent in front of the mirror to scribble something on a notepad.

"Tonight, okay. . . . I have it. . . ."

Clicking off the phone, she looked up. Harry was watching her in the mirror.

"That was Eaton . . . ," he said.

"Yes." Adrianna turned to face him.

"Where the hell is Danny?"

"Nobody knows. . . ." Her gaze drifted off to the TV—always half watching in case something happened, an ongoing habit, the disease of a field reporter—then back to Harry. "Roscani and his men went over the villa in Bellagio where he was supposed to be with a toothbrush just a few hours ago. . . . They found nothing."

"The police are certain it was Danny, not somebody else."

"As certain as they can be without having been on the hydrofoil themselves. Roscani's back here, in Como, coordinating Gruppo Cardinale forces. They're not leaving. That should say enough in itself. . . ." Adrianna tucked a sprig of still-wet hair behind an ear. "You look like you're going to melt. You can take your jacket off, you know. You want a drink?"

"No."

"I will . . ."

Crossing to a console, Adrianna opened it and took out a small bottle of cognac. Pouring most of it into a glass, she turned back.

Harry stared at her. "What do I do next? How do I get to Bellagio?"

"You're angry with me, aren't you? About what happened in Rome, about bringing Eaton into this."

"Yes and no. But I could never have gotten this far without your help or Eaton's. You both stuck your necks out, for your own reasons, but you did anyway. . . . The sex just made me feel a little cozier about it. So why don't we just forget it and you tell me what I'm supposed to do . . ."

"All right. . . ." Adrianna watched him for a moment, then, glass in hand, leaned back against the dressing table.

"You're to take the late hydrofoil to Bellagio. Check into the Hotel Du Lac across the street from the boat landing. The reservations have been made—Father Jonathan Roe of Georgetown University. You'll have the phone number of the man who runs Villa Lorenzi. His name is Edward Mooi."

"I'm to call him?"

"Yes . . ."

"What makes you think he knows where Danny is?"

"Because the police think he does."

"Then they'll have his phone tapped."

"And—what are they going to hear?" Adrianna took a tug at her drink. "An American priest offering to help simply because he's seen the news coverage and would like to do anything he can . . ."

"If I were him, I'd think the call was a setup. A police sting."

"So would I, except that between now and when you phone him, he'll get a fax sent from a religious bookshop in Milan. He won't know what it means at the time—neither will the police if they intercept it because it will look like an advertisement—but Edward Mooi is an educated man, and after you call, he'll go back and find the fax and look at it again, even if he has to dig it out of the trash. When he does, he'll understand."

"What fax?"

Setting down her glass, Adrianna fished a sheet of paper from a battered leather traveling bag on the bed and handed it to him. Then, putting a hand on her hip, she leaned back against the dressing table. With the movement, her robe came open. Not a lot, but enough for Harry to see part of one breast and a hint of the dark where her legs came together.

"Read it . . ."

Harry hesitated, then glanced at the paper.

!Read!
"*GENESIS 4:9*"
A new book by
Father Jonathan Roe

That was all. Neatly typed. Nothing else.

"You remember your Bible, Harry. . . . Genesis 4:9—"

"Am I my brother's keeper?" Harry dropped the paper on the bed.

"He's an educated man. He'll understand."

"Then what?"

"We wait. . . . I'll be in Bellagio, Harry. Maybe even before you are." Adrianna's voice became soft, seductive. Her eyes found Harry's and held there. "And I'll know how to reach you. . . . The phone in your pocket, you know." She paused. "The way we—did it in Rome . . ."

For a long moment Harry said nothing, just stood looking at her. Finally, he let his eyes fall the length of her body.

"Your robe is open . . ."

"I know . . ."

HE TOOK HER FROM BEHIND, the way she liked, the way he had in her apartment in Rome. The difference this time was that the lights were on and they were in the bathroom standing up. With Adrianna bent slightly at the waist, her hands on the edge of the marble sink, both of them facing the mirror, watching.

He could see her pleasure as he came into her. Saw it

intensify all the more with each deliberate stroke. He could see himself behind her. His jaw set. Firm. Becoming more so as the force and rapidity of his thrusting increased. In a way it was indecent, seeing his own face. It was almost as if he were doing it to himself. Except he wasn't.

"Yes," she breathed. "Yes—"

With her sound, his own being faded and he saw only her as she threw back her head, her eyes closed, gripping him with her secret muscles, magnifying each stroke for both of them.

"More," she whispered. "More. Harder. Yes. Break me, Harry. Break me . . ."

He felt his pulse go up and the heat of her body grow against his. Both of them glistening with sweat. It was like before. In her bed in Rome. Spots danced in front of his eyes. His heart pounded. The sound of her breathing was like a roar overlapping the slap of their flesh as it came together. Again and again. And again. Then suddenly she cried out and he saw her head dip between her shoulders. At the same time he ejaculated. It felt like a cannon. One that kept on firing, round after round, all on its own, with no control at all. And then his knees buckled and he had to catch himself on the edge of the sink to keep from falling. And he knew there was nothing left.

For either of them.

68

LI WEN ENTERED AS HE ALWAYS DID, THROUGH the front door, heavy leather briefcase in one hand, identification badge clipped to the lapel of his jacket, nodding to the half-asleep Chinese Army security officer sitting at a table just beyond. Then, opening another door, he turned down a hallway and walked by the main control room, where a lone female engineer kept one eye loosely on a back wall of gauges and meters that measured, among other things, pressure, turbidity, flow rates, and chemical levels, and the other on a magazine she was reading.

"Good morning," Li Wen said with authority. Instantly the magazine disappeared.

"Everything is in order?"

"Yes, sir."

Li Wen stared at her a moment longer, letting her know he was not pleased with the magazine business. Then, with a definitive nod, he turned, pushed through a door and went down a long flight of steps to the filter area on the floor below, a long, concrete reinforced room where the final stages of filtration took place before the water was pumped into the clear well for outflow into the city's water mains. The area was below ground level and felt immediately cool compared to the heat and humidity of the outdoors and even of the upper level.

The plant had been shut down for nearly six months for up-grading three years earlier but still had no air-conditioning. That, it was said, would be left for the new plant, the one to be built after the turn of the century. It was the same with most water-treatment and -filtration plants throughout China. They were old, and most in disrepair. Some, like this one, had been upgraded when the great water wheel in Beijing finally turned and the central committee provided funds. Small funds with big promises for the future.

What was true was that in some places the future had already arrived; and new ventures with western construction and engineering firms, such as the Sino-French hundred-and-seventy-million-dollar drinking-water plant in the city of Guangzhou, or the massive thirty-six-billion-dollar Three Gorges dam project along the Yangtze River, were well under way. But in the main, water-delivery and water-filtration plants across China were old, some bordering on the ancient, with hollowed-out trees serving as conduit pipes, hobbling along at best.

And at certain times of the year—as now, in the middle of summer when the long hot days provided ideal growing conditions for sun-fed algae and its accompanying biological toxins—the filtration plants became nearly ineffectual, providing little more than putrid lake or river water to the taps of Chinese homes.

It was, of course, why Li Wen was here—to oversee the quality of water flowing from Chao Lake, Hefei's primary water source to the city of a million. It was a job he had been doing day in and day out for nearly eighteen years. Eighteen years of never realizing money could be made from it. Real money, enough to flee the country and at the same time wreak havoc against a government he despised; a government that in 1957 had branded his father a "counterrevolutionary" when he protested against the corruption and abuses of power inside the Communist Party and had imprisoned him in a labor camp, where he died three years later, when Li Wen was five. Li grew up revering his father's memory while dutifully caring for a mother who never recovered from her husband's death or the public scorn surrounding his imprisonment. Li Wen had become a hydrobiological engineer only because he had an aptitude for science and simply followed the path of least resistance. Outwardly he seemed soft and faceless, a man without passion or emotion. Inwardly, he burned with rage against the state, secretly belonging to a group of Taiwanese sympathizers dedicated to the overthrow of the Beijing regime, and to the return of Nationalist rule to the mainland.

Unmarried and always traveling, he counted as his closest friend Tong Qing, an uninhibited, twenty-five-year-old computer programmer-artist he had met two years earlier in an underground meeting in Nanjing. It was she who had introduced him to the persuasive flower merchant Chen Yin, whom he had liked immediately. Through Chen Yin's familial connections in the central government, he had been able to travel widely, a hydrobiologist visiting various water treatment plants in Europe and North America to see how other governments did things. And through Chen Yin he had met Thomas Kind, who had taken him to the villa outside Rome where he had briefly met the man on whose mission he now worked—a giant of a man who dressed as a priest and whose name he was never told, but a man of power and position who had a unique design for the future of the People's Republic.

That meeting alone set Li Wen's entire future in motion, making the past year more exhilarating than any he'd ever known. At last and finally, he would avenge his father's death and he would be paid handsomely to do it. And afterward, through Chen Yin, he would be spirited out of the country and into Canada, with a new identity and a new life. There to sit and watch gleefully as the years turned and the government that had robbed him of his childhood, the government he so profoundly abhorred, slowly crumbled at the hands of the ardent revolutionary from Rome.

SETTING HIS HEAVY BRIEFCASE on a wooden bench, Li Wen looked back across the room toward the door through which he had come in. Certain he was alone, he approached one of the four two-foot-square cutouts where he could look directly into the treated water being pumped into the city's water mains. The water ran fast, but instead of being clear as it was in the winter months, it was cloudy and putrid smelling, the result of the summer heat and the buildup of sun-fed algae in Lake Chao. This was the thing the government had done nothing about, and the thing he was counting on.

Turning, he went quickly back to his briefcase. Opening it, he slipped on a pair of thin surgical gloves and then opened its large, insulated, inner compartment. A half dozen frozen gray-white "snowballs" sat in what looked like a Styrofoam egg crate, their coats just beginning to melt, glistening in the overhead light.

Glancing again at the door, Li Wen picked the egg crate from the case and carried it to the cutouts above the flowing water. Picking up the first "snowball," he reached over the side and dropped it in, feeling a triumphant flutter of his heart as he did. Then quickly he did the same with the rest, dropping them in one by one, and watching them whirl away to vanish in the swift flow of murky water.

As quickly, he turned back, put the egg crate and gloves in his briefcase and closed it. Then crossing to the cutouts once more, he lifted a vial from a metal case on the wall and took a sample of the water, then quietly went about the business of testing for what he was certain was its government-acceptable "purity."

69

Bellagio, Lake Como, Italy.
Monday, July 13, 10:40 P.M.

HARRY PICKED UP THE SMALL SUITCASE
Adrianna had given him when he'd left the hotel in Como
and walked with the handful of other late-night passengers
off the hydrofoil and up the landing toward the street. Ahead
was the Navigazione Lago di Como ticket booth, unmanned
at this hour and overhung by the dense summer foliage of the
lakeside trees around it. Past it, he could see the lighted street
and across it the Hotel Du Lac. Another minute, two at the
most, and he would be there.

The trip from Como—with stops at the small towns of
Argegno, Lezzeno, Lenno, and Tremezzo—had been nerve-
wracking. At each stop Harry had fully expected armed
police to come onboard, checking the identity of travelers.
But none had. And finally, after the stop in Tremezzo, with

Bellagio next, Harry started to relax like the rest of the passengers. For the first time in as long as he could remember, there was no sense of danger. No sense of being hunted. Nothing but the sound of the motors and the rush of water under the hull.

It was the same now as he walked up the landing behind the others, the way he might as a tourist, another passenger walking off a boat and into a lazy summer's night. He was tired, he realized, emotionally and physically. He wanted to lie down and turn off the world and sleep for a week. But this was hardly the place. He was in Bellagio. The heart of the Gruppo Cardinale search. And it wasn't only Danny they were looking for. He needed to be more guarded and alert than ever.

"Mi scusi, Padre."

Two uniformed policemen suddenly stepped out of the darkness. They were young and had Uzis slung over their shoulders.

The first policeman stepped smartly in front of him. Harry stopped, and the other passengers pushed around him, leaving him alone with the police.

"Come si chiama?"—What is your name?—he asked.

Harry looked from one to the other. This was it. He either crossed the line and played the role Eaton had set for him, or he didn't.

"Come si chiama?"

He was still thin, more gaunt than the Harry Addison in the video. Still wore the beard in the passport photo. Maybe it was enough.

"I'm sorry," he said, smiling. "I don't speak Italian."

"Americano?"

"Yes." He smiled again.

"Step over here, please." The second policeman said in English. Harry followed them across the walkway and into the light of the boat-ticket booth.

"You have a passport?"

"Yes, of course."

Harry reached into his jacket, felt his fingers touch Eaton's passport. He hesitated.

"*Passaporto.*" The first policeman said, brusquely.

Slowly Harry took the passport out. Handed it to the policeman who spoke English. Then watched as one and then the other studied it. Across the street, almost within touching distance, was the hotel, the sidewalk café in front of it busy with nightlife.

"*Sacco.*"

The first officer nodded at his bag, and Harry gave it to him without hesitation. At the same time, he saw a police car pull up in front of the hotel and stop, the man at the wheel looking in their direction.

"Father Jonathan Roe." The second policeman closed Harry's passport and held it.

"Yes."

"How long have you been in Italy?"

Harry hesitated. If he said he'd been in Rome or Milan or Florence or anywhere else in Italy, they would ask where he had stayed. Any place he named, if he could even think of one, could be easily checked.

"I came in by train from Switzerland this afternoon."

Both policemen watched him carefully, but said nothing. He prayed they wouldn't demand a ticket stub or ask where he had been in Switzerland.

Finally, the second spoke. "Why have you come to Bellagio?"

"I'm a tourist. I've wanted to come here for years. . . . Finally"—he smiled—"got the chance."

"Where are you staying?"

"The Hotel Du Lac."

"It's late. Do you have a reservation?"

"One was made for me. I certainly hope so . . ."

The policemen continued to watch him, as if they weren't certain. Behind them he could see the driver of the police car watching, too. The moment was excruciating, yet there was nothing for him to do but stand there and wait for them to make the next move.

Suddenly the second policeman handed him his passport.

"Sorry to have bothered you, Father."

The first gave him his bag and then both stepped back, motioning for him to go on.

"Thank you," Harry said. Then, sliding the passport into his jacket, he shouldered the bag and walked past them and up to the street. Waiting for a motor scooter to pass, he crossed to the hotel, knowing all too well the men in the police car were still watching him.

At the front desk, as the night clerk approached to register him, he took the chance and looked back. As he did, the police car pulled away.

70

A HANDSOME MAN WITH CLEAR BLUE EYES sat at a back table along the sidewalk café of the Hotel Du Lac. He was in his late thirties and wore loose-fitting jeans and a light denim shirt. He had been there for most of the evening, relaxing, occasionally taking a sip from his beer, and watching the people pass by in front of him.

A waiter in a white shirt and black trousers stopped and gestured at his nearly empty glass.

"*Ja*," Thomas Jose Alvarez-Rios Kind said, and the waiter nodded and left.

Thomas Kind no longer looked as he had. His jet-black hair had been dyed strikingly blond as had his eyebrows. He seemed Scandinavian or an aging but still very fit California surfer. His passport, however, was Dutch. Frederick Voor, a computer software salesman who lived at 95 Bloemstraat, Amsterdam, was how he had registered at the Hotel Florence earlier that day.

Despite the Gruppo Cardinale's announcement some

three hours earlier that the fugitive American priest, Father Daniel Addison, was no longer being sought in Bellagio and that his reported sighting there had been deemed erroneous, the roads in and out of town were still being closely watched. It meant the police hadn't given up entirely. Nor had Thomas Kind. He sat where he did out of experience, observing the people who came and went from the hydrofoils as they landed. It was a basic concept that went back to his days as a young revolutionary and assassin in South America. Know who you were looking for. Choose a place he would most probably have to pass through. Then, taking with you the arts of observation and patience, go there and wait. And tonight, like so many times before, it had worked.

Of all the people who had passed by in the hours he had been there, the most interesting, by far, was the bearded priest in the black beret who had arrived on the late hydrofoil.

THE NEARLY BALD, middle-aged night porter opened the door to room 327, turned on a bedside lamp, then set Harry's bag on a luggage rack next to it and handed Harry the key.

"Thank you." Harry reached in his pocket for a tip.

"*No, Padre, grazie.*" The man smiled, then abruptly turned and left, pulling the door closed behind him as he did. Locking it—a habit now—Harry took a deep breath and glanced around the room. It was small and faced the lake. The furnishings were well used but hardly shabby. A double bed, chair, chest of drawers, writing table, a phone, and a television.

Pulling off his jacket, he went into the bathroom. Turning on the water, he let it run cold, then wet his hand and ran it over the back of his neck. Finally he raised his head and saw his face in the mirror. The eyes were not the same as those that had peered so intently into another mirror in what seemed a lifetime ago, watching as he made love to Adrianna; they were different, frightened, alone, yet somehow stronger and more determined.

Abruptly, he turned from the mirror and walked back into the room, glancing at his watch as he did.

11:10

Crossing to the bed, he opened the small suitcase Adrianna had given him. In it was something the police had overlooked in their hasty search of the bag. A page torn from a notepad of the Hotel Barchetta Excelsior in Como, with the telephone number of Edward Mooi.

Picking up the bedside phone, he hesitated, then dialed. He heard it ring. Once, twice. On the third, someone picked up.

"*Pronto,*" a male voice answered.

"Edward Mooi, please—I'm sorry to be calling so late."

There was a silence, then:

"This is Edward Mooi."

"My name is Father Jonathan Roe from Georgetown University. I'm an American. I just arrived in Bellagio."

"I don't understand . . ." The voice was guarded.

"It's about the hunt for Father Daniel Addison. . . . I've been watching television—"

"I don't know what you're talking about."

"As an American priest, I thought I might be able to help where others couldn't."

"I'm sorry, Father. I don't know anything. It's all been a mistake. If you'll excuse me . . ."

"I'm at the Hotel Du Lac. Room three-two-seven."

"Goodnight, Father."

CLICK.

Slowly Harry clicked off his own phone.

Harry heard the thinnest crackle of static just before Edward Mooi hung up. It confirmed what he had feared. The police had been listening.

71

Bellagio. Tuesday, July 14, 4:15 A.M.

NURSING SISTER ELENA VOSO STOOD IN
the grotto's main tunnel listening to the lap of water against
the granite walls, hoping Luca and the others would come
back.

Above her, the ceiling rose at least twenty feet, maybe
more. And the wide corridor beneath it stretched another
hundred to the canal and boat landing at the far end. Rudimentary benches, now fractured and worn by the years, had
been hacked out of the natural stone walls and ran the full
length of it on either side. Two hundred people could sit
there easily. She wondered if that had been the purpose for
cutting the benches in the first place, as a site for numbers of
people to hide. If so, who had done it, and when? The
Romans? Or peoples before them or after? Whatever its ori-
gin, the cave or really series of caves, as one chamber opened
onto another, was now wholly modern—with electricity, air

vents, plumbing, telephones, a small kitchen and large central living room, off of which ran at least three private suites, decorated luxuriously and complete with opulent baths, massage rooms, and sleeping quarters. Somewhere there, too, though she hadn't seen it, was what was supposedly one of the most extensive wine cellars in all of Europe.

They had been brought there Sunday night by the soft-spoken, erudite Edward Mooi, moments after their arrival at Villa Lorenzi. Alone and at the wheel of a sleek, shallow-bottomed motorboat, Mooi had taken them south in darkness. Hugging the lake's shoreline for a good ten minutes, he had finally turned in through a narrow cut in what seemed the solid wall of a sheer cliff, then navigated through a tangle of rocks and overhanging foliage into the mouth of the cave itself.

Once inside, he had turned on the boat's powerful searchlight and taken them through a maze of waterways until they reached the landing, a thirty-foot platform cut out of the stone at the far end of the tunnel where she stood. Then their supplies had been unloaded and she and Michael Roark brought to the suite where he was now, two large rooms—one, a bedroom where she slept, the other a small living-entertaining area where Michael Roark was settled—the spaces divided by an ornate bathroom cut from the cavern walls and inlaid with marble and accented with gold fixtures.

The cave, or *grotto,* Mooi had told them, was on property belonging to Villa Lorenzi and had been discovered years earlier by its celebrated owner, Eros Barbu. His first venture had been to turn it into an immense wine cellar, and then he'd added the apartments, the construction done by workers imported from a villa he owned in southern Mexico and afterward returned there. It was a way of keeping the cave's existence secret, especially from the locals. At age sixty-four,

Eros Barbu was not only a highly successful and distinguished author but was equally celebrated as a man whose legend mirrored his name; his subterranean grotto becoming an intimate and most discreet destination for erotic dalliance with some of the world's most beautiful and prominent women.

But whatever the grotto's history, for Elena it now held only fear and aloneness. She could still see Luca Fanari's eyes bulging in horror and rage as he took the call. His wife was dead, tortured, her body left to burn to cinders in a fire that ravaged the apartment where they had lived all of their married life. Moments after hanging up, Luca was gone, returning to Pescara for her funeral and to be with their three children. Marco and Pietro had gone with him.

"God bless you," she had told them as they left for Bellagio and the first hydrofoil to Como, taking the only transportation they had—a small, outboard-powered dinghy.

And now she was alone with Michael Roark sleeping in the room behind her, praying to hear the sound of the outboard coming back. But there was no sound other than the gentle lap of the water against the rock walls.

She was turning back for the room, determined her only course was to pick up the telephone and call her mother general in Siena, tell her what had happened and ask what she should do, when she heard the distant rumble of a motorboat echo off the grotto's walls.

Certain it was Luca and the others, she walked, nearly ran, down the corridor toward the landing. Then she saw the bright beam of the searchlight, heard the cut of the engines, and then the sleek hull of the flat-bottomed motorboat slid into view. It was Edward Mooi.

THREE OF THEM CAME OVER THE BOAT'S
gunwale. Edward Mooi and a man and woman Elena had
never seen before.

"The men have gone," she said quickly.

"I know." Mooi's look was intent as he introduced her to
the couple with him. They were trusted, longtime employees
of Eros Barbu and had come to stay with Michael Roark
while she went into Bellagio.

"Bellagio?" She was startled.

"I want you to meet someone—a priest from the United
States—and bring him here."

"Here, to the grotto?"

"Yes."

Elena glanced at the man and the woman, then looked
back to Edward Mooi. "Why me?—Why not go yourself?"

"Because we are known in Bellagio and you are not . . ."

Again Elena looked to the man and woman. Salvatore and
Marta, Edward Mooi had called them. They said nothing,

only stared back at her. They were probably in their fifties. Salvatore was tanned, the woman, Marta, was not. Which meant he probably worked outside at the villa, while she worked inside. Both wore wedding bands, but there was no way to tell if they were married to each other. It made no difference, their eyes told everything. They were frightened and apprehensive and at the same time alert and determined. Whatever Edward Mooi asked, they would do.

"Who is this priest?" Elena asked.

"A relative of Michael Roark," Edward Mooi said quietly.

"No, he is not." Elena had already made up her mind when she said it. There was no fear, only anger at not having been told earlier, by Luca or Marco or Pietro or by her own mother general.

"There *is* no Michael Roark, or if there is, the man in there is not him." She pointed off, back toward the room where her patient slept. "He is Father Daniel Addison, the Vatican priest wanted for the murder of Cardinal Parma."

"He is in danger, Sister Elena, that's why he's here . . ." —Edward Mooi spoke calmly—"why he was given a new identity and moved as he was . . ."

Elena stared at him. "Why are you protecting him?"

"We were asked . . ."

"By whom?"

"Eros Barbu . . ."

"A world-famous writer is safeguarding a murderer?"

Edward Mooi said nothing.

"Luca knew and the others? My mother general?" Elena stared, incredulous.

"I . . . don't know. . . ." Edward Mooi's eyes narrowed. "What I do know is that the police are watching everything we do. That's why I asked you to go into Bellagio. If any of us went and met this priest, they would either arrest us all on the spot or wait and see where we went."

"This priest," Sister Elena said, "is Father Addison's brother. Yes?"

"I think he is."

"And you want me to bring him here . . ."

Edward Mooi nodded. "By land there is another way in that I will show you . . ."

"What if, instead, I went to the police?"

"You don't know for certain Father Daniel is a murderer. . . . And I have seen how you care for him. . . ." Edward Mooi's eyes were those of a poet. Fierce, yet at the same time trusting and sincere. "He is your charge, you will not go to the police."

Villa Lorenzi. 6:00 A.M.

HAIR DISHEVELED, BAREFOOT, AND IN A BATH-robe, Edward Mooi stood in the doorway of the caretaker's cottage and simply shrugged his shoulders, letting Roscani and his army—Gruppo Cardinale special agents, heavily armed uniformed *carabinieri*, along with an Italian army canine unit, five Belgian Malinois dogs and their handlers—have their second run at Villa Lorenzi.

Again they searched the palace-like main house, the adjoining sixteen-bedroom guest wing, the wing opposite, which was Eros Barbu's private quarters, the basements and sub-basements. The Malinois led them everywhere, hunting the scent of clothing flown in from Rome, and taken from Father Daniel's apartment on Via Ombrellari and from Harry Addison's belongings left behind at the Hotel Hassler.

Afterward they combed the huge domed structure behind the main residence, which housed the indoor swimming pool and tennis courts and, on the second floor, the immense, gilt-ceilinged, grand ballroom. And then the eight-car garage, the servants' apartments, the twin, single-story maintenance buildings, and finally, the three-quarter-acre greenhouse.

Roscani walked through it all. Tie loosened, shirt open at the collar against the early heat. One room after another, one building after another, directing the operation, alert to the actions of the dogs, opening closet doors himself, looking for access panels, looking between walls, under floors—his personal attention given to everything. At the same time his mind kept coming back to the murders in Pescara and the man with the ice pick. Who he was, might be. And in that, he sent an urgent request to INTERPOL headquarters in Lyon, France, for a list of terrorists and killers still at large thought to be in Europe; the list to include suspected whereabouts and, where possible, a personality profile.

"HAVE YOU SEEN ENOUGH, Ispettore Capo?" Edward Mooi was still in his bathrobe.

Roscani looked up, suddenly aware of where he was and of both men standing at the top of a flight of stairs inside Villa Lorenzi's boathouse. Outside, the morning sun painted a bright, shimmering surface across the still of the lake, while below, in semidarkness, two of the Belgian Malinois sniffed and grumbled at the gunwales of a large motorboat moored at the dock, their handlers letting them do as they pleased, four armed *carabinieri* watching closely as they did. Roscani turned to watch, and so did Edward Mooi, Roscani glancing at the South African as he did.

Finally the dogs gave up, one after the other, walking lazily around the dock sniffing at nothing. One of the handlers looked up and shook his head.

"*Grazie, Signore,*" Roscani said to Edward Mooi.

"Prego," Mooi nodded, then walked out and back along the path toward the villa.

"That's all," Roscani called to the dog handlers, and watched as they and their animals and the four *carabinieri* climbed the stairs, following in the direction Edward Mooi had gone, toward the house and the convoy of parked police vehicles.

Slowly Roscani started up the path after them. They had been there for more than two hours and nothing had been found. Two hours wasted. If he was wrong, he was wrong. And he needed to leave it and move on. Still—

Turning, he looked back. There was the boathouse and beyond it the lake. To his right he could see the dogs and the armed *carabinieri* almost to the villa. Edward Mooi was out of sight.

What had he missed?

To the left of the villa, between it and the boathouse was the stone landing with its ornate balustrade where the hydrofoil captain had said he put the fugitive priest and the others ashore.

Once again Roscani looked to the boathouse. Absently his fingers went to his mouth, and he took a pull from his phantom cigarette. Then, his eyes still on the boathouse, he dropped the imaginary cigarette, ground it out with his toe, and walked back and went inside.

From the top of the stairs he saw nothing but the motorboat moored to the dock below and the equipment needed to tend it. At the far end, the rectangular opening to the lake. The same as before.

Finally, he went down the stairs and walked along the dock beside the boat. Bow to stern. Stern to bow. Looking. For what, he didn't know. Then he climbed onboard. Studied the interior of the hull, the seats, the cockpit. The dogs had complained but found nothing. He could see nothing. A boat was a boat, and he was wasting his time. He was about to step over the side and back onto the dock, when he had one last thought. Crossing to the stern, he looked down at the twin Yamaha outboard engines. Kneeling, he reached over the side and gingerly ran his hand down the lower leg of each, touching the side panels between the power head and the water where the exhaust line ran.

Both were warm.

74

8:00 A.M.

ELENA VOSO CROSSED THE SQUARE AND started down the steps toward the lake. Shops catering mainly to tourists lined either side of the walkway down. Most of them were already open. Salespeople and customers alike, cheery, smiling, seeming happy about the prospects for the day.

In front of her Elena could see the lake. Boats criss-crossed on it. Across the street at the bottom of the stairs she could see the hydrofoil landing, and she wondered if the first hydrofoil had come yet, if Luca and Marco and Pietro were already in Como or maybe at the station, waiting for the train to Milan. At the bottom of the stairs was something else too—the Hotel Du Lac—and even now she wasn't certain what she would do when she got there.

After Edward Mooi left the grotto in the motorboat, Elena had taken Salvatore and Marta to where Michael Roark, or—and now she had to think of him this way—Father Daniel, was. He had been awake and moved up on one elbow, watching as they came in. Elena had introduced Salvatore and Marta as friends, saying she had to leave for a short while and they would care for him until she got back. Even though he was beginning to regain full use of his vocal chords and could talk for short periods of time, Father Daniel had said nothing. Instead his eyes had searched hers, as if somehow he knew she had found out who he was.

"You will be all right," she'd said finally and left him with Marta, who had mentioned that his bandages should be changed and said that she would do it herself, indicating she had some training in medical care.

And then Salvatore had led Elena into a part of the caves she had not seen before. A twisting, turning route through a series of stone corridors ending, finally, at a cage-like service elevator that took them up several hundred feet through a natural cut in the granite.

At the top they had emerged into a heavy thicket and walked down a forest path to a fire road. There Salvatore had helped her into a small farm truck, told her how to get to Bellagio and what to do once she reached it.

Well, now she had reached it and was almost to the bottom of the steps across from the Hotel Du Lac when she saw them—police. They were right in front of her—an ambulance and three police cars and a crowd of onlookers directly across the street near the boat landing at the edge of the lake. To her left was the little park with the public telephone she had been instructed to use to call Father Daniel's brother at the hotel.

"Someone drowned," she heard a woman say, and then other people pushed past her, coming down the steps, rushing to see what had happened

Elena watched for a moment, then glanced toward the telephones. Father Daniel was in her care, Edward Mooi had said. Maybe so, but reason told her that when she got the chance she should go directly to the police. Whether her mother general knew what was going on made no difference. Nor was it her business what Father Daniel had done or had not done. That was what the law was for. He was wanted for murder and so was his brother. There were the police. All she had to do was go.

And she did, moving away from the phones, crossing the street toward them. As she reached the far curb, a loud noise went up from the crowd at the water's edge. More people hurried past, anxious to see what was going on.

"Look!" someone said, and Elena saw police divers in the water near the boat landing lift a body from the lake. Policemen onshore hefted it from them and put it down on the landing. Another rushed to throw a blanket over it.

That breathless moment in time, that uncounted second, when the public glimpses the suddenly dead and becomes instantly silent, froze Elena Voso where she stood. The body fished from the lake was that of a man.

Luca Fanari.

75

HARRY WATCHED THE POLICE AND THE CROWD across the street a moment longer, then turned from his hotel room window to look back at the television. Adrianna in her L. L. Bean field jacket and baseball cap stood in a pouring rain outside the Geneva headquarters of the World Health Organization. A major story was coming, piecemeal, from mainland China. Unofficial reports from the city of Hefei in eastern China indicated that a major incident had taken place concerning the area's public water supply—thousands of people were rumored to have been poisoned and more than six thousand were already dead. Both Xinhua, the New China News Agency, and the Chinese Central Broadcasting Bureau dismissed the reports as unfounded.

Abruptly Harry hit the MUTE button and Adrianna was silenced. What the hell was she doing in Geneva reporting on an "unfounded" incident?

Unsettled, he glanced back out the window. Then at the bedside clock.

8:20 A.M.

No calls. Nothing. What had happened to Edward Mooi? Had he not reread the fax? And now Adrianna was in Geneva when she should have been in Bellagio. Crazily, he felt abandoned. Left in a tiny hotel room while the world went on.

He turned back to the window. As he did, a police car pulled up directly across the street. The doors opened, and three men in plainclothes got out and headed for the boat landing. Harry's heart stopped. The man walking first, leading the others, was Roscani.

"Jesus." Instinctively he twisted back from the window. At almost the same instant there was a knock at the door. Every nerve stiffened. The knock came again.

Quickly he went to the bed, opened the suitcase, and took out the sheet of paper with Edward Mooi's telephone number. Ripping it in pieces he went into the bathroom and flushed it down the toilet.

The knock came once more. Softer this time. Not the authoritative strike of the police. Eaton—of course. Harry relaxed, then walked to the door and opened it.

A young nun stood there.

"Father Roe?"

Harry hesitated. "Yes . . ."

"I am nursing sister Elena Voso . . ." Her English was accented with Italian but clear nonetheless.

Harry stared, unsure.

"I would like to come in."

He looked past her to the hallway. He saw no one.

"All right . . ."

Harry stepped back as she came in, then watched her turn and close the door behind her.

"You phoned Edward Mooi," Elena said, carefully.

Harry nodded.

"I've come to take you to your brother . . ."

Harry stared. "I don't understand . . ."

"It's all right. . . ." She could feel his caution, see his uncertainty. "I'm not with the police . . ."

"I'm sorry, I don't know what you're talking about."

"If you are not sure . . . follow me out. I will be waiting on the steps leading up to the village. Your brother is ill. . . . Please . . . Mr. Addison."

Harry nodded.

"I've come to take you to your brother."

Harry stared. "I don't understand."

"It's all right . . ." She could feel his caution, see his uncertainty. "I'm not sure, either. Please—"

"I'm sorry, I don't know what you are talking about."

"If you are not sure, then do not. But I will be waiting on the steps leading up to the village. Your brother is ill. Please . . . Mr. Addison—"

76

HARRY TOOK HER DOWN A BACK STAIRWAY.
At the ground floor, he opened the door to a rear hallway.

USCITA. Exit, the sign read. An arrow pointed off. Harry hesitated—he wanted to go out a rear or side door, anything but through the front and out onto the street where Roscani was. But there was only one sign, and he followed it, moving them off in the direction the arrow pointed. A minute later they pushed through a door and into the hotel lobby with the front door directly in front of them.

"Damn it," Harry breathed. People were at the front desk, checking in or out. Past them, a rotund man was in animated conversation with the concierge. Harry looked back. If there was another exit he had no idea how to find it. Just then the elevator doors opened, and two couples and a porter pushing a luggage cart came toward them. If they were going out, this was the time.

Taking Elena's arm, Harry timed his move to keep in step with the porter. As they reached the door he motioned for the man to go ahead. The porter nodded and pushed the luggage cart through. Harry and Elena came out just behind. The sunlight hit, and Harry turned them abruptly left along the sidewalk, walking with other pedestrians.

"*Buon giorno.*" A man tipped his hat. A young couple smiled at them. They kept on.

"Go up the steps to the left," Elena said calmly.

Then Harry saw Roscani coming up the walk from the water, the same way Harry had come last night. He was walking quickly, the other two plainclothes policemen at his heels. Harry moved closer to Elena, keeping her between himself and the police.

They were almost to the corner now, and Harry could see the steps Elena was talking about. Suddenly Roscani looked up. Directly at him. In the same instant, Elena began talking in Italian. He had no idea what she was saying. But she gestured ahead, using her hands, talking as if what they were doing and where they were going was hugely important. At the steps, she turned him abruptly left and up, still talking, sounding now as if she were scolding him, then, as quickly, smiling at an elderly man coming down the steps toward them.

Then they were in a mix of people on the stairs. Winding their way through them, passing shops and restaurants. It was only when they had reached the top that Harry looked back. Nothing. No police. No Roscani. Just shoppers. Civilians.

"Those men coming up from the landing were police," Elena said.

"I know." Harry looked at her as they moved on, wondering who she was, and why she was doing this.

77

9:10 A.M.

GRINDING GEARS, HARRY TURNED A CORNER, then, gritting his teeth, shifted again and accelerated down a narrow street. The farm truck was old and cranky, its clutch and manual shift worn and difficult. Crunching the gear box once more, he turned past a park, and then they were out of the city.

"Tell me about my brother." He took his eyes from the road and looked at Elena, calculating, to see if she really knew.

"His legs are broken, and he has been burned over parts of his head and upper body. He suffered a very serious concussion. But he is better now, and is beginning to take solid food and can talk a little. His memory comes and goes, which is normal. He's weak but is healing. I think he will be all right."

Danny was *alive!* Harry felt the breath go out of him. A rush of emotion followed, as the reality of it hit home. Suddenly he looked at the road in front of them. Cars were slowing, coming to a stop.

"Carabinieri," Elena said.

Harry's hand went to the shift lever. Immediately there was a loud wrench of grinding gears as he downshifted, coming to a halt inches behind a white Lancia stopped in a clog of vehicles pulled up at the police checkpoint.

Two uniformed *carabinieri* armed with Uzis checked each car as it came abreast and stopped. Two others stood to the side watching.

Now the car ahead of them was waved through, and Harry ground the truck into gear. It bucked raggedly forward, bouncing to a stop only after one of the *carabinieri* had jumped out of the way, yelling for Harry to halt.

"Jesus Christ."

The *carabinieri* came up, one on either side.

Harry glanced at Elena. "Talk to them. Say anything."

"Buon giorno." The *carabinieri* glared at Harry.

"Buon giorno." Harry smiled and Elena began. Speaking rapid-fire Italian. Gesturing between herself and Harry and the truck, talking to both policemen at once. In a matter of seconds it was over. The *carabinieri* stood smartly back, saluted, and waved them through. And with a grinding of gears and a sharp backfire, Harry steered past them, leaving all four police turning away in a cloud of blue smoke.

Harry watched the mirror, then looked to Elena.

"What did you tell them?"

"That the truck was borrowed and that we were on our way to a funeral and were late. . . . I hope it's not so . . ."

"So do I."

Harry looked back to the highway as it began to rise toward the distant cliffs, then instinctively glanced in the mirror. There was nothing but the checkpoint and vehicles being waved through one by one.

Slowly Harry took his eyes from the mirror and looked to Elena. She was staring at the road ahead, quiet, even introspective. Suddenly she turned and looked at him, as if she knew what he was thinking and was about to ask.

"Your brother's care was assigned to me by my convent."

"You mean you knew who he was? . . ."

"No."

"Did the people at your convent?"

"I—don't know . . ."

"You don't?"

"No."

Harry looked back to the road. She certainly knew who Danny was now. And she knew who Harry was, and still she had put herself in all kinds of potential trouble tap-dancing them through the police.

"You mind if I ask what seems like a silly question? . . . Why are you doing this?"

"That is something I have been asking myself, Mr. Addison. . . ." She glanced down the road and then back to Harry, her brown eyes suddenly intense and penetrating.

"You should know that when I came to Bellagio I was going to go to the police. To tell them about you and about your brother. And I almost did—except . . . the body they pulled from the lake in front of your hotel was that of a man who helped bring your brother to where he is. . . . Only hours ago he learned his wife had been murdered, and he left immediately to go back to his home. . . ." Elena paused, as if the memory of what she had seen was too heinous to talk about. Then Harry saw her gather strength, and she went on.

"They said he drowned. I don't know if that's true. . . . There were two other men with him. . . . I don't know where they are or what happened to them. . . . In result, I—made up my mind . . ."

"About what? . . ."

Elena hesitated. ". . . About my own future, Mr. Addison. . . . God gave me a job to do caring for your brother. . . . No matter what else has happened, it is something He has yet to dismiss me from. . . . The decision was really quite simple. . . ." Elena's eyes held on Harry, then she looked back down the road. "Those trees ahead—just past them is a dirt road to the right. Please take it."

78

10:15 A.M.

EDWARD MOOI STOOD NAKED, TOWEL IN HAND. Dripping from the bath.

"Who are you? What do you want?"

He had not heard the door open or had any idea how the blond man in jeans and light jacket had found his way to the second-floor apartment. Or how he had gotten past the Gruppo Cardinale police still outside and into the building. Or even onto the grounds of Villa Lorenzi, for that matter.

"I want you to take me to the priest," the blond man said quietly.

"Get out of here, now! Or I will call security!" Edward Mooi pulled the towel around him angrily.

"I don't think so." The blond man took something from his jacket pocket and set it on the white porcelain sink next to the poet.

"What am I supposed to do with that?" Mooi looked at what had been set on the sink. Whatever it was was wrapped in what looked like a dark green restaurant napkin.

"Open it."

Edward Mooi stared at him, then slowly picked up the napkin and unwrapped it.

"Oh, Lord!"

Heinously blue. Bloodied. Grossly swollen with bits of the green napkin fiber clinging to it—a neatly severed human tongue. Half gagging, Mooi threw it into the sink and backed away, terrified.

"Who are you?"

"The ambulance driver didn't want to talk about the priest. Instead he wanted to fight." The blond man's eyes were on his. "You are not a fighter. The television says you are a poet. That makes you an intelligent man. Which is why I know you will do as I ask and take me to the priest."

Edward Mooi stared. *This* was who they had been hiding Father Daniel from.

"There are too many police. We will never get past them—"

"We will see what we can do, Edward Mooi."

ROSCANI LOOKED AT THE OBJECT—or objects—intertwined in a single water-sodden mass of blood, flesh, and clothing pulled from the lake, discovered by the elderly owner of the villa on whose manicured grounds they now stood, while the tech-team people took photographs, made notes, interviewed the man who had come upon it.

Who could tell who they were, or had been? Except Roscani knew; so did Scala and Castelletti. They were the others—two, it looked like—who had been onboard the hydrofoil that brought Father Addison to Villa Lorenzi.

Damn, Roscani wanted a cigarette. Thought about bumming one from one of his detectives. Instead he pulled out a foil-wrapped chocolate biscuit from his jacket, unwrapped it and bit off a piece, then walked away. He had no idea how the men here were butchered, except that they were—butchered. And he would bet a year's cache of chocolate biscuits that it was the work of the man with the ice pick.

Moving to the water's edge, he stared out at the lake. He was missing something. Something of what had happened should be telling him something.

"Mother of God!" Roscani turned quickly and started back across the lawn toward the car. "Let's go! Now!"

Immediately Scala and Castelletti left the tech crew to follow him.

Roscani was walking, half running as he reached the car. Getting in, he snatched the radio from the car's dashboard. "This is Roscani. I want Edward Mooi taken into protective custody right now! We're on our way."

An instant later Scala swung the car in a wide arc, spewing gravel over the freshly cut lawn. Roscani was beside him. Castelletti in back. No one said a word.

79

10:50 A.M.

HARRY WATCHED AND LISTENED AS THE
sunlight faded to shadow and then darkness, and the wood-
and-steel cage lowered, creaking, between the rock walls.
Down there, somewhere, was Danny. Above was the dirt road
through the trees and the farm truck they had left hidden in the
brush near the edge of the wooded circle at the end of it.

One minute passed. Then two. Then three. The only
sounds were the creak of the cage and the distant hum of the
electric motor as the lift descended and they passed the occasional safety lamp mounted in the rock. With the coming and
going of the light, Harry could see the quiet nuance of
Elena's body under her habit, the strength of her neck held
high above her shoulders, the soft sweep of her cheek punc-
tuated by the angular bridge of her nose, a before unseen
sparkle in her eyes. Then suddenly something shifted his

attention away from Elena. It was an odor of mossy damp-
ness. Pungent and vividly familiar. One he hadn't smelled in
years.

Instantly he was transported to the afternoon of his thirteenth birthday. He was wandering alone in the woods after
school—woods with the exact same mossy-wet smell that
surrounded him now. Life had taken them all in a rush. In less
than two years he and Danny had lost their sister and father
to tragic accidents and seen their mother remarry and move
them into a house of chaos with a distant husband and five
other children. Birthdays, like other things personal, became
lost in a tide of confusion, uncertainty, and readjustment.

And though he tried not to show it, Harry was as lost and
dangling. Eldest son, older brother, he was expected to be
the leader of the household. But of which household, when
there were already two older boys in his adopted family who
seemed to run everything?

The whole thing made him reticent, afraid to step in any
direction for fear something else would happen and things
would become even worse than they were. The result was
that he quietly withdrew. With few friends in the school they
had been transferred to, he kept more and more to his own
company, reading mostly, or watching TV when someone
else wasn't, or, more often, just wandering as he was now.

This day was especially difficult—his thirteenth birthday,
the day he was officially a teenager and no longer a child. He
knew there would be no celebration at home—he doubted
the others even knew it was his birthday; the best he might
get in recognition would be a present or two from his mother
given to him with Danny there in her room, away from the
others and just before bedtime. It was, he understood, that
she was as lost herself, and simply afraid to single out her
own children in a much larger household and in front of a

husband she felt beholden to. Still, it made the celebration of his birth seem secretive and forbidden. As if he were hardly worth it, or, worse, as if he existed in name only. So the best he could do was wander in the woods and let the day pass, trying not to think about it.

That was—until he saw the rock.

Away from the trail and half hidden by brush, it caught his attention because something was written on it. Curious, he climbed over a log and approached it, pushing foliage aside as he went. When he reached it, he saw what was written—large, clear words freshly scratched in chalk.

WHO I AM IS ME

Instinctively he looked around to see if the person who had written it was nearby and watching. But he saw no one. Turning back, he studied the words again. And the longer he looked, the more he became convinced they had been put there solely for him. For the rest of the day and into the night he thought about it. Finally, just before he went to bed, he wrote them down in his school notebook. And when he did, they became his alone. It was his "Declaration of Independence." And in that one, single, momentous instant, he realized he was free.

WHO I AM IS ME

Who he was and what he became were in his hands and no one else's. And he determined to keep it that way, promising himself never to have to rely on anyone else again.

And mostly it had worked.

*   *   *

SUDDENLY BRIGHT FLUORESCENT light hit Harry in the face, jolting him from his memory. Immediately there was a solid bump as the cage touched the bottom of the shaft and stopped.

Looking up, he saw Elena staring at him.

"What is it?"

"You should know your brother is deathly thin. Don't be afraid when you see him . . ."

"All right . . ." Harry nodded, then reached forward and pulled the cage door open.

HE FOLLOWED HER QUICKLY down a series of narrow passageways lit on either side by ornate bronze sconces and marked on the floor by a line of green Athenian marble that showed the way. Above them, the ceiling heights rose and fell without warning, and more than once Harry had to hunch over just to get through.

Finally a course of short, abrupt turns brought them into what looked like a central corridor, long and wide, with benches cut into the ancient stone the length of it. Turning them left, Elena walked another twenty feet and stopped at a closed door. Knocking lightly, saying something in Italian, she pushed through.

Salvatore and Marta stood up suddenly as they entered. And then Harry saw him. Partway across the room. Asleep on a bed facing them. An IV strung from a rack above it. Gauze bandages covering part of his head and upper body. He was bearded like Harry. And, as Elena had warned, frightfully thin.

Danny.

80

HARRY APPROACHED THE BED SLOWLY AND looked down at his brother. There was no doubt who it was, no chance it could be someone else. The years they had gone without seeing each other, or how physically changed he was now, made no difference. It was a feeling, a familiarity, that went back to childhood. Reaching out, he felt Danny's hand. It was warm, but there was no reflex to his touch.

"Signore." Marta moved forward to Harry, looking at Elena as she did. "I . . . we had to sedate him."

Elena turned quickly, concerned.

"After you left he became frightened," Salvatore said in Italian, looking from Harry to Elena. "He pulled himself out of bed, was crawling out toward the water, dragging his legs when he found him. He wouldn't listen. I tried to pick him up, but he fought me. I was afraid he would hurt himself if I let him go . . . or drown if he fell into the water. . . . You had medicine here, and a hypodermic, my wife knew what to do."

"It's all right," Elena said quietly, then told Harry what had happened.

Harry looked back toward his brother, and slowly a grin crept over him. "Still the same tough little cookie, aren't you?" He looked back to Elena. "How long will he be knocked out?"

"How much did you give him?" Elena asked Marta in Italian. Marta told her and Elena looked back. "An hour, maybe a little more . . ."

"We have to get him out of here."

"Where?" Elena looked to Marta and Salvatore. "One of the men who brought Father Daniel was found drowned in the lake."

There was an audible sound as the couple reacted. Elena turned back to Harry.

"I don't believe he drowned on his own. I think the same person who killed his wife is here looking for your brother. So for now it is best we stay here. I know of nowhere else he would be as safe."

EDWARD MOOI guided the motorboat between the rocks and into the grotto entrance. Once inside, he turned on the searchlight.

"Put it out!" Thomas Kind's eyes flashed viciously in the bright light.

Immediately Edward Mooi touched a switch, and the light went out. At the same instant he felt something nick his ear. Crying out, he drew back, putting his hand to it. Blood.

"A razor, Edward Mooi. . . . The same one used for the tongue in your shirt pocket."

Mooi could feel his hand on the wheel and the lump in his shirt pocket where Thomas Kind had stuck the severed tongue as a reminder. He could sense too the familiar rocks as they slipped past on either side. He was going to die anyway. Why had he brought this madman here? He could have yelled for the police and run and taken his chances. But he had not. It was out of total fear and nothing else that he had done the man's bidding.

His life had been given to words and the creation of poetry. Reading his work, Eros Barbu had rescued him from a nothing life as a recorder of public records in South Africa, given him a place to live and a means to continue working. In return he asked only that he take care of the villa as best he could. And he had, and little by little his work had become known.

And then, at what was nearly the end of his seventh year at Villa Lorenzi, Barbu had made one more request. Protect a man who was coming by hydrofoil. He could have refused, but he did not. And because he had not, both he and that man were about to lose their lives.

Edward Mooi nosed the motorboat around a stand of rock in the dark. One hundred yards. Two more turns and they would see the lights and then the landing. The water here was deep and still. Slowly the poet's long black thumb reached up and flipped the emergency "kill" switch. The Yamaha outboards went silent.

The final action in the life of Edward Mooi was extraordinarily brief. His left hand pressing the motorboat's warning siren. His right pushing him up and over the side. The move of the razor across his throat as he fell was like silk. It mattered not. His prayers had been said.

SALVATORE HAD LEFT FATHER DANIEL'S chamber at the first scream of the boat siren, running down the central passageway toward the landing. When he saw only the dark of the channel and heard nothing more, he came back.

They must leave immediately, he said in Italian. Other than Eros Barbu himself, only Edward Mooi knew how to bring a boat in through the channels, and the boat had not come. The siren had been a signal, a warning.

If it had been the police Mooi was warning them about, they would have been there by now—Roscani and an army of Gruppo Cardinale people with him—and the media close behind. But since the boat siren, there had been only silence. So Mooi was telling them something else.

"Salvatore is right." Harry was suddenly looking at Elena. "We have to get out. And now."

"How? We can't take your brother up the elevator. Even if we could get him there, the cage is too small."

"Ask Salvatore if there is another boat."

"I don't have to ask. There is not. Luca and the others took the only one there was."

"Ask him anyway!" Harry could feel time closing in. "A raft. A float. Anything we can put Danny on to take him out by water."

Elena looked to Salvatore and repeated Harry's plea in Italian.

"*Forse,*" Salvatore said. "*Forse.*"

Maybe.

82

IT WASN'T A BOAT SO MUCH AS AN ALUMINUM skiff, flat bottomed, twelve feet long and five feet wide, and designed to be towed behind a boat to haul supplies or to take away garbage. Salvatore had found it near a smaller landing, around a turn in the canal, a hundred or more yards down from the first, propped up against a wall just outside a heavy door that led to Eros Barbu's legendary wine cellar. With it were two oars, and Harry and Salvatore carried it to the water and put it in, securing it to the landing with a rope.

Then Harry stepped in and tested it.

It floated, didn't leak, and held his weight. Bending, he set the oarlocks into place and slid the oars into them. "Okay, let's get him in."

Salvatore pushed the gurney forward, then he and Harry hefted it into the skiff, setting it sideways across the stern. Next, he handed Harry a bag holding a minimum of medical supplies. Then Harry helped Elena in and looked expectantly to Salvatore, but the Italian and his wife stepped back.

The skiff was too small for all of them, he said, Elena translating. There were markings on the walls high above the waterlines that would guide them out of the tunnels. Follow those and they would be all right.

"What about you?" Harry looked at Salvatore with concern.

Salvatore and Marta would ride the cage back up. Again Elena translated. They would meet them with the farm truck at a cove farther south on the lake. Glancing at Elena, he explained how to find it. Finally he looked back to Harry.

"*Arrivederci,*" he said, almost apologetically, as if he were abandoning them. Then he quickly took Marta's hand, and the two disappeared back into the cave.

83

THE NOTCHES WERE CUT INTO THE CAVERN

walls above the waterline, as Salvatore had said. Elena stood in the bow playing the beam of a flashlight on them as Harry rowed the skiff slowly down the channel.

Harry worked from the center, his back to Elena, his concentration on the oars, trying to keep them silent as they lifted from the water and then dropped back in.

"Listen—" Elena clicked off the flashlight.

Harry stopped, oars raised, the boat drifting. But he heard nothing other than the soft lapping of water against the rock walls as the skiff slid past.

"What was it?" Harry's voice was barely a whisper.

"I. . . . There—"

This time he heard it. A distant rumbling, the sound reverberating off the walls. Then it stopped.

"What is it?"

"Outboard motors. Run for a few seconds, then shut off."

"Who?"

"Whoever Edward Mooi warned us about. They're here, in the canals . . . trying to find us . . ."

Hefei, China. City of Hefei Water
Filtration Plant "A."
Still Tuesday, July 14, 6:30 P.M.

Li Wen stood back, calmly watching the people hover around the wall of gauges and meters measuring the pressure, turbidity, flow rates, and chemical levels. Why they were still standing there, he had no idea. The gauges and meters were still. The plant had been shut down completely. Nothing moved.

Zhu Yubing, governor of Anhui Province, merely stared, as did Mou Qiyan, deputy director of Anhui Province Water Conservancy and Power Department. The angry words, the accusations, had been made as the official word was given— Chao Lake had not been poisoned deliberately, by accident, by terrorists, or by anyone else; nor was pollution, caused by untreated water discharged from local farms and factories, the cause of the catastrophe; sun-fed algae, with its production of biological toxins, was. Both men had complained for years that this was a time bomb that had to be defused, a dangerous problem that had to be solved. But it never was. And now they stood in shock at this incredible horror. Putrid and deadly water pouring from the city taps like a plague before it had been shut off. The sheer numbers were beyond belief.

Chao Lake, water supply to nearly a million. In the last ten hours: Twenty-seven thousand, five hundred and eight confirmed dead. Another fifty-five thousand seriously ill. Thousands who ingested the water in common everyday circumstances still unaccounted for. The toll in sickness and death was mounting by the minute. And little could be done, even by the Chinese Army disaster teams, except take away the dead. And wait and count. The same as Li Wen watched them do now.

Lake Como, Italy. Same time.

The only sound was the lap of water against the rock. That and Danny's regular breathing. Elena stood frozen in the bow, while Harry let the skiff drift with the current, holding it just off the rock with his hands so it wouldn't scrape. Trying to keep it silent.

The dark was infinite. Impenetrable. Harry knew Elena's thoughts, her anxiety, were the same as his. Finally his whisper broke the silence. "Put your hand over the front of the flashlight. Let as little of the beam out as possible. Keep it high on the wall. If you hear *anything,* shut it off."

Harry waited and then the dark was cut by a narrow wand of light that searched the granite wall above them. For a long moment it inched over the ancient stone, looking for the directional markers but finding nothing.

"Mr. Addison—" Elena's whisper was abrupt, and Harry heard the fear in her voice.

"Keep the light moving."

Immediately, he pushed the skiff back from the wall, then eased the oars into the water and pulled gently. The craft moved forward against a barely perceptible current.

Elena could feel the perspiration on the palms of her hands as she watched the sliver of light play fruitlessly over the rock.

Harry watched it, too, trying not to think they had drifted

too far in the darkness and were moving deeper into the labyrinth. Suddenly Elena's light passed over notches cut in the stone, and he heard her stifle a cry.

"Okay, we're still okay," he whispered.

Twenty feet passed, then thirty. Then more notches.

"Turn the light down the channel."

Elena did. The rocky cavern went straight for as far as they could see.

"Put it out."

Immediately Elena snapped the flashlight off, then turned forward and peered into the dark in front of them, praying to see a dot of light that would mean the end of the canal and the way out to the lake. But she saw only blackness. Felt only the same cool damp of the air. Heard the light sound of the oars as Harry moved them forward.

Absently, she crossed herself. This was more of God's testing. But this time it wasn't about men or lust but about her own courage, her ability to persist under the most unbearable of situations while at the same time remaining strong and true to the patient in her charge.

"Yea, though I walk through the valley of the shadow of death," she said under her breath. "I will fear no—"

"*Sister Elena*—" Salvatore's voice suddenly echoed out of nowhere.

Elena started. Harry froze where he was, oars out of the water, the skiff drifting forward.

"Salvatore," Elena whispered.

"Sister Elena—" Salvatore's voice came again. "It's all right," he called in Italian. "I have the boat. Whoever was here is gone."

The white of Elena's eyes flashed in the dark as she turned toward Harry, translating what Salvatore had said.

"Sister Elena, where are you?"

Instantly Harry pulled in the oars, then grabbed at the passing wall of rock, slowing the skiff by hand. Stopping it. Then they heard the distant whine and rumble of motors. The boat and whoever was in it was coming up the channel toward them.

84

THOMAS KIND HELD THE EDGE OF THE RAZOR against Salvatore's throat as the motorboat moved slowly forward, the sound of the outboards echoing off the cavern walls. Behind them, Marta lay on the deck between the cockpit and the motors, blood still oozing from a tiny hole between her eyes.

Salvatore turned slightly to look at Thomas Kind. The right side of the blond man's face was raked with blood and torn skin where Marta had clawed him when he'd caught them, just as they'd reached the elevator cage. The fight had been short and quick. But she had done damage, and for that alone Salvatore Belsito was extraordinarily proud.

Yet Salvatore was not like his wife. Did not have her bravery or rage. It had been difficult enough for him to do what he had in lying to the police when they had twice invaded Villa Lorenzi. Difficult enough just to come to the grotto to care for the fugitive priest while the nun went in search of his brother. Salvatore Belsito was Villa Lorenzi's chief gardener, a gentle man who loved his wife and only cared about making things grow. Eros Barbu had given them both a home and jobs for as long as they cared to have them. For that he owed him a great deal. But not his life.

"Once more," Thomas Kind urged.

Salvatore hesitated, then again called out Elena's name.

THE STAB OF SALVATORE'S CALL resounded off the granite walls like a sound effect in a suspense movie. It was much louder, and much closer than before. Abruptly it was overridden by the throaty rumble of the outboards as the motorboat picked up speed.

"Go right!" Elena said behind Harry, the slim beam of her light following the marks on the stone walls as they reached an abrupt angle where the tunnel veered sharply right, nearly turning back on itself.

Harry pulled hard on the right oar, cutting the corner tightly. As he did, the left oar caught on the cavern wall and was nearly jerked out of his hand. Cursing under his breath, he recovered, felt the left oar touch water, and they were around.

Putting his back to it, he dug in with everything he had. The skin was raw on his hands, and the sweat ran down his forehead, stinging his eyes. He wished he could stop even for a moment to tear off the clerical collar. Throw it away so he could breathe.

"Sister Elena!!!!!!!"

Salvatore's cry came again in a rolling echo that followed them down the channel like a pursuing wave.

Suddenly a blinding light illuminated the entire waterway where they had just been like day. Harry could see the shadow of wall they had just come around and guessed they had ten seconds at most before the motorboat came around it too and entered the channel where they were.

Looking around wildly, he saw a canal in front of them that ran straight for almost twenty yards before cutting smartly to the left. There was little or no chance they would make it before the motorboat was around the corner and on top of them. Nor, despite some rugged outcropping of rock that fed into the channel, was there a place to hide.

"Mr. Addison! Look there!" Elena whispered. She was suddenly leaning forward, pointing off.

Ahead, to their left and a dozen yards away, Harry saw what she was pointing at. A dark shadow that might be the entrance to a cave or inlet. Three or four feet high at best, and not much wider. Just big enough—maybe—for the skiff to get through.

Behind them, the growl of the outboards suddenly rose. Harry looked back. The light was getting brighter. Whoever was at the controls was picking up the speed. Throwing his full body weight behind the oars, Harry drove toward the cave.

"We're going in!" Harry said over his shoulder at Elena. "Climb past me. Make sure his head doesn't hit."

Harry stopped rowing for the briefest second, feeling the brush of Elena's habit as she scrambled over him. Then he dug in again. As he did, the right oar twisted in his hands and came out of the water. The skiff swung sharply left. There was a metallic scrape as it hit the wall, then glanced off and back into the channel. Recovering, he pulled back toward the cave opening.

At the same time, he saw Elena look up to see the sleek prow of the motorboat slide past the outcrop of rock and turn into the channel where they were. Instantly, the powerful beam of the searchlight came around, sweeping mercilessly toward them as the boat turned fully into the waterway.

Harry glanced over his shoulder. They were right at the cave.

"Get down!" he said.

Crouching over, Harry jerked the oars inboard and the prow of the skiff slid into the opening, ceiling and sides clearing by only inches. Then he saw Elena duck, her hand on Danny's head. The stern slid through and they were inside.

Instantly, Harry was on his back. Grabbing the rock ceiling above them, pulling the skiff forward, hand over hand. Deeper into the cave. A heartbeat later the harsh beam of the searchlight swept past.

Abruptly the outboards throttled down. A half second later he saw the motorboat glide by. A blond man with a stark profile stood in silhouette to the far wall, one hand on the wheel, the other up tight under the throat of Salvatore Belsito. Then they were gone, the light trailing off with them, the boat's wake washing into the cave.

Immediately Harry put his hands out to the walls on either side to keep the skiff from banging off them. His heart pounding, he raised himself up and listened. One second. Then two. Then he heard the outboards stop. A moment later the wash subsided and everything was silent.

85

THOMAS KIND LET THE BOAT SWING IN A slow arc, bringing it around, letting it come to a stop facing the way they had come, his eyes searching the cavern in front of him—the glistening walls with their jagged outcroppings, the deep green-black water reflecting the illumination from the searchlight in a thousand different directions.

"Sit down . . ." Slowly he eased the razor from Salvatore's throat and nodded toward the bench along the gunwale behind him. The look in his captor's eyes was all the warning the Italian needed, and he did what he was told. Then he crossed his arms and tilted his head toward the irregular ceiling of the cave, letting his gaze fix there, fix anywhere but at the body of his wife at his feet, the body he had put there after Kind had made him carry it from where he had killed her, at the entrance to the elevator.

Thomas Kind glanced back at Salvatore, then reached into his jacket. From it he took a slender, black nylon pouch. Opening it, he took out a small electronic headset. Putting it on, adjusting the earpieces, he clipped a tiny microphone to his jacket collar and plugged the lead wire into a packet at his waist. There was the faintest click, and a tiny red glow rose from the monitor light beneath his fingers. His thumb ran over the volume control, and the sound came up immediately. Everything was amplified. The echo of the tunnel, the crisp lap of water against its walls. Listening intently, he swung the microphone slowly and deliberately across the canal. Wall left to wall right.

He heard nothing.

He panned back. Wall right to wall left.

Still nothing.

Leaning forward, he turned off the searchlight, and the cavern went dark. Then he waited. Twenty seconds. Thirty. A minute.

Again, he swung the microphone. Left to right. And then back. And then back again.

". . . wait . . ."

He froze at the sound of Harry Addison's voice, a whisper. He waited for more.

Nothing.

Ever so slowly, he swung back.

". . . without an IV . . . ," nursing sister Elena Voso said, her voice low and hushed like the American's.

They were there. Somewhere in the dark ahead of him.

Villa Lorenzi. Same time.

Roscani squinted in the bright sunlight of Edward Mooi's bedroom. The tech crew was still working the bathroom. Traces of blood had been found in the sink, the vague outline of a bare foot on the floor.

No one had seen the poet since he had returned to his

apartment following Roscani's early-morning search. None of the staff, none of the dozen *carabinieri* on posted guard. No one. Mooi, like Eros Barbu's motorboat, had simply vanished.

Through the window, Roscani could see two of the police boats on the lake. Castelletti was in one, coordinating the search on the water. Scala, a former army commando, had gone ashore with ten mountain-trained *carabinieri,* and they were walking the shoreline, south from the villa. It was assumed Mooi had not gone north, because that would have led him directly into Bellagio, where he was well known and where there were large numbers of uniformed police. So Scala had chosen the southern course, where coves and dense overgrowth provided cover where a boat could be hidden from view from both the lake and the air.

Turning from the window, Roscani left the room and went out into the hallway just as an aide arrived. Saluting, he handed Roscani a thick envelope, then turned and left. Opening it, Roscani quickly scanned its contents. The cover sheet bore the heading INTERNATIONAL CRIMINAL POLICE ORGANIZATION, with the familiar INTERPOL crest directly beneath, while the word *URGENTISSIMO* had been hand stamped on every page.

The pages were the INTERPOL reply to his request for information on the suspected whereabouts of known terrorists and, separately, the personality profiles of killers still at large and thought to be in Europe.

Pages still in hand, Roscani looked back into the room. Seeing Edward Mooi's bathrobe where it had been tossed on the bed, seeing the tech people still at work through the open door to the bathroom, he suddenly had the sense they were already too late. His ice picker had already been there.

HARRY HEARD THE SCRAPE OF THE HULL against rock in the dark and knew the blond man was working the boat back down the channel by hand, coming toward them. How did he know they were there? How could he be that close in all the miles of underground waterways? From the single glimpse Harry had as the boat passed going upchannel, Salvatore had seemed to be the man's prisoner, but even if he weren't, if he were there of his own free will, it would still be next to impossible for him to know where they were. Yet somehow he did. And he was only yards, maybe even feet, from the entrance to their hiding place.

The only thing to their advantage, if they had an advantage at all, was that the outcroppings of rock into the channel made the cave entrance difficult to see. Elena had seen it only because of the angle of the motorboat's searchlight as it turned into the channel. Without that, it would have appeared as nothing more than a shadow from an outcropping, a darkening above the waterline.

The sound came again. Closer than before. Wood or fiberglass scraping rock. Then again, closer still. Then it stopped, and Harry was certain the boat was directly in front of the entrance, so near that Elena, in the skiff's stern, could reach out a hand in the pitch black and touch it.

Harry held his breath, his senses electric, every nerve alive, waiting for what would happen next. And he knew Elena was the same, helpless, terrified, praying the boat and the men in it would move on.

THOMAS KIND STOOD SILENT, one hand holding the boat against the granite wall, the other pressing the headset to his ear as he listened. His upper body turned slowly, left to right, and then back, listening, but there was nothing.

Maybe they weren't here after all. Maybe he had been wrong in staying in this channel. Both the microphone and listening device were extremely sensitive. And the jagged rock walls and flat surface of the water were hard surfaces that acted like huge, multidirectional speakers that bounced sound everywhere. The voices could as easily have come from somewhere else. From the channel he had just left, or the one behind, which he had not yet ventured into.

THERE WAS A SOFT CREAK in the darkness just beyond her, and then Elena felt fresh air waft in from the channel. The motorboat was moving away from the entrance of the cave. The blond man was leaving. She crossed herself in relief, then whispered in the dark.

"He's gone . . ."

"Give him a few min—"

Suddenly, a loud, sharp wail echoed from the blackness inches away.

Elena froze where she was. A hand thrown to her mouth in horror.

The wail came again. Longer and louder than before.

"Jesus Christ!" Harry whispered.

Danny was waking.

87

A SHRILL WHINE ECHOED ACROSS THE CAVERN as Thomas Kind touched the starter. The twin two-hundred-and-fifty horsepower Yamahas thundered to life, and the searchlight came on full, swinging in a wide arc across the channel as Kind brought the motorboat's bow around sharply and roared back the way he had come. As quickly he cut the motors and let the boat drift, playing the light across the cavern walls.

HARRY DUG IN with his hands, grabbing at the rock overhead, pulling the skiff deeper into the recess. Beyond him, over his chest he could see the searchlight swing toward the mouth of the cave. In between, Elena was huddled against Danny on the flattened gurney that lay just below the top of the stern. Whatever sound Danny had made had stopped. He was still and breathing silently as before.

The light swung past the opening and moved on. In that brief second Harry saw more of the cave. It went straight back for another ten or fifteen feet before its height suddenly dropped and it narrowed sharply. There was no way to tell where it went from there. But it was all they had. That was, if the skiff would fit through it.

Thomas Kind swung the light back across the rock outcroppings. All he saw were the shadows where one ended and another began. But he'd heard the cry or whatever it had been. And this time there was no doubt where it had come from, somewhere here, along the wall in this section of the channel.

Now he swung the light back, his eyes intent, the deep scratches Marta had made on his face glistening in its spill.

Behind him, Salvatore sat in a kind of fascinated terror and watched, a spectator at a game. It was who Salvatore was, the most he could be.

There!

Thomas Kind saw it. The low ledge, the dark opening beneath it. Gratification tugged in a cruel smile as he turned the boat toward it.

THERE WAS A LOUD SCRAPE and then a dull bang as the skiff suddenly stopped.

"The flashlight. Quickly," Harry whispered.

The dull rumble of the outboards grew louder, and the light became appreciably brighter as it danced off the granite walls, moving toward them.

"Here!" Elena leaned toward Harry with the flashlight. Their eyes met for an instant, and then Harry took it, turning, playing it into the cave behind them.

The skiff had caught up against the passage entrance. With a little maneuvering, it would fit inside it. But after that, who knew? The blond man knew where they were and would stay there, waiting for them to come out. And if they went on, trying to find an exit at the far end. . . . If there was one. . . . If not, what then?

Suddenly the beam of the searchlight was full on them.

"GET OVER THE SIDE! NOW!"

Harry threw himself forward and sideways at the same time, felt his hand fill with material from Elena's habit, pulling her over the gunwale into the water in a hail of automatic-weapon fire.

Shoving her under the surface toward the passageway on the far side of the skiff, he looked back to see the skiff surrounded by the bright yellow-green of water roiling with gunfire. Bullets chewed up the cavern walls around him, whining shrilly off the heavy stern. It was only a matter of moments before they would cut through the thick aluminum and reach Danny.

Ducking under the water, Harry shoved the skiff hard from beneath, trying to turn it, get Danny out of the murderous line of fire.

Lungs bursting, using the underwater wall for leverage, he maneuvered the skiff around, fighting it backward and into the passage. Suddenly it caught against something, throwing Harry backward. He swam back, digging in against the underwater wall, trying to free it.

He couldn't. His chest was on fire. He had to have air. Pushing off, he came up. Broke the surface full in the beam of the searchlight. For an instant he saw the muzzle flashes. Thought he saw the face of the man behind them. Calm. Unemotional. Firing in short bursts.

Bullets tore past his head, shredding the thin aluminum bow. Half a breath. No more. Harry dove again.

Once more he used the rock for purchase, this time driving against the hull with his shoulder. Still nothing happened. He tried again. Then again. Once more, then he had to have air. This time he felt something give. Lungs exploding, he hit it again. The skiff broke free and jumped forward. He went after it, kept it moving. Then he had to come up.

He felt himself break the surface. Suck in fresh air. At almost the same instant, the firing stopped and the light swung away. And the place where they were went black.

"Elena . . ." Harry's voice rasped through the dark.

"Elena!" His second call, harder, more urgent. He imagined her hit by the gunfire and lying on the bottom, her lungs filled with water.

"I have hold of the boat. . . . I'm all right—" Her voice was close by and she was gasping, trying to get air.

"What about Danny—?"

"We're moving!" Elena's cry was sudden and frightened.

Harry felt the water become abruptly colder, the skiff start to move away from him. Somehow they'd entered an underground stream and were being swept along with it.

He went after the skiff in the dark, half swimming, half pushing off the rock walls. In a moment he caught up, grabbing hold as the boat picked up speed, the water taking them ever faster. Trapped, brutally pounded between the skiff and the passage's granite sides, he fought the rush of water past him, worked his way along the gunwales, hand over hand, toward the stern.

"Elena!" Harry shouted over the roar of the water and the banging of the skiff against the rocks.

No reply.

"Elena!—Where are you?—Elena!"

THOMAS KIND STRUGGLED WILDLY. SALVA-
tore was much stronger than he looked. The scarf taken from his wife's hair was twisted in his hands. Looped in a garrote around the blond man's neck. Pulling harder, the Italian pushed his knee into the small of Thomas Kind's back.

"Bastardo," he hissed. *"Bastardo."*

This was something Kind hadn't counted on, hadn't even considered from a man as insubstantial and spiritless as Salvatore Belsito. But he would not die because of it. Abruptly he let his body go limp and slumped forward, taking the Italian by surprise. Both men hit the deck at the same time. In a single motion, Thomas Kind pulled free, rolled to the side, and came up behind him. The razor flashed in his hand, and he grabbed the Italian by the hair, dragging his head back, fully exposing the length of his throat.

"That place—that cave where they were—" Thomas Kind took a breath and felt his pulse slow, come back to normal. "Where does it go?"

Deliberately the Italian's eyes crept up to fix on the blond man standing over him. Oddly, he was not afraid. "Nowhere . . ."

Abruptly the razor slid across the base of Salvator's nose. He cried out at the sudden gush of red that poured down over his lip and into his mouth.

"Where does it go?"

The Italian choked, tried to spit out his own blood.

"Like others in . . . here. . . . To an underground stream . . . and . . . then . . . back . . . to the lake."

"Where?—North of here, South. *Where?"*

Slowly a smile crossed Salvatore Belsito's face, a great, grand smile that was, in truth, his soul.

"I will not . . . tell you . . ."

89

HARRY HELD ELENA BETWEEN HIMSELF AND the skiff as it drove stern first against them, pushing them down through a thundering wash of narrow sluice that was dropping at an ever-increasing angle. The pitch black. The force of the water. His hands were raw and bleeding from trying to slow their speed against the unseen granite walls. He could feel Elena pressing against him, fighting to keep her head above water. As he was. If Danny was still inside the skiff—his gurney shoved against the stern—there was no way to tell.

Then suddenly there was nothing under them. Just air. He heard Elena scream. And he felt the skiff crush against him. Then they hit. Deep water. Blacker than before. The force sent him down. Twisting, spiraling, in a mass of turbulence. Then he felt himself touch bottom and push up, trying to swim to the surface.

And then he was up and through it. Choking, gasping, sucking in air. He saw light from somewhere cutting a ribbon through the dark.

"Elena!" he heard himself yell. "Elena!!"

"I'm here."

Her voice came from behind him. Startling him, making him swing around. In the light he saw her swimming toward him.

Abruptly he felt his feet touch ground, and he staggered forward to sprawl on a rocky shelf, gasping, exhausted. Outside he could see thick undergrowth and sunlight shimmering off the lake beyond it. Then he saw Elena move up on the rock shelf beside him, but she was looking off, past him, toward the water where they had just been. Real time came back, and he followed her gaze. Then he saw what she was looking at, and he could feel the chill cut through him.

Danny was like a ghost. Pale, almost transparent. Gaunt as death. Bearded and nearly naked. Bandages all but washed away. Lying only feet away, staring at him.

"Harry," he said. "Jesus H. Christ."

THE SOUND OF DANNY'S VOICE hung frozen in the close air of the water cave as the brothers stared at one another, half in sheer joy and half in disbelief that they were not only alive but together and face-to-face after so many years.

Finally Harry stood and quickly slid back down the rock to where Danny was. Bracing himself, he reached out.

"Take my hand," he said.

Slowly Danny reached up, their hands met, and Harry started to pull him up onto the ledge, sliding partway back into the water at the last moment to take special care of

Danny's broken legs that miraculously were still enclosed by the blue casts.

"Are you all right?" Harry asked as he crawled up beside him.

"Yes . . . ," Danny nodded weakly and tried to smile, and Harry could see the exhaustion beginning to overtake him. Then suddenly, and from behind them, came a loud unrestrained sob. Instantly both men looked up.

Elena sat on the rock ledge where Harry had left her. Her eyes were closed and her arms were pulled tight around her, while her entire body shuddered with sobs of enormous relief. Sobs she tried to hold back but could not.

Getting up quickly, his feet slipping on the damp rocks, Harry climbed up to where she was.

"It's okay," he said kneeling. Then, gently putting his arms around her, he pulled her close and held her against him.

"I'm—sorry . . . ," she managed, letting her head fall against his shoulder.

"It's okay," he said again. "*We're* all right, *all* of us."

Looking back toward the water, Harry could see Danny huddled on the rock ledge watching him. Yes, they were all right. But for how long? And what to do next?

90

Rome. Ambasciata della Repubblica Popolare Cinese In Italia—Embassy, People's Republic of China. Still Tuesday, July 14, 2:30 P.M.

THE DARK CADILLAC LIMOUSINE TURNED ONTO Via Bruxelles and drove past the nineteenth-century stone wall surrounding the grounds of the old Parco di Villa Grazioli, now a subdivision of apartment buildings and large private residences.

The limousine slowed as it approached an armored *carabinieri* car backed across the sidewalk. Farther down was another. In between was number 56. Turning in, the Cadillac stopped in front of a high green gate. A moment passed and then the gate slid back and the limousine entered, the gate closing again behind it.

Moments later United States ambassador to Italy Leighton Merriweather Fox walked up the front steps to the four-story, beige brick-and-marble structure that was the Embassy for the People's Republic of China. With him were Nicholas Reid, deputy chief of Mission; Harmon Alley, counselor for Political Affairs; and Alley's first secretary, James Eaton.

Inside, the mood was somber. Eaton saw Fox bow and shake the hand of Jiang Youmei, Chinese ambassador to Italy. Nicholas Reid did the same with Foreign Minister Zhou Yi, while Harmon Alley waited in turn to meet deputy Foreign Minister Dai Rui.

The topic among them, the discussion in every corner of the large light-green-and-gold reception room, was the same, the disaster in the Chinese city of Hefei, where the death toll from polluted drinking water had risen to a horrific sixty-two thousand and was still increasing.

Health officials had no estimate of where or when it would end. Seventy thousand. Eighty. No one knew. The filtration plants had been shut down. Fresh water was being flown, railroaded, and trucked in. But the devastation had already been done. The Chinese Army was on scene but was overwhelmed by the immensity of the task, by the most rudimentary logistics of dealing with so much sickness and death. And despite attempts at media control by Beijing, the whole world knew what was happening.

Leighton Merriweather Fox and Nicholas Reid were there to offer condolence and aid. Harmon Alley and James Eaton to assess the politics of the situation. It was the same worldwide: ranking diplomatic officials visiting the Chinese Embassy in the country to which they were assigned, offering help on one hand, assessing the political implications on the other. The speculation was whether Beijing was capable of safeguarding its people, or whether the fear that a simple drink of water could kill you, your family, and thousands of your neighbors in a single stroke would be enough to cause the provinces to pull away, choosing to rely upon themselves instead. Every foreign government knew Beijing was hovering on the precipice. The central government might weather Hefei, but if the same thing happened again anywhere else in the country, tomorrow, next week, or even next year, it would be the clap of thunder that would leave the People's Republic on the verge of total collapse. It was a nightmare every foreign government knew was China's deepest and most profound fear. Water had suddenly become her greatest weakness.

Which was why, in the name of human suffering and tragedy, the diplomats were gathered here at number 56 Via Bruxelles and in Chinese embassies around the world, hovering to see what would happen next.

Bowing politely, taking a cup of tea from a tray proffered by a young Chinese woman in a gray jacket, Eaton made his way across the crowded room, stopping now and then to take a familiar hand. As first secretary for Political Affairs, his presence here was not so much to offer sympathy to the Chinese, but rather to determine who else was there and doing the same. And now, as he chatted with the counselor for Political Affairs from the French Embassy, there was a stir at the main entry, and both men turned toward it.

What Eaton saw was not unexpected: the entrance of Vatican Secretariat of State Cardinal Umberto Palestrina, dressed in his emblem simple black suit with white clerical collar, and followed immediately by three others of the Holy See's ranking nobility, wearing their robes of office—Cardinal Joseph Matadi, Monsignor Fabio Capizzi, and Cardinal Nicola Marsciano.

Almost immediately the din of conversation faded, and diplomats stepped aside as Palestrina approached the Chi-

nese ambassador, bowed, and took his hand as if they were
the oldest and dearest of friends. That relations between Beijing and the Vatican hardly existed made little difference.
This was Rome, and Rome represented nine hundred and
fifty million Roman Catholics around the world. It was those
millions Palestrina and the others represented in the name of
the Holy Father. They were here now to offer sympathy to
the people of China.

Excusing himself from the French diplomat, Eaton
crossed the room slowly, watching Palestrina and the clergymen with him as they talked with the Chinese. Watching
with even greater interest as the group of seven left the room
together.

This was the second public interaction between the Vatican and ranking diplomats from China since the assassination of Cardinal Parma. More than ever, Eaton wished Father
Daniel Addison were there to tell him what it meant.

91

TRYING TO KEEP HIS SANITY AND AT THE same time praying to God to show him some way to stop the horror, Marsciano entered the small pale-green-and-beige parlor and sat down with the others—Palestrina, Cardinal Matadi, Monsignor Capizzi, Ambassador Jiang Youmei, Zhou Yi, and Dai Rui.

Palestrina was directly across from him, sitting in a gold-fabric armchair, speaking Mandarin to the Chinese. Every part of him, from the plant of his feet on the floor to the look in his eyes to the expressive way he used his hands, conveyed heartfelt empathy and vast concern for the tragedy playing out halfway around the world. He made his entire outpouring intimate and very personal, as if he were saying that if it were at all possible, he would go to Hefei and minister to the sick and dying himself.

It was a posture and generosity the Chinese took courteously and appreciatively, if not gratefully. But Marsciano—and, he knew, Palestrina as well—could see they were merely going through the motions. As much as their thoughts and concerns were with the people of Hefei, they were first and foremost politicians, and the focus of their attention was their government and its survival. Beijing, and what it did, was clearly under a world microscope.

Yet how, in their wildest nightmares, could they know, or even consider, that the prime architect of the disaster was neither nature nor a decaying water-filtration system, but instead the white-haired giant who sat only inches away, consoling them in their own language? Or that two of the three other highly distinguished prelates in the room with them had, in the last hours, become that architect's steadfast disciples?

If Marsciano had held any secret hope—now that the horror had started and Palestrina's "Protocol" was exposed for the awful and savage reality it was—that either Monsignor Capizzi or Cardinal Matadi would be rocked to his senses and take a forceful stand against the secretariat, it had been quashed by an internal letter of support, hand delivered that morning by both men to Palestrina personally (a letter Marsciano was asked to sign but refused), fully backing the secretariat's rationale for his actions. A rationale maintaining that Rome had sought rapprochement with Beijing for years, and for years the central government had spurned it; and would continue to spurn it for as long as they remained in power.

To Palestrina, Beijing's stance meant one thing—the Chinese had no religious freedom at all and never would have it. Palestrina's answer to that was simply that he was going to give it to them. The cost was irrelevant, those who died would be martyrs.

Obviously Capizzi and Matadi wholeheartedly agreed. Pursuit of the papacy was everything, and either would be foolish to defy the man who could put him there. In result, human life became merely a tool in that pursuit. And vile as it was now, it would get infinitely worse, because there were two more lakes yet to be poisoned.

Knowing what was to come, sickened by the awful hypocrisy and obscenity before him, unable to participate in it further, Marsciano suddenly stood. "If you will excuse me."

Palestrina started and looked up sharply in surprise. "Are you ill, Eminence?"

Palestrina's startled reaction made Marsciano realize how deranged the secretariat had become. He was playing his part so well he actually and truly believed what he was saying. At that moment the other side of him simply did not exist. It was a marvel of supreme self-deception.

"Are you ill, Eminence?" Palestrina said again.

"Yes . . . ," Marsciano said quietly, his gaze swinging directly to Palestrina and holding there for the briefest second, his profound contempt for the secretariat made explicitly clear but at the same time kept wholly private between them. Immediately he turned away and bowed graciously to the Chinese.

"The prayers of all of Rome are with you," he said and then left, crossing the room alone and walking out the door, knowing Palestrina watched him every step of the way.

92

MARSCIANO MIGHT HAVE LEFT THE ROOM
alone, but that was where his freedom ended. Protocol
forced him to wait for the others, and now, inside the limousine, there was silence.

Marsciano looked purposely out the window as the green
gate closed behind them and they turned onto Via Bruxelles—knowing, with the investments already in place, his
actions inside had all but sealed his fate.

Once again he thought of the three lakes Palestrina had
promised. Which two were to come after Hefei, and when,
only the secretariat knew. Palestrina's sickness and cruelty
were beyond comprehension. His just-witnessed act of self-
deception, incredible. When and how had an intelligent and
respectable man turned? Or had the monster always been
there and only sleeping?

Now the driver turned onto Via Salaria and slowed to a
crawl in heavy afternoon traffic. Marsciano could feel
Palestrina's presence beside him, and the eyes of Capizzi

and Matadi as they sat opposite watching him, but he acknowledged none of it. Instead his thoughts went to the Chinese banking head, Yan Yeh, remembering him not as an astute businessman who was, at the same time, an autocratic lifelong member of the Chinese Communist Party and prominent adviser to the party chairman, but rather as a friend and humanitarian, a man who could produce a cursory political diatribe one minute and in the next, talk about his personal concerns for health care and education and the well-being of the poor around the world; and then in the next, smile warmly and laugh and make small talk about Italian wine makers coming to the People's Republic to show them how it was done.

"—Do you often make telephone calls to North America?" Palestrina's voice echoed suddenly and sharply behind him.

Marsciano turned from the window to see Palestrina staring at him, his huge frame taking up most of the seat between them.

"I don't understand."

"Canada, in particular." Palestrina kept his eyes on Marsciano. "The province of Alberta."

"I still don't understand . . ."

"1011 403 555 2211," Palestrina said from memory. "You don't recognize the number?"

"Should I?"

Marsciano could feel the lean of the car as they turned onto Via Pinciana. Outside was the familiar green of the Villa Borghese. Abruptly, the Mercedes accelerated. Moving toward the Tiber. Soon they would be across it, turning onto Lungotevere Mellini, going toward the Vatican. Somewhere not far behind them was Marsciano's apartment on Via Carissimi, and he knew that he had seen it for the last time.

"It is the number for the Banff Springs Hotel. Two calls were made to it from your office on Saturday morning, the eleventh. Another, that afternoon, from a cellular phone signed out to Father Bardoni. Your private secretary. The man who replaced the priest."

Marsciano shrugged. "Many calls are made from my office, even on a Saturday. Father Bardoni works long hours, so do I, so do others. . . . I do not keep track of every telephone call . . ."

"You told me in the presence of Jacov Farel that the priest was dead."

"He is . . ." Marsciano's eyes came up and looked at Palestrina directly.

"Then who was brought to Bellagio, to Villa Lorenzi two days ago? On Sunday evening, the twelfth?"

Marsciano smiled. "You have been watching the television."

"The calls to Banff were made Saturday, and the priest was brought to Villa Lorenzi on Sunday." Palestrina leaned forward into the face of Nicola Marsciano, stretching the material of his jacket tight across his back.

"Villa Lorenzi is owned by the writer Eros Barbu. Eros Barbu is vacationing at the Banff Springs Hotel."

"If you are asking if I know Eros Barbu, Eminence, you are right. We are old friends from Tuscany."

Palestrina watched Marsciano carefully for a moment longer. Finally, he sat back. "Then you should be saddened to hear he has committed suicide."

93

Lake Como. 4:30 P.M.

BANGING AND PITCHING, HALF SLIDING, Harry worked the farm truck down the rutted and overgrown forest road toward the inlet where he hoped Elena and Danny were. Two hours had passed since he'd climbed up from the lake looking for the truck, and much of the terrain was now in late-afternoon shadow, and this changed the look of everything.

The going was not only slow and difficult, but also dangerous; the old truck had bad brakes and nearly bald tires, making it hard to control as it rattled and bounced, pitched and slid over the road that was barely a road at all. Almost every turn was a hairpin switchback, and at each he was certain he was going over the side, to be sent plunging through heavy undergrowth into a steep ravine on one side, or dropping like a stone to the lake several hundred feet below on the other.

It was at a high point that he saw the flotilla to the north, maybe thirty or forty boats at anchor or cruising slowly back and forth, held offshore by three larger craft that looked like cutters or guard boats, and he knew the police had found the grotto. Then, as he was starting down, negotiating the hairpin, he saw a helicopter suddenly rise up to circle over the top of the cliff where he'd been less than twenty minutes earlier.

Abruptly the entire scene vanished as the truck slid forward on the loose gravel. Pumping the brakes wildly, Harry swung the wheel back toward the road. But it did no good. The truck continued to slide. The edge was coming up. After that there was nothing but air and the water below. And then the right front wheel caught in a rut. The steering wheel snapped out of his hand. And, as if it had suddenly been mounted on a track, the vehicle swung sharply back and followed the path of the road, dropping behind a steep ridge and in under an umbrella of trees.

For another five minutes Harry fought both the truck and road, and then he was at lake level, where the road went on for another twenty yards, then ended abruptly in a growth of brush and high trees at the water's edge.

Parking on a hill behind a row of trees and making sure the truck couldn't be seen from the lake, Harry got out and walked along the water's edge, then pushed through the undergrowth to where he could see the dark shadow that was the entry to the cave. In the distance he could hear the helicopter circling. And he prayed that's where it would stay.

94

The grotto. Same time.

ROSCANI STOOD ON THE LANDING, LOOKING into the motorboat. A man and woman lay dead inside it. The woman had been lucky he hadn't used the razor—the way he'd used it on the man who lay beside her, or the way he'd used it on Edward Mooi, whose nearly headless body had been found floating in the inner channel.

Edward Mooi.

"Dammit!" he said out loud. "Dammit to hell!" He should have known he was the one who had hidden the priest. Should have gone back and pressured him the moment he'd found the engines on the outboard were still warm. But he hadn't, because the call had come about the dead men in the lake and he'd gone there instead.

Turning from the landing, letting the tech people work, he walked back down the grotto's main corridor past the ancient stone benches toward the room at the end where the priest had been kept, where Scala and Castelletti were now and where the body of a *carabiniere* had been brought from the maze of back passageways—another of the ice picker's victims, the ice picker who they now knew was blond and had scratches down his cheek.

"*Biondo*," the dying *carabiniere* had managed, his eyes glazed over, one hand grasping Scala's, his other clawing feebly at his own cheek.

"*Graffiato*," he'd coughed, his fingers still pulling at his cheek. *Graffiato*.

"*Biondo. Graffiato*."

Blond. And strong. And quick. And, they surmised, the skin on his face scratched as well, most likely by the finger nails of the murdered woman, under which fragments of skin had been found. Fragments that would be sent to the lab for DNA analysis. New technology, Roscani thought. But useful only when they had a suspect, when they could take a blood sample and see if they had a match.

Entering the room, he moved past Scala and Castelletti and went again into the room where the nun's personal belongings had been found.

Nursing sister Elena Voso, age twenty-seven, a member of the Congregation of Franciscan Sisters of the Sacred Heart; home convent, the Hospital of St. Bernardine in the Tuscan city of Siena.

Walking back to the main tunnel, Roscani ran a hand through his hair and tried to get some sense of the place itself. Eros Barbu's enormous wealth was everywhere, and yet the people who had hidden here, a nun and a priest, and the dead men who had protected them, were not wealthy. Why had Barbu allowed his property to be used as a hiding place?

It was a question Barbu himself would never answer. The Royal Canadian Mounted Police were now investigating his apparent suicide on a mountain trail overlooking Lake Louise in Banff. Death by shotgun in the mouth. Except that Roscani knew it was no suicide, but murder, done, he was certain, by a colleague of the blond ice picker, who knew where Barbu was and how to find him and had killed him either in retaliation for helping Father Daniel escape or in an effort to find out where he was. Perhaps it was even the same colleague who killed Harry Addison's boss in California. If that were so, the conspiracy was much broader and far-reaching than it first seemed.

In the distance, Roscani could hear the echo of the search dogs and their handlers leading the *carabinieri* teams probing the maze of tunnels for Elena Voso and the fugitive priest—and Harry Addison. He had no proof. It was a hunch and nothing else. But somehow Roscani sensed the American had been there and helped his brother to escape.

High above, a helicopter unit was coordinating Gruppo Cardinale teams on the ground combing the cliffs above the grotto. A clear set of footprints had been found outside the elevator shaft. And there were tire tracks of a vehicle driven in, parked, and then driven away. Whether any of it would lead them to the blond man or the fugitives it was too early to tell.

Whatever had happened, or would happen, one thing alone had become chillingly clear—Roscani was no longer dealing simply with a fugitive priest and his brother, but with people internationally connected, highly skilled, and with no reservation at all about killing. And anyone with even the slightest idea where the priest might be, or what he might know, had become a hard target seemingly reachable anywhere.

DANNY WAS ALONE AS HARRY CAME INTO THE
cave, sitting just back from the entrance, his broken legs in
their blue fiberglass casts twisted awkwardly in front of him.
He wore Harry's black jacket over the thin hospital gown he
had had on when they put him into the skiff.

Immediately Harry looked around. Where was Elena? He
looked back to find Danny staring at him, as if he weren't
quite sure who Harry was. And Harry knew the physical
exhaustion caused by the brutal ride through the grotto's
sluices was taking its toll. Danny had regressed, and it frightened him because he didn't know how far back he'd gone or
if he would have the strength to come back.

"Danny, do you know who I am?"

Danny said nothing, just continued to stare. Unsure,
uncertain.

"I'm your brother, Harry."

Finally, hesitantly, Danny nodded.

"We are in a cave in the north of Italy."

Danny nodded again. But the action was still vague, as if he understood the words but not what they meant.

"Do you know where the sister is?—the nun who is taking care of you. Where is she?"

For several seconds there was no reaction at all. Then slowly, deliberately, Danny's eyes shifted to the left.

Harry followed the movement across the cave to a bright, sunlit opening near the back. Leaving Danny, he crossed to it, started through, then stopped. Elena was half dressed, her habit around her waist, her breasts exposed. Startled, she quickly covered herself.

"Sorry," Harry said, then turned and went back inside.

A moment later and fully dressed, Elena followed him in, thoroughly embarrassed, trying to explain.

"I apologize, Mr. Addison. My clothing was still wet. I dried it out there on the rocks, as I did your jacket and your brother's gown. He was sleeping when I . . . was . . . not dressed . . ."

"I understand . . ." Harry found a way to smile, and it put her at ease.

"You came with the truck?"

"Yes."

"Harry—?" Danny cocked his head as Harry and Elena came closer.

Yes, it was Harry, he was sure. And Elena was with him, and that helped because she had been with him for a long time. And her presence gave him some kind of anchor to reality. Still, he felt weak. Thinking itself—where they were, how Harry came to be there—was a supreme effort. Abruptly the vision of Harry taking his hand and helping him out of the water came back. So, too, did the moment when they looked at each other and realized that after so much time they were together again.

"I . . ." Danny touched a hand to his head. "Not thinking . . . too . . . clear . . ."

"It's okay, Danny," Harry said gently. "It's going to be okay . . ."

"It's not unexpected, Mr. Addison," Elena said deliberately, her eyes going to Danny. "And I don't mind talking in front of the father, because he needs to understand it, too— he has been seriously hurt. . . . He was making progress, all this has set him back. . . . Physically I think he will be all right. . . . But he may have trouble with his words, his cognizance, or both. . . . How much will return, only time will tell." Now she looked to Harry.

"How far is the truck, Mr. Addison?" She was suddenly concerned with time, with the lengthening shadows outside the cave. "How far do we have to go to reach it?"

Harry hesitated, then looked to Danny. Afraid of upsetting or frightening him, he took Elena by the arm and led her toward the cave's entrance, telling her he'd show her the way from there.

Outside, he pointed to the rocks that kept the truck from being seen from the lake, then turned to face her.

"The police have found the grotto. They had a helicopter circling the top of the hill by the elevator shaft. Maybe that's the way the blond man got out—who knows? But they'll know Danny was there and that he was alive. . . ." Harry hesitated. "You left your things behind, Elena. They'll know who you are . . . and probably that I was there, too, because I wasn't very careful about what I touched.

"They'll search the tunnels and corridors, and when they don't find anything, they'll saturate this whole area looking for us.

"The road up out of here is impossible, but if we can get out before they come this far, and do it before dark, before I need to use headlights, we might make it. At least to the main road where we can mix in with other traffic. Hoping that when it does get dark, we can slip through their checkpoints like we did this morning."

"To go where, Mr. Addison?"

"With luck, the Autostrada at Como and then north to the Swiss border at Chiasso."

Elena studied him for the briefest moment. "And then where, Mr. Addison?"

"—I'm not sure . . ." Suddenly Harry was aware of Danny watching them intently from inside the cave. For the first time Harry saw him at a distance, and for the first time saw what he had become. Emaciated, broken. But still with fight, the same way Harry had always remembered him. Bullheaded sometimes, but always tough. Nonetheless, right now he was all but helpless.

Abruptly, Harry turned back to Elena. There were things she needed to understand before they went anywhere.

"You know that I am wanted for killing an Italian policeman. And that Danny is a prime suspect in the murder of the cardinal vicar of Rome."

"Yes."

Harry's eyes were suddenly intense and filled with strength. "It's important you understand that I did not kill the policeman. . . . What my brother did or didn't do, I don't know and won't until his mind is clear enough for me to ask him. . . . And even then, I don't know what he'll say, or won't. . . . But whatever happened, someone wants him dead. . . . Because of what he knows, for what he might tell. . . . That's why the blond man, maybe even the police. . . . And now they know he's alive, they'll not only come after him again, they will assume he's passed on whatever he knows to the people with him."

"You mean you and me, Mr. Addison . . ."

"Yes."

"Whether he has told us anything or not—"

"They won't ask." Harry finished the thought for her.

Suddenly, and out of nowhere, came the chunky thud of a jet helicopter's rotor blades slicing air. Taking Elena by the arm, Harry pulled her back into the cave's overhang just as the machine swept over the ridge above them. Moving out over the lake, it made a wide turn, then swung back the way it had come, disappearing over the treetops. Its sound vanishing with it.

Instantly Elena's eyes came back to Harry.

"I understand the situation, Mr. Addison, and I am prepared for whatever happens . . ."

Harry stared at her for the briefest moment.

"Okay," he said, then turned back into the cave for Danny.

96

ROSCANI SAW THE LAKE AND THEN THE TREE-tops as the helicopter swung in over the cliffs, taking one last careful look for himself, his father's way of doing things, as if because of it, he would succeed where everyone else had failed. But he didn't. He saw nothing but rock and trees and the water off to the left.

"Damn," he swore under his breath. They were down there somewhere, all of them. Father Daniel, the nun, the blond ice picker/razor man, and Harry Addison. Roscani's earlier hunch had been right: the American had been in the grotto. Fingerprints lifted from a medicine case in the room where Father Daniel had been confirmed it.

Roscani wouldn't allow himself to imagine how the American had slipped from them all and found the water caves before they did, or how he and the others had managed to avoid the blond man, which, it seemed, they had. On the positive side, a manhunt across all of Italy had narrowed down to an area of a few square miles. On the negative, he had two sets of fugitives—the Addison group and the blond killer—each with either extraordinary skill at avoidance, third-party help, or just plain luck. Roscani's job was to stop it all, pinch off any possible route of escape, and end it here as quickly as possible.

Ahead, as the pilot brought them north in growing twilight, he could see the buildup of the huge Gruppo Cardinale force he was putting in place to do it—hundreds of Italian Army, *carabinieri*, local police personnel—arriving at the tactical staging area on top of the cliffs above the grotto.

Abruptly, Roscani ordered the helicopter back to strategic headquarters set up hours earlier at Villa Lorenzi, his mind shifting to the next. Gruppo Cardinale was hunting two separate entities. The Americans and the nun he knew, but he had no idea who his murderous blond ice picker was. At this point, it was imperative he find out.

97

THE STEERING WHEEL CHATTERED UNMER-
cifully in Harry's hands. The truck shook, and the tires spun
in the gravel against the steep pitch of the hill, the truck inching upward but at the same time sliding sideways, bringing
them perilously close to the edge and the lake how many
hundred feet below. Then they were out of the gravel and
onto solid ground, the truck gained purchase, and Harry
guided it back toward the center of the road.

"So far, so good . . ." He half smiled and saw Elena
pressed against the far door, trying not to show her fear. And
Danny, jammed in between them, wholly exhausted, was
staring off at nothing, seemingly unaware of any of it. Immediately Harry glanced at the truck's primitive instrument
panel. Fuel. They had little more than a quarter of a tank, and
how far that would take them he didn't know.

"Mr. Addison, your brother needs fluids and food as
quickly as we can possibly get them."

By now, it was all but dark, and in the distance they could see the lights of traffic on the Bellagio road. The highway south would take them along the lake and back toward Como, where Harry wanted to go. How far it was or how many towns there were in between, he didn't know and neither did Elena.

"Does the Church here still practice sanctuary?" Harry asked suddenly, remembering that places of worship had provided asylum and safe haven for refugees and fugitives for centuries.

"I don't know, Mr. Addison . . ."

"Would they help us, at least for the night?"

"In Bellagio. Near the top of the steps. The Church of Santa Chiara. I remember it because it is Franciscan, and I belong to the Congregation of Franciscan Sisters. . . . If anyone would give us assistance, it would be there."

"Bellagio." Harry didn't like it. It was too dangerous. Better to take their chances going south along the lake, where the police might not yet be.

"Mr. Addison," Elena said quietly, her gaze falling to Danny, as if she knew what Harry was thinking, "we don't have the time."

Harry followed her gaze to Danny. He was asleep, his head dropped down, resting on his chest. Bellagio. Elena was right, they didn't have the time.

98

IN A BLAZE OF LANDING LIGHTS AND SWIRL-
ing dust, Roscani's helicopter set down on the driveway in
front of Villa Lorenzi.

Ducking the still-churning rotor blades, he crossed the
formal gardens and entered into the smoky chaos of the command post set up in the late Eros Barbu's grand ballroom.
Gilded, polished, and dripping with chandeliers, it was the
kind of place an invading army might have set up in, which,
in a sense, was exactly what it was.

Pushing through the clamor, answering a fusillade of
questions as he went, he glanced at the huge wall map with
the small Italian flags marking the checkpoints and worried,
as he had before, whether what they were doing, necessary
as it seemed, was too big, too loud, too unwieldy. They *were*
an army, and that made them think and act like an army, and
made them subject to the limitations of a large force; while
their prey, as they had proven so far, were essentially gueril-
las with the freedom of daring and creativity.

Going into a small office at the far end of the ballroom, he closed the door and sat down. There were calls waiting— from Taglia in Rome, Farel in the Vatican, his wife at home.

The call to his wife would be first. And then Taglia and then Farel. After that he would see no one for twenty minutes. He would take that time for himself. For *assoluta tranquillità*. His splendid silence. To be calm and to think. And then quietly go over the data he'd received from INTERPOL, to see if somewhere in those pages he could determine the identity of his blond man.

Bellagio. Hotel Florence. 8:40 P.M.

Thomas Kind sat at the dressing table in his room and looked at himself in the mirror. Astringent had cleaned the deep facial scratches made by Marta's clawing nails and drawn the wounds tightly enough to apply the makeup that he was now using to cover them.

He'd arrived back at the hotel a little before five after hitching a ride on the Bellagio road from two English university students on vacation. He'd been in a fight with his girl-friend, he'd told them; she'd lashed out, scratching his face, and he'd simply walked off—he was going back to Holland that night, and as far as he was concerned, she could go to hell. A half mile from the police checkpoint, he asked to be let out, saying he was still angry and wanted to walk it off. When the students had driven away, he'd left the road, crossed a field behind some trees, then come back to the road on the far side of the checkpoint. From there it had been less than a twenty-minute walk into Bellagio.

Coming into the hotel, he'd taken the back stairs to his room, then called the front desk to say he was checking out early in the morning and that whatever final payment was due should be added to his credit card and forwarded with the bill to his home in Amsterdam. Afterward, he'd looked at himself in the mirror and decided the thing to do was to take a shower and then change. And change he had.

Leaning toward the mirror, he touched mascara to his eyelashes, then dabbed once again at the eyeshadow. Satisfied, he stood back and looked at himself. He wore heels, beige slacks, and a loose white blouse under a lightweight blue linen blazer. Small gold earrings and a string of pearls finished the look. Closing his suitcase, he glanced once more in the mirror and then, pulling on a large straw hat, tossed the room keys on the bed, opened the door and left.

Thomas Jose Alvarez-Rios Kind of Quito, Ecuador, alias Frederick Voor of Amsterdam, was now Julia Louise Phelps, a real estate agent from San Francisco, California.

99

HARRY WATCHED ANXIOUSLY AS THE TWO
armed *carabinieri* waved the white Fiat on toward Bellagio,
then looked to the next car in line, motioning it forward and
then stopping it in the bright glare of the checkpoint's work
lights. Across, two more *carabinieri* worked the vehicles
leaving the city. Four more stood in the shadow of an
armored car at the roadside, watching.

Harry had seen the lights and knew what it was even
before the traffic in front of him began to slow. They'd been
more than lucky the first time, when it had been just he and
Elena going through the other way. Now, there were three of
them, and he held his breath, expecting the worst.

"Mr. Addison—" Elena was looking directly ahead.

Harry saw the car in front of them move off. Abruptly, an
armed *carabiniere* waved them forward. Harry felt his heart
pound, and suddenly there was sweat under his palms as his
hands gripped the wheel. Again the *carabiniere* waved them
forward.

Breathing deeply, Harry eased the clutch out. The truck moved ahead, then the policeman motioned him to stop. He did. Then two *carabinieri* came toward them in the purple-white of the checkpoint lights, one from either side. Both carried heavy flashlights.

"Christ!" Harry's breath went out of him with a rush.

"What is it?" Elena asked quickly.

"The same guy."

The *carabiniere* saw Harry, too. How could he forget? The old truck with the priest who had nearly run him over earlier that same morning.

"*Buona sera,*" the *carabiniere* said carefully.

"*Buona sera,*" Harry acknowledged.

The *carabiniere* lifted his flashlight and played it over the inside of the truck. Danny was still sleeping, still wearing Harry's black priest's jacket, slumped against Elena.

The other *carabiniere* was at Elena's window. Motioned her to roll it down.

Ignoring him, Elena looked to the *carabiniere* beside Harry.

"We went to a funeral. You remember?" she said in Italian.

"Yes."

"Now we are coming back. Father Dolgetta," she gestured at Danny, then lowered her voice as if trying not to wake him, "came from Milan to say the mass. You see how thin he is. He's been ill. He should never have come, but he insisted. And then what? A relapse. Look at him. We are trying to get him back and into bed before something worse happens."

For a long moment the *carabiniere* stared, his light playing over Harry again and then Danny.

"What would you like us to do? Get out and walk around? Wake him up? Make him walk, too?" Elena's eyes flashed angrily. "How long does it take for you to let people you already know pass?"

Behind them came a honking of horns. People impatient, waiting in line. Traffic backing up. Finally, the *carabiniere* snapped off his flashlight, nodded to his partner, then stepped back and waved them through.

ROSCANI BROKE OFF A PIECE OF CHOCOLATE,
bit into it, then closed the INTERPOL file.

Section one, fifty-nine pages, detailed twenty-seven men
and nine women as active terrorists with histories of Europe
as a workplace. Section two was twenty-eight pages of murderers still at large and thought to be in Europe: fourteen
altogether, all men.

Any of them could have blown up the Assisi bus. And any
of the men could be the charred body misidentified as Father
Daniel, the person who carried the Spanish Llama pistol. But
in Roscani's estimation, none of them had the same ingenious, erotic, and purely sadistic feel of his blond, scratch-
faced, ice picker/razor man.

Frustrated—damning himself for ever having quit smoking—he stood and opened the door of the tiny office he'd
retreated to and went back into Villa Lorenzi's grand ballroom. Walking through the tumult, looking around, he realized he had been wrong earlier. Yes, Gruppo Cardinale was

an army. It was too big. Too unwieldy. Called too much attention to itself. Made mistakes. But considering the situation, he was glad to have it. This was not a game he would like to have played alone, leading the search personally with the attitude of his father, as if he and he alone were capable of finding a solution. This was an arena where you needed a saturation force, a thousand eyes, open, alert, crawling over every inch of land. It was the only way to snap closed the trap and guarantee your quarry would not slip away again.

Bellagio. The Church of Santa Chiara.
10:15 P.M.

Harry sat with Danny in the dark of the parked truck waiting for Elena. She'd been gone for nearly half an hour, and he could feel the uneasiness building inside him.

Across the street, several teenagers walked by, joking and laughing, one strumming a guitar. A few moments earlier an elderly man had passed the same way, humming to himself and walking two small dogs. Now the sound of the teenagers faded, and quiet took over, heightening the isolation and raising the level of anxiety and the fear they would be caught.

Turning slightly, Harry looked at Danny sleeping on the seat beside him, his legs in the blue fiberglass casts pulled up under him in a fetal position. It was innocent and unknowing, the way a child might sleep. He wanted to reach out and touch him, tell him again that it would be okay.

Looking away, Harry glanced back up the hill toward the church, hoping to see Elena coming toward them. But there was nothing but the empty street and cars parked along either side of it. Suddenly a wave of emotion passed over him. It was deep and from far inside. It was the realization of why he was there. It was something still owed, a deliverance, the working out of a karma.

He was carrying out a promise made to Danny years before, just as he was leaving to go away to college. It was a time when Danny was more rebellious than ever, in constant trouble at home and at school and with the police. Harry's first year at Harvard was beginning in two days, and he was in the downstairs hallway with his suitcase, looking for Danny to say good-bye, when Danny came in. His face was dirty, his hair disheveled, the knuckles on his right hand raw from a fight. Danny looked at the suitcase and then at Harry, then started to push past him without a word. Harry remembered his hand snapping out, grabbing Danny hard and pulling him around. He could still hear his own words— "Just finish high school, all right?" he'd said strongly. "When you do, I'll come back and get you and take you with me. . . . I won't leave you here. I promise."

It was more than a promise, it was an extension of the covenant they had made years ago after the deaths of their sister and father and the too-soon, too-wrong remarriage of their mother, to help each other get out of that life and that family and that town, and to never come back to any of it. It was a pledge. A given. Guaranteed, brother to brother.

But for so many reasons it had never happened. And though it had never been talked about—or that circumstances had changed and Danny had gone off to the marines the day after he graduated high school—Harry knew nonetheless his not coming back was the real reason for their long alienation. He'd made a promise and never kept it, and Danny still held it against him. Well, he was keeping it now. Finally, he had come for his brother.

10:25

Another glance up the hill.

The street still dark and empty. The same as the sidewalks on either side. No Elena.

Suddenly the muted ringing of a telephone cut the silence. Harry started, looked around, wondering where it was coming from. Then he realized it was his cell phone stuffed inside the glove box, where he put it when he had gone into the grotto with Elena to find Danny.

Abruptly the ringing stopped. Then started again. Reaching over, opening the glove-box door, Harry took the phone out and clicked it on.

"Yes," he said carefully, knowing there was only one person who knew how to reach him.

"Harry—"

"Adrianna."

"Harry, where are you?"

Her voice had an inflection, a probing. Not of concern or warmth or friendship. It was business. She was back to the original deal, the one she had arranged for Eaton and herself—they got to talk to Danny first, before anyone else.

"Harry?"

"I'm still here."

"Is your brother with you?"

"Yes."

"Tell me where you are."

10:30

Quick glance up the street.

Still no Elena.

"Where are *you*, Adrianna?"

"Here in Bellagio. At the Du Lac. The same hotel you're still checked into."

"Is Eaton with you?"

"No. He's on his way here from Rome."

Suddenly headlights turned the corner at the top of the hill and started down. Police on motorcycles. Two of them. Cruising slowly, the streetlights glinting off their helmets, they were looking at the parked cars, the sidewalks. Looking for him and Danny.

"Harry, are you there?"

Harry heard Danny stir beside him. Christ, Danny, not now! Not like before, in the grotto.

"Tell me where you are. I'll come to you."

Danny stirred again. The police were almost there. Car lengths away. Less.

"Dammit, Harry. Talk to me. Tell me where—"
CLICK.

Harry snapped off the phone and slid his body over Danny's in the dark, below window level, praying he would be silent. Then, from somewhere under him, the phone rang again.

Adrianna was calling back.

"Christ," Harry breathed.

The ring was loud. Shrill. It sounded as if it were being blasted through a speaker. Desperately he fumbled under him, trying to find the phone in the dark. But it was caught between the folds of his shirt and Danny and the seat. Pulling his arms in, he tried to smother it with his body. Hoping to hell that in the stillness of the summer night the police couldn't hear it.

An eternity passed before the ringing stopped. And then there was silence. Harry wanted to look up, see if the police had passed. But he didn't dare. He could hear the thump of his heart. The thud of his pulse.

Suddenly there was a sharp knock on the window. A chill shot through him. His senses froze. The knock came again. Louder.

Finally. Terrified. Resigned. Harry raised his head.

Elena was looking in at him. A priest was with her, and they had a wheelchair.

AN ATTRACTIVE WOMAN IN A BLUE BLAZER
and large straw hat sat alone at a table near the front window of the bar of the Hotel Florence. From there she could see the waterfront and the landing where the hydrofoil would come in. She could also see the Gruppo Cardinale police near the ticket booth and on the landing itself, watching the people who waited for the boat.

Her back turned slightly to the crowd of the room, she took a cell phone from her purse and dialed a number in Milan, where the call was received by a special switching box and forwarded to another number and switching box in the coastal city of Civitavecchia, and from there to an unlisted number in Rome.

"*Si*," a male voice answered.

"This is *S*," Thomas Kind said.

"*Un momento*."

Silence. Then—

"Yes." Another male voice had come on. It was distorted electronically so that it could not be recognized. The rest of the conversation was held in French.

s: The target is alive. Possibly wounded. . . . And, it is unfortunate to report, escaped.

MALE VOICE: I know.

s: What do you want me to do?—I will resign if you like.

MALE VOICE: No. I value your resolve and proficiency. . . . The police know you are there and are looking for you, but they have no idea who you are.

s: So I presumed.

MALE VOICE: Can you leave the area?

s: With luck.

MALE VOICE: Then I want you to come here.

s: I can still pursue the target from where I am. Even with the police.

MALE VOICE: Yes, but why, when the moth has waked from its sleep and can be brought to the flame?

Palestrina pressed a button on a small box beside his telephone, then handed the receiver to Farel, who took it and hung it up. For a long moment the Vatican secretariat of state sat looking out across his sparsely lit marbled office at the paintings, sculptures, shelves of ancient books, at the centuries of history surrounding him in his residence on the floor beneath that of the papal apartments in the Palace of Sixtus V, the apartments where the Holy Father now slept, mind and body exhausted from the regimen of the day, trusting in his advisers to steer the course of the Holy See.

"If I may, Eminence," Farel said.

Palestrina looked at him. "Say what is on your mind."

"The priest. Thomas Kind cannot stop him, nor can Roscani with his huge force. He's like a cat who has not used up his lives. Yes, we may entrap him. . . . But what if he speaks out first?"

"You are suggesting one man could make us lose China."

"Yes. And there would be nothing we could do about it. Except to deny everything. But China would still be lost, and suspicion would live for centuries."

Slowly Palestrina swiveled his chair, turning to the antique credenza behind him and the sculptured figure that sat on it—the head of Alexander of Macedon, carved of Grecian marble in the fifth century.

"I was born the son of the king of Macedonia." He was talking to Farel, but his eyes were on the sculpture. "Aristotle was my tutor. When I was twenty, my father was assassinated and I became king, surrounded everywhere by my father's enemies. In a short while I learned who they were and had them executed, and then, gathering those loyal to me, I moved out to crush the rebellion they had begun. . . . In two years I was commander of Greece and had crossed the Hellespont into Persia with an army of thirty-five thousand Greeks and Macedonians."

Slowly, deliberately, Palestrina turned toward Farel, the angle at which he sat and the spill from the lamp on the credenza behind him making his head and Alexander's appear almost as one. Now his eyes found Farel's and he went on. And as he did, Farel felt a chill cross his shoulders and creep down his spine. With every word Palestrina's eyes grew darker and became more distant as he was drawn ever deeper into the character he was convinced he was.

"Near Troy I defeated a force of forty thousand, losing only one hundred and ten of my men. From there I pushed southward, meeting King Darius and the main Persian army of five hundred thousand.

"Darius fled in our wake, leaving behind his mother and his wife and his children. After that I took Tyre and Gaza and moved into Egypt, and thereby controlled the entire eastern Mediterranean coast. Next came Babylon and what was left of the Persian empire beyond the southern shores of the Caspian Sea into Afghanistan . . . and then I turned north into what is now called Russian Turkestan and Central Asia. . . . That was," Palestrina's gaze drifted off, "in 327 B.C. . . . and I had managed most all of it in three years."

Abruptly Palestrina swung back to Farel, the distance in him gone.

"I did not fail in Persia, Jacov. Priest or not, I will not fail in China." Immediately Palestrina's voice lowered, and his stare cut into Farel. "Bring Father Bardoni here. Bring him, now."

102

Bellagio. 10:50 P.M.

ELENA LAY IN THE DARK, LOOKING AT THE
square of light that came in through the small window high
on the wall above her.

They were in the *convento,* the friary, behind the church,
which served as housing for the priests. Except for Father
Renato, the short, affable priest who had gone to the truck
with her, and two or three others, the rest of the clergy were
away on retreat. It was a happenstance that provided her with
the tiny bedroom she was in and the one next to it, where
Father Daniel slept, and the similar room across the hall,
where Harry was.

She still regretted her delayed return to the truck and the
anxiety she knew she had caused Harry, but she'd had little
choice. Father Renato had been hard to convince, and it was
only when she reached her mother general by phone in Siena
and he had spoken to her personally that he'd relented and

gone with Elena, waiting with the wheelchair in the church's shadow until the police on motorcycles had passed.

Then they'd brought Father Daniel in, given him tea and rice pudding, and put him to bed. Afterward Father Renato had taken them to the *convento*'s tiny kitchen and served them a pasta-and-chicken dish left over from the evening meal. And then he had shown them the rooms where they could sleep and gone back to his room, warning them that tomorrow the priests would return and that they would have to leave before they did.

"Leave . . . ," Elena thought, her eyes still on the square of light high on the ceiling above her. "To go where?"

The thought, while deliberate, triggered something else—her own sense of freedom, or, rather, her lack of it. The turning point had come when she'd broken down so emotionally in the water cave, and Harry had left his brother to come to her and hold her and comfort her even though she knew he was exhausted and must have been at wits' end himself. A second moment had been even more pointed, when he'd returned with the truck and seen her standing naked outside the cave. It was something that, as she pictured it in her mind—the way he so quickly apologized and turned and went back into the cave—became no longer embarrassing but erotic. She wondered, if she were not a nun, whether, despite the seriousness and urgency of their situation, he might have let his eyes linger a little longer—after all, she was still young and had what she thought was a good figure.

Suddenly, and for the first time since she'd been in the hospital room in Pescara listening to the sound of Danny's breathing over the intercom, she found herself becoming sexually aroused. The night was still thick with heat, and she had taken off her habit and lay naked under the sheets. And now, as the feeling increased, she began to feel a warmth move through her. Reaching up, she touched her breasts.

Again she saw Harry step out of the cave, felt his eyes on her. In that moment she knew her feelings of wanting to be a woman in the fullest sense, wholly and physically, were real; the difference was, she was no longer afraid of them. If God had been testing her, it was not so much that He was challenging her inner strength or her spoken vows of chastity and obedience, but instead, helping her search for herself. Who she really was and wanted to be. And maybe that was the *why* of all this. And why Harry had come into her life. To once and for all help her make that decision. His presence and manner alone touched her in a way she had never before experienced. It was tender and fresh and reassuring and somehow lifted the guilt and sense of isolation her feelings had always brought her. It was like opening a door and finding that on the other side, life was safe and joyous and that it was all right to be alive, with the same passions and emotions other people had. That it was all right to be Elena Voso.

HARRY HEARD THE SOFT KNOCK, then saw the door open in the darkness.

"Mr. Addison," Elena whispered.

"What is it?" He sat up, quickly alert.

"Nothing is wrong, Mr. Addison. . . . Would it be all right if I came in?"

Harry hesitated, puzzled. "Yes, of course . . ."

He saw the door open a little more, and then the outline of her figure against the diminished light of the hallway outside, and the door closed behind her.

"I'm sorry to wake you."

"It's all right . . ."

There was just enough light for Harry to see her come

toward the bed. She was wearing her habit but was barefoot, and seemed excited and nervous at the same time.

"Please sit down," he said, and indicated the edge of the bed.

Elena looked at the bed and then quickly back to Harry.

"I would prefer to stand, Mr. Addison."

"Harry," he said.

"Harry . . ." Still nervous, Elena smiled.

"What is it?"

"I—I have come to a decision that I wanted to share with you . . ."

Harry nodded, still unsure what was happening.

"I—told you shortly after we met that God had given me a job to do in caring for your brother."

"Yes."

"Well, when it is done, I—" Elena stopped and Harry saw her dig down and find conviction. "I plan to petition my superiors for dispensation of my vows and to leave the convent."

For a long moment Harry said nothing. Finally he did. "Are you asking my opinion?"

"No, I'm stating a fact."

"Elena—," Harry said gently. "Maybe before you make a final decision you should realize that after what we've been through, none of us are thinking very clearly."

"I'm aware of that. I'm also aware that what we've gone through has helped clarify thoughts and feelings I've had for some time. Before any of this happened. . . . Most simply, I want to be with a man—and to love him in every way, and to have him love me in that way, too."

Harry studied her carefully, watched her breathe. Even in the dim light he could see the sparkle and determination in her eyes. "That's a very personal thing . . ."

Elena said nothing. Harry smiled. "Maybe what I don't understand is why you're telling *me*."

"Because I don't know what might happen tomorrow, and I want to have told someone who would understand . . . and because I wanted to tell *you,* Harry." Elena looked at him for a long moment, her eyes intent on his.

"Good night and God bless," she whispered finally and turned and left.

HARRY WATCHED HER cross the room in the dark, had just a glimpse of her as she opened the door and went out. She'd come to share something deeply personal with him, why exactly, he still wasn't sure. All he did know was that he'd never met anyone quite like her, but he also knew that if he was being drawn to her, this was not the time. The last thing they needed now was that kind of distraction. It was far too disruptive and, therefore, much too dangerous.

A STYLISH, HANDSOME WOMAN WEARING A
large straw hat stood in line with the other passengers, waiting as the hydrofoil approached the boat landing from the
dark of the lake.

At the top stairs above, four Gruppo Cardinale police in
flak jackets and carrying Uzis stood watch. Four more
patrolled the landing itself, studying faces of waiting passengers, searching for the fugitives. A spot check of papers confirmed that almost all of them were foreign tourists. Great
Britain. Germany. Brazil. Australia. The United States.

"Grazie," a young policeman said, as he handed Julia
Louise Phelps's passport back to her, then touched the brim
of his hat and smiled. This was no blond killer with a
scratched face, nor an Italian nun, nor a fugitive priest or his
brother. This was a tall, attractive woman, an American as he
had guessed, with a large straw hat and distinctive smile. It
was why he had approached her and asked for her papers in
the first place, not because she was a suspect, but because he
was flirting. And she had let him.

And then, as the hydrofoil docked and the passengers onboard disembarked, she put her passport back into her purse, smiled once again at the policeman, and, in the company of the other passengers, went onboard. A moment later the gangplank was pulled back, the engines revved, and the hydrofoil moved away.

The policemen on the landing and those at the top of the stairs watched it pick up speed, then saw the hull lift up out of the water as it moved out into the darkness of the lake, crossing to Tremezzo and Lenno, and then Lezzeno and Argegno, and finally back to Como. The hydrofoil *Freccia delle Betulle* was the last boat for the night. And, to a man, the police relaxed as they watched it go. Knowing they had done their job well. Confident that on their watch, not one of the fugitives had slipped past them.

Rome. The Vatican.
Wednesday, July 15, 12:20 A.M.

Farel opened the door to Palestrina's private office, and the young, bespectacled Father Bardoni entered, poised, unmoved by the hour or by being called there. Showing no emotion at all. Simply answering the summons of a superior.

Palestrina was behind his desk and motioned Father Bardoni toward a chair in front of him.

"I have called you here to tell you personally that Cardinal Marsciano has been taken ill," he said as the priest sat down.

"Ill?" Father Bardoni sat forward.

"He collapsed here, in my office, early this evening after attending a meeting at the Chinese Embassy. The doctors believe it to be a simple case of exhaustion. But they are not certain. As a result he is being kept under observation."

"Where is he?"

"Here, on the Vatican grounds," Palestrina said. "The guest apartments in the Tower of San Giovanni."

"Why is he not in a hospital?" From the corner of his eye, Father Bardoni saw Farel step forward to stand near him.

"Because I chose to keep him here. Because of what I believe to be the reason for his 'exhaustion' . . ."

"Which is?"

"The ongoing dilemma of Father Daniel." Palestrina watched the priest carefully. So far he was showing no outward display of emotion, even now, at the mention of Father Daniel.

"I don't understand."

"Cardinal Marsciano has sworn he was dead. And perhaps he still does not believe, as the police do, that he is not. Moreover, new evidence suggests that Father Daniel not only lives but is well enough to continually avoid the authorities. All of which means that he is probably able to communicate in one way or another—"

Palestrina paused, looking at the priest directly, making certain there would be no confusion interpreting what he said next.

"How joyous it would make Cardinal Marsciano to see Father Daniel alive. But since he is under the care of physicians and unable to travel, it follows that Father Daniel should come, or be brought, if it is necessary, to visit him here, at the apartments of San Giovanni."

It was here that Father Bardoni faltered, casting a quick, furtive glance at Farel—a sudden, instinctive reaction, to see if Farel fully sided with Palestrina and backed Marsciano's imprisonment. And from his cold, impassive stare, there was no doubt whatsoever that he did. Recovering, he looked back to Palestrina, incensed.

"You are suggesting that I know where he is? And could get that message to him? That I could somehow engineer his coming to the Vatican?"

"A box is opened," Palestrina said easily. "A moth flies out. . . . Where does it go? Many people ask that same question and hunt for it. But it is never found because, at the last minute, it moves, and then moves again, and then again. Most difficult when it is either ill or injured. That is, unless it has help . . . from someone sympathetic, a famous writer perhaps, or someone in the clergy . . . and is attended to by a gentle hand schooled in such things. A nurse perhaps, or a nun, or one and the same . . . a nursing sister from Siena— Elena Voso."

Father Bardoni didn't react. Simply stared, vacantly, as if he had no idea what the secretariat of state was talking about. It was a deliberate orchestration to cover his earlier lapse, but it was too late, and he knew it.

Palestrina leaned forward. "Father Daniel is to come in silence. To speak with no one. . . . Should he be caught along the way, his answer—to the police, to the media, even to Taglia or Roscani—is that he simply does not remember what happened . . ."

Father Bardoni started to protest, but Palestrina held up a hand to silence him, and then he finished, his voice just loud enough to be heard.

"Understand—that for every day Father Daniel does not come, Cardinal Marsciano's mental outlook will worsen. . . . His health declining with his spirit, until there comes a point where"—he shrugged—"it no longer matters."

"Eminence." Father Bardoni was suddenly curt. "You are speaking to the wrong man. I have no more idea where Father Daniel is or how to reach him than you."

Palestrina stared for a moment, then made the sign of the cross. *"Che Dio ti protegga,"* he said. May God protect you.

Immediately Farel crossed to the door and opened it. Father Bardoni hesitated, then stood and walked past Farel and out into the darkness.

Palestrina watched the door as it closed. The wrong man? No, Father Bardoni was not. He was Marsciano's courier and had been all along. The one responsible for getting Father Daniel out of the hands of medical personnel and to Pescara after the bus explosion and guiding his movements ever since. Yes, they had suspected—followed him, had his phone line tapped, even suspected he was the man who had hired the hydrofoil in Milan. But they had been unable to prove anything. Except he had erred in glancing at Farel, and this had been enough. Palestrina knew Marsciano commanded strong loyalty. And if Marsciano had trusted enough in Father Daniel to confess to him, he would have trusted in Father Bardoni to help save the American's life. And Father Bardoni would have responded.

And so, he was not the wrong man, but the right one. And because of it, Palestrina was certain his message would be sent.

3:00 A.M.

Palestrina sat at a small writing table in his bedroom. He was dressed in sandals and a silk scarlet robe that, with his physical poise and enormous size and his great mane of white hair, gave him the look of a Roman emperor. On the table in front of him were the early editions of a half dozen world newspapers. In each the lead story was the ongoing tragedy in China. To his right, a small television tuned to World

News Network showed live coverage from Hefei, at the moment the picture was of truckloads of troops of the People's Liberation Army entering the city. They were dressed in coveralls, their hands gloved, their wrists and ankles taped, their faces hidden by bright orange filtration masks and clear protective goggles to safeguard—as a similarly dressed on-camera correspondent explained—against the transfer of bodily fluids and the spread of disease as they rushed to help manage the still-multiplying volumes of dead.

Glancing off, Palestrina looked at the bank of phones at his elbow. Pierre Weggen, he knew, was at this moment in Beijing in a friend-to-friend conversation with Yan Yeh. Solemnly—and with no hint whatsoever that the idea was any other than his alone—Weggen would be laying the early seeds of Palestrina's blueprint to rebuild all of China's water systems. He was trusting the Swiss investment banker's station and longtime association with the president of the People's Bank of China would be enough for the Chinese businessman to embrace the idea and take it directly to the general secretary of the Communist Party.

Whatever happened, when the meeting was ended and the proper courtesies had been said, Weggen would call and let him know. Palestrina glanced at his bed. He should sleep, but he knew it was impossible. Standing, he went to his dressing room and changed into his familiar black suit and white clerical collar. Moments later he left his private apartments.

Purposely taking a service elevator, he went unseen to the ground floor, and from there out a side door and into the dark of the formal gardens.

He walked for an hour, maybe more, lost in thought, doing little more than wandering. Along the Avenue of the Square Garden to the Central Avenue of the Forest and then back, pausing for some time at Giovanni Vasanzio's seventeenth-century sculpture *Fontana dell' Aquilone*, the Fountain of the Eagle. The eagle itself, the uppermost piece on the fountain—the heraldic symbol of the Borghese, the family of Pope Paul V—was, to Palestrina, something entirely different: symbolic, enormously personal and profound, it brought him to ancient Persia and the edge of his other life, touching his entire being in a way nothing else could. From it, he drew strength. And from that strength came power and conviction and the certitude that what he was doing was right. The eagle held him there for some time and then finally released him.

Vaguely, he drew away, moving off in the dark. In time, he passed the two INTELSAT earth stations for Vatican Radio and then the tower building itself, and then continued on, across the endless green stage maintained by an army of full-time gardeners, through ancient groves and pathways, along the manicured lawns. Past the magnolias, the bougainvillaeas. Under the pines and palms, oaks and olives. Past seeming miles of carefully trimmed hedges. Surprised now and then by a shower of water thrown up by the booby traps of nighttime sprinklers set on automatic timers with no mind but the inching of the clock.

And then a lone thought turned him back. In the faint light of day, Palestrina approached the entry to the yellowbrick building that was Vatican Radio. Opening the door, he climbed the interior steps to the upper tower and then stepped out onto its circular walkway.

Resting his massive hands on the edge of the battlement, he stood and watched day begin to rise over the Roman hills. From there he could view the city, the Vatican Palace, St. Peter's, and much of the Vatican gardens. It was a favorite place and one that not so coincidentally provided physical security should he ever need it. The building itself was on a hill some distance from the Vatican proper and therefore easily defended. The exterior walkway where he stood encircled the entire building, putting anyone approaching in clear view; and gave him a vantage point from which he could direct his defenders.

It was a fanciful sentiment perhaps, but one he took increasingly to heart. Especially in light of the singular thought that had brought him there—Farel's observation that Father Daniel was like the cat that had not used up its lives, the one man alone who could make him lose China. Before, Father Daniel had been an unwelcome glitch, a festering sore to be eliminated. That he had been able to elude both Thomas Kind and all of Roscani's men, and continued to do so, touched a chord deep in Palestrina that terrified him—his secret belief in a dark and pagan netherworld and the mystic depraved spirits who dwelled there. These spirits, he was certain, were responsible for the sudden onslaught of crippling fever and his subsequent cruel death at the age of thirty-three when he lived as Alexander. If it were they who were guiding Father Daniel—

"No!" Palestrina said out loud, then deliberately turned from his perch and left, walking back down the stairs and out into the gardens. He would not allow himself to think of the spirits, now or ever again. They were not real but rather of his own imagination, and he would not let his own imagination destroy him.

104

Hefei, China. Wednesday, July 15, 11:40 A.M.

BUREAUCRACY AND CONFUSION AND HIS OWN position as water-quality inspector had delayed Li Wen from leaving the filtration plant. But finally he had done so by simply walking out of the angry turmoil of arguing politicians and scientists, and leaving. And now, heavy briefcase in one hand, the other pressing a handkerchief against his nose in a futile attempt to keep out the stench of decaying bodies, he worked his way up Changjiang Lu. Walking in the street one moment, on the sidewalk the next. Alternately moving between a flow of backed-up ambulances and emergency vehicles and the hordes of frightened, confused people desperate to find a way out of the city, or looking for relatives, or waiting in dread to feel the first chills and nausea that meant the water they had drunk earlier, that they had been told was safe, had poisoned them, too. And most were doing all three at the same time.

Another block and he passed the Overseas Chinese Hotel, where he had stayed and left his suitcase and clothing. The hotel was no longer a hotel but now Anhui Province's Anti-Poisoning Headquarters; it had been taken over in a matter of hours, with guests abruptly thrown out of their rooms, their luggage hurriedly stacked near the front of the lobby, some of it spilling out onto the street. But even if he had time, Li Wen would not go back there anyway. There were too many people who might recognize him, stop to ask him questions, delay him further. And the one thing Li Wen could not afford was further delay.

Head down, doing his best to avoid looking at the horror-stricken faces of the people around him, he walked the few remaining blocks to the railroad station, where army trucks waited in long lines to pick up the hundreds of soldiers arriving by train.

Soaked with sweat, lugging his briefcase, he pushed around soldiers and dodged military police, each step becoming more laborious than the last, as his decidedly out-of-shape forty-six-year-old body battled the strain of the last days, the persistent heat, and the putrid, inescapable odor of rotting corpses, which, by now, permeated everything. Finally, he reached the *jicun chu,* the left-luggage room, and collected the battered suitcase he'd checked early Monday when he'd first arrived; a suitcase containing the chemicals he would need to prepare more of his "snowballs."

Doubly weighted now, he went back into the station, pushed through the platform entrance gate, and walked another fifty yards to the track area already jammed with refugees waiting for the next trains out. In fifteen minutes his train would come. The soldiers arriving on it would pile off, and he and the others would rush on. Because he was a government official, he would have a seat and for that he was extraordinarily grateful. After that, he could sit back and for a time relax. The trip to Wuhu would take nearly two hours, and then he would change trains for Nanjing, where he would spend the night at the Xuanwu Hotel on Zhongyang Lu as planned. It was there he would rest and let himself begin to feel his accomplishment and sense of retribution over the hated, dogmatic government that had so long ago killed his father and robbed him of his childhood.

Feel it and enjoy it, and wait to receive the order that would send him to his next objective.

105

Bellagio. Gruppo Cardinale Headquarters,
Villa Lorenzi. Wednesday, July 15, 6:50 A.M.

SHIRT OPEN AT THE NECK, HIS JACKET OFF,
Roscani looked out across the grand ballroom. A skeleton
staff worked as they had in the hours since midnight, when,
at the lack of any action at all, he had sent only the most critical of them off to the second floor to sleep in the cots
brought in by the army. Personnel were still out in the field,
and Castelletti had taken off in the helicopter at first light,
while Scala had left before then to go back to the grotto with
two of the Belgian Malinois and their handlers, still not convinced that they had searched all of it.

At two A.M. Roscani had put in a call for an additional
eight hundred Italian Army troops and then gone to bed himself. By three-fifteen he was up and showered and back in
the same clothes he had worn for two days. By four he'd
decided they'd all had enough.

At six A.M. an announcement was broadcast over local radio and television and read in early parish masses. In exactly two hours, at eight o'clock sharp, the Italian Army would stage a massive door-to-door search of the entire area. The phrasing had been simple and direct: the fugitives were there and would be uncovered, and anyone found harboring them would be considered an accomplice and prosecuted accordingly.

Roscani's move was more than a threat, it was a ploy to make the fugitives think they might have a chance if they made their move before the deadline, and it was why Gruppo Cardinale police and army troops had moved into position a full thirty minutes before the announcement was made; silently watching and waiting, hoping one or all of them would cut from their hiding places and run.

6:57

Roscani glanced at Eros Barbu's elaborate rococo clock on the wall over the silent bandstand, then looked to the men and women at the computer terminals and phone banks, sifting information, coordinating the Gruppo Cardinale personnel in the field. Finally, he took a sip of cold, sweet coffee and went outside, glancing again around the elaborate ballroom as he did.

Outside, Lake Como was still, as was the air. Walking toward the water, Roscani turned and looked back toward the imposing villa. How anyone could afford to live in such a place and in the style of Eros Barbu boggled the mind, especially the mind of a policeman. Still, he wondered, as he had earlier, what it would have been like to be part of it. Invited there to dance and listen to the music of a live orchestra and perhaps, he smiled, to be just a little bit decadent.

It was a contemplation that faded as he walked along the gravel that bordered the lake, and his thoughts again turned to the INTERPOL dossier that had provided him no information whatsoever on his blond ice picker/razor man. At almost the same moment, he became aware of a strong scent of wild flowers. The odor was far more pungent than pleasant, and instantly he was transported back four years to when he had been temporarily assigned to a branch of the Ministero dell'Interno's Antimafia section working to break a series of mafia murders in Sicily. He was in a field outside Palermo with several other investigators examining a body a farmer had found facedown in a ditch. It was the same early morning as it was now, the air crisp and still, the peppery smell of the wild flowers dominating the senses as they did here. When they rolled the body over and saw that the throat had been cut from ear to ear, a shout went up from all of the investigators at once. To a man they knew who their killer was.

"Thomas Kind," Roscani said out loud, a chill punching through him from his head to his feet.

Thomas Kind. He'd never even thought of him. The terrorist had been out of the public eye for at least three years, maybe more, and thought to be ill or retired or both and living in the relative safety of Sudan.

"Christ!" Roscani was suddenly turning, running back toward the villa. It was seven-forty in the morning. Twenty minutes exactly before the door-to-door sweep was to begin.

106

Bellagio. The car-ferry landing. Same time.

HARRY WATCHED THE HEAVILY ARMED *CARA-binieri* questioning the man and woman in the dark Lancia in front of them. Immediately the police ordered the man out of the car and walked with him as he opened the trunk. Finding nothing, the police waved the couple on. Then as the Lancia drove across the ramp and onto the ferry, the police turned toward them.

"Here we go," Harry said under his breath.

Five of them were in a white Ford van with Church of Santa Chiara neatly stenciled on the doors. Father Renato was at the wheel with Elena beside him. Harry, Danny, and a young, almost baby-faced priest, Father Natalini, sat in back. Elena was dressed in a business suit and wearing tortoise-shell glasses, her hair pulled back tightly and twisted in a bun. The priests were in their everyday black with white clerical collars. Danny wore glasses as well, and he and

Harry, still bearded, were also in black. Long black coats buttoned to the throat with black zucchettos on their heads. They looked like rabbis, which was the idea.

"I know them," Father Renato said quietly in Italian as the *carabinieri* came to either window.

"*Buon giorno,* Alfonso. Massimo."

"Padre Renato! *Buon giorno.*" Alfonso, the first *carabiniere,* was tall and hulking and physically intimidating, but he smiled broadly as he recognized the van and Father Renato and then Father Natalini. "*Buon giorno, Padre.*"

"*Buon giorno.*" Father Natalini smiled from where he sat beside Danny.

For the next ninety seconds Harry felt as though his heart was coming to full arrest as Father Renato and the policemen chatted in Italian. Once in a while he caught a word or phrase he understood. "*Rabbino.*" "*Israele.*" "*Conferenza Cristiano/giudea.*"

The rabbi business had been Harry's idea. It was straight out of the movies. Crazy and preposterous. And sitting there, breathless, terrified, waiting for the *carabinieri* to suddenly stop talking and order them all out of the van the way they had the man in the Lancia, he wondered what the hell he must have been thinking. Still, they'd had to do something, and quickly, after Elena had come hurriedly into his room before dawn with Father Renato, saying her mother general had arranged a place for them to stay just over the border in Switzerland.

With the approval of his superior, Father Renato had agreed to help get them there—but he had no idea how. It was while Harry was dressing that he'd absently looked in the mirror and seen his growth of beard and remembered Danny's. It was nuts, but it might work, considering they had bluffed their way through police checkpoints twice before;

and because Father Renato and Father Natalini were not only clergy but also locals who knew everyone, including the police.

And then there was the L.A. thing. Harry might have been Catholic, but one didn't move far in the entertainment business without having Jewish friends and clients. He'd been invited to Passover seders for years, had shared uncountable breakfasts at Nate and Al's deli in Beverly Hills, an oasis for Jewish writers and comedians; gone regularly with clients visiting relatives to the ethnic neighborhoods around Fairfax and Beverly, Pico and Robertson. More than once he'd marveled at the similarity of the yarmulke to the Catholic skullcap, the zucchetto, the black coats of the rabbis to those of bishops and priests. And now, for better or worse, he and Danny had become visiting rabbis from Israel, touring Italy as part of an ongoing discourse between Christians and Jews. Elena had become an Italian guide and translator from Rome, traveling with them. Though God forbid anyone should ask her, or them, to speak Hebrew.

"*Fuggitivo*," one of the *carabinieri* said sharply. Bringing Harry back with a rush.

"*Fuggitivo*," Father Renato nodded, adding a succinct, fiery reply in Italian. Obviously both *carabinieri* agreed with what he said, because they suddenly stepped back, saluted, and waved the van forward.

Harry looked to Elena, then saw Father Renato shift into gear. Felt the van move forward. Up onto the ramp and across it into the hold of the ferry. Turning back, he saw the policemen advance on the next vehicle in line. Saw the occupants made to get out, show identification, while the vehicle itself was aggressively searched.

None in the van dared look at another. Just waited in silence for an agonizing ten minutes before the last car came on board, the gangway doors closed, and the ferry got under way.

Harry felt the sweat run down his neck, trickle from his armpits. How many more of these could they get away with? How long would their luck, if that's what it was, hold?

THE FERRY HAD BEEN STEP ONE, sailing for Mennagio at seven fifty-six, exactly four minutes before the Italian Army sweep of the entire peninsula would begin, and fifteen minutes after Salvatore Belsito's farm truck had been found parked on a street a half mile from Santa Chiara. Father Natalini had left it there just before six, carefully wiping the steering wheel and gearshift clean of his fingerprints, then walking quickly back to Santa Chiara.

Step two, the crossing of the border from Italy into Switzerland, would have been more difficult, if not impossible, because neither Father Renato nor Father Natalini knew Gruppo Cardinale personnel at the border checkpoint. What saved them was that Father Natalini had grown up in Porlezza, a small town inland from Mennagio, and knew as only a native could know, the narrow country roads that wound and twisted through the hills and rose up into the Alps; roads that enabled them to bypass the Gruppo Cardinale checkpoint at Oria and brought them into Switzerland unmolested at ten twenty-two in the morning.

The Vatican. The Tower of San Giovanni.
11:00 A.M.

MARSCIANO STOOD AT THE GLASS DOOR, THE only opening in the room to admit daylight; and, other than the locked and guarded entry door from the hallway outside, its only exit. Behind him, the television screen he could no longer bear to watch glowed like an all-seeing eye.

He could turn the TV off, of course, but he hadn't and wouldn't. It was a trait of character Palestrina understood all too well in Marsciano, which was why he'd ordered the twenty-inch Nokia left behind when he'd had the formerly luxurious one-room apartment stripped of all but its essentials—bed, writing table, chair—and ordered the apartment itself shut off from the rest of the building.

"The death toll in Hefei has reached sixty thousand, six hundred and is still rising. There remains no estimation where the number will end."

The field correspondent's voice was crisp behind him. Marsciano did not need to see the screen. It would be the same color graphic they used every hour to project the number of deaths, as if they were doing exit polls projecting votes in an election.

Finally, Marsciano pulled the door open and stepped out onto the tiny balcony. Fresh air touched him, and, mercifully, the resonance of the television diminished.

Grasping the iron safety railing, he closed his eyes. As if not seeing would somehow lessen the awfulness. In his darkness he saw another vision—the cold, conspiratorial faces of Cardinal Matadi and Monsignor Capizzi watching him dispassionately from their seats inside the limousine on the drive back to the Vatican from the Chinese Embassy. Then he saw Palestrina pick up the car phone and quietly ask for Farel, the secretariat's gaze rising up to hold on Marsciano's as he waited for the Vatican policeman to come on the line. And then came the secretariat's soft-spoken words—

"Cardinal Marsciano has been taken ill in the car. Prepare a room for him in the Tower of San Giovanni."

The chilling remembrance made Marsciano suddenly open his eyes to where he was now. Below, a Vatican gardener was looking up at him. The man stared for a moment and then turned back to what he had been doing.

How many hundreds of times, Marsciano thought, had he come to the tower to visit foreign dignitaries staying in its ornate apartments? How many times had he looked up from the gardens below, as the worker had, to see this curious little platform on which he stood, never giving a thought to how darkly sinister it was?

Hanging like a diver's platform forty feet off the ground, it was the only opening in the cylindrical wall from top to bottom. An exit that led nowhere. Surrounded by a thin, iron safety railing, the platform was hardly wider than the door itself and no more than two feet across. The sheer wall above it rose another thirty feet to the point where the windows of the other apartments jutted sharply out. Looking upward, one could not see past those windows, but Marsciano knew they were near the top, and above them was a circular walkway and then the tower's turreted crown.

In other words, there was no way up or down or to the sides, making no reason for the platform at all. Except as a place to stand and breathe the air of Rome and marvel at the green of the Vatican gardens below. After that there was nothing. The rest of this distant corner of the *Vaticano* was surrounded by a high, fortified wall built in the ninth century to keep barbarians out and at other times, as now, serving to keep people in.

Slowly, Marsciano slid his hands from the rail and went back inside to the confines of his room and the television screen that was the center of it. On it he saw what the world saw: Hefei, China—a live helicopter shot of Chao Lake and then, in a cavalcade of horror, an aerial view of a series of huge circus-like tents, one after the other, erected in city parks, alongside factories, on open land outside the city proper; and the offscreen correspondent explaining what they were—makeshift morgues for the dead.

Abruptly, Marsciano turned off the sound. He would watch but he could listen no longer; the running commentary had become unbearable. It was a scorecard on which his personal crimes—done, he reminded himself over and over, as if in some desperate attempt to save his sanity, because Palestrina had held him hostage to his love of God and the Church—were tallied, one after the other in minute-by-minute detail.

Yes, he was guilty. So were Matadi and Capizzi. They had

all let Palestrina loose to commit this outrage. What was worse, if anything could be worse than what he was seeing now, was that he knew Pierre Weggen was well into his work on Yan Yeh. And the Chinese banker, sensitive and caring as Marsciano personally knew he was, would be truly horrified by what appeared to be an act of nature gone amuck in human hands, and would pressure his superiors in the Communist Party, with all he had, to listen to Weggen's proposal to immediately rebuild China's entire water-delivery and -filtration infrastructure. But even if they agreed to meet with Weggen, the politics would take time. Time. When there was none. When Palestrina was already moving his saboteurs to the second lake.

108

Lugano, Switzerland.
Still Wednesday, July 15, Noon.

ELENA HAD NOT REALLY LOOKED AT HARRY
since she'd helped him dress Danny and get him into the van.
He wondered if she'd been embarrassed by coming to him
the way she had and telling what she did and now didn't
know what to do about it. What surprised him was the extent
to which the whole thing had affected him, and continued to
affect him. Elena was a bright, beautiful, ballsy, and caring
woman who had suddenly found herself and wanted the freedom to express it. And from the way she'd presented herself—coming barefoot into his room in the dark and talking
in the intimate way she had—in his mind there was no doubt
she'd wanted him to be the one to help her do it. The trouble
was, as he'd told himself then, this was not the time, and he
had to stop thinking about it—other things were far too
pressing. So now—as they wound down out of the hills from

the north and turned along Lake Lugano to drive into Lugano itself, Viale Castagnola, across the Cassarate River, and up Via Serafino Balestra to the small, storied, private home at Via Monte Ceneri, 87—he deliberately turned his attention to what had to be done next.

It was a given that they couldn't keep traveling as hunted criminals from one place to another, trusting that somehow someone would help them. Danny needed a place safe enough and secure enough to rest and recover to the point where he could talk to Harry in a thoughtful, coherent manner about the murder of the cardinal vicar of Rome. Moreover, and as important, they needed to acquire powerful legal representation. And those two things, Harry knew, had to be his only priorities.

"WE HERE?" Danny asked weakly as Father Renato set the hand brake and turned off the engine.

"Yes, Father Daniel." Father Renato half smiled. "Thankfully."

Getting out, Elena saw Harry glance at her briefly as he opened the van's sliding door and then he turned away as Father Natalini brought the wheelchair from the back. Father Daniel had said almost nothing during the trip, just stared out the window at the passing countryside. Elena was certain he was still exhausted from the events of the past forty-eight hours. He needed to eat and then to sleep for as long as he could.

Elena stepped back, watching as Harry and Father Natalini hefted Danny into the wheelchair then carried him up the steps into the second-floor living room of the house on Via Monte Ceneri. What had happened the night before made her feel more awkward than embarrassed. In the exhilarated, emotional rush she'd had when she'd gone to Harry, she'd revealed more about herself and her feelings than she'd intended, or at least more than was appropriate when she was yet to give up her vows. But she'd done it nonetheless, and there was no taking it back. The question was how to act now. It was why she had been unable to look at him directly all day, or to say more than the few words that were necessary. She just didn't know how.

Suddenly the door at the top of the stairs opened, and their hostess appeared.

"Come in quickly," Veronique Vaccaro said and stepped back to make way for them.

Once they were inside, she immediately closed the door and looked at everyone in turn, as if sizing them up. Diminutive, temperamental, and middle-aged, Veronique was an artist and sculptor who dressed in earth colors and whose quickly spoken sentences came in a bewildering mix of French, English, and Italian. Abruptly she looked to Father Renato.

"*Merci.* Now you must go. *Capisce?*"

No offer to rest, use the washroom, even a glass of water. No, he and Father Natalini had to go.

"A vehicle from a Bellagio church parked in front of a private house in Lugano? Might as well call the police and tell them where you are."

Father Renato smiled and nodded. Veronique was right. And as he and Father Natalini turned to leave, Danny surprised everyone by suddenly perking up and moving his wheelchair forward to take their hands.

"*Grazie. Grazie mille,*" he said with genuine gratitude, understanding what the two men had risked to bring them there.

And then the priests were gone, and Veronique, saying she was preparing something for them to eat, left, passing one of half a dozen large abstract sculptures that sat like characters in the small, sunny room, and disappeared through a doorway on the far side of it.

"Father Daniel should rest," Elena said almost the moment she had gone. "Let me ask Veronique where."

Harry watched her cross the room and push through the same door Veronique had used. He stared at the closed door for a moment longer, then turned to Danny—the two bearded and in black, with the black zucchettos on their heads, looking the way they were supposed to, like rabbis.

Until now Harry had held back, trying to give his brother as much time as he needed to heal, both physically and mentally. But Danny's sudden responsiveness in thanking the priests made Harry begin to suspect that Danny was stronger and more cognizant than he was letting on. And now alone with him, he felt a rush of anger. He didn't need Danny keeping him in the dark and at bay for reasons of his own. He'd been through enough for him already. Whatever the truth was, the time had come to get it out.

"You called me, Danny. You left word on my answering machine. . . . Do you remember?" Abruptly Harry took off his zucchetto and stuck it in his pocket.

"Yes . . ."

"You were scared to death of something. It was a hell of a way to say hello after so many years—especially on an answering machine. . . . What were you afraid of?"

Slowly Danny's eyes traveled over Harry's face. "I want you to do me a favor."

"What?"

"Get out of here right now."

"Get out of here?"

"Yes."

"Just me. By myself?"

"If you don't, Harry, . . . they'll kill you . . ."

Harry stared at his brother. "Who is 'they'?"

"Just go. Please."

Abruptly Harry looked off, his gaze going around the room. Then his eyes came back to Danny. "Maybe I should fill you in on what you either don't remember or don't know. . . . We're both wanted for murder, Danny. You for—"

"—killing the cardinal vicar of Rome, and you for shooting a Rome detective," Danny finished for him. "I saw a newspaper I wasn't supposed to see . . ."

Harry hesitated, trying to find the way to put it. Finally he just said it. "Did you kill the cardinal, Danny?"

"Did you kill the cop?"

"No."

"Same answer." Danny's reply was direct and unwavering.

"The police have a lot of evidence, Danny. . . . Farel took me to your apart—"

"Farel?" Danny cut him off sharply. "That's where your evidence came from . . ."

"What do you mean?"

For a long moment Danny said nothing, then glanced off. It was a retreat, a look that meant he'd said too much already and it was as far as he was going to go.

Shoving his hands in his pockets, Harry looked off at Veronique's collection of sculptures. Finally he turned back.

"You were in a bus explosion, Danny. Everybody thought you were dead. . . . How'd you get out?"

Danny shook his head. "Don't know . . ."

"Not only got out," Harry pressed him. "You managed to stuff your Vatican ID, your passport, and your glasses in somebody else's jacket . . ."

Danny said nothing.

"The bus was going to Assisi. Do you remember that?"

"I . . . go there often." Danny's eyes flashed anger.

"Do you?"

"Yes!—Harry, just get out of here. Now. While you still can."

"Danny—we haven't talked in years. Don't make me go yet." Picking up the chair again, Harry turned it around beside Danny and sat down on it backward.

"Who were you afraid of when you called me?"

"I . . ."

"Farel?"

"—I don't know . . ."

"You do know, Danny," Harry said quietly. "That's why they tried to kill you on the bus. And why the blond man followed you to Bellagio and then into the grotto."

Danny glanced off, then looked at the floor.

"Somebody got you out of the hospital and to Pescara. Got Elena's mother general involved. . . . She got Elena into it—and now Elena's life is as much on the line as ours . . ."

"Then take her with you." Still, Danny stared at the floor.

"Who helped you, Danny?"

Danny didn't react.

Harry pushed harder. "Cardinal Marsciano?"

Suddenly Danny's head came up, his eyes fierce.

"How do you know about Cardinal Marsciano?"

"I saw him, Danny. More than once. He warned me to stay away. Not to look for you. Before that, he tried to convince me you were dead." Harry paused, then pushed again. "It's Marsciano, isn't it? He's orchestrated everything . . ."

Danny stared at his brother. "I don't recollect any of it, Harry. Calling you. Why I was going to Assisi. Who helped me. None of it. Blank. Zip. Nothing. No memory at all. Is that clear?"

Harry hesitated but didn't waver. "What's going on inside the Vatican?"

"Harry,"—Danny's voice dropped off—"get the hell out of here before you get killed."

109

ROSCANI IGNORED THE MUFFLED WHINE OF the helicopter's jet engine as the machine banked sharply over the gray sprawl of Milan and headed southeast, toward Siena; his whole focus on the just-received INTERPOL fax in his lap. Most of which he already knew.

```
THOMAS JOSE ALVAREZ-RIOS KIND
   INTERPOL PROFILE: One of the
world's most notorious terrorists.
Celebrated murderer of French
antiterrorist police. Violent crimi-
nal. Fugitive. Request to apprehend
and detain. Extremely dangerous.
 OFFENSES: Murder, kidnapping, bomb-
ing, taking of hostages, aircraft
hijacking.
   NATIONALITY: Ecuador.
```

Roscani skipped down.

    TRAITS: Master of disguise. Mul-
tilingual, esp. Italian, French,
Spanish, Arabic, Farsi, English,
American English. Highly individual-
istic. Works alone. Nonetheless, has
extensive terrorist connections
worldwide.
    OTHER: Self-styled revolutionary.
    LAST RESIDENCE: Khartoum, Sudan.
    FINAL COMMENTS: Excessive
sociopath. Killer for hire. Available
to highest bidder.

Those were the official profile notes. Hand scrawled on
the bottom was a more personal message:

  "Subject is not known to have traveled outside
    Sudan.
  Per your request French Intelligence is
    investigating.
  Will notify immediately on confirmation."

"I can tell you right now," Roscani said to himself as he
folded the slim dossier and put it on the seat beside him,
"he's not in Sudan, he's in Italy."

Reaching into his jacket, he pulled out a large piece of
biscotti wrapped in plastic and secured by a rubber band.
Opening it, he bit into it with the same absent abruptness he
would have used to light a cigarette, his thoughts going to
the Milan city morgue, where he'd been a half hour earlier.

The body of one Aldo Cianetti, age twenty-six, a fashion designer, had been found in the storage closet of a women's washroom at a service-station stop on the A9 Autostrada halfway between Como and Milan. His throat had been cut and the wound stuffed with paper towelettes. Four hours later Cianetti's new, dark green BMW was found parked near the Palace Hotel in Milan.

"Thomas Kind," Roscani had said to no one in particular. Investigators might prove him wrong, but he doubted the killer was anyone but his ice picker/razor man. Somehow he had avoided the Gruppo Cardinale dragnet and made it from Bellagio to Milan, along the line hitching a ride with the young Cianetti and then killing him. And where had he gone from Milan? Or was he still there, hiding?

But the larger question was why he had come back into Italy and the heat of an all-out police hunt when as easily he could have crossed into the relative safety of Switzerland and moved on from there. Why? What was so important in Italy that he risk everything?

Lugano, Switzerland. 2:00 P.M.

Harry pulled back a chair, and Elena sat down. "Thank you," she said, still without looking at him. The table setting was for two, with fresh melon and prosciutto and a small carafe of red wine. Veronique had ushered them out onto the covered bougainvillaea-framed terrace after they had fed Danny and put him to bed in a room on the floor above where they were now. Demanding they sit down and eat, she had gone quickly back inside, leaving them alone for the first time since the night before, when Elena had been in Harry's room.

"What happened between you and your brother?" Elena asked as Harry sat down opposite her. "You had words. I could tell the way you both reacted when I came back into the room."

"It was nothing. Brothers being brothers, that's all. . . . We hadn't talked in a long time . . ."

"If I were in your position, I would have talked about the police. And I would have talked about the killing of the cardinal vicar of—"

"You're not in my position, though, are you?" Harry cut her off sharply. What had gone on between his brother and him was something he didn't care to share with her. Not right now, anyway.

Elena looked at him briefly, then, demurring, picked up her knife and fork and began to eat. As she did, a slight breeze picked up her hair, and she had to reach up with one hand to settle it.

"—I'm sorry. I didn't mean to snap at you like that. . . . There are just things that . . ."

"You should eat something, Mr. Addison. . . ." Elena kept her eyes on the plate in front of her. Cutting a small slice of melon, she did the same with a piece of prosciutto, then very slowly set the utensils down and looked up and quietly changed the subject.

"I want to . . . apologize for—last night . . ."

"It's all right," Harry said gently. "You only said what you felt."

Elena's eyes held his. "Still, I am sorry . . ."

"Look—" Harry started to say something, then pushed back from the table and crossed the terrace to look out over a sweep of orange-and-white-tile rooftops that fell to the city and Lake Lugano below.

"Whatever you need or feel, or"— he looked back her— "whatever I might feel in return, we can't get into. I've told myself"—his voice became gentler—"and now I'm telling *you*. It's why I snapped at you a moment ago. We're in trouble, a lot of it, and we have to get out. Veronique may be an extraordinary woman, but we're not safe here. By now Roscani will know we've slipped him. Lugano is too close to the Italian border. It won't be long until the Swiss police are everywhere. If Danny could walk it might be different, but—" Suddenly Harry stopped.

"What is it?"

"I . . ." Harry's gaze drifted off. "This is Wednesday. Monday, a friend of mine got out of a car in Como and left on foot to walk here, to Lugano. It wasn't far, but it wasn't easy either, because the police were looking for him, too, and he was a cripple and on crutches." Now he looked back. "But he went anyway. Smiled and went, because he believed he could do it and because he wanted to be free. . . . His name is Hercules. He's a dwarf. . . . I hope to God he made it."

Elena smiled gently. "I hope he did, too . . ."

Harry looked at her for a long moment, then abruptly turned to look out over the city once again. Purposely, he kept his back to her, all but overwhelmed by a wave of emotion. For some reason, the combination of everything that had happened—finding Danny alive, being with Elena, and the vision of Hercules bravely swinging off in the Como twilight sent an enormous yearning for life—to live it fully and to old age—sweeping over him.

He had never realized until that moment how extraordinary human beings could be, or, just by being with her, how truly beautiful Elena was. To him, she was purer, more magnetic, and more real than anyone he could ever remember. Maybe the first real person he had known, or allowed himself to know, since childhood. And if he wasn't careful, all of his protestations would be wasted, because he would fall hopelessly in love with her. And if he did, it could kill them all.

Suddenly a loud chime from the hallway inside jolted Harry from his reverie. He swung around to look. So did Elena. There was silence and then the chime rang again. Someone was downstairs at the front door.

A half second later, Veronique entered and went to the intercom. Pushing a button, she spoke into it, listened, then pressed the buzzer, letting whoever it was into the building.

"Who is it?" Harry came into the hallway behind her. Elena followed.

Veronique looked up.

"Someone to see your brother," she said quietly, then went to the door and opened it.

"Who knows he's even here?"

Harry could hear footsteps coming up the stairs. One person, maybe two. A man, the step was too heavy for a woman. Who was it? The blond man? A trick, set up by the Bellagio priests. Give the killer clear operating room away from Roscani's people. Or maybe they had made a deal with the Swiss police, and it was a detective coming up to check things out. Why not?—the priests were poor, and there was still a considerable reward for their arrest. Maybe the clergymen couldn't take the money, but Veronique certainly could, easily funneling a share back to them.

Harry glanced over his shoulder at Elena, nodding toward the upper floor. In an instant she had slipped past him, going up the stairs to where Danny was.

The footsteps were louder. Whoever it was had climbed almost to the top of the stairs. Harry started past Veronique to close the door and lock it.

"It's all right." Veronique stopped him.

Then, whoever it was was there, almost to the top. One man, alone, mostly in shadow. Not the blond man—someone else, taller, dressed in jeans and a light sweater. Then he stepped through the door. And Harry saw the dark curly hair, the familiar black eyes behind black-rimmed glasses.

Father Bardoni.

REVEREND MOTHER CARMELA FENTI WAS
sixty-three and petite. Her eyes sparkled and she was full of
humor, and yet, at the same time, filled with deep concern.
Sitting in her cramped, austere office on the second floor of
the Hospital of St. Bernardine in Siena, she poured that concern to Roscani, the same as she had earlier to the Siena
police; telling him that early in the evening of Monday, July
6, she'd received a call from Sister Maria Cupini, Administrator of the Franciscan Hospital St. Cecelia in Pescara,
telling of an Irishman with no apparent kin who had been
injured in an auto accident. He had suffered a severe concussion, burns, and other serious trauma. Sister Cupini was
short of staff. Could Mother Fenti help?

Yes, and she had. And that was all Mother Fenti knew
until the police had come to talk with her. It was not her practice to keep in touch with her charges when they were sent to
other hospitals.

ROSCANI: Do you know Sister Cupini personally?

MOTHER FENTI: No.

ROSCANI: Mother Fenti [Roscani paused, studying the administrator, then went on], Sister Cupini told the police in Pescara that she never made the call. She also said, and hospital records bear her out, that she knew of no such victim admitted to Hospital St. Cecelia during that time. She did concede, however, that an unnamed male patient had been admitted without her knowledge and stayed for approximately seventy-two hours, cared for by his own medical attendants. Quite conveniently, no one seems to know who admitted him or how the admission was arranged.

MOTHER FENTI: Ispettore Capo, I know nothing of the practices or operation of St. Cecelia's. I know only what I was told and led to believe.

ROSCANI: Let me add that the Pescara police have no record of a serious automobile accident occurring at any point during that time period.

MOTHER FENTI: I only know what I was told by a Franciscan sister and led to believe. [Mother Fenti opened a drawer and took out a worn ledger. Turning several pages, she found what she wanted and pushed the book across to Roscani.] These are my own handwritten telephone records. There [she pointed a finger at mid-page] you will see that the call came to me on July sixth at seventen P.M. and ended at seven-sixteen. The caller's name and position is listed at the far right. Sister Maria Cupini. Administrator, Hospital St. Cecelia, Pescara. It was written in pen as you can see. Nothing has been changed.

Roscani nodded. He had already seen telephone company records documenting the same information.

MOTHER FENTI: If the woman I spoke with was not Sister Cupini, why did she say she was?

ROSCANI: Because someone who understood the procedure was trying to find a private nurse to care for the fugitive priest, Father Daniel Addison. A nurse who turned out to be your Sister Elena Voso.

MOTHER FENTI: If that is true, Ispettore Capo, where is she? What has happened to her?

ROSCANI: I don't know. I was hoping you did.

MOTHER FENTI: I do not.

Roscani stared for a moment and then stood and went to the door.

ROSCANI: If you don't mind, Reverend Mother, there is someone else who needs to hear what I have to say.

Roscani opened the door and nodded to someone outside. A moment later a *carabiniere* appeared. With him was a proud, gray-haired man about Mother Fenti's age. He wore a brown suit and white shirt and tie. And though he was trying hard to look strong and impassive, it was clear he was shaken, if not afraid.

ROSCANI: Mother Fenti, this is Domenico Voso, Sister Elena's father.

MOTHER FENTI: We know each other, Ispettore Capo. *Buon pomeriggio, Signore.*

Domenico Voso nodded and sat down in a chair brought forward by the *carabiniere.*

ROSCANI: Reverend Mother, we have told Signore Voso what we believe has happened to his daughter. That she is somewhere now caring for Father Daniel, but that we believe she is a victim rather than an accomplice.

Nonetheless, I want you both to know she is in a very dangerous circumstance. Someone is trying to kill the priest and will most likely kill anyone found with him. And this person is not only capable but extremely vicious.

Roscani looked to Domenico Voso, and as he did, his entire mood and body language changed: he became the father he was, knowing how he would feel if one of his own children were out there, the prey of Thomas Kind.

ROSCANI: We don't know where your daughter is, Signore Voso, but the killer very well might. If you know where she is, I beg of you to please tell me. For her sake . . .

DOMENICO VOSO: I don't know where she is. I wish with the heart of all my family that I did. [His eyes flashed to Mother Fenti, pleading.]

MOTHER FENTI: Nor do I, Domenico. I have already said so to the *ispettore capo*. [She looked to Roscani.] If I hear, if either of us hears, you will be the first to know. [Now she stood.] I thank you for coming.

MOTHER FENTI KNEW where Elena Voso was. Domenico Voso did not. That was how Roscani felt as he sat at a desk in a back room of *carabinieri* headquarters in Siena twenty minutes later. She knew. And she denied it. Never mind that a father's heart was torn out.

Amiable and sparkly-eyed as she was, at heart she was a tough and very savvy old bird, strong enough to let Elena Voso be killed to protect whomever she was answering to. And she was answering to someone, because as prominent a figure as she was, by no means was she powerful enough to be doing this on her own. A mother general in Siena did not flaunt her authority in both the faces of the Catholic Church and the nation of Italy.

And even though he was certain the anonymous patient admitted to the hospital in Pescara had to have been Father Daniel, he knew Sister Cupini would stand by her claim of not knowing about it because it was the story Mother Fenti had invented for her. Clearly it was Mother Fenti who was running things here. And she would not give in. What he had to do, and quickly, was find a way around her.

Sitting back, Roscani took a sip of cold coffee. As he did, a way, or, rather, a conceivable way, came to him.

EuroCity Train #55. 4:20 P.M.

JULIA LOUISE PHELPS SMILED LIGHTLY AT the man in the first-class seat across from her, then turned to the window and watched the rural land ease to cityscape. In a matter of a few miles, open land became apartment buildings, warehouses, factories. In fifteen minutes Julia Phelps, or rather Thomas Kind, would be in Rome. Then, a taxi from the station to the Majestic Hotel on Via Veneto. And then, a few minutes later, another. Taken across the Tiber to the Amalia, the former *pensione* on Via Germanico—which was small, homey, and discreet. And comfortably close to the Vatican.

Only one part of the trip from Bellagio to Rome had been troublesome—the killing of the young designer he'd met on the hydrofoil and coaxed into giving him a ride to Milan when he'd learned the man had a car in Como and was driving there. What should have been a short, simple late-night automobile trip suddenly turned onerous when the young man began making jokes about the seeming impotence of the police and their inability to catch the fugitives. He'd looked at Thomas Kind too seriously, studying his large hat, his clothing, his overdone makeup that covered the scratches on his face, then half playfully suggesting that one of the fugitives could be dressed just like him, pretending to be a woman. A killer who could slip away unnoticed, right under the noses of the police.

In times past, this was something Thomas Kind probably would have let go. But not in the mental state he was in now. That the designer could be a dangerous witness had been almost irrelevant; the thing that had jumped out foremost was the uncontrollable urge for killing that the suggestion of danger had aroused in him. And the intensely erotic gratification that went with it.

This sensation, which had once been vague and all but unnoticeable, had grown markedly in the last weeks; beginning with the murder of the cardinal vicar of Rome and increasing in passion and fervor with his acts in Pescara and Bellagio and then inside the grotto. How many had it been?—seven killed, within hours? One on top of the other on top of the other.

And now, here on this train entering Rome, he was desperately hungering for more. His emotions, his entire being, suddenly and intractably pulled toward the man in the first-class seat across from him. The man was smiling, flirting, but doing absolutely *nothing* that was in any way threatening.

My God, he had to stop it!

Abruptly he looked away and back out the train's window. He was ill. Terribly, mentally ill. Maybe even insane. But he was Thomas Jose Alvarez-Rios Kind. Who the hell could he talk to? Where on God's earth could he go for help where they wouldn't catch him and throw him into prison? Or, worse, see his weakness and shun him for the rest of his life.

"*Roma Termini*"—the metallic voice crackled over the speaker system. The train slowed as it came into the station, and people stood to collect their luggage from the overhead racks. Julia Louise Phelps didn't have the chance to take hers down; the man she had smiled at did it for her.

"Thank you," Thomas Kind said in an American accent and sounding singularly feminine.

"*Prego,*" the man replied.

And then the train stopped, and they departed. One more smile between them. Each going his own way.

112

Lugano, Switzerland. Same time.

HARRY KNOCKED ON THE BEDROOM DOOR, then opened it, and he and Elena went in. Danny was alone, sitting on the edge of the bed intently watching the small television that sat on an antique table nearby.

"Where is Father Bardoni?" Harry asked. It had been more than two hours since the priest had gone upstairs to talk with Danny. Finally Harry had had enough of waiting. He would talk to Father Bardoni himself.

"He's gone," Danny said, still preoccupied with the television.

"Where?"

"Back to Rome."

"He came all the way from Rome and then left. Just like that?"

Danny said nothing. Just continued to watch the TV. The pictures on it were being broadcast live from China. It was night now in Hefei, and there was an eerie silence. Media reporters were saying nothing, only watching. As were the armed soldiers in goggles, masks, and protective clothing who kept them behind barricades. In the distance two separate but distinct red-orange glows were clearly visible against the black sky. Words were not needed. Closer shots, unimaginable. With rescue workers overwhelmed, mass burning of corpses had been ordered to prevent the spread of disease. In the lower right-hand corner of the screen was a muted graphic.

Last official death toll: 77,606

"My God . . . ," Danny breathed. This was the first he knew about what had happened in China. He'd come on it by accident after Father Bardoni had left and he'd switched on the TV, looking for news about the police search for Harry and himself.

"Danny—?" Harry was behind him, prodding him.

Suddenly, Danny picked the remote from the edge of the bed and pointed it at the TV.

CLICK.

The screen went dark.

Danny looked to Harry, and then to Elena. "Would you leave us, please, Sister," he said quietly in Italian.

"Of course, Father . . ." Elena glanced briefly at Harry and then left.

As the latch clicked into place, Danny looked to his brother.

"Cardinal Marsciano is ill. I have to go back to Rome. . . . I need your help."

"Rome?" Harry was incredulous.

"Yes."

"Why?"

"I just told you."

"No, all you said was that Cardinal Marsciano was ill, you didn't tell me anything." Harry glared at his brother. Instantly they were back to the conversation they'd had earlier when Danny shut down completely.

"I said before that I can't talk about it . . ."

"Okay, you can't. Let's try something else. . . . How did Father Bardoni know you were here?"

"Sister Elena's mother general . . ."

"All right. Go on."

"Go on about what?" Danny asked flatly. "I *have* to get to Rome, that's all. . . . I can't walk. Can't even go to the bathroom without help . . ."

"Then why didn't you go with Father Bardoni?"

"He had to get back. He was taking a plane from Milan. . . . I could hardly be seen in an airport, could I, Harry?"

Harry ran a hand across his mouth. Danny was not only lucid, he was determined.

"Danny, our pictures are all over television. In every newspaper. How far into Italy do you think we'd get?"

"We got here, we can get there."

Harry studied his brother, trying to find the answer he wasn't getting. "A little while ago you warned me to leave here before I got killed. Now you're asking me to jump right back into the furnace. What changed it?"

"A little while ago I didn't know the situation."

"What *is* the situation?"

Danny said nothing.

Harry kept on. "Inside the Vatican. What the hell is all this about?"

Still Danny said nothing.

"Marsciano wanted me and everybody else to believe you were dead." Harry kept pushing. "He was protecting you. . . .

He said, 'They will kill you both. Your brother for what he knows. You, because they will believe he has told you.' Now you can add Elena to that. . . . If you want me to put my life and yours and hers on the line, then you can fucking well tell me the rest."

"I can't . . ." Danny's voice was barely a whisper.

"Give me a reason." Harry was hard, even brutal, determined to get an answer.

"I—" Danny hesitated.

"I said, give me a reason, dammit."

For a long moment there was silence, then finally Danny spoke. "In your business, Harry, it's called client-counselor privilege. In mine it's called confession. . . . Now do you understand?"

"Marsciano confessed to you?" Harry was stunned. Confession was something he'd never considered.

"I didn't say who or what, Harry. I simply told you why— I can't talk about it."

Harry turned away to stare out the small window at the end of the room. For once in their adult lives he wanted them on the *same side*. Wanted Danny to trust him enough to tell him the truth. But now it was clear he couldn't.

"Harry," Danny said quietly. "Cardinal Marsciano is being held prisoner inside the Vatican. If I don't go, they'll kill him."

Harry turned back. "Who is 'they'?—Farel?"

"The Vatican secretariat of state. Cardinal Palestrina."

"Why?" Harry breathed.

Danny shook his head ever so slightly. "—can't tell you."

Abruptly Harry crossed back, toward Danny's bed. "They want you for Marsciano, that's the deal, isn't it?"

"Yes. . . . Except it's not going to work that way," Danny said. "Father Bardoni and I are going to get the cardinal out.

That's why he went back alone, to start setting things up, and because we couldn't take the chance of traveling together and us both getting caught."

"You are going to get Marsciano out of the Vatican?" Harry stared in disbelief. "Two men, one of them a cripple, against Farel and the Vatican secretariat of state? Danny, this isn't just two powerful men you're fighting, it's a country."

Danny nodded. "I know . . ."

"You're crazy."

"No. . . . I'm methodical, I think things through. . . . It can be done. . . . I was a marine, remember. I learned a few tricks . . ."

"No." Harry said sharply.

"No, what?" Danny sat up quickly.

"No, period!" Harry was intense, decisive. "It's true, I didn't come back for you in Maine all those years ago, but I'm making up for it now—New York to Rome, to Como, to Bellagio, to wherever the hell we are now.—Well, here I finally am . . . and I'm getting you the fuck out. But not to Rome, Geneva. . . . I'm going to try to get us there and arrange a surrender to the International Red Cross. And hope to hell that much spotlight will give us at least some rational measure of protection."

Abruptly Harry crossed to the door. He had his hand on the knob when he looked back to Danny. "I don't care about the rest of it, brother of mine, I am *not* going to lose you. . . . Not for Marsciano or the Holy See, and not to Farel or Palestrina or anyone else . . ." Harry's voice dropped off. "I am *not* going to lose you to them, the way I lost Madeline to the ice . . ."

Harry stared at Danny for a long moment, making sure he understood. Then he opened the door and started out.

"Who I am is me!" Danny's voice exploded behind Harry,

stabbing into him like a knife. Harry stopped short, frozen where he was. When he turned back, Danny's eyes were riveted on his.

"Your thirteenth birthday. You saw it chalked on a rock in the woods when you walked home from school, the same long way around you always took when you didn't want to come home. And that day, especially, you didn't want to come home."

Harry could feel his legs turn to rubber. "*You* put it there . . ."

"It was a present, Harry. The only one I could give. You needed to trust in yourself, because that's all any of us had. And you did. And you ran with it. You built your life around it. And you did a helluva job. . . ." Danny eyes danced over Harry's face, studying him. "Getting to Rome means everything to me, Harry. . . . I'm the one who needs a present now. . . . And you are the only one who can give it."

For the longest moment Harry just stood there. Danny had reached into the pack and pulled out the trump card, the only one he had left. Finally Harry stepped back into the room and closed the door.

"How the hell are we going to get to Rome?"

"These . . ."

Danny picked up a flat manila envelope from the bedside table and slid out what was inside—long, narrow white license plates emblazoned with the black letters *SCV 13*.

"Vatican City plates, Harry. Diplomatic plates. Very low number. No one will stop a car with those on it."

Slowly Harry looked up.

"What car?" he said.

5:25 P.M.

THE RABBI LOOK WAS OUT, THE PRIEST LOOK
back in. Once again Father Jonathan Arthur Roe of Georgetown University, Harry was making his way through the
rush-hour streets of Lugano, looking for the rented gray
Mercedes Father Bardoni had supposedly left parked on Via
Tomaso across the tracks and up the hill from the railroad
station.

Following Veronique's directions, he took the funicular
up to the Piazza della Stazione and then crossed to the railroad station itself and went inside. Keeping his head down,
doing his best to avoid looking at people directly, he worked
his way through the crowds waiting for trains, trying to find
a place where he could cross the tracks to the stairs leading
up to Via Tomaso.

His mind was on Rome and getting there without getting
caught. And what to do about Elena. It was a mental turmoil
that left him totally unprepared for what happened next, as
he turned a corner inside the station.

Uniformed police, six of them, suddenly materialized out

of a crowd directly in front of him, walking forcefully toward a train that had just come into the station. But it wasn't just the police—it was who they had with them: three prisoners in chains and handcuffs. The second, and now passing directly in front of Harry, was Hercules. The shackles were making it all but impossible for him to move on his crutches, but he was doing it anyway. And then he saw Harry, and their eyes met. Even as they did, he abruptly looked away, protecting Harry from any happened glance from the police that might make them single him out, wonder why he recognized one of their prisoners. And then they were gone, Hercules hustled with the others, up the steps and onto the train.

Harry saw him a moment later as one of the police took his crutches and helped him into a seat beside a window. Immediately, Harry pushed through the crowd, moving alongside the train toward the window. Hercules saw him coming and quickly shook his head, then looked away.

Station chimes sounded, and with Swiss precision the train moved off, leaving the station exactly on time. Heading south for Italy.

Harry turned away, stunned, absently looking for the stairs to Via Tomaso. The whole thing had taken no more than sixty seconds. Hercules had looked pale and resigned until he had seen Harry, and then everything seemed to change as he worked to protect him. For a moment at least, life and the fire of it, had seemed to come back to him. What he had regained, if fleetingly, had been a purpose.

Siena, Italy. Police headquarters. 6:40 P.M.

It had come to this. An unlit cigarette held between the fingers. Then, once in a while, snuggled into the corner of the mouth for a minute or two. But that, Roscani promised himself, was as far as it would go. No matter how much more frustrating or anxious things became from here on in, he would not go for the match. In a ceremonial gesture for himself, and just to make sure, he took the one packet of matches he had from his jacket pocket, tore one match off, then put the packet into an ashtray, struck the lone match, and touched it to the others. For the briefest moment he felt a pang of remorse, then, as quickly, turned back to the telephone company print-outs spread across the desk in front of him and went over them again. Logs were numbered in date/time order, the path of telephone calls coming to and going from Mother Fenti's office and the private number in her apartment, from the day of the Assisi bus explosion up through today. Thirteen days altogether.

Two police researchers stationed in the hallway to assist Roscani saw him suddenly turn, pick up the telephone, and dial. He waited for a moment, then said something and hung up. Abruptly he stood up and walked across the room, an unlit cigarette put in his mouth, taken out, then put back in. Suddenly the phone rang. He turned and came back quickly, immediately picking it up. Nodding, he scrawled something on a piece of paper, underlined it, then said something brief and hung up. A half second later, he threw the cigarette into a wastebasket, snatched up the paper, and headed out the door.

"I need one of you to drive me to the helicopter pad," he said as he came into the hallway.

"Where are you going?" The first researcher was already up and on his feet, moving with Roscani down the hallway.

"Lugano, Switzerland."

114

Lugano. Same time.

A DARK GRAY MERCEDES WITH VATICAN CITY license plates and two priests in the front seat left Lugano in an early evening darkened by rain. Passing the hotels along the lakefront, the Mercedes turned onto Via Giuseppe Cattori, then headed west toward the N2 motorway that would take them south to Chiasso and then into Italy.

Elena sat in back, watching Danny give Harry directions as he read from a map in the glow of the light above the rearview mirror. There was tension between the brothers. She could see it and feel it. What it was exactly she didn't know, and Harry hadn't mentioned it, only given her the opportunity to stay behind, but she had refused. Where the brothers were going, she was going. It was a given, and she told Harry so, reminding him she was a nurse and Father Daniel was still in her care. Moreover, she was Italian and they were going back into Italy and, if Harry didn't remember, that was something that had proven beneficial more than once in the past. And when Harry smiled ever so slightly at her pluck and determination, it was clear she was coming with them.

As they reached the motorway, Danny abruptly reached up and shut off the map light, settling back out of sight as he did. Suddenly Harry was the only one Elena could see.

Lighted by the dim of the instrument panel, he became the entire focus of her attention. The tense movement of his fingers over the steering wheel. His concentration on the road in front of him. That same aura of uneasiness grew as he sat back, then leaned forward again against the restraint of the seat harness, a discomfort not with the car but with where it was going. Rome, it was obvious, was not his idea.

"Are you all right?" Harry asked quietly.

Elena looked up and saw he was watching her in the mirror.

"Yes . . ." Her eyes fastened on his, and they studied each other in silence.

"Harry." Danny's voice suddenly warned over the metronome of the wipers.

Instantly Harry's eyes left Elena and went to the road. The traffic in front of them was slowing. Then came the distinct pink-white glow of mercury-vapor lamps against the turbid night sky.

"The Italian border." Danny sat up, alert, attentive.

Elena saw Harry's hands tighten on the wheel. Felt the Mercedes slow as he touched the brakes. Then he glanced at her once more, his eyes holding for the briefest instant before he looked back to the road ahead.

115

Beijing. Thursday, July 16.

PIERRE WEGGEN'S BLACK CHAUFFER-DRIVEN limousine entered Zhongnanhai Compound, the private complex where China's most preeminent leaders resided, shortly after one in the morning. Five minutes later, the Swiss investment banker was being shown into a large living room in the home of Wu Xian, general secretary of the Communist Party, by the solemn president of the People's Bank of China, Yan Yeh.

The general secretary stood to meet Weggen as he came in, taking his hand genuinely and introducing him to the half dozen ranking members of the Politburo waiting to hear the details of his proposal; among them were the heads of the Ministry of Construction, the Ministry of Communication, and the Ministry of Civil Affairs. What they wanted to know was the full extent of it, how it might be accomplished, at what cost and in how short a time.

"Thank you for your hospitality, gentlemen," Weggen began in Chinese. And then, extending his deepest sympathies not only to those present but to the country as a whole and especially the people of Hefei, he began to lay out his recommendations for a very rapid and highly visible rebuilding of the country's water-delivery systems.

Taking a chair to one side, Yan Yeh sat down and lit a cigarette. Deeply shaken by the horror of what had happened and exhausted from the events of the day, he remained hopeful that the men gathered here in the early-morning hours would see that the plan Weggen was presenting was vital to national security and national interests. He hoped they would bury their pride and political infighting, along with their suspicions of the West, and undertake to endorse the project and begin work as quickly as was humanly possible—before the same thing happened again.

There was something else, too, and more personal. Whether it was spoken of or not, everyone in China who knew of the incident in Hefei was fearful of the drinking water, especially the water that was drawn from the lakes; and as powerful and influential a leader as he was, Yan Yeh was no different. Only three days before, his wife and ten-year-old son had left to visit his wife's family in the lake city of Wuxi. And hours earlier he had called her to tell her the tragedy at Hefei had been a lone incident, reassuring her, as the public was being reassured, that the quality of the drinking water across the country was being heavily monitored. And that the government was well into taking a plan of action that, if it followed his counsel, would hastily rebuild the nation's entire water system. More than anything, Yan Yeh had made the call simply to talk to his wife and calm her fears and tell her he loved her. And secretly, he hoped he was right, that Hefei had been an isolated incident.

But somehow, in the pit of his stomach, he knew it wasn't.

Rome, Vatican City. Wednesday, July 15, 7:40 P.M.

Palestrina stood by the window in his library office and looked out on the crowds that still filled St. Peter's Square enjoying its ambience and the day's last hours of light.

Turning from the window he looked back across his office. On the credenza behind his desk, the marble head of Alexander stared out eternally, and Palestrina looked at it almost wistfully.

Then, in an abrupt change of mood, he crossed to his desk, sat down, and lifted the telephone from its console. Clearing a line, he punched in a number and waited, listening as a switching station in Venice took the call and automatically forwarded it to a station in Milan, which in turn rang a number in Hong Kong and was immediately switched to Beijing.

THE CHIRP OF CHEN YIN'S cell phone brought him quickly from a sound sleep. By the third ring, he was out of bed and standing naked in the dark of his bedroom above his flower shop.

"Yes?" he said in Chinese.

"I have an order for an early-morning delivery to the land of fish and rice," an electronically altered voice said in Chinese.

"I understand," Chen Yin said and hung up.

PALESTRINA LET THE PHONE SLIDE back into its cradle, then slowly swiveled in his chair to look again at the marble presence of Alexander. He had used Pierre

Weggen's close friendship with Yan Yeh—a casual probing about the Chinese banker's daily life, his friends and family—to select the second lake. A fertile area of water and mild climate and booming industry called "the land of fish and rice," it was south of Nanjing and little more than a few hours' train ride for the poisoner Li Wen. The lake was called Taihu. The city was Wuxi.

116

HARRY WATCHED IN THE MIRROR, FEELING the response of the Mercedes' acceleration as they left the checkpoint. Behind him he could see the glow of the mercury-vapor lamps, the taillights of cars moving north as they slowed to a stop, the mass of Italian Army vehicles and *carabinieri* armored cars. This had been a major checkpoint, two hours south of Milan. Unlike the roadblock at Chiasso, where they'd just been waved through, barely slowing, here they had been slowed to a stop with heavily armed soldiers approaching the car from both sides. That was until an army officer had suddenly pointed to the license plates, glanced at the priests in the front seat, and quickly waved them past.

"Wise ass." Danny grinned at him as darkness enveloped the car and they were safely away.

"Just because I waved the guy a thanks?"

"Yeah, just because you waved the guy a thanks. What if he hadn't liked it and decided to pull us over? Then what?"

Harry glanced in the mirror at Elena, then looked to his brother. "Then you could have explained to him what the hell was going on and why we had to get to Rome. Maybe he would have even sent the army with us . . ."

"The army wouldn't go into the Vatican, Harry. . . . Not the Italian Army, not any army . . ."

"No, just you . . . and Father Bardoni . . ." Harry's voice had a decided edge.

Danny nodded. "Just me and Father Bardoni."

Rome. The Church of San Crisogno, Trastevere section. Thursday, July 16, 5:30 A.M.

Palestrina stepped from the back of the Mercedes and into the mist of early-morning light. Glancing around protectively at the deserted street, one of Farel's black-suited men moved ahead of him, crossing the sidewalk to open the door to the eighteenth-century church. Then he stepped back, and the Vatican secretariat of state entered alone.

Palestrina's footsteps echoed as he approached the altar and then, crossing himself, knelt to pray beside the only other person there—a woman in black, a rosary in her hand.

"It has been a long time since my last confession, Father," she said without looking at him. "Could I confess to you?"

"Of course." Palestrina crossed himself again and stood. And then he and Thomas Kind walked away toward the dark singularity of the confessional.

117

Lugano, Switzerland. The house at Via Monte Ceneri, 87. Still Thursday, July 16. Same time. A clear morning after the rain.

ROSCANI WALKED DOWN THE STEPS AND BACK into the street. His suit was more than wrinkled, he had a stubble beard, and he was tired. Almost too tired to think the way he needed to think. But more than that, he was angry and tired of being lied to, especially by women who, on the outside at least, should have been respectable. Mother Fenti for one, and, here in Lugano, the sculptor and painter Signora Veronique Vaccaro, an iconoclast in middle age who swore through the night and into the early morning hours that she knew nothing of the fugitives and refused to waver from her story. Then she had abruptly and indignantly gone to bed, leaving the police to worry among themselves. And worry they did, especially Roscani, who insisted the chief

Swiss investigator who had first interviewed Veronique Vaccaro go over his entire findings again.

Exhaustively he had, saying the Swiss police had found
nothing to indicate the house had been occupied during Signora Vaccaro's short absence. However, neighbors had
reported seeing a white van with lettering on the doors
parked in front of the entrance for a short time at midday the
day before. And two young boys taking their dog for a walk
in the rain after dinner that night had said they'd seen a big
car, a Mercedes, the older boy proudly swore, parked in front
as they'd left their house. But it had not been there when
they'd come back. And Signora Vaccaro's alibi, one impossible to corroborate, was that she had come home only
moments before the police arrived, returning from a camp-
ing/sketching trip alone in the Alps.

It was no better with Castelletti and Scala, who had
closed the investigations in Bellagio with the interrogation
of Monsignor Jean-Bernard Dalbouse, French-born parish
priest of the Church of Santa Chiara, and his staff, clerical
and laypeople alike. The end result of exhaustive questioning was that each and every one denied having received a
call from a cell phone in Siena at 4:20 A.M. the day before. A
cell phone registered to Mother Fenti.

Liars. They were all liars.

Why?

It was driving Roscani crazy. Every one of them risked
going to jail and for a long time. Yet none of them had even
begun to crack. Who, or what, were they protecting?

Leaving Veronique's house, Roscani walked the street
alone. The neighborhood was quiet, its residents still asleep.
Lake Lugano stretching in the distance was also still, glassed
over, from this distance not even a ripple. What was he doing

out there? Looking for clues the others had missed? Once again becoming the bulldog of his father's legacy? Going in circles until he had some kind of answer? Or, did he have a sense that this was where he should be? Like some kind of magnet drawn toward a pile of sawdust and a lost nail. Throwing off the notion, telling himself he was out there for the fresh air, for a moment of *assoluta tranquillità,* he pulled a battered cigarette pack from his jacket, once again twisted an unlit cigarette into the corner of his mouth, and turned back for the house.

Five paces later he saw it. It was on the edge of the road, under an overhanging bush that kept last night's rain from soaking it through. A flat manila envelope with the impression of a tire tread on it.

Tossing away his cigarette, Roscani bent over and picked it up. More ragged than it had first appeared, it looked as if a wet tire had run over it, caught it up and turned it several revolutions before speed had thrown it off. There was an impression in its surface, as if something stiff and hard had once been inside.

Going back to the house, Roscani went inside and found Veronique Vaccaro—still incensed from her long night and the continued presence of the police—sitting in her kitchen in a bathrobe, one hand around a cup of coffee, the other drumming fingers on the table as if that in itself would make the authorities leave once and for all. Politely he asked for a hair dryer.

"It's in the bathroom," she said in Italian. "Why not use the bath, too, and take a nap in my bed."

With a half smile at Castelletti as he passed him, Roscani went into Veronique's bathroom, took down the hair dryer and played it over the envelope until it dried.

Castelletti came in and stood behind him, watching as Roscani smoothed the envelope on the edge of the sink, and pushed a pencil back and forth across it, as one might do in the creation of a rubbing. Little by little the image of what had been inside appeared.

"Jesus Christ." Suddenly Roscani stopped.

Raised on the envelope in front of them were the highly select letters and number of a diplomatic license plate.

SCV 13

"Vatican City," Castelletti said.

"Yeah," Roscani looked at him. "Vatican City."

118

Rome.

IT WAS JUST BEFORE FIVE IN THE MORNING
and still dark when Danny signaled Harry to stop in front of
Via Nicolò V, 22, an old, well-kept three-story apartment
complex on a tree-lined street. Locking the Mercedes, Harry
and Elena took Danny in his wheelchair up the small elevator to the top floor, where Danny took a set of keys from an
envelope Father Bardoni had given him in Lugano. Choosing one, he opened the door to Piano 3a, a spacious rear
apartment.

Once they were inside, Danny, visibly wearied from the
long drive, had gone to bed. Then Harry, taking brief stock of
the surroundings and warning Elena to let no one in but himself, left.

Following Danny's instructions, he drove the Mercedes to
a street several blocks away, where he removed the Vatican
City license plates and replaced them with the original ones.

Then, locking the keys inside, he walked off, the Vatican plates hidden inside his jacket. Fifteen minutes later, he was back at number 22 Via Nicolò V, taking the elevator up to the apartment. It was almost six o'clock in the morning, little more than half an hour before Father Bardoni was to meet them there.

Harry liked none of it. The idea that Danny, in his condition, and Father Bardoni could succeed in freeing Marsciano from wherever he was being held inside the Vatican was insane. But Danny was determined and so, evidently, was Father Bardoni. What that meant to Harry was one thing alone: Danny would try and Danny would be killed—which was obviously Palestrina's plan.

Furthermore, if Farel had framed Danny for the murder of the cardinal vicar, and if Farel was working for Palestrina, then Palestrina himself had to have orchestrated the killing. And Marsciano knew about it or he wouldn't be Palestrina's prisoner now. All of which made it obvious the confession had been Marsciano's. So, by killing Danny, Palestrina would wipe out the only trail that could lead back to him.

And whom could Harry tell—Roscani? Adrianna? Eaton? Tell them what? What he had was nothing more than conjecture. Moreover, even if he had proof, the Vatican was a sovereign country and not bound by the laws of Italy. Meaning, that outside the Vatican itself, no one had the legal authority to do anything. Still—and this was Danny's agony—if they did nothing, Marsciano would be killed. And Danny was going to do everything he could to prevent that, even if it cost him his own life.

"Shit," Harry said to himself as he came into the apartment and locked the door behind him. He was in as much damn trouble as Danny. Not just because he was his brother, but because he'd promised Danny he wouldn't lose him to anyone the way he'd lost Madeline to the ice. Why did he do that? Why the hell did he keep making these kinds of promises to his brother?

"I have not been to Rome often and so was not certain where this place was . . ."

Harry's introspection was cut short as Elena came eagerly toward him.

"What do you mean?"

"I'll show you."

Leading him into the living room, Elena took Harry to a large window on the far side of it. The pale of the early light revealed what they could not have seen in the dark when they arrived, a view that looked directly across a street toward a high, yellow-brick wall that ran as far as Harry could see in both directions. On the far side of it to the right, and deep in shadow, were a number of nondescript buildings, and to the left what looked like the tops of trees, as if the wall enclosed some kind of large park.

"I don't understand . . ," Harry said, unsure of Elena's interest.

"It's the Vatican, Mr. Addison . . . part of one side of it anyway."

"Are you sure?"

"Yes, I have toured the gardens just over the wall."

Harry looked back, trying to find a landmark he could recognize, get some sense of where they were in relation to the public front and St. Peter's Square. Still, he couldn't get his bearings. He was about to question her again when he looked up and a chill came over him; what he had taken for skyline was a huge building still in shadow, but its top was full in sunlight. He was looking directly at St. Peter's itself.

"Christ," he said under his breath. Not only had they landed in Rome unmolested, they had also been given the keys to a piece of real estate barely a stone's throw from Marciano's prison.

For the briefest moment Harry rested his head against the glass and closed his eyes.

"You are tired, Harry . . ." Elena's voice was hushed, comforting, in the way a mother might talk to her child.

"Yes," he nodded, then opened his eyes to look at her.

She was still in the business suit the priests had found for her in Bellagio, still had her hair pulled back. Yet it struck Harry that this was the first time he was seeing her not as a nun but as a woman.

"I slept during our drive here, you did not," she said. "There is another bedroom here. . . . You should sleep . . . at least until Father Bardoni comes."

"Yes . . . ," Harry started to say. Then, out of nowhere, he realized that he had a major problem. Elena. The gravity of what Danny and Father Bardoni were planning had suddenly become dangerously real, and he couldn't let Elena stay and be part of it.

"—Your parents are alive . . . ," he said cautiously.

"What does that have to do with sleep?" Elena cocked her head, looking at him with the same caution.

"Where do they live?"

"Tuscany . . ."

"How far is it from here?"

"Why?"

"It's important . . ."

"Roughly two hours by car. We passed through it on the Autostrada."

"And your father has a car. He drives?"

"Why?"

"Does he have a car?" Harry said again, harder and more directly. "Does he drive?"

"Of course."

"I want you to call him and ask him to come to Rome."

Abruptly Elena felt fire shoot through her. She leaned back against the wall and crossed her arms defiantly in front of her.

"I cannot do that."

"If he leaves now, *Elena*," Harry said, emphasizing her name, as if to silence her protest, "he can be in Rome by nine. Nine-thirty at the latest. Tell him to pull up in front of the building and stay in the car. That when you see him, you'll come down and get in and he is to drive away immediately. No one will ever know you were here."

Elena could feel the fire grow hotter, her indignation rise. How dare he? She had feelings and she had pride. And she was not about to call her *father*, of all people, to have herself be picked up like some red-faced schoolgirl left abandoned in the big city the morning after.

"I am sorry, *Mr. Addison*," she said, bristling, "but my duty is to care for Father Daniel. And I will stay with him until I am formally relieved of that duty."

"That is very easy, *Sister* Elena." Harry glared at her. "You are hereby formally, reliev—"

"By—my—mother—general!" The veins stood out in Elena's neck.

A shattering silence followed. The two staring at each other. Neither realizing this was their first lover's quarrel— and that one of the lovers had just drawn a deep line in the sand. Yet who would blink first was never answered.

CRASH!

Suddenly the kitchen door flew open, slamming hard off the wall behind it.

"Harry!—"

Danny came through the doorway fiercely. Thrumping

the wheels of his wheelchair with both hands, his eyes wide with alarm, a cell phone in his lap.

"I can't reach Father Bardoni. I have three numbers for him. One's a cell phone he always has with him. I've tried them all! No answer!"

"Danny, take it easy."

"Harry, he was supposed to be here fifteen minutes ago! If he was on his way, he'd at least be picking up the cell!"

119

HARRY TURNED THE CORNER ONTO VIA DEL
Parione and started down the block. By his watch it was now
seven-twenty-five, nearly an hour after Father Bardoni was
to have met them at the apartment. As he walked, he tried the
cell number again with the phone Adrianna had given him.

Still nothing.

Common sense told him that for one reason or another
Father Bardoni had simply been delayed. It was no more
complicated than that.

Ahead was number 17, Father Bardoni's building. Behind
it, Danny had said, was an alley and, off it, an old wooden gate
to the rear entrance of the building itself. To the left of that
entrance, and under a potted red geranium, he'd find the key.

Turning down the alley, Harry walked twenty yards and
then saw the gate. Opening it, he crossed a small gravel
courtyard. The pot was where it was supposed to be. Under it
was the key.

* * *

FATHER BARDONI'S FLAT, like the one they were staying in, was on the top floor, and Harry took the back stairs to it quickly. Outwardly, he was still thinking nothing unusual had happened and that there was a simple explanation for Father Bardoni's tardiness. But inwardly, he felt the same as Danny had when he'd burst through the kitchen door.

Dread.

Then Harry was at the top of the stairs and turning down a narrow hallway, stopping as he reached Father Bardoni's door. Taking a breath, he put the key in the lock and started to turn it. It wasn't necessary. The door was unlocked, and swung open.

"Father—?"

There was no reply.

"Father Bardoni—" Harry stepped into a darkened hallway. In front of him was a small living room. Like the one in Danny's apartment, little more than utilitarian.

"Father—?"

Still nothing.

To his right was a narrow hallway. There was a door halfway down and one at the end. Both were closed. Taking a breath, he put his hand on the knob to the first door and turned it.

"Father?"

The door swung open to a bedroom. It was little and cramped, with a small window at the back. The bed was made. A phone was on a small table beside it. That was all.

Turning, Harry started out, then he saw a cell phone on the floor next to the bed. The phone Father Bardoni "always has with him"?

Suddenly Harry was aware of his own presence. Something felt very wrong, as if he didn't belong there. Stepping out of the room, he turned ever so slowly to the other door.

What was there? Everything in him told him to leave right then. Walk away. Do anything but open that door.

But he couldn't.

"Father Bardoni," he said again.

Silence.

Reaching for his handkerchief, he put it around the knob.

"Father Bardoni," he said loud enough to be heard on the far side of the door.

No reply.

Harry could feel the sweat on his upper lip. The pound of his heart. Slowly he turned the knob. There was a click at the latch and then it opened. He saw the worn white tile of a bathroom floor and then the sink and a corner of the bathtub. Reaching up with his elbow, he pushed the door open the rest of the way.

Father Bardoni sat in the tub. He was naked. His eyes open, staring.

"Father?"

Harry stepped forward. His foot touched something. The priest's black-rimmed glasses were on the floor. Harry's eyes came back to the tub.

There was no water in it.

"Father?" he said under his breath, as if he hoped for a response of some kind. All he could think of was that the priest had started to take a bath and had had a heart attack or seizure of some kind before he'd had a chance to run the water.

One more step forward.

"OH, GOD!"

Harry's heart shot into his mouth, and he backed away quickly, staring wide-eyed in horror. Father Bardoni's left hand had been cut off at the wrist. There was hardly any blood at all. Just a stump where the hand used to be.

120

Milan. Same time.

ROSCANI SAW THE RUNWAYS OF LINATE
Airport below them and at the same moment felt the helicopter begin to descend. Information had come at him in a
rush even as he had left Lugano; more was coming in now.
Castelletti and Scala, in the seats behind him, were alternately talking over the radio and compiling notes.

Curled in Roscani's hand was the piece he'd been waiting
for, a brief but very telling fax from INTERPOL headquarters in Lyon, France. It read:

> French Intelligence has determined
> Thomas Jose Alvarez-Rios Kind is not
> in Khartoum, Sudan, as previously
> believed. Current whereabouts
> unknown.

Immediately Roscani had an ARREST AND DETAIN
order sent out from Gruppo Cardinale headquarters in Rome

to all police agencies throughout Europe. Additionally, Thomas Kind's most recent photograph had been rushed to the worldwide media along with a brief, declaring Kind as a fugitive wanted by Gruppo Cardinale in connection with both the murder of the cardinal vicar of Rome and the bombing of the Assisi bus. The part about the bus had come to Roscani the moment he'd suspected Kind. It was his trademark, known to police and intelligence agencies worldwide, which he used time and again when he was in a position of employing trigger men instead of doing the job himself. It was simply "kill the killer"—let the man or woman do the job and then get rid of him or her as expeditiously as possible, leaving no channel back to Kind himself or to those who had hired him.

It was the reason for the Spanish Llama pistol found at the scene of the burned bus. Kind had put a killer onboard to get rid of Father Daniel and then he'd blown up the bus to eliminate the killer and leave no trace back. The trouble was the gunman's timing was off and it hadn't worked. But the gun and the blown bus together pointed right at Thomas Kind.

And now, with information Castelletti and Scala were getting from Milan, the police there were bringing things to a fast closure. Aldo Cianetti, the fashion designer found murdered on the Como-to-Milan section of the Autostrada, had been onboard the last hydrofoil from Bellagio and seen talking with a woman wearing a large straw hat—a woman a young Bellagio policeman recalled as having both an American passport and accent—and had left the boat with her when it had docked in Como.

Meanwhile, investigators in Milan had moved out in a grid pattern from the street near the Palace Hotel where Cianetti's dark green BMW had been found. A short distance away was Milano Centrale, Milan's main railroad station.

Time of death had been estimated at sometime between two and three in the morning. And police canvassing ticket sellers on duty at the station between two and five A.M. had found an outspoken middle-aged female railroad employee who had sold a ticket to a woman in a large straw hat just before four in the morning. The woman's destination had been Rome.

Woman? It had been no woman, it had been Thomas Kind.

There was a roar and light bump as the helicopter touched down. And then the doors were opened, and the three policemen were ducking under the rotor blades and running across the tarmac toward the chartered jet that would take them to Rome.

"The SCV 13 diplomatic plates are what we thought," Castelletti shouted as they ran. "One of the low-numbered plates assigned to cars chauffeuring the pope or high-level cardinals. No one plate is designated to any person in particular. SCV 13 is currently assigned to a Mercedes which is away from the Vatican grounds being serviced."

The Church.

The Vatican.

Rome.

The words pierced Roscani's mind. He heard the roar of jet engines and felt himself pushed back into his seat as the aircraft hurtled down the runway. In twenty seconds they were up and airborne, with the sound of the landing gear closing into the fuselage beneath them. What had begun with an investigation into the assassination of the cardinal vicar of Rome was returning there, full circle.

Loosening his seat belt, Roscani plucked the last cigarette from its tattered pack, put the empty pack back in his jacket pocket, then stuck the cigarette in his mouth and looked out. Here and there the sun glinted off something on the ground, a lake or a building, as all of Italy seemed to bask under a cloudless sky. It was an ancient land. Beautiful and serene, yet trampled endlessly by scandal and intrigue that operated on every level. Was any land or history free of it? He doubted it. But he was Italian, and the country beneath him his. And he was a policeman, charged with enforcing its laws and seeing justice done.

He saw Gianni Pio, his friend and partner and godfather to his children, as he was taken from his car, drenched in his own blood, his face shot away. Saw the bullet-riddled body of the cardinal vicar of Rome, and the burned hulk of the Assisi bus. Remembered the butchery done by Thomas Kind in Pescara and Bellagio. And wondered what justice meant.

Yes, the crimes had been committed on Italian soil where he had the power to do something about them. But inside the Vatican walls he had no authority at all. And once his fugitives were behind them, there would be nothing he could do but turn his evidence over to Gruppo Cardinale's prosecutor, Marcello Taglia. Once he did, justice would no longer be his. Instead, it would belong to the politicians. And, in the long run, that would be the end of it. He remembered well Taglia's words about their investigation into the assassination of the cardinal vicar, warning of "the delicate nature of the whole thing and the diplomatic implications that could rise between Italy and the Vatican."

In other words, if it so chose, the Vatican could get away with murder.

121

HARRY'S FIRST IMPULSE HAD BEEN TO GO
back to where he'd left the Mercedes, break the window and
retrieve the keys, and get Danny and Elena out of the apartment on Via Nicolò V.

"He's dead. They mutilated him," he told Danny over the
cell phone. "Who the hell knows what he told them? They
could be on the way there now!" Harry was half walking,
half running, trying not to draw attention to himself as he
came out of the alley behind Father Bardoni's apartment and
turned down the street. Heading back the way he'd come.

"Harry," Danny said quietly. "Just come in. Father Bardoni would have told them nothing."

"How the hell do you know?"

"—I just do . . ."

LESS THAN THIRTY MINUTES LATER, Harry
came into the building. Carefully checking the entryway, he
looked at the elevator, then took the front stairs, feeling they

were safer than the little elevator box where he could be trapped.

Danny and Elena were in the living room when he came in. He could feel the tension and the electricity. For a moment no one said anything. Then Danny motioned toward the window.

"I want you to take a look, Harry."

Harry glanced at Elena, then went to the window.

"Look to the left, follow the wall," Danny said. "Far down is the top of a round brick tower. It's the Tower of San Giovanni, where Cardinal Marsciano is being held. He's in the center room halfway up on the far side. It has a glass door that goes out to a small terrace. It's the only opening in the wall."

The tower was perhaps a quarter of a mile away, and Harry could see the top of it clearly—a high, circular tower, turreted on top, made of the same ancient brick as the wall inside which it stood.

"We're the only ones left to do it," Danny said quietly.

Harry turned slowly.

"You and me and Sister Elena."

"Do—what?"

"Get Cardinal Marsciano out . . ." Whatever emotion Danny had shown earlier, when he couldn't reach Father Bardoni, he'd put away. Father Bardoni was dead; they had to move on.

Harry shook his head. "Uh-uh, not Elena . . ."

"I want to, Harry." Elena was looking directly at him. There was no doubt at all she meant it.

"Of course you do. Why wouldn't you?" Harry looked from Elena to Danny. "She's as crazy as you are."

"There's no one else, Harry . . . ," Elena said softly.

Abruptly Harry looked to Danny. "Why are you so certain we're safe here . . . that Father Bardoni didn't tell them?—I saw him, Danny. If it was me, I would have told them anything they wanted to know."

"You have to believe me, Harry . . ."

"It's not you. It's Father Bardoni. I don't have that much trust."

Danny looked at his brother for a long moment in silence; when he finally spoke it was in a way that tried to make Harry understand there was more to what he was saying than simply the words he was using.

"This apartment building belongs to the owner of one of the largest pharmaceutical manufacturers in Italy. All he had to know was that Cardinal Marsciano requested a private place for a few days and it was done with no questions . . ."

"What's that got to do with Father Bardoni?"

"Harry, the cardinal is one of the most beloved men in Italy. . . . Look who helped him, and at what risk to themselves. I . . ."—Danny hesitated, then went on—"I became a priest because I was as lost and confused after I came out of the marines as I was before I went in. . . . By the time I came to Rome, I was just as lost. . . . Then I met the cardinal, and he showed me a life that was inside me that I never knew existed. Over the years he guided me, encouraged me to find my own convictions, spiritual and otherwise. . . . The Church, Harry, became my family . . . and the cardinal I loved like a father. . . . It was the same for Father Bardoni. It's why he would have told them nothing . . ."

The image of Father Bardoni in the bathtub was too strong: a man being tortured yet saying nothing. Shaken and moved, Harry ran a hand through his hair and had to look away. When he did, his eyes found Elena's. They were tender and loving and told him she understood what Danny had said—and knew he was right.

"Harry—"

The sharpness of Danny's voice brought him around and back to his brother. It was only then he saw the television was on in the background.

"There is something else. . . . If I didn't believe it before, Father Bardoni's murder confirmed it. . . . Do you know what is going on in China?"

"A catastrophe, a lot of people dead. I don't know. I haven't exactly had a lot of time to watch the TV. What the hell are you talking about?"

"In Bellagio, Harry. When we were waiting in the truck for Sister Elena to come for us. You got a call on a cell phone. . . . It woke me. . . . I heard you say two names, Adrianna and Eaton."

"What about it?" Harry still didn't understand.

"Adrianna Hall. James Eaton."

Harry was both surprised and puzzled. "They were the people who helped me get to you. How the hell do you know them?"

"It doesn't make any difference. What's important is that you get in touch with them both as fast as you can." Abruptly Danny moved his wheelchair toward his brother. "We have to stop what's going on in China."

"Stop what?" Harry didn't understand.

"They're poisoning the lakes, Harry. . . . One has already been done. . . . There are two more to go . . ."

"What? Who's poisoning the lakes? From what little I know, it was an act of nature."

"It's not," Danny said quickly, then glanced at Elena before looking back to Harry. "It's part of Palestrina's goal . . . for the Vatican to control China."

Harry felt the hairs stand up on the back of his neck. "That was what the confession was about, wasn't it? . . ."

"It was a part of the confession . . ."

Elena crossed herself, "Mother Mary . . . ," she said under her breath.

"A little while ago WNN ran a recap story on Hefei," Danny kept on, pressing strongly. "At two minutes and twenty-odd seconds past eight, there was a clip from the Hefei water-filtration plant—I know the time because I looked at my watch. In that clip was the face of a man who, if he isn't doing the poisoning, knows who is."

"How do you know that?" Harry whispered.

"I saw him last summer at a private retreat outside Rome. He was there with another man, waiting to see Palestrina. Not many Chinese are invited to a Vatican retreat." Danny was as intense as Harry had ever seen him.

"Adrianna Hall can roll the tape back to the second and find that picture. The man is short and standing to the left, and he's got a briefcase in his hand. When she has it, have her get it to Eaton as fast as she can."

"What is Eaton going to do with it? He's a minor embassy official."

"Harry, he's Rome station chief of the CIA."

"What?" Harry was dumbfounded.

Danny didn't waver. "I've been in Rome a long time, Harry. . . . Where I work, there are levels of international diplomacy where things are known. . . . Cardinal Marsciano has guided me into rooms most people would never know existed . . ."

Both Harry and Elena could see Danny's anguish. Bound by the Seal of Confession, he was jeopardizing his soul by revealing anything he had heard in it. Yet hundreds of thousands of lives were at stake, and he had to do something. And in doing it, he had to trust not in canon law, but in God.

Danny wheeled his chair back a little, never taking his eyes from Harry. "I want you to go out of the building now.

Call Adrianna Hall first, and do it from a pay phone. Then go to another pay phone and call Eaton. Tell him what I told you and that Adrianna is getting him the footage. Tell him to inform Chinese Intelligence—tell him they have to find the man with the briefcase. Underline that speed is everything. Otherwise the people in Beijing are going to have a couple of hundred thousand more dead to answer for . . ."

Harry hesitated for the briefest moment, then his finger pointed off. "There's a phone right there, Danny. Why not tell Eaton yourself?"

"He can't know where I am or you are . . ."

"Why?"

"Because I'm still a U.S. citizen, and because a threat to China is a matter of national security. He'll want more from me, and he'll do whatever he has to do to get it. . . . Even if it means illegally taking all three of us into custody. . . . If he does"—Danny's voice faded to a hoarse and exhausted whisper—"Cardinal Marsciano will die."

Elena saw the look in Harry's eyes. Saw him stare at his brother for a long time before he slowly nodded and said, "Okay." She knew in her heart Harry felt what they were doing was wrong, even ill advised. But she had also seen him accept without a word Danny's special reverence for Cardinal Marsciano, understanding why he would risk everything to save him.

By going along, Harry had not only shown his brother how much he loved him, but in doing so had made—possibly for the first time in their adult lives—their mission the same: slip into the venerable city, free the prince imprisoned in the tower, and then escape alive. It was gallant, medieval, foolhardy, and would have been difficult enough even with Father Bardoni's help. But Father Bardoni was dead, and so his part of the burden rested solely on Harry. And Elena could feel him trying to work it out, to determine where they were now, where they could go from here. Suddenly Harry glanced at her, holding her eyes for a moment, then opened the door and left, still dressed the way he had been most all the time she'd known him, as a priest.

122

Beijing, China. Zhongnanhai Compound.
Still Thursday, July 16, 3:05 P.M.

YAN YEH SPENT THE DAY IN HORROR. THE FIRST
reports had begun coming in from Wuxi just before ten that
morning. A dozen serious cases of uncontrolled nausea, diarrhea, and vomiting had been reported to number 4 People's
Hospital within a fifteen-minute span. At nearly the same
time, similar reports came in from the number 1 and number
2 People's Hospitals. By eleven-thirty the Hospital of Chinese Medicine was coordinating an epidemic. Seven hundred cases reported, two hundred and seventy-one deaths.

Immediately the water supply had been shut down, and
emergency service personnel along with police put on alert.
The city was on the verge of panic.

By one in the afternoon there were twenty thousand poisoned. And eleven thousand four hundred and fifty of those
were dead. Among them were Yan Yeh's mother-in-law and

two of her brothers. That much he had been able to find out. Where his wife and son were, or if they were dead or alive, he had no idea. Even the towering influence of Wu Xian, general secretary of the Communist Party, had proven ineffectual in trying to find out. But what had happened was enough. Pierre Weggen had been summoned to the Zhongnanhai Compound.

Now, just after three, with still no news of his family, a solemn, deeply shaken Yan Yeh sat down with his Swiss friend at a table with Wu Xian and ten other grim-faced ranking members of the Politburo. The conversation was brief and to the point. It had been agreed to let the Swiss investment banker bring together the consortium of companies he had earlier proposed to immediately begin a leviathan ten-year plan to thoroughly and completely rebuild China's entire system of water and power delivery. Haste and efficiency were everything. China and the world must know Beijing was still in control and doing everything possible to protect the future health and well-being of its people.

"*Women shenme shihou neng nadao hetong?*" Wu Xian said to Weggen, finally and quietly.

When can we have the contract?

123

HARRY'S CALLS TO ADRIANNA AND EATON had been made from public phones on streets two blocks apart and had been short and crisp. Yes, Adrianna had told him, she knew the piece of news tape he was talking about. Yes, she could find the sequence. Yes, she could get a copy of the tape to Eaton. But why? What was in the footage that was so important? Harry didn't respond, simply asked her to do it, saying that if Eaton wanted her to know, he would tell her. Then he'd said thank you and hung up, even as she was yelling, "Where the hell are you?"

Eaton had been a little more difficult, delaying Harry, talking around him, asking if he was with his brother and, if so, where they were. And Harry knew he was tracing the call.

"Just listen." Harry had cut him off abruptly, then gone on to describe the piece of video as Danny had, telling him that there were three lakes in China to be poisoned; that the Chinese with the briefcase, in the sequence at the Hefei water-treatment plant, was their man; that Chinese Intelligence should be informed immediately; and that Adrianna was getting him the footage.

"How do you know this?—Who's behind the poisoning?—What is the reason?" At the end Eaton's questions had been direct and rapid-fire. And Harry had replied that he was only delivering a message.

And then, as he had with Adrianna, he had simply hung up and walked off and kept walking as he was now, turning down Via della Stazione Vaticana, a priest alone proceeding down a sidewalk beside the Vatican walls, nothing unusual in that. Above him were the arches of what looked like an ancient aqueduct that might have brought water to the Vatican sometime in the past. What were there now, what he hoped he would soon see, were railroad tracks that led from the main rail line in to massive gates, and then through them and into the Vatican railroad station.

"By train," Danny had said when Harry asked how he and Father Bardoni had planned to get Marsciano out of the Vatican. The station and tracks were rarely used anymore. An Italian supply train used them to deliver heavy goods every once in a while, but that was all. In other days the tracks had provided the means for the pope to travel by train out of Vatican City and into Italy. But those days had long since ended. All that was left were the gates, the station, the tracks, and a rusting freight car sitting on a siding near the end of the line, which was a short concrete tunnel that went nowhere. Only God and the walls themselves knew how long the boxcar had been there.

Before he'd left Rome for Lugano, Father Bardoni had called the head of the railroad station and told him Cardinal Marsciano hated seeing the freight car and, ill or not, wanted it removed immediately. A short while later a call had come back from a subordinate to say that at eleven o'clock that Friday morning, a work engine would come for the old car.

And that was the plan. When the car left, Cardinal Marsciano would be inside it. It was as simple as that. And since it had been a subordinate who had called, Father Bardoni was certain the matter had been treated merely as another duty in line with many. Security would be alerted, but only to expect the switch engine; again, a conversation between underlings, and something far too mundane to reach Farel's office.

Now Harry was walking up the hill coming up toward the top level of the aqueduct. He kept moving, looking ahead.

Reaching the track level, he turned back and saw it—the main line curving to the left, the rails shiny from constant use, and the spur line to the right, its double set of rails rusted and leading directly toward the Vatican walls.

Harry turned and looked behind him, his gaze following the tracks down the main line toward Stazione San Pietro. He had ten minutes to get there and look around, make certain he wanted to go through with it. If he didn't, if he changed his mind, he could leave before they got there. But he wouldn't leave, he'd known that when he made the call. At ten-forty-five he was to meet Roscani inside the station.

124

The Vatican. The Tower of San Giovanni.
Same time.

"YOU ASKED TO SEE ME, EMINENCE." PALEST-
rina stood in the doorway of Marsciano's cell, his massive
body filling most of it.

"Yes."

Marsciano stepped back, and Palestrina came into the
room. As he did, one of his black suits stepped behind him,
to close the door and stand beside it, guardlike. He was
Anton Pilger, the young man with the perpetual smirk and
eager face, who, only days earlier, had been Marsciano's driver.

"I wanted to speak to you in private," Marsciano said.

"As you wish." Palestrina lifted a huge hand, and Pilger
suddenly snapped to attention, then turned on his heel and
left, a move not of a policeman, but of a soldier.

For a long moment Marsciano stared at Palestrina, as if
trying to see behind his eyes, then slowly his hand moved out

from his body and he pointed a finger toward the silent television nearby. The pictures on it, a horrible replay of those in Hefei—a convoy of trucks jammed with People's Liberation Army troops. Hordes of people crowding the streets on either side of them as they passed. The camera cutting to a field reporter dressed much like the troops, his voice not heard because of the muted television, but obviously attempting to describe what was happening.

"Wuxi is the second lake." Marsciano's face was ashen. "I want it to be the last. I want you to stop the next."

Palestrina smiled easily. "The Holy Father has been asking for you, Eminence. He wanted to visit. I told him you were very weak, and that it was best that for the time being you rested."

"No more deaths, Umberto," Marsciano whispered. "You already have me. Stop the horror in China. Stop it and I will give you what you have wanted from the beginning . . ."

"—Father Daniel?" Palestrina smiled again, this time benevolently. "You told me he was dead, Nicola . . ."

"He is not. If I ask him, he will come here. Call off the last lake and you can do with us as you wish. . . . The secret of your 'Chinese Protocol' passing with us."

"Very noble, Eminence. But, unfortunately, too late on both counts . . ." Palestrina turned to glance for a moment at the television, then he looked back.

"The Chinese have capitulated and have already asked for the contracts. . . . Even so"—Palestrina added, smiling distantly—"in war there is no pulling back; the campaign must be concluded according to plan . . ." Palestrina hesistated long enough for Marsciano to know any further argument would be in vain, and then he continued. "As for Father Daniel. No need to summon him, he is on his way to see you. May even be in Rome as we speak."

"Impossible!" Marsciano shouted. "How could he even know I was here?"

Again Palestrina smiled. "Father Bardoni told him."

"No! Never!" Marsciano was flushed with anger and outrage. "He would never give up Father Daniel."

"But he did, Eminence. . . . Ultimately he became convinced that I was right and that you and the cardinal vicar were wrong. That the future of the Church is worth more than the life of one single man, no matter who he is—Eminence . . ." Palestrina's smile faded. "Have no doubt, Father Daniel will come."

Marsciano had never hated in his life. But he hated now, with everything in him.

"I do not believe you."

"Believe what you wish . . ."

Slowly Palestrina slipped his hand into the pocket of his priest's jacket and took out a dark velvet drawstring purse. "Father Bardoni sends his ring to you as proof . . ."

Setting the purse on the writing table next to Marsciano, Palestrina fixed his eyes on the cardinal, then turned and walked to the door.

Marsciano did not see Palestrina leave. Did not hear the door open or close, or even the click of the lock as it was turned. His eyes were frozen on the dark velvet pouch in front of him. Slowly, his hand trembling, he picked it up and opened it.

Outside, a gardener looked up sharply at the sound of a hideous scream.

125

10:42 A.M.

ROSCANI WALKED ALONE DOWN VIA INNO-
cenzo III. It was hot, and getting hotter as the sun moved
higher overhead. In front of him was Stazione San Pietro.
He'd stepped from the car a half block back, leaving Scala
and Castelletti to go on to the station. They were to come in
separately from either side, one arriving before Roscani, the
other just afterward. They would be looking for Harry Addison, but doing nothing to apprehend him unless he ran. The
idea was to give Roscani room to operate comfortably one
on one with the fugitive, to keep the thing as easy and
relaxed as it could be; but at the same time to position themselves in such a way that if he did bolt, one or the other
would be in his path. There were no other police, no back-
ups. It was what Roscani had promised.

Harry Addison had been good. His call had come into the
Questura switchboard at ten-twenty. He'd said simply:

"My name is Harry Addison. Roscani is looking for me."

Then he'd given his cell-phone number and hung up. No time to trace. Nothing at all.

Five minutes later Roscani called him from where he had been since his plane had touched down in Rome and he and Scala and Castelletti had rushed there—the crime scene in Father Bardoni's apartment.

ROSCANI: This is Roscani.

HARRY ADDISON: We should talk.

ROSCANI: Where are you?

HARRY ADDISON: The train station at St. Peter's.

ROSCANI: Stay there. I'll meet you.

HARRY ADDISON: Roscani, come alone. You won't know me, I look different. If I see any police, I'll leave.

ROSCANI: Where in the station?

HARRY ADDISON: I'll find you.

ROSCANI CROSSED THE street, closing in on the station. He remembered how he'd first planned to come upon Harry Addison. Alone, with a gun. To kill him for murdering Gianni Pio. But things had turned wildly, and with a complexity he could never have imagined.

If Harry Addison was here, in the station as promised, he was still outside Vatican territory. So, Roscani hoped, was Father Daniel. Perhaps he had a chance yet, before the whole thing crumbled into the hands of Taglia and the politicians.

HARRY SAW ROSCANI come in and cross the lobby, then walk out to stand near the tracks. Stazione San Pietro was small, a depot serving a small circuitous route through Rome. There were few people. Looking around, he saw a man in a sport coat and tie who might be a plainclothes policeman. But he had noticed the man a few moments earlier, before Roscani had come in, and that made it hard to tell.

Leaving the station by another door, he walked around to the side, and came down the platform from another angle, slowly, without energy. A priest waiting for his train; a priest who had purposely left his false identification tucked under the bottom of the refrigerator in the kitchen of the apartment on Via Nicolò V.

Through an open door, he saw another man come into the station. His shirt was open at the throat, but he wore a sport coat like the first man.

Now Roscani saw him, watched him approach.

Harry stopped, a dozen feet away. "You were supposed to come alone."

"I did."

"No, there are two men with you." Harry was guessing, but he thought he was guessing correctly. One man was still in the station, the other had come out onto the platform and was watching them.

"Keep your hands where I can see them." Roscani's eyes were frozen on Harry's.

"I'm not armed."

"Do as I say."

Harry moved his hands out from his waist. It felt awkward and uncomfortable.

"Where is your brother?" Roscani's voice was flat. No emotion at all.

"He's not here."

"Where is he?"

"He's—someplace else. . . . . In a wheelchair. His legs are broken."

"Other than that, he's all right?"

"Mostly."

"The nurse is still with him? Sister Elena Voso?"

"Yes . . ."

Harry felt a thud of emotion as Roscani said Elena's name. He'd been right when he'd said they would identify her from what she'd left behind in the grotto. And now he knew they were treating her as a willing accomplice. He didn't want her to be this involved, but she was anyway, and there was nothing he could do about it.

Abruptly, he glanced behind him. The second man had come out onto the platform, keeping his distance, the same as the first. Beyond him, a group of teenagers waited for a train, chattering, laughing. But it was the police who were closest.

"You don't want to take me in, Roscani, not now, anyway."

"Why did you call me?" The policeman continued to stare at him. He was strong and very focused. The same as Harry remembered.

"I told you, we need to talk."

"About what?"

"Getting Cardinal Marsciano out of the Vatican."

126

THEY DROVE THROUGH MIDDAY TRAFFIC.
Harry and Roscani in back. Scala up front, with Castelletti
driving. Along the Tiber, and then across it and through city
streets to the Colosseum, down Via di San Gregorio past the
ruins of the Palatine and the ancient Circus Maximus, and
then down Via Ostiense and into the EUR, Esposizione Uni-
versale Roma—a grand tour of Rome, a way to talk and not
be seen.

And Harry did talk, laying it out for them as simply and
succinctly as he could.

The one person, he told them, who could reveal the truth
behind the murder of the cardinal vicar of Rome, the killing
of Gianni Pio, and, very probably, the explosion of the Assisi
bus was Cardinal Marsciano, who was being held incommu-
nicado and under the threat of death inside the Vatican by
Cardinal Palestrina.

Harry knew this because his brother, Father Daniel Addison, had told him. It was all he knew, a revelation from one

brother to another. But it was only a scratch on the surface; the real substance, the details, had been told to Father Daniel by Marsciano in confession, a confession secretly recorded by Palestrina.

Because of what Father Daniel had learned, Palestrina ordered him killed; but even before that, to keep leverage over Marsciano, Jacov Farel had set Father Daniel up, planting evidence to make it look as if he was the assassin of the cardinal vicar. And later, when Palestrina suspected Father Daniel was still alive, it was very probably he, through Farel, who had okayed the murder of Pio; because immediately afterward, they had taken Harry away and tortured him, trying to make him tell where Father Daniel was.

"That was when the video was made, when you asked your brother to give himself up," Roscani said quietly.

Harry nodded. "I was still in shock from the torture, I was told what to say over a headset."

For a long time Roscani did nothing, simply sat and studied the American.

"Why?" he said, finally.

Harry hesitated. "—Because there's something else," he said. "Another part of Marsciano's confession . . ."

"What other part?" Roscani suddenly leaned forward.

"—It has to do with the disaster in China."

"China?" Roscani tilted his head as if he didn't get it. "You mean the mass deaths?"

"Yes . . ."

"What does that have to do with what's happened here?"

This was the beat Harry was looking for. As much as Danny loved and cared for Marsciano, it was crazy to think that he and Danny and Elena alone could free him. But with Roscani's help they might have a chance. Moreover—the emotional part of it aside—the truth was, Cardinal Marsciano was the only one whose testimony could vindicate Danny and Elena and him. It was the reason Harry was here, why he had taken the chance and called Roscani.

"Whatever I said, Ispettore Capo, would only be hearsay and therefore useless. . . . And, as a priest, my brother can say nothing at all. . . . It's Marsciano who knows everything . . ."

Roscani sat back abruptly, pulling a crushed cigarette pack from his jacket. "So, we ask Cardinal Marsciano, he tells us on the record what, before, he would say only in confession, and everything is resolved."

"—Maybe, yes," Harry said. "His situation is a great deal different than it was."

"You're speaking for him?" Roscani said quickly. "You're saying he *will* talk to us. He will name names and give us facts."

"No, I'm not speaking for him. I'm only saying that he knows and we don't. . . . And won't, unless we get him out of there and give him the chance."

Roscani sat back. His suit was wrinkled and he needed a shave. He was still a young man but looked tired and older than he had the first time he and Harry had met.

"Gruppo Cardinale police blanket the country," he said softly. "Your photograph is on television and in the newspapers. A substantial reward offered for your arrest. How did you manage to get from Rome to Lake Como . . . and back?"

"Dressed as I am now, as a priest. . . . Your country has a great reverence for the clergy. Especially if they are Catholic."

"You had help."

"Some people were kind, yes . . ."

Roscani looked at the crumpled pack of cigarettes in his hand, then slowly crushed it and held it in his tightened fist.

"Let me tell you a truth, Mr. Addison. . . . All the evidence is against you and your brother. . . . Even if I said I believed you, who else do you think would?" He gestured toward the front. "Scala? Castelletti? The Italian court? The people of Vatican City?"

Harry kept his eyes on the policeman, knowing that to do anything else would make it seem as if he were lying.

"Let me tell *you* a truth, Roscani. Something only I would know because I was there. . . . The afternoon Pio was killed I was called from my hotel by Farel. His driver took me to the country, near where the bus exploded. Pio was there. There was a scorched gun some boys had found. Farel wanted me to see it. Insinuated it had belonged to my brother. It was more pressure on me to tell Farel where Danny was. . . . The trouble was, at that time I didn't even know if he was alive let alone where he was . . ."

"Where is the gun now?" Roscani asked.

"You don't have it?" Harry was surprised.

"No."

"It was in an evidence bag in the trunk of Pio's car . . ."

Roscani said nothing. Just sat there, watching him with no expression at all. No expression, but his mind was churning. Yes, it had been the truth. How could Harry Addison even know about the pistol if he hadn't been there? And he had been genuinely surprised the police didn't have the gun. And the other things he said rang true with most of Roscani's own investigation—from the missing gun to bits and pieces of a high-level struggle going on inside the Vatican.

What he said also answered why so many people had sheltered, cared for, and protected Father Daniel and lied about it: because Cardinal Marsciano had asked them to.

Marsciano's shadow was huge. A Tuscan farm boy with roots deep in the Italian soil, a man of the people who had been loved and admired as a priest long before he'd risen to his high place inside the Church. It was a given that when such a man asked for help, it would be dispensed without question, a "why?" never asked, that it had been done never revealed.

And Palestrina, as evil architect of it all—somehow, for some reason, involved in the mass deaths in China—and as a major figure in global diplomacy, was certain to have contacts that could have put him in touch with an international terrorist like Thomas Kind.

Furthermore, Cardinal Marsciano controlled the real purse strings of the Holy See, the type of huge financial base Palestrina would need to realize some immense ambition.

Harry could see Roscani weighing what he had said and wondering whether to believe him. To win him over, to have him fully on his side with no doubts at all, Harry knew he had to give him something else.

"A priest who worked for Cardinal Marsciano came to Lugano where we were hiding," Harry said, his eyes locked on Roscani's, "and asked my brother to come back to Rome. He did that because Cardinal Palestrina threatened to kill Marsciano if he didn't. So he came and told us. He arranged for a Mercedes and provided Vatican license plates and a place for us to stay when we got here. . . . This morning I went to his apartment. He was dead. His left hand had been cut off. . . . I was scared as hell and ran away. . . . I'll give you the address, you can—"

Roscani cut him off. "We know about the license plates, Mr. Addison, and we know about Father Bardoni."

"*What* do you know?" Harry kept going. "That it was Father Bardoni who found my brother still alive in the pandemonium of the hospital after the bus explosion? Found him, and got him out of there in his own car. Took him to the home of a doctor friend outside Rome and saw that he was cared for until he could make arrangements for the hospital in Pescara and the people to protect him there?—Do you know that, Ispettore Capo?" Harry stared at Roscani, letting what he'd said penetrate, then his manner softened and he finished. "You have to believe I'm telling you the truth about the rest."

Castelletti was turning now, heading up Viale dell'Oceano Pacifico and back toward the Tiber.

"Mr. Addison, do you know who killed Father Bardoni?" Roscani asked quietly.

"I have a good idea. The blond man who tried to kill us in the grotto in Bellagio."

"Do you know who he is?"

"No . . ."

"Does the name Thomas Kind mean anything to you?"

"Thomas Kind?" Harry felt the name stab through him.

"Then you know who he is—"

"Yes," he said. It was like asking if he knew who Charles Manson was. Not only was Thomas Kind one of the most publicized, brutal, and elusive outlaws in the world, to some he was one of the most romantic. "Some," meaning Hollywood. In the last months, four major movie and television projects had been announced with Thomas Kind spinning as the central character. And Harry knew firsthand, because he'd been involved in negotiating two of them, one for a star, the other for a director.

"Even if your brother weren't confined to a wheelchair, he is in a very dangerous situation. . . . Kind is ingenious in finding people he wants to find. As he proved in Pescara and Bellagio, and now here, in Rome. I would suggest you tell us where he is."

Harry hesitated. "If you take Danny in, it's even more

dangerous. Once Farel knows where he is, they'll kill Marsciano and then they'll send somebody after Danny wherever you've got him. Maybe Kind, maybe somebody else . . ."

Roscani hunched forward, his eyes on Harry. "We'll do our best not to let that happen."

"What does that mean?" Suddenly a red flag went up. Harry's palms felt sticky, and there was sweat on his upper lip.

"It means, Mr. Addison, there is no *evidence* that what you've said is true. There is, however, substantial evidence to prosecute both you and your brother for the crimes of murder."

Harry's heart jumped for his throat. Roscani was going to arrest him right then. He couldn't let it happen. "You are willing to let the prime witness be killed without any attempt to stop it?"

"There *is* nothing I can do, Mr. Addison. I have no authority to send people into Vatican territory. No power to arrest, if I did. . . ." Roscani's words, how he said them, at least showed Harry that he *did* believe his story. At least he wanted to.

"If we tried to extradite any of them," Roscani continued, "Marsciano, Cardinal Palestrina, or Farel, . . . it wouldn't work. In Italy it is the judge who must prove a suspect guilty 'beyond a reasonable doubt.' The investigator's mandate, my mandate"—he gestured toward the front—"and that of Scala and Castelletti and the others of Gruppo Cardinale is to collect evidence for the prosecutor, for Marcello Taglia. . . . But there is no evidence, Mr. Addison, and therefore no grounds whatsoever. . . . And with no grounds, to accuse the *Vatican?*" Roscani's voice trailed off. "You are a lawyer, you should understand."

Roscani's eyes had remained on Harry the entire time. And in them Harry saw volumes: anger, frustration, emasculation, a sense of personal failure. Roscani was fighting himself and his own position.

Slowly, Harry pulled away from Roscani to see Scala and Castelletti in pale silhouette to the glare of the midday Roman sun. He could feel the same emotion in them. They had come to the end of the line. Politics and law had overridden justice. The only thing they could do was what their jobs allowed. And that meant prosecuting him and Danny. As well as Elena.

In that moment Harry knew that it had come back to him. That somehow he had to turn it around or they were all lost. He and Danny and Elena and Marsciano.

Deliberately, he looked back to Roscani.

"Pio and the cardinal vicar. . . . The killings in Bellagio and the other places. . . . All the crimes were committed on Italian soil . . ."

"Yes," Roscani nodded.

"If you had Cardinal Marsciano. And if he would talk to you and to the prosecutor about those crimes. If he named names and said why. Would you have enough for extradition?"

"It would still be very difficult."

"But it might work."

"Yes. Except that we don't have him, Mr. Addison. And we can't get him."

"What if I could?"

"You?"

"Yes."

"How?"

Scala turned in his seat. Harry saw Castelletti find him in the mirror.

"At eleven o'clock tomorrow morning, a work engine is

going into the Vatican to pick up an old freight car and bring it out. . . . Father Bardoni set it up as a way to try and get Marsciano out. . . . Maybe I can find a way to still make it happen. I would need your help. But it would be on this side of the Vatican walls."

"What kind of help?"

"Protection for me and my brother and Sister Elena. By you three. Nobody else. I don't want Farel finding out. . . . You give me your word nobody will be arrested until we're through, and I'll take you to where they are."

"You are asking me to break the law, Mr. Addison."

"You want the truth, Ispettore Capo. So do I . . ."

Roscani glanced at Scala, then looked back to Harry. "Continue, Mr. Addison . . ."

"Tomorrow, when the engine takes that freight car out of the Vatican, you follow it until it stops. If it works, Cardinal Marsciano and I will be inside it. You take us back to where Danny and Sister Elena are. Give Danny and the cardinal time together alone, whatever it takes, until he is ready to make a statement. Then you come in with your prosecutor."

"What if he chooses to say nothing?"

"Then our agreement's over and you do what you have to do."

For a long moment Roscani sat stone-faced, and Harry wasn't sure if he would give him what he was asking or not. Finally, he spoke.

"My part is easy, Mr. Addison. . . . But I have grave doubts about you. It's not just getting a man into a freight car. First you have to get him out of where he is, and in doing that you will have to deal with Farel and his people. And then, somewhere, is Thomas Kind."

"My brother was a marine," Harry said quietly. "He'll walk me through it."

Roscani knew it was crazy. And knew that Scala and Castelletti felt the same. But unless they went in with him themselves—which was impossible, because if they did and were caught, it would make for a major diplomatic incident—there was nothing they could do but stand back and wish him well. It was a gamble and a bad one. But, ultimately, the only one they had.

"All right, Mr. Addison," he said quietly.

Harry felt the relief but tried not to show it. "Three more things," he said. "First, I want a handgun."

"Do you know how to use it?"

"Beverly Hills Gun Club. Six months' training in self-protection. One of my clients made me do it."

"What else?"

"Climbing rope. A long length that can support two men without breaking."

"That's the second. What's the third?"

"You have a man in jail. The police took him by train from Lugano and back to Italy. He's wanted for murder, but a fair trial would prove self-defense. I need his help. I want him out."

"Who is he?"

"He's a dwarf. His name is Hercules."

"PIANO THREE-A," HARRY SAID.

"All right." Roscani nodded and Harry got out of the car.
He waited for a moment, watching the policemen drive
away, then went inside. He had done what he had done,
Roscani knew where they were, and now he had to tell
Danny.

"ADRIANNA HALL notified. Eaton notified. Just as you
asked—"

"And the police *notified*." Heatedly Danny turned away in
his wheelchair. Moved it across the room to stare blankly
and angrily out the window.

Harry didn't move, just stood watching his brother,
uncertain what to do.

"Please, Harry, let it wait until later . . ."

Elena put her hand on Harry's arm. She wanted him to go
to one of the bedrooms, lie down and rest. He'd been without
sleep for more than thirty hours, and she could hear the raw
edge in his voice, see the emotional roller coaster of the last
weeks in his eyes, and knew he had nothing left. He'd come

back telling them about his calls to Adrianna and Eaton and his meeting with the police. The help he'd asked for that they could not give. He told them what Roscani had threatened and the agreement he'd made with him instead. He told them about Hercules. And about Thomas Kind. But Danny seemed to have heard only the part of it he wanted to hear— that the police and the state prosecutor would be waiting when they came back with Marsciano. As if the cardinal were some kind of spy or prisoner of war just waiting to deliver the intelligence he had gathered on the enemy.

"Danny—" Harry pulled away from Elena and walked toward his brother, his weariness propelling his intensity. "I understand your anger, and I respect how you feel about the cardinal. But for Christ's sake, open your mind enough to understand Marsciano is all that stands between us and prison. If he doesn't talk to the police and to the prosecutor, all of us"— Harry's hand shot out, pointing toward Elena— "Elena included, are going to go away for a very long time."

Slowly Danny turned from the window and looked at his brother. "Cardinal Marsciano will not bring down the Church, Harry," he said calmly and quietly. "Not for you, for Sister Elena, for me, not even for himself."

"What about—for the truth?"

"Not even for that . . ."

"Maybe you're wrong."

"I'm not."

"Then I think, Danny"—Harry's voice had the same quiet of his brother's—"the best we can do is try to get him safely out and then let him decide. . . . If he says no, he says no. . . . Fair?"

There was a long silence, then, "Fair," Danny whispered.

"Okay . . . ," Harry said and then, exhaustion overtaking him, turned to Elena. "Where do I sleep?"

128

The Vatican. The Tower of San Giovanni.
Same time.

CARDINAL MARSCIANO SAT IN A STRAIGHT-backed armchair, staring trancelike at the television screen five feet in front of him. Its sound was still turned off. A commercial played now. It was animated. Whatever was being sold did not penetrate.

Across the room was the velvet purse Palestrina had left him. The hideous thing inside it affirmation, as if more were needed, of the secretariat's descent into total madness. Barely able to look at it let alone touch it, Marsciano had tried to get them to take it away, but Anton Pilger had merely stood in the doorway and refused, saying nothing could be brought in or taken out without specific orders, and there were none. With that he had said he was sorry and closed the door, the sound of the bolted lock as it clicked into place, by now, almost ear shattering.

Abruptly a graphic flashed on the television screen in front of Marsciano. It played over a map of China that high-lighted both Wuxi and Hefei.

As of 10:20 P.M. Beijing time:
WUXI, CHINA—FATALITIES: 1,700
HEFEI, CHINA—FATALITIES: 87,553

Immediately the picture cut to Beijing. A field reporter was standing in Tiananmen Square.

Marsciano picked up the remote:

CLICK.

The sound came up. The reporter was speaking in Italian: A major announcement regarding the disasters in Hefei and Wuxi was imminent, he said. Speculation centered on an announcement to the provinces of an immediate and massive rebuilding of China's entire water and power infrastructures.

CLICK.

The reporter spoke on in silence. Marsciano put down the remote. Palestrina had won. He had won, yet there was still to be a third city, another mass poisoning. What hell was this?

Seeing what had already happened, knowing what was yet to come, Marsciano closed his eyes and wished Father Daniel *had* died in the bus explosion, so that he never would have known of the horror caused by Marsciano's loathsome weakness and inaction against Palestrina. Wished he had died then rather than be killed here by Farel's thugs when he came looking for Marsciano—after China had already hap-pened.

Turning from the cold cruelty of the television screen, Marsciano looked across the room. Early-afternoon sunlight radiated through the glass door, beckoning him toward it. Besides sleep and prayer, the door had been his only solace.

From it, he could look out over the Vatican gardens and see a pastoral world of peace and beauty.

Going there now, he pulled aside the curtains to stand at the glass, watching the sunlight stream through the trees to make a grand chiaroscuro of the landscape beneath. In a moment he would turn from the doorway to kneel at his bed and beg—as he had so often in the last days and hours—God's forgiveness for the terror he had helped create.

His mind on his prayers, he was about to turn back when suddenly the beauty he looked upon vanished. What he saw in its place shook him to his soul. It was an image he had seen a hundred times before, but never had it filled him with the revulsion it did now.

Two men walked toward him along a gravel pathway. One was huge physically and wore black. The other was older and much smaller and dressed in white. The first was Palestrina. The other, the one in white, was the Holy Father, Giacomo Pecci, Pope Leo XIV.

Palestrina was animated as they walked. Chatting, gesturing with infectious energy. As if the world and everything in it were filled with joy. While the pope, beside him, was, as always, enamored by his charisma and utterly trusting. And because of it, wholly blind to the truth.

As they drew closer, Marsciano felt a chill creep across his shoulders and ease like frozen breath down his spine. For the first time, and with profound horror, he saw who this *scugnizzo*, this common street urchin from Naples, as Palestrina called himself, really was.

More than a grand, beloved, and all-persuasive politician. More than a man who had risen to the second most powerful position in the Roman Catholic Church. More, even, than a corrupt, increasingly mad, and paranoid being, prime architect of one of the most gruesome civilian massacres in history. The smiling, ruddy-cheeked, white-haired giant who walked through Eden's dappled sunlight with the Holy Father ravished in his spell was darkness itself, a whole and complete incarnation of evil.

$$\boxed{129}$$

8:35 P.M.

"MR. HARRY!" HERCULES BLURTED AS HARRY
opened the door to Piano 3a and Roscani gestured for him to
enter. In complete surprise the dwarf swung into the apartment on his crutches, with Roscani, Scala, and Castelletti
following.

Closing the door and locking it, Castelletti remained
alongside it while Scala, with a glance at Danny and Elena,
walked off and through the rest of the apartment.

"The climbing rope you asked for is in the hallway outside," Roscani said.

Harry nodded, then looked to Hercules hanging on his
crutches in front of Castelletti, open-mouthed and totally
baffled.

"Come in and sit down, please. . . . This is my brother,
Father Daniel, and this is Sister Elena . . . ," he said to both
Roscani and Hercules, introducing the priest in a wheelchair

and an attractive young woman beside him as if both men had been invited there for dinner.

Hercules followed Harry across the room as bewildered as ever and with no idea at all of what was going on. All he knew was that he'd been suddenly hustled away from a work detail in the central jail and told he was being transferred to another prison. Fifteen minutes later he was being whisked across Rome in the backseat of a dark blue Alfa Romeo with the top cop of Gruppo Cardinale sitting next to him.

"Nobody else," Scala said, coming back into the room, looking at Roscani. "One door through the kitchen to a rear stairway. Single-bolt lock on the door. Anybody tries to come in from the roof, he's going to have to break glass and make a lot of noise doing it."

Roscani nodded, then, with a studied glance at Danny as if he were trying to get the measure of him, looked to Harry. "Hercules is signed out in a transfer from one jail to another. The paperwork got mixed up on the way. . . . This time tomorrow, I want him back."

"This time tomorrow you may have all of us," Harry said. "What about the handgun?"

Roscani hesitated, then abruptly looked to Scala and nodded. Opening his jacket, Scala took a semiautomatic pistol from his waistband and gave it to Harry.

"Nine-millimeter Calico parabellum. Sixteen-shot magazine," he said in heavily accented English. Then he pulled a second clip from his pocket and gave it to Harry as well.

"The serial numbers have been filed off," Roscani said flatly. "If you get caught, you don't remember where you got it. If you say anything about what's gone on here, it will be denied completely and your trial will become more difficult than you could ever imagine."

"We've only met once, Ispettore Capo," Harry said. "The

day you picked me up at the airport. . . . The others here have never seen you . . ."

Roscani's eyes crossed the room. He looked at Hercules. At Elena. Then at Danny and, finally, at Harry.

"Tomorrow," he said, "the freight car is to be taken from the Vatican to a siding between Stazione Trastevere and Stazione Ostiense, where it will be left to be picked up later. We will follow it the entire way. When the work engine leaves, we will come in.

"As for the rest. . . . My advice is to avoid Farel's men at all cost. . . . There are too many and they have too much communication . . ."

Roscani slipped a 5 × 7 color photograph from his inside jacket pocket and gave it to Harry.

"This is Thomas Kind, as of three years ago. I don't know if it will help, because he changes his appearance as often as most of us change clothes. Dark hair, blond, man, woman— he speaks a half dozen languages. If you see him—"

"Roscani." Harry cut him off. He was staring at the photograph the policeman had given him, remembering the face, where he had seen it before. It had been illuminated for a split second just after the ear-shattering roar of gunshots. Pale and cruel with the deepest blue eyes he had ever seen. "It was him," he said, looking up to Roscani. "It was Thomas Kind who shot Pio."

For the longest moment Roscani was silent, then he finished what he had started to say before. "If you see him, don't even think, just pull the trigger. And keep pulling it until he's dead. Then walk away. Let Farel take credit for it." Roscani paused and glanced around the room. "One of us will be outside all night if you need us."

Harry nodded. "Thank you," he said and meant it.

Roscani glanced once more at the others. *"Buona fortuna,"* he said, then looked to Scala and Castelletti.

A moment later the door closed behind them and they were gone.

Buona fortuna. Good luck.

130

Wuxi, China. Friday, July 17, 3:20 A.M.

FLASH!

Li Wen grimaced in the brilliant pop of the strobe light,
trying to look away. A hand pushed him back.

FLASH! FLASH! FLASH!

He had no idea who these people were. Or where he was.
Or how they had found him in the shoving, terrified mass on
Chezhan Lu as he made his way toward the railroad station.
He'd merely been trying to leave Wuxi, after a frenzied discussion with officials at Water Treatment Plant number 2.
The water he'd tested just after daybreak that morning had
shown alarming levels of blue-green algae toxin, the same as
Hefei. And he'd said so. But the only result of his warning
was a rush of local politicians and safety inspectors to the
scene. By the time the arguments were done and the city's
water-treatment plants along with the water intake systems

from Taihu Lake, the Grand Canal, and Liangxi River were shut down, a full-scale emergency was in process.

"Confess," a voice commanded in Chinese.

Li Wen's head was jerked back and he looked into the face of an officer of the People's Liberation Army, but instantly Li Wen knew he was more than that. He belonged to the *Guojia Anquan Bu*, the Ministry of State Security.

"Confess," he said once again.

Suddenly Li Wen was shoved face forward toward papers spread out on a table before him. He stared at them. They were the pages of formulas, received in the Beijing hotel from the American hydrobiologist James Hawley, and had been in his briefcase when he had been caught and arrested.

"The recipes for mass murder," the voice said again.

Slowly Li Wen looked up. "I have done nothing," he said.

Rome. Thursday, July 16, 9:30 P.M.

Scala sat in a chair, watching his wife and mother-in-law play cards. His children—ages one, three, five, and eight—were asleep. He was home for the first time in what seemed like months and wanted to stay there. If for no other reason than to hear the women talk and smell the smell of the apartment and know his children were as close as the next room. But he couldn't. He was to relieve Castelletti outside the apartment on Via Nicolò V at midnight, taking the watch until Castelletti came back with Roscani at seven. Then he would have three hours to sleep before he met them again at ten-thirty and they waited for the work engine to go into—and then come out of—the Vatican through the monstrous iron doorway in its immense walls.

Scala was starting to get up, to go into the kitchen and make fresh coffee, when the phone rang.

"*Si*," he said, picking up quickly.

"Harry Addison is in Rome . . ." It was Adrianna Hall.

"I know . . ."

"His brother is with him."

"I . . ."

"Where are they, Sandro?"

"I don't know . . ."

"You do know, Sandro, don't lie. Not on this one, not after all these years."

All these years—Scala flashed back to the time when Adrianna was a young reporter newly assigned to the Rome bureau. She was about to break a story that would have rocketed her career forward but would have greatly jeopardized a murder case he was about to close. He'd asked her to hold her story back, and with great reluctance she had. But because of it she had become *fidarsi di,* someone to trust. And he had trusted her, secretly slipping her privileged information over the years, and she had responded with information of her own that helped the police. But this time it was different. What was happening here was much too dangerous, with too much at stake. God help him if the media learned the police were helping the Addison brothers.

"I'm sorry. I have no information. . . . It's late, you understand . . . ," Scala said quietly and hung up.

131

10:50 P.M.

THEY SAT AT THE KITCHEN TABLE, LISTENING to Danny, his hand-drawn map of Vatican City in front of them, surrounded by coffee cups and bottles of mineral water and the remains of the pizza Elena had gone out alone to get.

"Here is the goal. Here is the mission," Danny said for the twentieth time, walking them through it again, as Harry had told Roscani he would, talking not as a priest but as a highly trained marine.

"The tower is here, the railroad station here."

Once more Danny jabbed his finger at his diagram of Vatican City, looking up from his wheelchair at Harry, Elena, and Hercules in turn, making certain they were watching, understanding each step. As if this were the first time he had gone over it.

"A high wall here," he continued, "runs southeast along a narrow paved road leading from the tower for maybe sixty yards. Then it ends. On the right is the main wall"—abruptly, Danny pointed off—"the one we can see from the window." Now he looked back to the faces at the table.

"At the end of the wall, there's a gravel path through the trees that will bring you to Viale del Collegio Etiopico, the boulevard of the Ethiopian College. A right there and you are at a low wall and almost on top of the station.

"Everything keys to the timing. We can't try to get Marsciano out too soon, or we'll give them time to swarm the place. But we have to be out of the tower and inside the railroad car *before* they open the gates at eleven to let the engine in. That means he has to be out of the tower at ten-forty-five and inside the railroad car by ten-fifty-five, no later, because by then the stationmaster or one or two of his men will be coming out to make sure the gates are opening properly.

"Now"—Danny's index finger went back to the drawing—"you come out of the tower and for some reason—Farel's men, Thomas Kind, an act of God, who knows, but for some reason—you can't follow the wall? Take the road directly in front of you through the Vatican gardens. Several hundred yards down, you'll see another tower building, which is Vatican Radio. As soon as you see it, turn right. The cut across will bring you back to the Viale del Collegio Etiopico and then the wall above the station. Follow the road along the wall for maybe thirty yards. By then you'll be at track level. The freight car will be right there, between the station and the turn-around tunnel at the end. Cross the tracks to the far side of the car, away from the boulevard. All that's there is another set of tracks and then the wall. Pull open the doors—and they may take some work because they're old and rusted—then climb in. Close the doors. And wait for the engine. . . . Any questions?"

Once again Danny looked around the table, and Harry had to marvel at his attitude, his precision, focus. Whatever melancholy he had had before had been pushed aside completely. He might as well have had "The Few, The Proud" stenciled on his forehead.

"I have to pee," Hercules said, and standing, gathered his crutches and swung off out of the room.

This was hardly a time to smile, but Harry did. It was Hercules' way. Brusque, funny, and all business, whatever that business was. Earlier, the moment the police had gone, Hercules had looked to Harry, totally perplexed, and said, "What the hell is this?"

And soberly, in front of Danny and Elena, Harry had explained how Cardinal Marsciano was being held against his will inside the Vatican as part of a secret coup and that he would be killed if they didn't get him out. They needed an inside man, someone who could get to the tower unseen. That man, they hoped, was Hercules, and that was the reason for the climbing rope. Harry had ended it by telling him that if he went along he would be risking his life.

For the longest moment Hercules had remained stone-faced, staring at nothing. And then his eyes had gone around the room. Looking from one to the other to the other. Finally his face slowly twisted into an enormous grin.

"What life?" he'd said loudly, his eyes gleaming. And in that moment, he'd become one of them.

132

11:30 P.M.

SCALA CAME OUT OF HIS APARTMENT, GLANCED briefly around, then crossed to an unmarked white Fiat. Looking around once more, he got in, started the engine, and drove off.

A moment later a dark green Ford pulled away from the curb a half block down. Eaton was behind the wheel, Adrianna Hall beside him. Turning left onto Via Marmorata, they followed Scala through light traffic to Piazza dell'Emporio and then across the Tiber on Ponte Sublicio. Then, dropping back in traffic, they followed him north, along the river's western bank. A few minutes later Scala turned west through the Gianicolo section, only to go north again on Viale delle Mura Aurelie.

"He's not taking any chances about being followed . . ." Eaton dropped the Ford behind a silver Opel, keeping a guarded distance between himself and Scala's Fiat.

For the Italian detective to suddenly refuse Adrianna information was a cue in itself that something major and highly secret was going on. It was out of character for Scala to shut her out—it had been Scala himself who tipped Adrianna to Father Daniel's suspected presence in Bellagio hours before it was announced, meaning just days ago he was still including her. His deliberately evasive maneuvers now only added to a series of rapid-fire happenings that suggested whatever was going on inside the Vatican was fast coming to a head.

Eaton and Adrianna reviewed all of it: The sudden and mysterious illness of Cardinal Marsciano, last seen Tuesday leaving the Chinese Embassy seemingly in good health. Even their combined efforts provided little more information than the formal Vatican press release announcing his sickness and saying he was under the care of Vatican physicians.

The abrupt return of Roscani, Scala, and Castelletti to Rome from Milan.

The murder early this morning of Marsciano's personal aide, Father Bardoni. Not yet announced by the police.

Also this morning—Harry Addison's terse calls, traced to public telephones near the Vatican, alerting them to the situation in China. To which they had responded immediately, and which within hours resulted in the clandestine arrest and interrogation of a government water-quality inspector named Li Wen.

And again this morning—the surprising announcement of the suspected reemergence in Italy of the long-silent celebrated terrorist Thomas Kind, and the all-points arrest-and-detain order put out for him by Gruppo Cardinale.

Suddenly Scala took a sharp left ahead of them, turning right after a half block, and then making a quick left and accelerating off. Adrianna could see Eaton smile slightly as he kept up with him. Changing gears, accelerating, then dropping back, using the skill and training demanded of the professional spy he was. Up until tonight both he and Adrianna had had to sit back and wait, hoping Harry Addison would lead them to Father Daniel. Now the police were doing it. Why and what was unfolding, they didn't know, but with the disaster in China now seemingly interconnected with the Vatican intrigue, they were certain they were on the edge of monumental, breaking history.

"The police are going to make it difficult." Eaton slowed. Ahead of them Scala made a sharp right down a darkened residential street.

Adrianna said nothing. She knew that at another time and in another situation Eaton would have called in two or three of his Italian operatives and had Father Daniel kidnapped. But not now, not in the presence of the police and not with a clumsy post—Cold War CIA under the stony-cold microscope of both Washington and the world. No, they could only do what they'd been doing all along, wait and watch and see what happened. And hope that something would happen, and that they could get Father Daniel alone.

133

Friday, July 17, 12:10 A.M.

PALESTRINA WOKE FROM HIS SLEEP WITH A
cry. He was soaked with sweat, his arms out in front of him
in the darkness, still trying to push the thing away. This had
been the second night in a row when shadowy spirits had come
toward him in a dream. There were many of them and they carried a heavy, unclean blanket to cover him, a blanket he knew
was filled with disease, the same disease that had caused the
fever that killed him before, when he was Alexander.

It was a moment before he realized that what had waked
him was not only the terror of his dream but the ringing of the
phone at his bedside. Abruptly the ringing stopped, then
started again, the multiline phone lighting up a private number
only one person had, Thomas Kind. Quickly he picked up.

"*Si . . .*"

"There has been a setback in China," Kind said evenly in
French, deliberately trying not to alarm Palestrina. "Li Wen

has been detained. I have taken care of the situation. There is nothing to concern yourself with other than the business of the coming day."

"Merci," Palestrina said, aghast, and hung up. Suddenly he shivered, the coldness real and reaching deep inside him. The spirits were not a dream, they were real and getting closer. What if something happened and Thomas Kind failed to "take care of the situation" and the Chinese found out? It was not impossible—after all, it was Thomas Kind who had failed to kill Father Daniel.

Suddenly a new horror stabbed through him—that Father Daniel was still alive not because of luck but because the spirits had sent him, and sent his brother as well. They were Death and their appointment was with Palestrina. Not only that, as the moth comes to the flame, Palestrina was bringing them right into his own lair.

12:35 A.M.

Harry opened the door to the kitchen and turned on the light. Crossing to the counter, he double-checked the battery charger, making certain life was being pumped into the ultra-slim batteries of the cell phones. They had two of them, the one that had been in the apartment and the one Adrianna had given Harry. In the morning when they left for the Vatican, Danny would carry one, Harry the other. It was how they would communicate when they went in after Marsciano, trusting that between the masses of tourists and Vatican personnel, random conversations would be difficult, if not impossible, for Farel to monitor, even if he knew they were there.

Satisfied the charger was working, Harry turned out the light and started back into the hallway.

"You should sleep." Elena stood in the open doorway of her room, directly across from the bedroom Harry was sharing with Danny. Her hair was brushed back and she wore a thin cotton nightshirt. Farther down the darkened hallway was the living room, and they could hear Hercules snoring loudly as he slept on the couch.

Harry moved closer. "I don't want you to go with us," Harry said, quietly. "Danny and I and Hercules can handle it alone."

"Hercules has his own job, and someone has to take Father Daniel in the wheelchair, and you can't be two places at once . . ."

"Elena. . . . It's too unpredictable and too dangerous . . ."

The light from the bedside lamp behind her shone through the material of her nightshirt. She was wearing nothing at all underneath. She moved closer, and Harry could see the rise and fall of her full breasts under the nightshirt as she breathed.

"Elena, I *don't* want you to go," Harry said definitively. "If something were to happen—"

Reaching up, Elena gently pressed her fingers to his mouth. Then, in almost the same motion, slid her fingers away and brushed her lips against his.

"We have now, Harry," she whispered. "Whatever happens, we still have now. . . . Use it to love me . . ."

134

1:40 A.M.

FIFTEEN MINUTES LATER THAN THE LAST
time Danny had looked at his bedside clock. If he'd slept in
those minutes, he didn't know. Harry had come in only a few
moments earlier and gone to bed. It had been more than an
hour since he'd gone out to check the battery chargers.
Where he had been or what he had been doing in the meantime he didn't know, but he assumed he had been with Elena.

He had seen electricity building between them since Bellagio, and he knew that at some point it had to spark. It made
little difference that she was a nun. Danny had known almost
from the time she had come to care for him in Pescara that
Elena was not the kind of woman who could continue to live
the lifelong, cloistered, contemplative life required of her.
That she should fall in love with his brother, of all people,
was something he could never have foreseen under the
wildest circumstances. And these—he half-grinned in the

dark—were, far and away, the most turbulent circumstances that anyone could have ever foreseen. Turbulent and—the grin abruptly faded—terribly, terribly tragic. In his mind he saw the man with the gun on the bus to Assisi, felt again the explosion. Remembered the fire, the screaming, the confusion, the bus swinging wildly out of control. Remembered his reflex reaction of getting up, sticking as much of his identification as he could in the gunman's jacket. Abruptly that vision left, and he saw Marsciano through the wire mesh of the confessional, heard the pained sound of his voice. *"Bless me Father, for I have sinned . . ."*

Abruptly Danny turned away, put his head to his pillow, trying to drown out the rest of it. But he couldn't. He knew every word by heart.

ADRIANNA STIRRED at the sound and looked up. Eaton was getting out of the car, straightening his beige summer suit jacket, then walking off along the sidewalk toward where Scala was parked. She saw him sidestep the throw of a streetlight, all the while looking up at the dark loom of the apartment building partway down the street, then he disappeared in the darkness. Immediately her eyes went to the dull orange illumine of the dashboard clock and wondered how long she had been dozing.

2:17 A.M.

Now Eaton came back, sliding into the seat beside her.

"Scala still there?" she asked.

"Sitting in the car, smoking . . ."

"No lights on in the apartment building?"

"No lights." Eaton looked over at her. "Go back to sleep. You'll know when something happens."

Adrianna smiled lightly. "I used to think I loved you, James Eaton . . ."

"You loved the office, not the man . . ." Eaton looked back at the apartment building.

"The man, too, for a while." Adrianna pulled her loose-fitting denim over-shirt around her, then curled up on the seat. For a long time she watched Eaton watch the building, then finally she drifted off.

Beijing, China. Still Friday, July 17, 9:40 A.M.

"JAMES HAWLEY. AN AMERICAN HYDROBIO-logical engineer," Li Wen said in Chinese. His mouth was dry and he was soaked with sweat. "He . . . he lives in Walnut Creek, California. The procedure came from him. I . . . I . . . didn't know what they were. I . . . thought they were a new test . . . for wa . . . water toxicity . . ."

The man in the army uniform who stared at Li Wen across the hard wooden table was the same man who had demanded he confess what he had done six hours earlier in Wuxi. The same man who had handcuffed him and accompanied him on the military jet to Beijing and taken him here to this brightly lit cement-block building somewhere on the air base where they had landed.

"There is no James Hawley of Walnut Creek, California," the man said softly.

"Yes, there is. There *has* to be. I did not have the formulas, *he* did."

"I repeat . . . , there is no James Hawley. It has been confirmed by the American authorities."

Li Wen felt the breath go out of him as suddenly he realized he'd been played for the fool the entire time. If something went wrong he alone was the one who would pay for it.

"Confess."

Slowly Li Wen looked up. Just behind the man at the table was a videocamera, its red light on, recording what was happening. And behind the camera he could see the faces of a half dozen uniformed soldiers—military police, or, worse, men like his interrogator, members of the Ministry of State Security.

Finally he nodded, and looking directly into the camera, told how he had introduced his "snowballs"—the deadly, nonmonitored constituent polycyclic, unsaturated alcohol—into the water systems. Explaining extensively and in scientific terms the details of the formula, what it was designed to do, and how many it was expected to kill.

As he finished, wiping sweat from his forehead with the palm of his hand, he saw two of the uniformed men suddenly step forward. In an instant they had him on his feet and he was marched through a door and down a dimly lit concrete corridor. They went for twenty or thirty feet before he saw a man step out of a side door. The soldiers froze in surprise. In an instant the man had stepped forward. He had a pistol in his hand, a silencer on the barrel. Li Wen's eyes went wide. The man was Chen Yin. His finger squeezed back on the trigger and he fired point-blank.

PTTT! PTTT!

Li Wen was blown backward, his body twisting away from the soldiers, his blood splattering across the wall behind him.

Chen Yin looked at the soldiers and smiled, then started to back away. Suddenly his grin turned to horror. The first soldier was raising a submachine gun. Chen Yin backed away.

"NO!" he screamed. "NO, YOU DON'T UNDERSTA—"

Suddenly he turned and ran for the door. There was a sound like a dull jackhammer, the first shots spinning Chen Yin around, the last taking off the top of his head just over his right eye. He, like Li Wen, was dead before his body hit the ground.

136

Rome. 4:15 A.M.

HARRY WAS IN THE BATHROOM SHAVING, getting rid of the beard. It was dangerous because he would be exposing the face the public knew from the Gruppo Cardinale television spots and from the newspapers. But he had no choice. Few if any Vatican gardeners, Danny had said, wore beards.

Hercules sat at the kitchen table watching tiny whiffs of steam rise from the steaming cup of black coffee he held between his hands. Elena was across from him, as silent as he, her coffee untouched.

Fifteen minutes earlier Hercules had left the bathroom—a treat so rare and luxurious he'd spent half an hour there to enjoy all of it, sit and wash in a tub of hot water, and shave as Harry was now. And when Harry was done, that would give them something else in common. Not only bold and brave crusaders about to march on a foreign land, but they would also both be freshly shaven when they did. A little thing maybe, but like a uniform, it added to the brotherhood and tickled Hercules no end.

SCALA SAW THE FRONT DOOR open and the two come out. The only distinction between Harry Addison and an ordinary priest on his way to early mass was the long coil of climbing rope over his shoulder. That, and the dwarf who swung alongside him on crutches, his movements strong and smooth, like those of a gymnast.

Scala saw them cross onto Viale Vaticano and then turn left in the darkness, moving west, along the Vatican wall toward the tower of San Giovanni. It was twenty minutes to five in the morning.

EATON—SITTING BEHIND the wheel of the Ford, using a monocular nightscope—saw them leave, too. The crippled dwarf as much a puzzle as the coil of rope.

"Harry and a dwarf." Adrianna was awake and alert and had glimpsed them in the brief seconds when they'd passed under a streetlight before vanishing again in the dark.

"But no Father Daniel, and Scala hasn't made a move." Eaton put away the nightscope.

"Why the rope? You don't think they're—"

"Going in after Marsciano?" Eaton finished Adrianna's sentence. "And the police are letting them . . ."

"I don't get it."

"Neither do I."

A PICKUP TRUCK RATTLED PAST CARRYING firewood. Then the street was dark again, and Harry and Hercules stepped from the angle in the Vatican wall they had hidden behind.

"You know what that wood is for, Mr. Harry?" Hercules whispered. "Pizza ovens all over the city. Pizza." He winked. "Pizza." Abruptly he gave Harry his crutches and turned to the wall. "Boost me up."

With a glance back down the street, Harry picked Hercules up by the waist and lifted him toward a ledge that ran the length of the wall halfway up. Hercules strained to reach it, then did. In an instant he was up and balancing on it.

"Crutches first. Then the rope."

Crutches handed overhead, Harry tossed the coil of rope. Grabbing it, Hercules shook out a few feet, put a loop around his shoulder and dropped the free end to Harry.

Taking hold, Harry felt it tighten. Above him, Hercules smiled, then waved him up. Ten seconds later Harry had come up the wall and stood on the ledge beside him.

"No legs, Mr. Harry, but the rest of me like granite, eh?"

"I think you like this." Harry half grinned.

"We are in search of the truth. And no goal is more honorable, is it, Mr. Harry?" Hercules' eyes bore into Harry's, the pain of a lifetime in them. Then, as quickly, he looked to the top of the wall.

"Another boost, Mr. Harry. This time is trickier. Lean your back to the wall and keep your balance or we both go down."

Putting his back against the wall, Harry dug his heels into the narrow stone ledge.

"Go," Harry whispered. Immediately he felt Hercules' hands on his shoulders, felt him pull up. Then the rope coil brushed across his chest, and Hercules' deadened feet banged over his face, then his weight vanished. Quickly Harry looked up. Hercules was kneeling on top of the wall.

"Crutches," he said.

"How's it look?" Harry handed them up.

One arm tucked through his crutches, Hercules peered over the side and into the Vatican gardens. The tower loomed behind some trees, not thirty yards away. Turning, he gave Harry the thumbs up.

"Good luck."

"See you inside." Hercules winked.

Then Harry saw him twist a turn of rope over a jutting corner of the wall, jab his arm through the crutches and disappear over the top.

For the briefest second Harry hesitated, then with a look back down the street, he jumped. Hitting the ground, he rolled over once and was up. Brushing off his jacket, tugging the black beret over his forehead, he walked quickly back down Viale Vaticano, the way he had come. Scala's Calico automatic was in his belt, Adrianna's cell phone in his pocket. Ahead of him, the buildings were stark black against the eerie pale of the brightening sky.

138

6:45 A.M.

WEARING THE BLACK SUIT AND WHITE SHIRT of Farel's guard, his hair black and cut short, Thomas Kind leaned against the balustrade on the outside walkway at the top of the Dome of St. Peter's, looking out over Rome. Two hours earlier he'd learned the situation in Beijing was over, the contracts he'd put out on Li Wen and Chen Yin satisfied. The first had been carried out by an unsuspecting Chen Yin himself, the second done swiftly but expensively through a contact in the North Korean secret police with close ties to the Chinese Ministry of State Security. Li Wen had been brought to a military airfield in Beijing for questioning. A source had been paid to leave a door open and look the other way as Chen Yin entered. Chen Yin had done his job, fully expecting to simply turn and walk away unmolested. That was when the second contract kicked in and the whole thing ended.

That left only the business of Father Daniel and those with him. At Palestrina's order and with Farel's blessing, Thomas Kind had spent most of yesterday with five members of the black-suited Vigilanza whom the Vatican policeman had carefully chosen himself. Outwardly they carried the same initial credentials as all of the specially chosen Swiss Guards. They were Catholic and Swiss citizens, but comparisons stopped there. Where the others had previously been exemplary members of the Swiss Army, these five simply had the word "military experience" next to their names. Secondary records showed why. All had been recruited by Farel himself and then used as his or Palestrina's personal guard. Three had been members of the French Foreign Legion and discharged with prejudice before the expiration of their five-year terms. The other two had had troubled childhoods, had been in and out of prison before Swiss Army service, and had later been discharged from the Swiss Army for aggravated assault, one with intent to commit murder. That one had been Anton Pilger. Moreover, all five had been brought into the Vigilanza within the last seven months, making Thomas Kind wonder if perhaps Palestrina had foreseen this kind of problem and therefore his need of the five black suits. But whatever Palestrina's motive, Kind had accepted the selection, met them, and then, handing out photographs of the Addison brothers, laid out his plans.

The brothers' sole purpose in coming, he told them, was to free Cardinal Marsciano. The idea then was to guard the tower from a distance, letting the brothers approach it in any way they chose. Once they were inside, the trap would simply be closed, the brothers shot on the spot, their bodies put into the trunk of an unmarked car and driven to a farmhouse in the countryside outside Rome, where they would be discovered a day or two later, killed by people unknown.

From his perch at the top of St. Peter's, Thomas Kind looked down to the empty square below him. In another hour people would start to come. From then on, the crowds would grow almost by the minute as the multitudes from around the world came to visit this holy and ancient place. It was curious, he thought, how much calmer and less mad and desperate he was since he'd come here. Perhaps there was indeed something spiritual here after all.

Or perhaps it was because he was helped by distance, as the one orchestrating the killing as opposed to doing it himself. And he began to rationalize and think that if he stopped killing altogether, retired from it completely, he would get well. The idea was frightening, because it was finally admitting that he was ill, agreeing that he was both seduced by and addicted to the act of murder. But like with any illness or addiction, he knew the first step in the cure was recognizing it. And since there was no professional he could turn to for help, he would have to become his own physician and prescribe the necessary treatment.

Looking up, he let his eyes drift toward the distant banks of the Tiber. The plan he had outlined for the black suits was more serviceable than remarkable, but they were hardly fighting a Third World War, so, under the circumstances and with the men he had chosen, it would do. The thing now was to watch, and wait for the brothers to come.

And then would begin the first step in his healing: orchestrate the plan while letting the others execute it.

139

THE CLINK OF GLASS AND SMELL OF RUM AND
spilled beer filled the kitchen. There was a final gurgle as
Elena emptied the last bottle of Moretti double-malt beer
into the sink. Then, running the tap, she rinsed the bottle,
collected the four other Moretti bottles she'd already emptied, and brought them to the table where Danny worked.

In front of him was a large ceramic mixing bowl with a
pour spout. In it, mixed proportionally, were two simple ingre-
dients from the kitchen: 150-proof rum used for cooking, and
olive oil. On the table to his right were a pair of scissors and a
box of pint-sized plastic Ziploc bags; and to the right of that,
the work that was already done—ten large cloth table napkins,
cut in quarters, then soaked in the rum-and-oil mixture and
rolled up tightly like little tubes. These he was carefully plac-
ing with oily, rum-soaked fingers into the plastic bags, and
then sealing them. Forty in all, four to a bag, ten bags.

Finishing, he wiped his hands with a paper towel, then
took the Moretti bottles from Elena and placed them on the

table in front of him. Picking up the mixing bowl, he carefully poured the remainder of the liquid into each.

"Cut another napkin," he said to Elena as he worked. "We'll need five dry wicks, about six inches long, rolled tightly."

"All right." Picking up the scissors, Elena glanced at the clock over the stove.

ABRUPTLY ROSCANI TOOK THE unlit cigarette out of his mouth and shoved it in the Alfa's ashtray. Another moment and he knew he would have pushed in the lighter. Glancing at Castelletti beside him, he looked in the mirror and then to the broad avenue ahead of them. They were driving south, along Viale di Trastevere, and Roscani was more troubled than he had been throughout the entire night, when he couldn't sleep; he was thinking about Pio and how much he missed him and how much he wished he were with them right now.

For the first time in his life, Roscani was lost. He had no idea if what they were doing was right. Pio's magic was that he would have looked at the whole thing differently than any of them, and they would have talked it through and in the end found some way that made it work for everyone. But Pio wasn't there, and whatever magic they might hope for they would have to find themselves.

The Alfa's tires squealed loudly as he took a sharp right, and then another. On their left were the railroad tracks, and absently Roscani searched for the work engine. But he saw nothing. Then they were there and turning down Via Nicolò V, moving toward Scala's white Fiat parked at the end of the street across from number 22.

140

"ROSCANI AND CASTELLETTI," ADRIANNA SAID said as the blue Alfa Romeo pulled in and stopped behind the Fiat.

Now the Fiat's door opened, and they saw Scala get out and go to the Alfa. The men chatted for a few moments, then Scala went back to the Fiat and drove off.

"This is a timing thing," Eaton said. "Harry Addison goes out two hours ago and doesn't come back. Now Roscani shows up. He's gotta be waiting for Father Daniel to make the next move and make certain nothing happens when he does—"

There was a shrill chirp as Eaton's beeper suddenly went off. Immediately he picked a two-way radio off the seat beside him and clicked it on.

"Yes—"

Adrianna saw his jaw tighten as he listened.

"—When?"

Eaton's jaw strained more, and she could see him grind his teeth.

"Not a word from our office, we know nothing about it. —Right." Abruptly he clicked off and stared into space.

"Li Wen confessed to poisoning the lakes. A few minutes later he was shot and killed by an assailant who was then killed by the security force. Convenient?—Whose stamp does that echo?"

Adrianna felt the chill. "Thomas Kind . . ."

Eaton turned back toward the apartment building. "I don't know what the fuck Roscani's thinking, but if he lets them go into the Vatican after Marsciano, there's every chance somebody's going to get killed, especially if Thomas Kind is in there waiting."

"James," Adrianna warned suddenly. An abrupt movement down the street had caught her eye.

Roscani was getting out of his car, looking around, a cell phone to his ear. Castelletti was getting out, too, walking along the sidewalk, an automatic held down alongside his leg. He was looking up at the buildings on either side of the street as if he were Secret Service.

Now Roscani was talking into the phone, nodding, then looking up and motioning to Castelletti. Immediately they both got back into the Alfa.

At the same moment the front door to number 22 Via Nicolò V opened, and a bearded man in a wheelchair and wearing a Hawaiian shirt was pushed into the morning sunshine by a young woman in jeans and sunglasses. The man had a camera case in his lap, the woman carried another over her shoulder.

"It's fucking *him*," Adrianna breathed. "The woman has to be Elena Voso."

There was an abrupt squeal of tires as Roscani swung the Alfa from where it was parked. Cutting directly across the street, he swerved sharply, then pulled abreast of the wheelchair couple, slowing and staying with them as they moved along the sidewalk toward the Vatican as if they were tourists out for an early stroll.

"Christ, he's going to baby-sit them right into St. Peter's."

Eaton was turning the ignition key, starting the engine, his fingers already tugging at the gearshift. Slowly he eased the green Ford out and down Via Nicolò V. He was angry and frustrated and helpless; the most he could do without creating an international incident was keep the Alfa in sight.

THEY WERE TURNING NOW, moving from Largo di Porta Cavalleggeri onto Piazza del Sant' Uffizio, a stone's throw from the southern colonnade and the entrance to St. Peter's Square. Instinctively, Roscani glanced in the mirror. A green Ford was twenty or thirty yards behind them. It was moving slowly, at the same speed they were. Two people were in the front seat. At his glance, the person in the passenger seat suddenly looked down. Then he saw Elena turn the wheelchair left, heading directly for the colonnade. Again, Roscani looked in the mirror. The Ford was right there, swinging left behind him. Then abruptly it turned right and sped off and out of sight.

141

EATON RACED ON FOR TWO SHORT BLOCKS,
then turned a quick left and then left again onto Via della
Conciliazione. Accelerating past a tour bus, he cut sharply
into the right lane and brought the Ford to an abrupt stop in a
taxi zone directly across from St. Peter's.

In an instant he and Adrianna were out of the car, ignoring
the angry shouts of a cab driver for leaving the Ford in the
taxi zone, and dodging traffic as they ran toward the crowded
square. Reaching it, they pressed desperately through the
mass of tourists, looking for a woman pushing a wheelchair.
Suddenly a loud claxton horn signaled a warning. They
looked up to see a small shuttle bus bearing down on them,
leaving the square. Lettering on the shuttle's front read
Musei Vaticani—Vatican Museums. Beneath it was the
familiar blue logo with the white wheelchair that was the
international symbol for the handicapped. Quickly they
stepped out of the way, letting it pass. As it did, Adrianna

caught the briefest glimpse of Father Daniel seated at a window near the front. Then the shuttle turned onto the street and crossed the piazza where they had left the car.

FIFTY YARDS AWAY, Harry traversed the square in a crowd heading for the basilica, Scala's pistol in his waistband, the black beret pulled almost rakishly over his forehead, and the papers Eaton had provided in his pocket identifying him as Father Jonathan Roe of Georgetown University, just in case. Unseen beneath the priest's clothing, he wore chinos and a work shirt. Clothes Father Bardoni had left in the apartment on Via Nicolò V.

Reaching a flight of steps, he climbed them with the crowd and then stopped. In front of him several hundred more people were massed, waiting for the doors to the basilica to open. It was now eight-fifty-five. The doors would be opened at nine. Two hours exactly before the work engine came. Head down, praying someone wouldn't suddenly look over and recognize him, Harry took a deep breath and waited.

HERCULES CROUCHED IN THE BATTLEMENTS
of the ancient fortified wall abutting the Tower of San Giovanni. He was at the rampart's far end, right at the tower
itself and maybe twenty feet beneath its tiled, circular roof.

It had taken nearly three hours to work his way up the far
side of the wall, handhold to handhold, using the morning
shadows to hide him. But then he'd made the top and scrambled to where he was now, cramped and thirsty, but precisely
where he was supposed to be and when he was supposed to
be.

Below, he could see two of Farel's black-suited men hidden in bushes near the tower entrance. Two more waited
behind the cover of a high hedge across the narrow roadway.
The main door, directly beneath him, appeared unprotected.
How many more black-suited men were inside the tower he
had no way of knowing. One, two, twenty, none? What was
clear was what Danny had predicted: the black suits would

stay back and out of sight, spiders hoping their prey would unwittingly lurch into their web.

Danny! Hercules grinned. He liked that, calling a priest by his first name, the way Mr. Harry had. It made him feel like part of the family, one in which he somehow wished he belonged. And for now, for today at least, he decided he did belong. It was that important. The stalwart dwarf who'd been abandoned by his family shortly after his birth and who had made his own way ever since, taking life as it came, all the while refusing to be its victim, suddenly found himself longing to belong. It surprised him because the pain and want were much more acute than he could have imagined. It told him one thing: he was much more human than he supposed, no matter what he looked like. Harry and Danny had included him because they needed him for what he could do, and that, in itself, gave him purpose and dignity for the first time in his life. They had entrusted him with their lives, and Elena's life, and that of a cardinal of the Church. Whatever happened, at whatever cost to himself, he would not let them down.

Squinting against the glare of the sun, he looked down the narrow road toward the railroad station, the way they would go later. Almost directly across, beyond the bushes where the second group of black suits were secreted, he could see the landing pad for the papal heliport. In the other direction, to his right and beyond the trees, was another tower building, Vatican Radio. He looked at his watch.

9:07 A.M.

Danny and Elena came in through the main entrance to the Vatican museums with the three other wheelchair couples who had been on the shuttle bus with them: a retirement-age American couple—the man in an L.A. Dodgers baseball cap who kept staring at Danny and his New York Yankees cap, as if he either recognized him or had had enough of museums and touring and simply wanted to talk baseball; his wife, plump and smiling pleasantly, pushing him in the wheelchair; a father and his son, probably twelve, wearing leg braces, seemingly French; a middle-aged woman caring for an elderly white-haired woman, apparently her mother, and apparently English, though it was hard to tell because the older woman was so abrupt with the younger.

One by one they went through the line to buy museum tickets and then were instructed to wait for the elevator that would take them all to the second floor.

"Stop over there. Closer to the door," the white-haired English woman snapped at her daughter. "Why you insisted on wearing that dress when you know I don't like it is beyond me."

Elena adjusted the camera bag over her shoulder, glancing at Danny's as she did. They were nondescript black nylon camera bags any tourist might carry, but inside them, instead of cameras and film, were cigarettes and matchbooks; the olive oil and rum-soaked rags rolled up and packed in the plastic Ziploc bags; and the four Moretti beer bottles—two in each case—plugged and wicked, with the same incendiary fluid.

There was a dinging sound, a light came on, and the elevator door opened. They waited while a few people got out, and then entered, squeezing in together, with the white-haired woman pushing ahead.

"We will be first, if you don't mind."

And she was, and in the order of things, this made Elena

and Danny last, forcing them to press in against the others, with the doors closing against their backs. Had they been first, or even second or third, and turned around like the others, Danny might have seen Eaton, with Adrianna. Seen him turn from the ticket window and glimpse them inside the elevator just as the doors closed.

143

HARRY WALKED SLOWLY INSIDE THE BA-
silica, moving just behind a cascade of Canadian tourists,
stopping, as they did, to look at Michelangelo's *Pietà*, his
impassioned statue of the Madonna with the dead Christ.
Then he eased away from the Canadians to the center of
the nave, casually studying the interior of the towering
dome, finally bringing his gaze down to the papal altar and
Bernini's *Baldacchino*, the grand canopy over it.

Then, following Danny's directions, he moved off alone.

Crossing to the right, passing the wooden confessionals,
looking easily at the sculptures of the saints Michele Arcan-
gelo and Petronilla, he reached the monument of Pope
Clement XIII. Just past it, he found a protrusion of wall.
Turning measuredly around it, he saw a decorative drapery
that looked as though it hung from a solid wall.

Glancing back and seeing no one, he pushed quickly
through it to a narrow hallway and walked to the door at the
end of it. Opening it, he walked down a short stairway to

another door at the bottom and went out, finding himself instantly out of doors and squinting in the bright sunshine of the Vatican gardens.

9:25 A.M.

9:32 A.M.

Elena pushed open the emergency exit door, carefully holding it with her foot, while she put a piece of clear plastic tape over the latch to make certain it wouldn't lock behind her.

Satisfied, she stepped out into the daylight and let the door close behind her. Then she walked off, glancing up at the second floor of the building she had just come out of, where she had been moments before when she'd left Danny alone in a hallway outside a men's rest room near the entrance to the Sistine Chapel—the same hallway to which she would return a few minutes later.

Adjusting the camera bag over her shoulder, she walked quickly across a small courtyard and out into a convergence of tended walkways, lawns, and ornamental hedges that was one of the many entrances to the Vatican gardens. Ahead, on her right, was the split stairway rising to the Fountain of the Sacrament.

She moved toward it quickly but carefully, looking around every so often as if unsure where she was going, knowing that if she was stopped she would say simply that she had taken a wrong door from the museums and was lost.

Climbing the stairs to the right, she entered the area of the fountain proper and turned right again to see a number of large planters near the base of a conifer. Again, she looked around, puzzled, as if she were indeed lost. Then, seeing no one, she took a black nylon waist pack from her camera case and tucked it carefully behind the planters at the base of the tree. Standing, she looked around once more, and went back the way she had come, passing through the courtyard, then pulling open the door and peeling the tape from the latch. Reentering the building, she let the door close behind her, and then took the stairs to the second floor.

ired. Standing, she looked around once more, and went back the way she had come, passing through the courtyard, then pulling open the door and popping the tape from the latch. Reentering the building, she let the door close behind her, and then took the stairs back to the third floor.

9:40 A.M.

DANNY OPENED THE DOOR TO THE MEN'S room stall cautiously and peered out. Two men stood at urinals, another was picking his teeth in the mirror. Opening the stall door wider, he wheeled himself to the men's room door and tried to push it open. It didn't work. Someone was on the other side trying to come in. Danny looked back. The other men were still there. Neither was watching him.

"Hey!" A voice came from the far side of the door.

Danny moved back, not knowing what to expect, his hand going to the camera bag to fling it if he had to.

The door swung open and another man in a wheelchair came through from the other side—the American from the shuttle bus, wearing the L.A. Dodgers cap. The man stopped dead in the doorway, the two of them chair to chair facing each other.

"You really a Yankees fan?" The man was looking at his baseball cap, a mischievous twinkle in his eye. "You are, you're crazy."

Danny looked past him into the hallway. People moved back and forth in a steady stream. Where was Elena? They were on a tight clock. Harry would already be outside crossing the Vatican gardens looking for the waist pack.

"I just like baseball. I collect a lot of caps." Danny moved his wheelchair back. "You come in. I'll go out."

"What teams you like?" The man didn't budge. "Come on, talk the game. Tell me the teams. Which league, American or National?"

Suddenly Elena appeared in the hallway behind the Dodgers fan.

Danny looked at the man and shrugged. "Since we're in the Vatican I guess I ought to pick the Padres as my favorite. . . . I'm sorry, I have to go."

The man grinned broadly. "Why, sure, pal, go ahead." Abruptly he pushed into the men's room and Danny went out.

Elena took the wheelchair and they started off. Then suddenly Danny put his hand on the wheels, slowing the chair.

"Stop," he said.

Eaton and Adrianna Hall were crossing at the far end of the hallway in a crowd, alert, moving quickly, looking for someone.

Danny looked over his shoulder at Elena. "Turn around, go the other way."

IF THERE HAD BEEN A PHONE BOOTH HARRY would have felt like Superman. There was no phone booth, just a low wall with dense shrubbery behind it across the roadway from St. Peter's where he'd come out. It was here he ducked out of sight and stripped off the beret and priest's clothing, revealing the chinos and work shirt underneath.

Then, burying the priest's outfit in the thick of the bushes, he scooped up a handful of the powdery dirt at his feet and dusted it over his chest, rubbing the remainder off on his thighs. Then he moved from the bushes, waited for a small black Fiat to pass on the narrow roadway and stepped out, hoping to hell he looked enough like a gardener to pass if anyone saw him.

Resolutely, he walked down the short sweep of manicured lawn and crossed the road to the Fountain of the Sacrament. Getting his bearings, he took the short stairway to the right. At the top he stopped and looked quickly around. He saw no one. Directly before him were the planters and pine tree Danny had designated. As he moved toward them his coolness left. Suddenly he was aware of his own breathing, felt the awkward press of the Calico automatic in the waistband under his shirt, felt his pulse begin to race.

Now he was at the planters at the base of the tree. Anxiously, he glanced around, then knelt. His hand touched nylon and he could feel the breath go out of him in relief. It meant not only that Danny and Elena were there, but also that the bulky package he'd decided not to wear at the last minute, for fear it might raise the suspicion of security guards inside St. Peter's, had been safely delivered.

Glancing around once more, he stood and slipped into the tree's shadow. Loosening his shirt, he fastened the waist pack underneath at his waist and repositioned the Calico inside the pull of its strap. Then, tucking his shirt back in, letting it fall loosely at his waist to cover the pack's bulge, he walked off and back down the steps. The whole thing had taken no more than thirty seconds.

9:57 P.M.
The Tower of San Giovanni. Same time.

There was the cruel sound of the lock turning and then the door to Marsciano's apartment opened and Thomas Kind entered. Anton Pilger was in the hallway behind him, hands crossed in front of him, staring in. He stayed there as Kind crossed the room.

"*Buon giorno,* Eminence," he said. "If I may."

Marsciano stood back silently as Kind looked carefully around the room, then went into the bathroom. A moment later he came out and crossed to the glass doorway. Opening the doors, he stepped out onto the tiny balcony. Putting his hands on the railing, he looked down at the gardens below and then up, overhead, at the sheer brick wall leading to the roof.

Satisfied, he came back in and closed the glass doors and for a moment studied Marsciano.

"Thank you, Eminence," he said, finally. Crossing the room, he went out immediately, pulling the door closed behind him. Marsciano shuddered at the sound of the lock turning. By now it was a grating that had become almost unbearable.

Turning away, he wondered why the assassin had visited him for the third time in the last twenty-four hours, and each time had gone through the exact same motions.

"WHEN YOU REACH THE FAR DOORWAY, TURN right," Danny said as Elena pushed him through the Room of the Popes, the last of the rooms of Borgia Apartments.

There was a rush and anxiousness to Father Daniel that Elena hadn't seen before. The abrupt turning in the hallway outside the men's rest room, the urgency in his voice now. It was more than concentration on what they were doing. It was fear.

Passing through the doorway, she turned him right, as he had said, moving him down a long corridor. Halfway down on the left was an elevator.

"Stop there," Danny said.

Reaching it, they stopped and Elena pushed the button.

"What's wrong, Father? Something happened—what is it?"

For a second Danny watched people move past, going from one gallery to another, then he looked up at her sharply.

"Eaton and Adrianna Hall are in the museum looking for us. We can't be found by either of them."

Abruptly the elevator door opened. Elena started to push him in when they heard an all-too-familiar voice behind them.

"We will be first, if you don't mind."

Looking, they saw the pushy white-haired woman in the wheelchair and her dutiful middle-aged daughter from the shuttle bus. For the second time they were face-to-face with a couple from that bunch. And Danny wondered if it was a curse.

"Not this time, madam. I'm sorry." Danny looked at her with a glare and Elena pushed him into the elevator.

"Well, I never—," the woman ranted. "I shall not ride in same lift with you at all, sir."

"Thank you."

Danny leaned forward and punched a button, and the door slid closed in the woman's face. As the elevator started down, Danny reached in his pocket and took out the set of keys Father Bardoni had given him in Lugano. Sliding one into a lock underneath the panel of elevator buttons, he turned it.

Elena watched the elevator pass the ground floor and continue down. When it stopped, the door opened onto a dimly lit service corridor. Danny took the key out and pushed a button that read LOCK.

"Okay. Out and to the left and then to the corridor immediately to the right."

Fifteen seconds later they were moving into a large mechanical room housing the museum's massive ventilating equipment.

10:10 A.M.

THE MARBLE FLOORS, THE SMALL COVERED
wooden benches, the semicircular rose marble altar with its
bronze crucifix, the bright stained-glass ceiling. The Holy
Father's private chapel.

How many times had Palestrina been here before? To
pray alone with the pope or with the few select guests who
might have been invited to join them. Kings, presidents,
statesmen.

But this was the first time he had been summoned on the
spur of the moment to pray alone with the Holy Father. And
now as he came in, he found the pope seated in his bronze
chair in front of the altar, head bent in prayer.

He looked up as Palestrina approached. Outstretching his
hands, he took Palestrina's in his and studied him, his eyes
intense and filled with worry.

"What is it?" Palestrina asked.

"This is not a good day, Eminence." The pope's voice was
barely audible. "There is a sense of foreboding. And dread

and fearfulness in my heart. It was there on arising and has sat perched on my shoulder ever since. I don't know what it is, but you are a part of it, Eminence . . . a part of whatever this darkness is. . . ." The pope hesitated and his eyes probed Palestrina's. "Tell me what it is . . ."

"I do not know, Holiness. To me the day seems bright, and warm with the summer sun."

"Then pray with me that I am wrong, that it is only a feeling and will pass. . . . Pray for the salvation of the spirit . . ."

The pope stood from his chair and both men knelt before the altar. Palestrina bowed his head as Pope Leo XIV led them in prayer, knowing that whatever the Holy Father felt, he was wrong.

The forbidding horror that had begun in the early morning hours as Palestrina had waked from his nightmare of the disease-bringing spirits, even as Thomas Kind was calling to tell him of the situation with Li Wen, had turned suddenly and inconceivably to good fortune.

Less than an hour earlier, Pierre Weggen had called to tell him that despite the revelation that the lakes had been deliberately poisoned—by, in the official words of the Chinese, "a mentally ill co-worker and water-quality engineer"—Beijing had decided to go ahead with the massive plan to rebuild the country's entire water-delivery system. It was a gesture designed to comfort and unite a traumatized, still-fearful, and unsettled nation, and at the same time show the world the central government remained in control. It meant that despite everything Palestrina's "Chinese Protocol" was in place and would not be turned back. In addition, what Thomas Kind had promised he had delivered—with the deaths of Li Wen and Chen Yin, any chance that a road might be discovered that would lead from China to Rome was closed forever. And under Thomas Kind's sure hand, the final chapter removing the last possible connection would soon be written here, inside the Vatican, as the moth comes to the flame—neither Father Daniel nor his brother were Death sent by the spirits, but simply a worry that had only to be eliminated.

So the Holy Father was mistaken, and the thing sitting perched on his shoulder was not the shadow of Palestrina's death but the emotional and spiritual infirmities of an old and fearful man.

148

10:15 A.M.

ROSCANI BIT DOWN RESTLESSLY ON A
knuckle and watched as the work engine came slowly down
the track toward them. It was old and creaky with oily soot
muddying most of the once bright green paint beneath.

"It's early," Scala said from the backseat.

"Early, late. At least it's here," Castelletti said, sitting in
front with Roscani.

They were watching from Roscani's blue Alfa parked on
the roadside halfway between the railroad spur to the gates
in the Vatican wall and Stazione San Pietro. As the green
engine drew closer, they could hear a grating of steel on steel
as the engineer applied the brakes and the rumbling machine
began to slow. A moment later it drifted past them, slowing
even more. Then it stopped. A brakeman jumped from it and
walked up the track to the spur. They saw him unlock a
mechanical hand switch, then reach up and tug on a steel bar

connecting it to the rail switches. A moment later he waved to the engine. There was a puff of brown diesel exhaust from the smokestack and it moved forward onto the spur. When it had gone far enough, the brakeman signaled, and it stopped. Then he threw the switch back the way it had been and climbed back onboard the engine.

Scala leaned forward against the front seat. "They go in now, it's going to fuck up everyone's timetable inside."

Castelletti shook his head. "They won't. It's the Vatican. They'll sit there until precisely the time it takes to open the gates and go inside at eleven on the dot. No Italian trainman is going to risk pissing off the pope by being early or late."

Roscani glanced at Castelletti, then looked back to the work engine. He was increasingly troubled by what he had done. Maybe he had wanted justice too much and had let some part of him reason the Addisons could somehow deliver it to him. But the more he thought about it, the more he realized they were all crazy. And he most of all for letting it happen. The Addisons might think they were prepared for what they were getting into, but the truth was, they weren't, not when they were going up against Farel's black-suited secret service, never mind someone like Thomas Kind. The trouble was—and he knew it—his insight had come too late, the event had already begun.

10:17 A.M.

Danny was out of his wheelchair and on the floor, his legs in the blue fiberglass casts twisted out awkwardly from his body. In front of him was a large blanket of crumpled newspaper. On top of it, he placed the last of eight of the rolled olive-oil-and-rum-soaked rags, setting them side by side and approximately eight inches apart and directly in front of the main air intake for the Vatican museums' central ventilating system.

"Oorah!" Danny said to himself. "Oorah!" Ready to kill! The ancient Celtic battle cry the marines had taken as their own. It was both arousing and chilling and came from the soul. Everything to now had been the setup, here and now was where it all began. Emotionally he had shifted gears, working himself up to where he needed to be, his mind-set become that of a warrior.

"Oorah!" he said again under his breath as he finished, then looked over his shoulder to Elena standing at a work sink behind him, waiting with a battered galvanized bucket containing a dozen water-soaked equipment-maintenance towels.

"Ready?"

She nodded.

"Okay."

With a glance at his watch, Danny lit a match and touched it in turn to the rags. Instantly they caught, throwing up a cloud of oily brown smoke and igniting the newspapers. Twisting abruptly left, Danny picked up more of the crumpled newspapers and fed them on top of those already burning. In seconds he had a roaring inferno.

"Now!" he said.

Elena came in a rush. Wincing against the heat and flame, they took the wet towels from the bucket, laying them one by one across the top of the fire.

Almost instantly the flames died away. In their stead was a thick billow of heavy brown-and-white smoke, all of it drawn, not into the room, but into the ventilating system. Satisfied, Danny pushed back, and Elena helped him into the wheelchair. As she did, he looked up at her.

"Next," he said.

149

10:25 A.M.

HARRY STOOD IN THE DEEP SHADE OF PINE trees just east and north of the Carriage Museum, waiting until a gardener's electric cart passed. When it did, he stepped out, cursing and fumbling with the stuck zipper on the waist pack inside his shirt. Finally, it came open and he reached in to take out a Ziploc bag. Opening it, he pulled out one of the rolled, oily rags, then closed the bag again and put it back in the waist pack.

In the distance near St. Peter's he could see two white-shirted Vigilanza patrolmen walking along the road away from him and toward the Ufficio Centrale di Vigilanza, the Vatican police station, a building that he now realized was probably no more than a hundred yards from the railroad station.

Harry watched for a half second more, then, quickly kneeling, he pulled together a large mound of pine needles, placed the rolled oily rag near the bottom and lit it. Immediately it flared up, igniting the tinder-dry needles around it. Counting to five, he smothered the fire with more pine needles. Instantly the flames turned to smoke. Then, as the flames flared again, he piled on several heavy armloads of soaking leaves gathered from beneath a freshly watered hedgerow nearby.

It was then he heard the first wail of warning sirens coming from the direction of the Vatican museums. Dumping a final armload of wet leaves onto the fire and seeing the smoke billow up, he glanced around, then walked quickly up the hill toward the Central Avenue of the Forest.

ELENA STARED BLANKLY ahead, waiting for the elevator to stop. She tried not to hear the sirens or think of the mass anxiety of the people or the damage the smoke might do to the priceless art—"little, if any," Father Daniel had told her. Then she realized the elevator had stopped and the doors were opening. As they did, the smell of smoke mixed with a clang of warning bells and shrieking fire alarms.

"Let's go!" Danny urged, and she pushed the wheelchair out into the corridor in front of them. Suddenly they were in a rush of frenzied tourists being urged on by white-shirted Vigilanza.

"The doors at the far end," Danny said.

"All right," Elena said. She could feel the adrenaline pump through her as she moved the wheelchair forward through the clamor and thickening smoke. Abruptly, and for no reason, her thoughts went to Harry and how he had looked at her without saying a word just as he and Hercules were leaving the apartment in the early-morning darkness. It was a look not of concern or even fear, but of love. Deep, even profound, there was no real way to describe it, except that it had been there and it had been for her, and it would stay with her for the rest of her life, wherever she was and no matter what happened.

"Out here," Danny said suddenly.

The urgency in his voice brought her back to the instant. She was following his direction, pushing him forcefully through a rush of people into an outer courtyard, the screaming sirens drowning out the yells of people pouring out the myriad of doors right along with them. She could see Danny opening the camera bag—taking out three of the oiled rags, then three matchbooks whose covers had been inserted with nonfiltered cigarettes that would act as fuses, and then the covers tucked back in again to hold the cigarettes tight.

"Over there." He was indicating the first of three large trash receptacles, each twenty yards apart.

Smoke was now drifting out from every open window and doorway. And everywhere people rushed and shoved to get out, afraid, yelling, uncertain.

Taking the matchbooks between oily fingers, Danny inserted them separately into the rags.

"Slow it up," he said as they neared the first trash container. Elena did. Danny lit a match to the first cigarette fuse, made certain it caught, then glancing around, dropped it into the receptacle.

"Okay."

They moved on to the second and did the same. And then again at the third.

Behind them the first cigarette burned down to the match pack. With a tiny *whoosh* it ignited, and, in turn, set fire to the oil-and-rum rag, setting the mess of collected refuse aflame.

"Back inside," Danny yelled over the shriek of sirens and blaring alarms.

Elena wheeled the chair toward the nearest open doorway, where mountains of people continued to pour out with the smoke that was now heavier than ever.

They could see a half dozen helmeted, ax-carrying, and rubber-jacketed *vigili del fuoco*—Vatican firemen—running along the edge of the roof above them looking for flames. It meant that as yet they had not discovered the source of the smoke. Now one of them stopped and pointed and yelled something. They saw others stop, too, and look in the same direction. And they knew the other trash containers were burning as well.

Now they were at the doorway.

"Scusi! Scusi!" Elena yelled at the crowd, forcing the wheelchair into their midst. Miraculously, enough of them moved out of the way for her to push through. And then they were inside. Pushing along an interior hallway, moving with a river of people going that way, Elena saw Father Daniel pull the cell phone from his shirt pocket and dial.

"Harry—where are you?"

"Top of the hill. Number two is burning."

Harry was moving quickly through a heavy growth of conifers toward the northwest corner of the gardens, trying not to think that it was working and that only three of them were doing it. Planning, surprise, and determination of the individual, Danny had emphasized over and over, were at the heart of any successful guerrilla action, and so far he was right.

Fifty yards behind him he could see the towers of Vatican Radio. To his right, another fifty yards downhill, heavy smoke began to billow from behind a high hedge, where he had just been. Beyond that he could already see the smoke from his first fire rising slowly.

"No wind, Danny," Harry said into the cell phone. "All this stuff's going to hang around."

"You should be near the shut-off valves."

"Right."

Harry pushed through an opening in a protective hedge to find the plumber's Christmas tree, the low twist of piping that came up from underground and held the control valves for what appeared to be the main water shut-off. But, according to Danny, it wasn't; it was only an intermediary shut-off, aged and almost never used. And unless the maintenance engineers on duty were old-timers, they probably had no idea of its existence. Still, if one shut it down, it turned off the water to all of the Vatican from that point out, which meant to all of the buildings below, including St. Peter's, the museums, the Vatican palace, and the administrative buildings.

"I'm on top of them. Twin valves, one opposite the other."

ELENA TILTED DANNY BACKWARD in the chair, taking them down a flight of stairs and deeper into the smoke.

"How badly rusted?" Danny coughed strongly against the smoke.

"Can't tell." Harry's voice crackled through the phone.

Elena stopped at the bottom of the stairs and opened her own camera case. Coughing, wiping her tearing eyes, she took out two dampened handkerchiefs and spread them open. Pulling one over Danny's nose and mouth, she tied it behind his head like a bandana. Then she did the same for herself and pushed them forward and into the Chiaramonti Gallery of Sculptures. The portrait busts of Cicero, Heracles with his son, the statue of Tiberius, the colossal head of

Augustus, all were lost in the fog of smoke and mass confusion as people rushed both ways down the long, narrow gallery at the same time. All looking for a way out.

"Harry—" Danny hunched over into the phone.

"First one's okay.—The second's—"

"Shut it down now!"

"As soon as I can, Danny—"

Harry grimaced, the second of the two wheels was rusted, and it took everything he had. Finally it gave all too fast, and he pitched sideways against the Christmas tree, ripping the skin from his knuckles and tossing the phone a dozen feet away.

"Shit."

THEIR BANDANAS MAKING them look like Old West bandits, Elena turned Danny sideways and pulled him back, avoiding a half dozen Japanese tourists running hand in hand toward them like a train, yelling, choking, crying with the smoke like everyone else. As she did, she glanced out one of the narrow windows and saw a phalanx of blue-shirted men in berets and armed with rifles run into the courtyard outside.

"Father," she said, alarmed.

Danny looked. "Swiss Guard," he said, then turned back to the phone, as Elena moved them forward again.

"Harry—"

"HARRY—"

"What?—"

Harry was bent over, recovering the tossed phone and at the same time sucking on his bloody knuckle.

"What's wrong?"

"The fucking water's off, okay?"

Danny put up a hand as they reached the far end of the gallery. Elena stopped the wheelchair. In front of them was a closed gate to the gallery beyond. The Galleria Lapidaria, the Gallery of Inscriptions. As far as they could tell, no one was inside.

For the first time they were alone, the crowd, the rush, the panic moving in the opposite direction.

"I'm going for fire three. Are you out of there?" Harry's voice came through the phone.

"Two more stops."

"Hurry the hell up."

"The Swiss Guards are outside in force."

"Forget the last two stops."

"We do, you'll have Farel and the Swiss Guards all over you."

"Then stop talking and do it."

"Harry." Danny looked back. Through the window he could see the Swiss Guards pulling on gas masks, and firemen with breathing tanks and fire axes.

"Eaton is somewhere here. Adrianna Hall is with him."

"How the hell did—?"

"I don't know."

"Jesus Christ, Danny, forget Eaton. Just get the hell out of there!"

150

"IT'S A DIVERSION." THOMAS KIND STOOD on the roadway just below the tower, watching the smoke from the Vatican museums billow up, talking into the two-way radio in his hand. In the distance he could hear the scream of emergency vehicles en route from various Rome City locations.

"What will you do?" Farel's voice came back at him.

"My plans have not changed. Nor should yours either." Suddenly Thomas Kind clicked off, and turned back for the tower.

HERCULES CROUCHED in his perch, tying the last of the heavy knots in the snout of his climbing rope, and watched Thomas Kind come back up the pathway toward the tower, radio in hand, talking into it as he came. Below, he saw the black suits on the far side of the hedge.

Hercules waited for Thomas Kind to pass the tower. Then, crutches tied together by a short length of rope and tossed over his shoulder, he moved up on the wall, hesitated briefly, and whirled a length of rope with its heavily knotted snout over head. Standing up fully, balancing almost on air, he flung the rope up and over the roof.

The knotted end settled around a heavy iron railing, then fell back. As the rope went slack Hercules glanced around once more. In the distance he could see the smoke from Vatican buildings, and over the hill beyond the trees in front of him, still more smoke rising.

Standing, he whirled the rope once more and let it fly. Again it came back slack and he cursed himself. And threw it again.

On the fifth toss it snagged, and he tested his weight on it. The tension held and he went up, grinning, straight up the side of the tower, crutches dangling from his back. Moments later he disappeared from sight over its red-and-white-tile roof.

"DAMMIT!" EATON CHOKED AGAINST THE smoke, handkerchief to his mouth, watery eyes searching the courtyard from the upper window of the Gallery of Tapestries, watching for wheelchairs in the mass exodus. He had already seen two of the handicapped people and discounted them. Where the hell Father Daniel and the nurse were in this confusion was impossible to tell.

Smoke, coughing, tearing eyes, and the panic around them aside, none of it was keeping Adrianna from rattling into her cell phone. She had two camera crews outside, one in St. Peter's square, the other at the entrance to the Vatican museums. Two more were on the way, and a Skycam helicopter pulled from the Adriatic coast, where it had been covering an Italian Navy exercise, was due any minute.

Suddenly Eaton was pulling her around, taking the phone from her, covering it with his hand.

"Tell them to watch for a bearded man in a wheelchair being cared for by a young woman," he said urgently. "Tell them he's suspected of starting the fire or whatever. Tell them if they spot him to keep him in sight and let you know right then. Thomas Kind gets to him first, it's over."

Adrianna nodded and Eaton gave her back the phone.

GRIMACING AT THE PAIN in his legs, Danny struggled up in his wheelchair and pressed his full weight against the window frame. For a moment nothing happened. Finally, there was a loud creak. The old casing gave and the window swung open just enough to see out and onto the Belvedere Courtyard. The fire department was directly across, and the throw at this angle, awkward. Still—

Opening the camera bag, he took out one of the oil-and-rum-filled beer bottles, with the short wick sticking from the neck. Now he looked up to Elena, her face barely visible behind the bandana covering it.

"You all right?"

"Yes."

Danny glanced back, then raised the bottle and touched a match to the wick.

Leaning back, he counted to five.

"Oorah!" he grunted and flung the bottle through the open window. Outside, a resounding crash was followed by a wall of flame as the shattering glass spread burning oil across the pavement and into the shrubbery beneath the window.

"Other side," he said quickly, pulling the window closed, sitting back down.

Two minutes later a second bottle exploded on the gravel near the Courtyard of the Triangle—the closest point yet toward the papal palace—like the first firebomb, sending a sheet of flame across the open ground and igniting the brush around it.

FAREL'S OFFICE WAS PANDEMONIUM. THE
fire chief was on the telephone, demanding to know what the
hell was going on, screaming that water pressure had been
reduced to a dribble everywhere when the first bomb
exploded outside the fire department. Instantly the chief's
tone changed. Were they under a terrorist siege or not? He
was not sending his fire fighters against armed terrorists.
That was Farel's job.

Farel well knew and was already scrambling his black
suits toward the museums to assist the fully armed regi-
ment of Swiss Guards, leaving only the six, including
Thomas Kind and Anton Pilger, to keep the trap at the
tower. It was then that the second firebomb went off.

No more chances could be taken. This might be the
Addisons, it might not.

"The water is your problem, Capo." Farel ran a sweaty
hand across his shaved head.

"The Vigilanza and Swiss Guards will get the public to

safety. My concern is one thing alone. The safety of the Holy Father. Nothing else matters." With that he hung up and started for the door.

HERCULES COULD SEE Harry's fourth fire go up. Then he saw him cross out of the smoke and start toward the tower, then duck behind a row of ancient olive trees and disappear.

Securing the rope in a double twist around the iron railing at the top of the tower, then letting it slip through his fingers, Hercules eased himself down the steep pitch of roof to the edge and looked over. Some twenty feet beneath him he could see the small platform that stuck out from Marsciano's prison room. And twenty, thirty feet below that was the ground. Easy enough, unless people were shooting at you.

Across the way he saw another fire go up. And then another, the thick smoke filtering the sunlight and turning the landscape blood red. Suddenly the bright morning had become dark. The combination of Harry's fires, the smoke from the museums, and the absolute lack of wind had, in the matter of the last few minutes, come together and turned Vatican Hill into an eerie, nearly invisible, foglike dreamscape, a choking, ghostly canvas where objects floated free-form and disembodied, where seeing more than a few feet in any direction was all but impossible.

Beneath him Hercules could hear coughing and gagging. Then, for a briefest moment the smoke cleared and he saw the two black suits nearest the front door move quickly away toward where the others were hidden, desperate to find fresh air.

At the same time he saw a figure dart across the road in the direction of the railroad station and into the tall hedges on the far side. Slinging off his crutches, Hercules moved up on his knees, waving them over his head. A moment later Harry's head popped up. Hercules used the crutches to point across the roadway, where the four black suits were gathered. Harry waved back, then the smoke came again, and he vanished from sight. Fifteen seconds later, bright red flame shot up from the spot where he had been.

10:38 A.M.

Roscani, Scala, and Castelletti stood beside the blue Alfa, watching the smoke and listening to the sirens, like most all of Rome. The police radio gave them more, the ongoing exchanges between Vatican Police and Fire and Rome City Police and Fire. They had heard Farel himself call for a helicopter for the pope, not to land on the helipad at the rear of the Vatican gardens but on the ancient roof of the papal apartments.

At almost the same moment, they saw a puff of diesel smoke from the work engine. Then a second puff came, and the little green engine began to inch forward toward the Vatican gates. That the pope was being evacuated, as was most of the Vatican proper, had no bearing on orders. The railroad wasn't on fire, and no one had called them back. So, forward they went, wanting only to retrieve an aging freight car.

"Who has a cigarette?" Abruptly Roscani turned from the train to look at his policemen.

"No, Otello," Scala said. "You quit, you can't start again . . ."

"I didn't say I was going to light it." Roscani snapped harshly.

Scala hesitated. He could see Roscani's disquiet. "You're

worried about the whole thing, especially what happens to the Americans."

Roscani looked at Scala a moment longer. "Yes," he said, half nodding, then turned and walked away by himself. Back down the track, stopping finally to watch the work engine as it crept toward the Vatican wall.

worried about the whole thing, especially what happens to the American."

Roscani looked at the train engineer. "Yes?" he said, half nodding, then turned and walked away by himself, back down the track, stopping at [?] with the work engineer as it crept toward the Vatican.

$$\boxed{\textbf{153}}$$

10:40 A.M.

A DARK MERCEDES LIMOUSINE WAS PARKED in the shadow of a hedgerow near the tower, the car to take the bodies of the Addison brothers out of the Vatican.

Thomas Kind sat inside, behind the wheel and out of the smoke. He had known from the first fire the brothers were coming. At first he thought it was a simple diversion, and then had come more fires and then the blanket of smoke and he knew he was dealing with someone with definitive military training. He knew Father Daniel had been a skilled marksman and a member of an elite unit in the U.S. Marine Corps; but the smoke and effectiveness of it were telling him the priest had been with a group such as Force Recon, which was schooled in deep insurgency. If so, he would have trained with the Navy SEALS, who are schooled to do with a small number of men what a major force might do, and who rely almost entirely on the individual.

What it meant was the Addisons were much more inventive and dangerous than he thought. It was a musing abruptly brought to life when suddenly Harry Addison darted past an opening in the hedge directly in front of him and vanished back into the smoke moving toward the tower.

Thomas Kind's immediate response was to go after Harry right then and kill him himself. And he was starting to, his hand already on the car door, when he pulled himself back. His reaction had been uncontrolled and flush with urgency. It was the old feeling, and it terrified him. This was what he had thought about earlier when he had admitted to himself that he was ill and decided to distance himself from the act.

There were other men here who were paid and waiting to do the job. He needed to let them and refuse to become involved himself. If he did, he would be all right.

Abruptly he lifted his two-way radio. "This is *S*," he said into it, *S* now his official command designation. "Target B is dressed in civilian clothes and moving alone on the tower. Let him get inside and then eliminate him immediately."

HIDDEN IN THE VEGETATION at the bottom of the tower, Harry looked up through the smoke. He could just see Hercules. Again the dwarf pointed toward the far bushes where the black suits had gone. Acknowledging, Calico in hand, he moved. In an instant he was at the heavy glass tower door, throwing it open and going inside. Closing it behind him, he locked it and turned quickly to look at what was there. A small foyer, with narrow stairs leading up, a tiny elevator.

Glancing over his shoulder at the door, he pressed the elevator button and waited for the door to slide open. When it did, he reached inside and clicked the lock switch into place. Then, using the Calico as a hammer, he brought the grip down hard on the top of the switch, breaking it off and disabling the elevator.

Quickly, he turned back, glanced again at the door, and then started up the stairs.

He was halfway up when he heard them trying to get past his lock and in through the door. It would be only a matter of seconds before they would break the glass and come in after him.

He looked up. Another dozen steps and stairs turned abruptly to the right. Quickly he climbed them, stopping at the corner and easing around, Calico first, ready to fire. There was nothing. The stairs simply continued up to the next floor, maybe twenty steps higher.

Suddenly he heard the crash of glass below. Then the door slammed open, and he glimpsed two men in black suits come in and start up the stairs, guns drawn. Quickly he darted around the corner and stopped. Slipping the Calico into his belt, he opened the waist pack and took out the olive-oil-and rum-filled Moretti beer bottle. He could hear the footsteps as the men raced up the stairs behind him.

Lighting a match, he touched it to the wick in the bottle, counted—one, two. Suddenly he stepped out, flinging the bottle at the feet of the first man. The crash of glass and whoosh of flame were buried in a hail of gunshots. Bullets chewed up the stairs beside Harry, wanged off the ceiling and walls. Then the shooting stopped. In its place came the sound of the men below screaming.

"This time you're out of luck," a heavily accented voice barked from above.

Harry whirled, pulling the Calico free. A familiar figure was coming down the stairs toward him. Young, black suited, eager, deadly. Anton Pilger. A large gun was in his hand, and his finger closing on the trigger.

Harry was already firing, pulling the Calico's trigger. He kept on pulling it, making Pilger's body seem to dance on the stairs where it was, his own gun firing into the steps at his feet, his expression one of surprise and puzzlement.

Finally, his legs gave out and he slid backward against the stairs. There was a crackle from the radio in his jacket. But that was all. In the deathly silence that came next Harry knew that he had heard the voice before. Suddenly he understood what Pilger had said about luck. He had tried to kill Harry before and failed. It had been in the sewer, after he had been tortured and before Hercules found him.

Then Harry bent over, taking Pilger's radio and moving on up the stairs in a daze, only now realizing the truth of why he was there, why he had done all of this. It was because he loved his brother and because his brother needed him. There was no other reason.

10:45 A.M.

MARSCIANO WAS PRESSED BACK AGAINST
the wall when he heard the lock turn in the door. He'd heard
the gunshots outside in the hallway. The breaking glass
and the screaming. His prayers were twofold. That Father
Daniel was coming for him. And that he wasn't.

Then the door banged open and Harry Addison stood
there.

"It's all right—," he said quietly and closed the door
behind him, locking it.

"Where is Father Daniel?"

"Waiting for you."

"There are men outside."

"We're going out anyway."

Glancing around, Harry saw the bathroom and went in. A
moment later he came out carrying a wetted hand towel.

"Put this over your nose and mouth." Harry handed
Marsciano a towel, then went quickly to the glass doors and

threw them open. Heavy smoke wafted in. At the same time, an apparition dropped from the sky.

Marsciano started. A tiny man with a huge head and larger chest stood on the balcony, a rope harness slung around him.

"Eminence." Hercules smiled, bowing his head respectfully.

THOMAS KIND'S RADIO picked it up the same time it came over Adrianna's cell phone, her open line patched into the radio communication between her crews.

"I don't know if anybody cares in all this, but the railroad gates are open in the Vatican wall, and a work engine's going toward it."

"Skycam, are you sure?" Adrianna was talking to her helicopter pilot, who was just coming in over Vatican territory from the south.

"Affirmative."

ADRIANNA TURNED QUICKLY from the phone and looked to Eaton. "The Vatican railroad gates are open, a work engine's going in."

Eaton stared. "Christ—it's how they're getting Marsciano out!"

"SKYCAM, STAY ON THE ENGINE. Stay on it!" Thomas Kind heard Adrianna finish and click off.

Suddenly he was turning the key, starting the Mercedes engine. There had been no communication from any of the men inside the tower, and he couldn't wait longer to find out what had happened. Throwing the car in gear, he fishtailed out of the gravel path and onto the narrow road beside the tower wall. Peering through the smoke and ash, he accelerated. Suddenly bushes were flying past. Then there was a loud bang as he sideswiped a tree and slid sideways into the thick of a hedgerow. Where the road had turned he had no idea. Violently, he threw it in reverse. There was a roar of engine and the whine of tires. The car shuddered but didn't move. Flinging open the door, he saw the wheels spinning on the green of the torn shrubbery as if it were ice.

Cursing in his native Spanish, he climbed out, choking against the smoke, and ran off on foot in the direction of the station.

155

10:48 A.M.

DANNY AND ELENA CAME OUT INTO THE
smoke through an emergency door on the ground floor of the
Apostolic Library.

"Left," Danny commanded through his handkerchief, and
Elena turned them that way along the narrow road to the gardens.

"Harry," Danny spoke urgently into the cell phone.

Nothing.

"Harry, can you hear me?"

There was a hiss on the other end, as if the line were still
open. Then:

CLICK. The line went dead.

"Dammit!" Danny said out loud.

"What's the matter?" Elena pressed, sudden fear for
Harry jolting her.

"Don't know . . ."

*   *   *

HARRY, HERCULES, AND MARSCIANO huddled in silence on Marsciano's platform, peering over the side in the smoke.

"You're sure they're there?" Harry said to Hercules.

"Yes, down there just past the door."

Just as Hercules dropped from the roof to the platform he had seen two of the black suits take position on either side of the door. But now the settling smoke made it impossible to see.

"Send them away." Harry was suddenly pulling Anton Pilger's two-way radio from his belt, giving it to Hercules.

Taking it, Hercules clicked on, winking at Harry as he did. "They've come down the outside of the tower by rope!" he said urgently in Italian. "They're moving toward the helipad!"

"*Va bene*,"—Okay—a voice came back.

"The helipad! The helipad!" Hercules barked for good measure, then abruptly shut the radio off.

Beneath them was a scurrying, and then they glimpsed one man and then another move off at a dead run away from the tower.

"Now!" Harry said.

"Eminence," Hercules said. The rope suddenly twisted in his hands; he made one loop and brought it over Marsciano's shoulders, then a second around his waist. A moment later Hercules was balanced on the rail and Harry was helping Marsciano onto it. Then, turning it through the steel of the railing, he held on and stepped back, lowering both men to the ground.

"Mr. Harry!" Hercules voice floated up. Harry saw the rope tighten from the ground and knew Hercules was guiding it. Taking hold, he swung up on the railing, then went over himself. An instant later, a shot rang out and the rope half severed. For a moment Harry just hung there, and then the rope broke and he dropped like a stone to the ground.

The wind knocked out of him, he looked up at the sound of a scream. Hercules had a black suit at the edge of the bushes, his steel-like arms around the man's neck.

"Look out!" Harry yelled.

The black suit still had his gun, and Hercules didn't see it. It was coming up against the side of Hercules' head.

"GUN!" Harry yelled again, pushing himself up, rushing up toward them.

There was a tremendous report as the pistol went off just as Hercules wrenched. There was a hideous scream and both men fell back.

Harry and Marsciano arrived at the same moment. The black suit lay still, his head twisted at a terrible angle. Hercules was on his back, blood covering half his face.

"Hercules." Harry moved quickly, kneeling down, looking at him. "Jesus God," he whispered, his hand moving in to feel his neck for a pulse.

Then Hercules opened one eye, and his hand reached up and wiped the blood from the other. Abruptly he sat up, blinking the blood away. A second wipe from his hand took a huge smear of the blood from his face. A clear flesh wound with the sheer white of a powder burn ran, like an arrow, up the side of it.

"Can't kill me," he said. "Not like that."

In the distance came the sound of a train whistle. Finding a crutch, Hercules pulled himself up.

"The engine, Mr. Harry." Blood or not, Hercules eyes danced. "The engine!"

156

ADRIANNA CAME OUT OF THE BUILDING TO see Eaton running up the road behind St. Peter's, then he vanished like a wisp in the smoke.

"Skycam, what do you have on the engine?" she spat into the phone as she ran, cutting up the hill and across the grass toward the Palace of the Government, the Vatican's city hall. She was three minutes, maybe four, from the railroad station.

ELENA PULLED DANNY BACK into the overhang of a tree near the Church of San Stefano and waited for the helicopter to pass over. It did, then abruptly swung back toward the station.

At the same moment, Danny's cell phone chirped.

"Harry—"

"We have Marsciano with us. What about the engine?"

Elena could feel the pound of her heart at Harry's voice. He was all right, at least for the moment.

"Harry—," Danny said, "we've got air cover. I don't know who it is. Go the other way, come down by Vatican Radio and in past the Ethiopian College. By then we'll be closer, and I can see what the hell's going on."

10:50 A.M.

"Stay here!" Roscani yelled at Scala and Castelletti. Then, turning, he ran down the track after the little oily-green engine just as it chugged in through the open gates and vanished in the massive hang of smoke.

For a moment Scala and Castelletti stood open-mouthed, watching him. Little by little Roscani had been walking down the track following the engine, but his move and the quickness of it had caught them by surprise. Suddenly they started to run after him. A dozen yards later they stopped as they saw him reach the opening in the wall and disappear into the gloom. From where they stood, it looked like the entire Vatican was either on fire or fully under siege.

Suddenly an Italian Army helicopter roared in directly overhead. At the same time Farel's voice crackled loudly over the radio, identifying himself and telling the WNN Skycam helicopter to vacate Vatican airspace immediately.

"DAMMIT," ADRIANNA SAID at the order. Then she heard the rotors overhead crank up and her Skycam pull away.

"Keep south of the wall," she shouted into the phone. "When that engine comes out, stay with it!"

FOR SOME REASON THE WORK engine had stopped just outside the open gates, and Roscani crossed the tracks behind it quickly, moving to his right and past the station. Coughing, his eyes tearing with the smoke, he pulled open his jacket and slid a 9mm Beretta automatic from his belt. Straining to see, he went up the road in the direction of the tower. What he was doing was totally illegal, but he didn't care. The law was fucked and could go to hell. He'd made the decision in an instant as he walked down the tracks after the work engine and saw the huge gates pull back for it. The open portal in the wall was all he needed, and he went for it just like that, all fire and emotion and the knowledge that he *had* to do *something*.

And now, as he fought the smoke and tearing eyes and just tried to breathe, he prayed to God he wouldn't lose his bearings and get lost, that he would somehow find the Addisons before Farel's gunmen or Thomas Kind did.

THOMAS KIND RAN FORWARD, Walther *mascinen pistole* in hand, wiping his eyes, trying not to cough with the acrid smoke. It was already hard enough to see anything, and the physical act of coughing jarred and threw him off even more.

Running across the lawn, jumping a low hedge, he suddenly lost his bearings and stopped. It was like being on a mountain on skis in a whiteout. Up, down, or sideways, everything was the same.

He could hear emergency sirens far to his left. Above, and also to the left, was the heavy thud of rotors from what he assumed was the Italian Army jet helicopter circling to land on the roof of the papal palace. Pulling up his radio, he spoke into it in Italian.

"This is *S*. Copy."

Silence.

"This is *S*," he said again. "Copy."

*   *   *

HERCULES SWUNG ALONGSIDE Harry and Marsciano as they made their way quickly along the narrow road toward Vatican Radio. The two-way radio in Hercules' belt spat with Thomas Kind's voice.

"Who is that?" Marsciano asked.

"I think someone we want nothing in the world to do with," Harry said, knowing, without knowing, that it was Thomas Kind. Harry coughed, looking at his watch.

10:53 A.M.

"Eminence," he said suddenly. "We have five minutes to get past the Ethiopian College to the tracks and into the railroa—"

"Mr. Harry!" Hercules suddenly cried out.

Harry looked up. A black suit stood directly in front of them, less than five feet away in the smoke. He had a huge pistol in either hand—revolvers. He stepped forward. He was tall and youthful and had wavy hair. He looked for all the world like a young Dirty Harry.

"Put your gun on the ground," he said to Harry in English with a thick French accent. "The waist pack, too."

Slowly Harry eased the Calico out and set it on the ground, then unclasped the waist pack and let that fall, too.

"Harry—" Danny's voice jumped out from the cell phone in his belt.

"Harry!"

At that moment something happened that startled them all. A light breeze wafted across, lifting the smoke ever so slightly. At the same time came the distant sound of the work engine's whistle as it passed through the gates. The black suit suddenly smiled. The train was coming, the trio in front of him would never make it.

It wasn't much, just a tiny moment, and what Hercules had been looking for. In a single motion he shifted his weight to his left crutch and flung the right.

The black suit cried out in surprise as the crutch struck his right hand sending one gun flying off. Recovering, he swung the other gun toward Harry, his finger closing on the trigger. At the same instant Hercules threw himself forward. Harry saw the gun buck in the black suit's hand, heard its heavy report just as Hercules crashed into him, knocking them both to the ground.

Harry's fingers found the Calico. What happened next was in flashes. Split seconds. Pieces. Bits. Passion. Fury. Harry was across the ground and on the black suit. Arm around his neck. Tearing him off Hercules. Then suddenly the black suit wrenched free.

In an instant he had Harry by the hair with both hands and was jerking him forward, slamming his forehead hard into Harry's with a vicious head butt. Harry saw a stabbing bolt of light and then blackness. A split second later, his vision returned to see the Calico in the black suit's hand inches from his face.

"Fuck you!" the black suit screamed, his finger squeezing the trigger.

Immediately there was a thundering gunshot. Followed in lightning succession by three more horrendous blasts. Harry saw the black suit's entire head explode in what seemed like slow motion. Then his body arched and he fell back, the Calico dropping to the grass beside him.

Harry whirled, looking up.

Roscani was coming down the hill toward them, his

Beretta pointed directly at the dead black suit, as if there were some chance the man might actually get up again.

"Harry, the engine!" Danny's voice came out of a fog from the cell phone at Harry's waist.

Harry got to his feet, picking up the Calico as Roscani came nearer. He started to say something, then froze, staring up the hill behind him.

"Look out!" Harry yelled.

Roscani spun. The two black suits Hercules had sent running toward the helicopter pad were rushing toward them. They were thirty yards away, coming through the smoke.

Roscani glanced at Hercules. His face was ashen, his hand over his stomach, a circle of blood widening from it.

"Get out of here!" Roscani yelled, turning and dropping to one knee. His first shot hit the lead black suit in the shoulder, spinning him around, the second kept coming.

Behind him Harry heard a barrage of gunshots. He could feel bullets whizz by inches away as he bent to pick Hercules from the ground. As he did, he suddenly remembered Marsciano.

"Eminence—," he said, looking up.

There was no one. Marsciano was gone.

ROSCANI LAY PRONE IN THE GRASS. THE first black suit was fifteen yards away sprawled on his back and moaning, the second was facedown in the grass not more than ten feet from Roscani, his eyes open but lifeless, blood slowly oozing from a hole between his eyes.

Taking a chance there had been only the two, Roscani rolled over and looked down the hill in the direction Harry had carried Hercules. He could see only the swirl of smoke that instead of dissipating was becoming thicker.

Getting up cautiously, he glanced around for more black suits, then went to the dead man in front of him. Taking the man's gun, Roscani slipped it in his belt, then moved off toward the black suit still lying moaning on the ground ahead.

10:55 A.M.

"Danny." Harry's urgent voice came over the open phone line. "Where are you?"

"Close to the station."

"Get on the freight car. I've got Hercules, he's been shot."

Elena stopped. They were at the edge of the trees and behind a hedge across from the Vatican City Hall and the Mosaic Studio. Directly ahead was the railroad station, and to the right of it she could see a part of the freight car. Then came the blast of an air horn, and a dirty, bright green work engine chugged slowly into view. Abruptly it stopped, and a lone man with white hair walked out from the station, a clipboard in his hand. Stopping at the track he seemed to note the number painted on the engine, then moved to it and climbed aboard.

"I don't know if Hercules is going to make it."

Elena glanced at Danny. They could both hear the fear, the desperation in Harry's voice.

"Danny." Harry's voice came again. "Marsciano's gone."

"What?"

"I don't know where, he went off on his own."

"Where were you when he did?"

"Near Vatican Radio. We're passing the Ethiopian College now. . . . Elena, Hercules is going to need you."

Elena leaned into the phone. "I'll meet you, Harry. Just be careful . . ."

"Danny—Roscani's here, so is Thomas Kind. I'm sure he knows about the train. Watch it."

"DON'T MOVE!" Roscani commanded, his Beretta held military style in both hands and pointed at the moaning black suit.

As he drew closer, Roscani could see the man on his back. One leg was twisted under him, and his eyes were closed. Now he could see a bloodied hand limp across his chest; the other was out of sight beneath him. The man was going nowhere. In the distance came the sound of the train whistle. It was the second blast within seconds. Roscani turned quickly, looking through the smoke in its direction. Harry and Hercules had to be going toward it. Maybe Marsciano, too, and Father Daniel and Elena Voso. That meant there was every chance Thomas Kind was going there as well.

Instinct made Roscani turn back. The black suit was raised up on an elbow, an automatic in his hand. Both men fired at the same time. Roscani felt a jolt. His right leg collapsed under him, and he went down. Rolling over, he came up on his stomach firing. There was no need, the black suit was dead, the top of his skull blown away. Grimacing, Roscani struggled to his feet, then, crying out, slumped back down. A patch of red spread across the beige material of his upper pant leg. He'd been shot in his right thigh.

THERE WAS A deafening roar, and the whole building shook.

"Va bene,"—Okay—crackled through Farel's radio.

Farel nodded and two jumpsuited Swiss Guards carrying automatic rifles pushed open the rooftop door. And they went out into smoky daylight, the guards first and then Farel, holding firmly onto the Holy Father's arm, guiding the white-clad old man out.

A dozen more heavily armed Swiss Guards were on the ancient rooftop as they crossed it, moving hastily toward the Italian Army helicopter balanced on the edge of the terrace wall, its rotors slowly turning. Two army officers waited in its open doorway, two of Farel's black suits with them.

"Where is Palestrina?" the pope asked Farel, looking around, fully expecting his secretariat of state to be waiting to leave with him.

"He said to tell you he would join you later, Holiness,"

Farel lied. He had no idea where Palestrina was. Had not communicated with him in the last half hour at all.

"No." The Holy Father suddenly stopped at the helicopter's open door, his eyes fixed on Farel's.

"No," he said again. "He will not join me. I know it, and he knows it."

With that, Giacomo Pecci, Pope Leo XIV, turned away from Farel and let the black-suited Vigilanza help him into the helicopter. Then they and the Italian Army officers followed him onboard. The door closed, and Farel moved back, waving to the pilot.

A thundering roar was followed by an immense blast of wind, and Farel and the Swiss Guards ducked away as the machine lifted skyward. Five seconds, ten. And then it was gone.

158

MARSCIANO HAD SEEN THE TOWERING FIG-
ure through the smoke at the same moment Hercules had
thrown his crutch at the black suit. Seen him come up the hill
on the far side of the Vatican Radio tower, moving steadily
toward it. In that instant Marsciano knew he would not be on
the train when it left. Father Daniel or not, Harry Addison
and the curious, miraculous dwarf or not, there were other
things here. Things that he, and he alone, had to deal with.

PALESTRINA NO LONGER wore the simple black
suit with its humble clerical collar; instead, he was dressed
in the vestments of a cardinal of the Church. A black cassock
with red piping and red buttons, a red sash at his waist, a red
zucchetto on his head. A gold pectoral cross that hung from a
gold chain around his neck.

He had paused at the Fountain of the Eagle on his way
there, finding it easily, even in the dense smoke. But for the
first time ever, the aura of the great heraldic symbol of the

Borgheses, which had always touched him so deeply and so personally, from which he had drawn strength and courage and certitude, failed him. What he gazed upon was not magic, did not feed the secret warrior-king in him, as it always had. What he gazed upon was the ancient statue of an eagle. A sculpture. An adornment atop a fountain. Nothing.

A great breath was expelled from within him, and, hand over nose and mouth against the horrid, acrid smoke, he moved on toward the only refuge he knew.

He could feel the thrust of his giant body as he moved up the hill. Feel it even more as he threw open the door and started up the steep, narrow marble stairway toward Vatican Radio's upper floors. More still as he pushed, heart pounding, lungs bursting, to kneel finally on the black marble floor before the altar of Christ in the tiny chapel just off the empty and vacant broadcast rooms.

Empty. Vacant.

Like the eagle.

Vatican Radio was his spire. Self-chosen. The place from which to command the defenses of the kingdom. The place from which to broadcast to the world the greatness of the Holy See. A Holy See more exalted than ever—one that controlled the appointment of bishops, rules for the behavior of priests, the sacraments, including marriage, the establishment of new churches, seminaries, universities. One that over the next century would be joined, little by little—hamlet to town to city—by a new flock representing one-quarter of the world's population, making Rome again the centerpiece of the most powerful religious denomination on earth. To say nothing of the enormous financial leverage to be garnered through control of that country's water and power, which in turn would govern when and where and what could be built or grown, and by whom. In a very short time a once-powerful saying would become the new and lasting one—— and all because Palestrina had had the keenness to foresee and create it. *Roma locuta est; causa finita est.* "Rome has spoken," it translated; "the matter is settled."

Except that it was not. The *Vaticano* was under siege, part of it burning. The Holy Father had seen the darkness. The Eagle of the Borghese had given him nothing. He had been right about Father Daniel and his brother the first time. They *had* been sent by the spirits of the netherworld; the smoke they had created was filled with darkness and disease, the same that had killed Alexander before. So it was Palestrina and not the Holy Father who was mistaken: the thing perched on his shoulder was not the emotional and spiritual infirmities of an old and fearful man but indeed the shadow of death.

Suddenly Palestrina raised his head. He'd thought he was alone. He was not. There was no need to turn. He knew who it was.

"Pray with me, Eminence," he said softly.

Marsciano stood behind him.

"Pray for what?"

Slowly Palestrina rose up and turned. Looking at Marsciano, he smiled gently. "Salvation."

Marsciano stared.

"God has intervened. The poisoner has been caught and killed. There will be no third lake."

"I know."

Palestrina smiled once more and then slowly turned back to kneel again in front of the altar and make the sign of the cross. "Now that you know, pray with me."

Palestrina felt Marsciano step behind him. Suddenly he grunted. And there was a piercing light brighter than any he had ever seen. He could feel the blade pierce the center of his neck. Between his shoulder blades. Feel the strength and rage in Marsciano's hands as he pressed it down.

"There *is* no third lake," Palestrina cried. His chest heaved, his massive hands and arms clawing, flailing behind him to reach Marsciano. But unable to.

"If not today, tomorrow. Tomorrow you would find a way to create another horror. And after that, another. And then another." In his mind Marsciano saw only the anguish of a face seen in close-up on his television screen only moments before Harry Addison had come. It had been that of his friend Yan Yeh as the Chinese banker was led to a waiting car in the Beijing compound after having been informed of the deaths of his wife and son, poisoned by the water in Wuxi.

Staring blindly at the altar cross, over the white blaze of Palestrina's hair in front of him, Marsciano felt the ornate letter opener in his hands as he pushed down, twisting slowly and with all his might as he did, driving it deeper into the neck and body that roiled and writhed like some monstrous serpent trying to escape.

Then he heard Palestrina cry out and felt his body shudder once against the blade, and then he was still. A huge breath escaped Marsciano and, letting go, he stumbled back. Bloodied hands before him. His heart pounding. Horrified at what he had done.

"Holy Mary, Mother of God"—his voice was a whisper—"pray for us sinners, now and at the moment of our death . . ."

Suddenly, he felt a presence and looked around.

Farel stood in the doorway behind him.

"You were right, Eminence," he said softly, and closed the door behind him. "Tomorrow he would have found another lake . . ." Farel's eyes went to Palestrina and he stared for a long moment before he looked back to Marsciano.

"What you did had to be done. I had not the courage. . . . He was, as he said, a street urchin, a *scugnizzo* . . . nothing more."

"No," Marsciano said. "He was a man and a cardinal of the Church."

159

10:58 A.M.

EATON STOOD NEAR THE BACK CORNER OF the railroad station, breathless and sweating, trying to stifle a coughing fit from the inhaling of smoke. The scant breeze that had come helped some but not enough, except that it had cleared the air just a little, enough for him to see what he saw now—Harry Addison coming down the grassy slope to his right, carrying the dwarf he'd left the apartment on Via Nicolò V with in his arms. He was half walking, half running, using a stand of trees that lined the roadway to the rail station for cover.

Fifty feet in front of him, Eaton saw the green engine inch toward an old and rusting freight car, which, he was certain, had to be the escape wagon. Glancing back he saw the rusty tracks leading out through the open gates in the Vatican wall. Now he looked back, searching for Father Daniel. If he could find him, that opening was the way he would take him, one way or another, even if he had to carry him.

Crossing behind the station, Eaton came onto the tracks with his back to the open gate. In front of him he saw the white-haired, white-shirted stationmaster standing on the platform watching the work engine near the freight car. The man was a problem, as was the two-man crew he'd seen on the engine. But none of them were half the problem he saw now. Adrianna, suddenly, and from nowhere, was crossing the grassy hill toward Harry Addison and the dwarf.

He saw Harry stop when he saw her. Then heard him yell something, as if to tell her to go away. But it made no difference. She kept coming, and now she reached them and was moving alongside, looking at the dwarf in Harry's arms then back to Harry himself. Whatever she said or was saying, Harry Addison kept going, heading downhill, toward the tracks.

"Dammit," Eaton swore under his breath, his eyes moving off again, searching for Father Daniel.

"ADRIANNA, GET OUT OF HERE! You don't know what the fuck you're doing!" Harry yelled, half stumbling with Hercules in his arms.

"I'm going with you, that's what the fuck I'm doing."

They were almost at the bottom of the hill. Almost to the tracks. Harry could see the green work engine nose to nose with the freight car, its engineer and brakeman with their backs to them working at the couplings. Saw the white-haired stationmaster turn and go back inside.

"Your brother's in the freight car, isn't he? The trainmen don't know it, but that's where he is."

Harry ignored her. Kept walking, praying the trainmen wouldn't look up and see them. Hercules grunted and Harry looked down at him. The dwarf smiled feebly.

"The Gypsies are going to meet the train when it stops. . . . Don't let the police have me, Mr. Harry. . . . The Gypsies will bury me . . ."

"Nobody's going to bury you."

Suddenly the trainmen were walking away from the coupling, moving toward the engine.

"They're getting ready to leave!" Immediately Harry was pulling Hercules tight to his chest. Starting to run the short distance to the tracks. Adrianna stayed right with him.

Ten seconds later they were there. Crossing the tracks behind the freight car, running alongside it, out of sight of the trainmen.

Harry's eyes watered, his lungs on fire from the smoke and exertion of carrying Hercules. Where the hell were Danny and Elena? What had happened to Roscani? Then they were at the freight car door and he stopped. It was open.

"Danny. Elena—"

No reply.

Suddenly the train whistle sounded. They heard the engine's diesel rev up. A puff of brown-black exhaust rising from its smokestack.

"Danny—," Harry called again. Nothing.

Again the train whistle. Harry glanced at his watch.

11:00 A.M. exactly.

No time, they had to get into the car and do it now.

"Get in." Harry looked quickly to Adrianna. "I'll hand him up."

"All right—"

Putting both hands on the freight car's floor, Adrianna pulled herself up and in. Then she turned and Harry set Hercules in her arms.

The dwarf coughed, grimacing as she strained to lift him. Then she had him up, and Harry was coming into the dimly lit car behind her. Suddenly he froze.

Thomas Kind stood directly in front of him. Elena was with him, eyes wide with fright, an ugly machine pistol to her head.

160

11:04 A.M.

SCALA LEANED ON THE HOOD OF ROSCANI'S blue Alfa, a set of binoculars trained on the distant gates. All he could see was the slight bend of the tracks as they curved inside the wall and a small part of the station but that was all. Behind it everything, despite the new breeze, was still thick smoke. Castelletti stood halfway down the tracks in front of him, staring at the same gape in the wall. Despite the wail of sirens, they had heard the gunshots, and as much as they knew their job was to wait for the train to come out and follow it to where it stopped, both had to work with all they had not to rush in after Roscani. But they couldn't, and they knew it. All they could do was watch and wait.

"YOU HAVE A GUN, Mr. Addison. Please give it to me."

Harry hesitated; Kind pushed the machine pistol up under Elena's ear.

"You know who I am, Mr. Addison. . . . And what I will do . . ." Thomas Kind's voice was calm, a slight smile crossing his lips.

Slowly Harry reached into his belt and lifted out the Calico.

"Put it on the floor."

Harry did, then stood back.

"Where is your brother?"

"I wish I knew . . ." Harry's eyes went to Elena.

"She doesn't know either," Thomas Kind said with the same calm. Elena had been alone, running to the freight car, when Kind suddenly came down over the edge of the wall and grabbed her, demanding to know where Father Daniel was. She had no idea, she told him defiantly. The father had gone one way, she another. She was a nurse, Father Daniel's brother was bringing a wounded man to the train. And that was where she was headed, to give the service that was needed.

It was at that moment, when he had Elena by the arm and saw both the dread and the fiery resolve in her, that Thomas Kind felt the sudden savage rush of his addiction come back. He could taste it in his mouth and feel the arousal it gave him. In that instant he knew his retreat from it had ended.

"We are going to find your brother, Mr. Addison," Thomas Kind said thinly, his calmness turned to ice.

Harry barely heard, his attention on Elena; he was staring at her, trying somehow to comfort her while at the same time find a way to get her out of Kind's grasp. Then, out of nowhere, a man appeared in the freight car's open doorway.

It was Eaton. "*Vigili del fuoco!*" Fire department, he said quickly and with authority.

"What are you doing here?" Eaton demanded in Italian. He was playing it very carefully, not looking at Thomas Kind at all, but addressing them as a group, as if the machine pistol in Kind's hand didn't exist.

"Taking a journey." Kind smiled easily.

Eaton's automatic appeared from nowhere. The move was professional, calculated, and controlled, going for a single shot between the terrorist's eyes.

Thomas Kind barely blinked. A short burst from the machine pistol took Eaton just under his nose, blowing him out of the freight car doorway backward and across the tracks in a wash of blood and bone, and sending the automatic flying out of sight.

Elena stiffened in horror. Kind tightened his hand over her mouth.

Adrianna remained frozen where she was. She showed no expression at all. Hercules was on the floor in between Harry and Adrianna, Kind and Elena, his breath held, knowing what they all knew: another squeeze of Kind's finger and any or all of them were dead.

161

"ADRIANNA—" SUDDENLY THE VOICE OF THE Skycam pilot came through Adrianna's open phone line, the sound tinny and distant, coming from the cell phone in her jacket pocket.

"Adrianna—we're holding just outside the Vatican wall at fifteen hundred feet. The train hasn't moved. You still want us to stay on it?"

"Let the women go. . . . Let them take Hercules . . . ," Harry said again.

Suddenly Elena moved toward Hercules. Kind swung the gun.

"Elena!" Harry yelled.

Elena froze where she was. "He's going to die if he doesn't get help."

"Adrianna—," the Skycam came again.

"Tell him to get off the train and cover the crowds outside St. Peter's," Kind said quietly. "Tell him."

Adrianna stared at Thomas Kind for a long moment, then lifted the telephone and did as she was told.

Kind took a step toward the door and looked up. Saw the Skycam helicopter break its holding pattern, fly east and then swing north to hover over St. Peter's. Thomas Kind looked back. "Now, we're going to get out of the train car and go into the station."

"He can't be moved . . ." Elena was looking up at Kind, pleading for Hercules.

"Then leave him."

"He'll die."

Harry saw Kind's finger dance nervously over the machine pistol's trigger.

"Elena, do as he says."

THEY MOVED ALONG the tracks quickly, Kind keeping Elena close, then Harry and Adrianna. Suddenly there was movement at the front of the engine. Two sets of feet were suddenly turning and running away.

Thomas Kind took a half step forward. The train's engineer and brakeman were dashing toward the open gate in the Vatican wall. Kind's eyes swung back to freeze on Harry in a deadly warning not to move, then he simply skewed the machine pistol sideways, turned to look, and fired two short bursts. The brakeman and then the engineer went down like suddenly dropped sacks of flour.

"Mother of God!" Elena crossed herself.

"Move," Kind commanded, and they crossed in front of the engine. "In there," he said next, indicating a painted door leading into the station itself.

As they moved, Harry saw the wide open gate in the Vatican wall, and, at the far end of the overpass, where the old tracks met the main line, a parked car with two men standing outside it, looking toward them.

Scala. Castelletti.

Roscani was still somewhere inside. *Where?*

THE PAIN IN HIS leg excruciating, Roscani alternately walked, then stopped to rest, then walked on again, his right hand pushing hard, as a pressure point against the wound in his thigh. He thought he was moving toward the railroad station, but he was no longer sure, the smoke and the trauma of his wound working to disorient everything. Still, with the Beretta in his free hand, he stumbled determinedly on.

"Halt! Hands up!" a voice suddenly barked out of the smoke in Italian.

Roscani froze where he was. Then he saw a half dozen men with rifles step out of the gloom in front of him. They had blue shirts and wore berets. They were Swiss Guards.

"I am a policeman!" Roscani yelled back. He had no idea whether they were under Farel's direct orders or not, but he had to take the chance they were not in the same group as the black suits.

"I am a policeman!"

"Hands up! Hands up!"

Roscani stared, then slowly raised his hands. A moment later the Beretta was jerked away. Then he heard one guard speak into a two-way radio.

"Ambulanza!" the man ordered urgently. *"Ambulanza!"*

THOMAS KIND shut the railroad station door behind them, and suddenly they were inside the cavernous building that had once been the pope's marble-walled gateway to the world. Daylight streamed in from the windows above, sending a cascade of brightness like theater spotlights along the center of the floor. But other than that and the dim light coming from the window looking out to the tracks, the inside was dark and cool. And, if it mattered, preciously free from the smoke.

"Now." Kind released his grip on Elena and stepped back, looking at Harry. "Your brother was coming for the train. Since it's still here, we will assume he is still coming."

Harry's eyes traveled over Kind slowly, as if he were trying to find a spot where he was most vulnerable. Then, behind Kind and through an open door, he saw a white shirt suddenly move out of sight. The trouble was he gave it too much attention.

"So?" Kind said sharply. "Perhaps your Father Daniel is here already. . . ." Abruptly he raised his voice. "You, in the office, come out!"

Nothing happened.

Slowly Adrianna shifted position, moving a step closer to Kind. Harry looked at her, wondering what she was doing. She looked back and shook her head.

"Come out!" Kind commanded again, "Or I will come in."

Time froze, and then a shock of white hair slowly appeared. And then they saw the rest of the stationmaster. White shirt, black trousers. A man easily in his late sixties. Kind motioned him forward. The man came out slowly. Frightened, staring, confused.

"Who else is here?"

"—No one . . ."

"Who opened the gates?"

The man raised a hand and pointed to himself.

Harry could see Kind's eyes move back in his head and he knew he was going to shoot. "Don't!"

Kind looked at him. "Where is your brother?"

"Don't kill him, please . . ."

"Where is your brother?"

"—Don't know . . . ," Harry whispered.

Kind half smiled, his finger squeezed the trigger and there was the muffled sound of a jackhammer.

Elena watched in horror as the stationmaster's white shirt exploded in red. The old man held his stance for a moment then staggered backward, and, turning, fell sideways into the doorway of his office.

Abruptly Harry pulled Elena to him, turning her away from the terror.

Again Adrianna moved her position, another step closer to Thomas Kind.

"You want my brother, I'll take you to him." Harry said abruptly. There was no doubt at all that Thomas Kind was altogether insane, and if Danny suddenly showed up, he'd kill them all in a blink.

"Where is he?" Thomas Kind slid a fresh clip into the machine pistol.

"Outside—near the gate. The train was going to stop to pick him up . . ."

"You're lying."

"No."

"Yes. The gates open and close into the wall. There's nothing there. No place to wait."

Suddenly Kind was aware of Adrianna's drawing closer and he turned toward her.

"Careful—," Harry warned.

"What are you doing?" Kind said.

"Nothing . . ." She moved closer still, a half step, no more. Her eyes were locked on Kind's.

"Adrianna, don't." Again Harry warned her.

Adrianna stopped. She was five feet from Kind, no more. "You are the one who killed the cardinal vicar of Rome."

"Yes."

"In the last few minutes you killed four more people . . ."

"Yes."

"And when you find Father Daniel you'll do the same to him . . . and then us . . ."

"Perhaps . . ." Thomas Kind smiled, and Harry could tell he was enjoying every moment of it.

"Why?" Adrianna said sharply. "What does it all have to do with the Vatican and the poisoning of the lakes in China?"

Harry looked at her, wondering what she was doing. Why she was pressing Kind when he had the gun and she had nothing at all to gain.

Then he realized. The same instant Kind did.

"You're taping this, aren't you? You're wearing a lipstick camera, you've got a video rolling . . ." Kind smiled, wholly amused, amazed at his own revelation.

Adrianna smiled. "Why don't you answer the question and then we'll talk about it . . ."

The next happened in a nanosecond. Thomas Kind lifted the machine pistol. There was the sound of the dull jackhammer. A look of complete surprise swept over Adrianna. She half stumbled, then fell backward.

Elena froze in horror. Thomas Kind moved forward, lost in his own actions. Harry could see the veins bulge in his neck and forehead as he stepped over Adrianna's body. Firing at it, no longer in bursts but a single shot at a time. Dropping down to a squatting position he smiled and shot her again, then again, almost as if he were making love to her.

It was all too fast. Too violent, too perverse. No time for

Harry to react. It was just he, Elena, and Thomas Kind. In the center of the floor of an enormous room. Void of furniture. No place to run. To hide at all.

Then Harry did move. Directly for Kind. Kind saw him and stepped around, bringing the machine pistol up as he did.

"HARRY!"

Danny's voice suddenly echoed across the empty station. Harry froze.

So did Kind, his eyes searching the empty depot.

Abruptly Harry stepped into the line of fire, directly between Kind and Elena and the door behind them.

"Elena, get out. Now!"

Harry's eyes were locked on Kind's. His voice full of urgency.

Elena turned, slowly, reluctantly.

"GET OUT!!!"

Suddenly, she broke. Running for the door. In a moment she was across the room and through it.

"THOMAS KIND!" Once again Danny's voice echoed. "LET MY BROTHER GO!"

Kind felt the touch of his palm against the machine pistol's grip. His eyes continued to search. Dark, to the bright spots of sunlight in the center of the floor, back to the dark of the room.

"SHE'S GONE, KIND. YOU'RE DONE ANYWAY. YOU KILL MY BROTHER YOU GAIN NOTHING. I'M THE ONE YOU WANT."

"Show yourself!"

"LET HIM GO, FIRST."

"I count to three, Father. Then I start to take him apart in pieces. One—"

Through the window Harry could see Elena climb the stairs to the engine. He wondered what the hell she was doing.

"Two—"

Suddenly a series of short, loud train whistle bursts rocked the station. Kind ignored it. Dropped the machine pistol toward Harry's knee caps.

"Danny!" Harry yelled. "What's the word?—What's the word, Danny?"

Harry's eyes swung to Thomas Kind. "I know my brother better than he thinks." Harry kept his eyes on the terrorist. "What is it, Danny?—the word!" He yelled again, his voice bouncing in a thousand echoes off the empty station's stone walls.

"OORAH!"

Suddenly Danny appeared from behind a partition near the back, his wheelchair in deep shadow. Harry saw him push off with both hands. Disappearing into a circle of ultrabright sunlight streaming through the high windows.

"OORAH!" Harry yelled back. "OORAH!"

"OORAH!"

"OORAH!"

Kind saw nothing but blinding light in front of him! Then Harry began walking toward him.

"OORAH! OORAH!" he chanted, his eyes fixed on the terrorist. "OORAH! OORAH!"

Suddenly Kind swung the machine pistol at Harry. At the same time Danny rolled forward in the wheelchair. There seemed to be flame in his lap.

"OOOO RAHHHHHH!"

Danny's Celtic yell thundered off the hardness of the marbled walls, and the wheelchair moved into view.

"NOW!" Harry yelled.

Kind swung the machine pistol toward Danny, just as he hurled the last of the beer bottles. One. And then two. And they crashed flaming at Thomas Kind's feet.

For the briefest moment Thomas Kind felt the jump of the machine pistol in his hand and then he couldn't see. Fire was everywhere. Turning, he started to run. But to run he had to breathe, and without realizing, he inhaled the burning sear, sucking the flames deep, igniting his lungs. There was pain like nothing he'd ever experienced. There was no air to breathe either in or out, not even to scream. All he knew was that he was on fire and he was running. And then time itself began to slow. He could see the outdoors. The sky above him. The looming open gate in the Vatican wall. Curiously and despite the terrible pain that now seemed to exist in every part of him, he felt a deep peace. Never mind what he had done with his life or what he had become; for Thomas Jose Alvarez-Rios Kind, the disease that had ultimately usurped his soul was being terminated. That the cost was enormous didn't matter, in a matter of moments he would be free.

THE TRAIN WHISTLE still sounding, Scala and Castelletti ran down the track. The gunshots, the train whistle with no train appearing. The hell with it, they were going in. Then they stopped. A man on fire was running through the open gates coming down the tracks toward them.

The policemen watched as the man ran on. Another ten feet, fifteen. Then he slowed, stumbled a few feet more and collapsed on the tracks. He was no more than a hundred feet into Italy.

162

HARRY HEARD THE MASSIVE IRON GATES thud closed in the wall behind. In front of him an ambulance pulled in through a sea of blue-shirted, heavily armed Swiss Guards and drove rapidly onto the dock beside the station. Backing up, it stopped next to the work engine. Then the paramedics and the doctor with them rushed to where Elena knelt with Hercules. In no time they had inserted an IV and moved him onto a stretcher; and then the dwarf was lifted up, put in the ambulance, and it was gone, driving off through the army of Vatican soldiers.

Watching it go, Harry felt as if some part of him were leaving with it. Finally he turned away only to find Danny watching him from his wheelchair. The look in Danny's eyes told him he knew they had been seeing the same thing; the déjà vu of someone they cared for deeply, put into an ambulance and driven away as they stood helplessly by and watched. It had been twenty-five years since that terrible Sunday when their sister's body had been taken from the icy pond, put blanket-wrapped into the ambulance by the fire chief, and driven away in the shivering semidarkness. The only differences now were that quarter century and that they were in Rome, not Maine, and that Hercules was still alive.

Suddenly Harry realized in the confusion that he had forgotten Elena. Turning, he saw her standing alone, her back to the work engine, watching them both, all but unaware of the force of soldiers around them. It was as if she understood something of great significance was going on between the brothers and was hesitant, even afraid, to intrude. In that moment she became the dearest person he had ever known in his life.

Automatically, and without the slightest conscious thought, he went to her. And in front of Danny and the mass of faceless blue shirts surrounding them, he kissed her— gently and with all the love and tenderness he had.

163

THAT AFTERNOON AND INTO EVENING HARRY and Elena and Danny sat in a small private waiting room at the Hospital of St. John. Harry held Elena's hand, while his mind danced everywhere. Mainly, he tried not to think. The men he'd killed, or the men others had killed. Eaton, even Thomas Kind. The worst was Adrianna. The first night they'd been together he'd sensed she was afraid to die. Yet everything she did, every story she covered, seemed to be about death in one way or another, from the war in Croatia to the refugees escaping the bloody civil wars in Africa, to the business right here and the story of the assassination of the cardinal vicar of Rome. What had she said to him? Something like if she'd had children she never would have been able to do what she did. Who knew?—maybe that was what she really wanted but simply didn't know how to make it work, a home, children, and her job. She couldn't have all three, so she chose the one that seemed to give her the most out of life, and probably it had. Until it killed her.

*   *   *

JUST BEFORE THE DINNER HOUR, and dressed in civilian clothes, Cardinal Marsciano joined them. An hour later, Roscani came, pale and in a wheelchair, brought from his room in another wing of the hospital by an orderly.

At five minutes to ten the waiting room door opened and a surgeon, still in his surgical scrubs, entered.

"He will be all right," he said in Italian. "Hercules will live . . ."

There was no need for translation. Harry knew right away.

"*Grazie*," he said getting up. "*Grazie*."

"*Prego.*" Glancing around the room, the surgeon said he would have more information later, then nodding, turned and left, the door closing behind him.

The collective silence that followed was vast and deep, touching each one of them. That the dwarf from the sewers would recover was a bright and joyful note in a long, twisted, and painful journey they had all shared, no matter how disparately. That it was over, for the most part, was something that had yet to sink in. Yet it *was* over, the tidying up already well under way.

In a blink Farel had personally taken over and become a one-man damage control, as much to protect himself as the Holy See. In a matter of hours the chief of the Vatican police had called a press briefing that was broadcast live on Italian state television. In it he announced that late this morning the infamous South American terrorist Thomas Jose Alvarez-Rios Kind had instigated a bold and murderous fire-bombing rampage inside the Vatican in a presumed attempt to reach the pope himself. In the process, he had shot to death World News Network correspondent Adrianna Hall and Rome CIA station chief James Eaton, who had been nearby and gone to her aid. Meanwhile, in an attempt to protect the Holy Father, the Vatican's beloved secretariat of state, Cardinal Umberto Palestrina, had suffered a massive heart attack and died. Farel closed the briefing with a terse pronouncement that Thomas Kind had become the only suspect in the murders of the cardinal vicar of Rome and the Italian police detective Gianni Pio and in the bombing of the Assisi bus; and, finally, that he had been killed when a firebomb exploded as he was trying to ignite it. No mention at all was made about Roscani's presence inside Vatican territory.

ROSCANI LOOKED AROUND the room. He had left his own hospital room and come there personally to inform the Addisons and Elena Voso about Farel's press announcement and tell them that no charges would be made against them. Marsciano's presence had been a surprise, and for a short time he hoped that he might find a way to get the prelate to talk to him privately about what had really happened concerning the murders of both the cardinal vicar of Rome and Palestrina, the employment of Thomas Kind, and the horror in China. But the cardinal had squashed that ambition quickly with a simple apology—saying that he was sorry but because of the circumstances, questions regarding the state of the Holy See would be addressed only through official Vatican channels. It meant that what Marsciano really knew he was not about to disclose to anyone, now or ever. And, having no choice, Roscani accepted it and turned back to the others.

What surprised him was that though he could have left then, he didn't. Tired as Roscani was from his ordeal, he had stayed, waiting with the rest for word of Hercules' condition. It was more than something he felt he should do, it was something he wanted to do. Maybe it was because he felt he was as much a part of it all as they were. Or maybe he just wanted to be with them because in some crazy way Hercules had gotten to him, and he cared as much as they did. In the exhausted, confused state they were all in, who the hell knew about anything? At least he'd given up smoking, and that had to be good for something.

Pushed in his chair by the orderly, Roscani went to each of them, taking their hands, saying if there was anything he could do to please call on him. Then he said goodnight. But he wasn't quite done; purposely he made Harry the last and asked him to come to the door with him.

"Why?" Harry tensed.

"Please," Roscani said. "It's a personal thing . . ."

With a glance at Danny and Elena, Harry took a breath and went with him. At the door they stopped.

"The video they made of you," Roscani said, "after Pio was killed."

"What about it?"

"At the end—whoever made it cut something out. A last word or phrase. I tried to figure out what it was. I even had a lip-reading expert look at it. She couldn't get it either. . . . Do you remember what you said?"

Harry nodded. "Yes . . ."

"What was it?"

"I'd been tortured, it took me that long to realize what was going on. I wanted help, I called out a name."

Roscani was as much in the dark as ever. "Whose name did you call?"

Harry hesitated. "Yours."

"Mine?"

"You were the only person I knew who could help."

Slowly Roscani grinned.

So did Harry.

Epilogue

Bath, Maine.

THE PACT HAD BEEN TO LEAVE AND NEVER come back. But two days after the state funeral for Cardinal Palestrina, Harry and Danny did come back. With Harry manning the carry-ons and Danny hobbling on crutches—flying to New York and then Portland, Maine, and driving up from there on a bright summer day.

Elena had gone home to be with her parents and tell them of her plans to leave the convent and then to go to Siena and request dispensation of her vows, and afterward to join Harry in Los Angeles.

Harry drove the rented Chevy through the familiar towns of Freeport and Brunswick and finally into Bath. The old neighborhood had changed little, if at all, the white clapboard houses and faded shingle cottages brilliant in the July sunshine, the big elm and oak trees flush with summer growth as stately and timeless as ever. Passing Bath Iron

Works, the ship-building yard where their father had worked and died, they drove slowly south in the direction of Boothbay Harbor, then veering off Route 209, Harry took the fork onto High Street and shortly afterward a right onto Cemetery Road.

The family plot was on a grassy knoll on a hill overlooking the distant bay. It was as they both remembered, well tended, quiet, and peaceful with the chirp of birds in the nearby trees the only sound. Their father had bought the parcel with savings just after Madeline was born, knowing there would be no more children. The plot was for five, and three rested there now. Madeline, their father, and their mother, who had stipulated in her will that she be buried not with her new husband but with Madeline and the father of her children. The last two plots were for Harry and Danny if they chose.

Before, it would have been unthinkable for either brother to consider being buried there. But things had changed, as the two of them had. And who knew what life was yet to bring? It was lovely and tranquil, and in a way the idea was comforting and brought things full circle.

They left it like that, tender and up in the air, discussed but not discussed, in the way siblings talk of such things.

A day later Danny flew out of Boston for Rome and Harry for Los Angeles, their lives sadder, richer, wiser, and immeasurably changed. Together they had ventured into a nightmare and managed to come out of it alive. In the process they had collected a crazy, improbable, ragtag little band that included a nun, a crippled dwarf, and three exceptional Italian policemen and had become a team, working together for the first time since boyhood.

Heroes?—Maybe. . . . They had saved Marsciano's life and prevented further untold thousands of innocent deaths in China. . . . But there was the other side of it, too, the horror they had not been able to stop. And for that there would always be sorrow and emptiness and heartache. Yet it was over and in the past, and there was nothing they could do to change it. What they had to do now was try to pick things up somewhere where they had left off. Each with his own extended family—Danny with Cardinal Marsciano and the Church, Harry with the madness that was Hollywood, appended hugely by an entirely new and fantastic core that was Elena. And each with the all-so-real cognizance that he had a brother again.

AT THREE-THIRTY in the afternoon, Friday, July seventeenth, Giacomo Pecci, Pope Leo XIV, ensconced under heavy guard at his summer refuge at Castel Gandolfo, in the Alban Hills near Rome, was informed of the violent happenings inside the Vatican walls, culminating with the death of Umberto Palestrina.

At six-thirty that same evening, nearly eight hours after he had left by helicopter, the Holy Father returned by car to the Vatican. By seven, he had gathered his closest advisers for a prayer mass for the dead.

On Sunday, at noon, the bells of Rome tolled in mourning for Cardinal Palestrina. And on the following Wednesday a massive state funeral was held for him inside St. Peter's Basilica. Among the thousands in attendance was the newly appointed secretariat of state for the Holy See, Cardinal Nicola Marsciano.

At six o'clock that same evening Cardinal Marsciano met privately with Cardinal Joseph Matadi and Monsignor Fabio Capizzi. Immediately afterward he went to pray with the Holy Father in his private chapel, and later the two dined alone in the papal apartments. What was said there or transpired between them is not known.

* * *

TEN DAYS LATER, on Monday, July twenty-seventh, Hercules had recovered sufficiently to be released from the hospital of St. John and sent to a private rehabilitation center to recuperate.

Three days after that, murder charges against him were quietly dropped. A month later he was released from the rehabilitation center and given a job and a small apartment in Montepulciano in Tuscany, where he lives today as an overseer of an olive grove owned by Elena Voso's family.

IN SEPTEMBER, Gruppo Cardinale ranking prosecutor Marcello Taglia officially announced that the late terrorist Thomas Jose Alvarez-Rios Kind was the assassin of Rosario Parma, cardinal vicar of Rome, and that he had acted alone, with the participation of no other groups or governments. With that announcement the Italian government formally disbanded Gruppo Cardinale and closed its investigation.

The Vatican maintained total silence.

On October first, exactly two weeks after prosecutor Taglia's formal announcement, Capo del Ufficio Centrale Vigilanza Jacov Farel took his first holiday in five years. While trying to cross the border between Italy and Austria in his private car he was arrested and charged with complicity in the murder of the Italian policeman Ispettore Capo Gianni Pio. Today, he awaits trial for that murder.

The Vatican remains without comment.

There Was One Other Thing—

Los Angeles. August 5.

IN THE MIDST OF A RIOTOUS WORKLOAD after his return—including hammering out a contract for a sequel to *Dog on the Moon*—and innumerable hour-long conversations with Elena in Italy as she prepared in body and soul to move to Los Angeles, Harry was increasingly troubled by the memories of a conversation he'd had with Danny on the drive from Maine back to Boston.

It had begun with Harry thinking about unanswered questions. And in light of his restored relationship with his brother and because of what they had experienced together and the secrets they still shared, he felt it completely natural to ask Danny to help him clarify a few things.

HARRY: You called me early Friday morning Rome time and left word on my answering machine that you were scared and didn't know what to do. "God help me!" you said.

DANNY: Right.

HARRY: I assume it was because you had just heard Marsciano's confession and were horrified by it and by what the repercussions might be.

DANNY: Yes.

HARRY: What if I had been home and had answered the phone? Would you have told me about the confession?

DANNY: I was a mess, I don't know what I would have told you. That I had heard a confession, maybe. Not what was in it.

HARRY: But you didn't get me, so you left word and a few hours later you were on a bus to Assisi. Why Assisi? There was hardly a church inhabitable after the earthquakes.

(It was here Harry remembered Danny's beginning to get uncomfortable with his questions.)

DANNY: It didn't make any difference. It was a terrible time, the bus was going and Assisi was my solace. It always had been. . . . What are you getting at?

HARRY: That maybe it wasn't just solace, that maybe you were going there for another reason.

DANNY: Like what?

HARRY: Like to meet someone.

DANNY: Who?

HARRY: Eaton.

DANNY: Eaton?—Why would I be going all the way to Assisi to see Eaton?

HARRY: You tell me . . .

DANNY: [Big smile.] You're wrong, Harry. It's that simple.

HARRY: He was trying very hard to get to you, Danny. By providing me with false papers he was sticking his neck way out. He could have gotten into a hell of a lot of trouble if he got caught.

DANNY: It's the business he was in . . .

HARRY: He got killed trying to find you. Maybe even protect you.

DANNY: It's the business he was in . . .

HARRY: What if I said the real reason you went to Assisi all those years was not for solace but to deliver information . . . to Eaton . . .

DANNY: [Big incredulous grin.] Are you suggesting I was the CIA's man in the Vatican?

HARRY: Were you?

DANNY: You really want to know?

HARRY: Yes.

DANNY: No. . . . Anything else?

HARRY: No . . .

But there was, and finally Harry had to find out. Closing his office door, he picked up the phone and called a friend at *TIME* in New York. Ten minutes later he was talking to the magazine's CIA expert in the Washington bureau.

What were the chances, he wanted to know, of the Central Intelligence Agency's having a mole inside the Vatican. The response was a laugh. Very unlikely, he was told. But possible? Yes, possible.

"Especially," the *TIME* correspondent explained, "if someone assigned to watch Italy was concerned about the Vatican's influence on the country, particularly after the Vatican banking scandals of the early 1980s."

"Banking—and/or where they had their"—Harry chose the word carefully—"investments?"

"Right. . . . Decide if that information was important enough, and if it was, then place an operative as close to the source as possible."

Harry felt the chill begin to slide down his spine. *Close to the source,* he thought—as in private secretary to the cardinal who manages the Holy See's investments.

"Might," he went on, "this someone watching Italy be the Rome station chief?"

"Yes."

"Who would know about it?"

"There's a very guarded category of operative called HUMINTS—an acronym for Human Intelligence, people who are deep cover plants. Deeper still, and in a situation as sensitive as Vatican-U.S. relations more likely, are people known as NOCs—an acronym for Non-Official Covers. Operatives like this are so concealed and protected even the director of Central Intelligence might not know. A NOC would be recruited directly by someone like a station chief for a very precise positioning. In all likelihood they would have been recruited sometime earlier so that they could work their way to a position of trust with no suspicion whatsoever."

"Could an operative like this be . . . someone in the clergy?"

"Why not?"

HARRY DIDN'T REMEMBER getting off the phone, or leaving his office, or walking in the August heat and smog along Rodeo Drive or even where or how he crossed Wilshire Boulevard. All he knew was that somehow he was in Neiman-Marcus and a very attractive young woman was showing him ties.

"I don't think so." Harry shook his head at a proffered Hermès tie. "Why don't I just look around on my own . . ."

"Sure." The woman smiled at him with the kind of flirtatious glow he used to do something about. But not now, maybe not ever again. Today was Wednesday. Saturday he was going back to Italy to meet Elena's family. Elena was all he thought about, saw in his dreams, felt with every breath. That was until now, after the phone call to the *TIME* correspondent, and on the way here, when he had the sudden and all-too-clear memory of facing Thomas Kind in the Vatican railroad station and boldly telling him across his murderous machine pistol—"I know my brother better than he thinks."

NOC, Non-Official Cover—so concealed and protected even the director of Central Intelligence might not know.

Danny. Jesus H. Christ, maybe he didn't know him at all.

By the year 2000, 2 out of 3 Americans could be illiterate.

It's true.

Today, 75 million adults... about one American in three, can't read adequately. And by the year 2000, U.S. News & World Report envisions an America with a literacy rate of only 30%.

Before that America comes to be, you can stop it... by joining the fight against illiteracy today.

Call the Coalition for Literacy at toll-free **1-800-228-8813** and volunteer.

Volunteer Against Illiteracy. The only degree you need is a degree of caring.

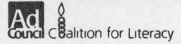

Ad Council Coalition for Literacy

Warner Books is proud to be an active supporter of the Coalition for Literacy.